Also by Cecelia Holland

FICTION

Home Ground (1981)

City of God (1979)

Two Ravens (1977)

Floating Worlds (1975)

Great Maria (1974)

The Death of Attila (1973)

The Earl (1971)

Antichrist (1970)

Until the Sun Falls (1969)

The Kings in Winter (1968)

Rakóssy (1967)

The Firedrake (1966)

FOR CHILDREN

The King's Road (1970)

Ghost on the Steppe (1969)

THE SEA BEGGARS

The SEA BEGGARS

Cecelia Holland

ALFRED A. KNOPF   New York   1982

Library of Congress Cataloging in Publication Data

Holland, Cecelia [date]
The sea beggars.
1. Netherlands—History—Wars of
Independence, 1556–1648—Fiction. I. Title.
PS3558.O348S4 1982   813'.54   81–48115
ISBN 0–394–50406–2   AACR2

FIRST EDITION

For Spike van Cleve,
and his blue filly

You can blow out a candle,
But you can't blow out a fire,
Once the flames begin to catch,
The wind will blow it higher.

—Peter Gabriel, "Biko"

Historical Note

THE REVOLT of the Dutch against the Spanish monarchy in the late sixteenth century was the first of a long series of national revolutions that changed the nature of government and shaped the societies we now live in. Its impact on the English is clearly visible in Shakespeare's and Marlowe's writings and was obviously an influence on the English revolts of 1648 and 1688, direct forerunners of the American and French revolutions of the next century.

In a time dominated by the personalities of mighty individuals, the revolt of the Dutch stands out as the action of an entire people. Yet it produced at least one great man, William of Nassau, William the Silent—the Prince of Orange, one of those rare people in history about whom the more I learn the more I admire him. For these reasons, and the deeper one of its being a struggle between freedom and autocracy, tolerance and ideology, the Dutch revolt is the first real modern event.

The Netherlands—the Low Countries, what we now call Belgium, Luxembourg, and Holland—began in the Middle Ages as a cluster of dozens of autonomous provinces along the banks, swamps, and estuaries of the three great rivers, the Rhine, the Maas, and the Shelde, that empty their waters into the North Sea. In the fourteenth century the dukes of Burgundy, striving to create a separate state between France and Germany, acquired the Provinces one by one, by marriage and conquest. Still the region remained a patchwork of local governments. Here and there great cities sprang up, centers of commerce and finance. Elsewhere the Dutch reclaimed swamp and wasteland and the shallows of their coastline for farms.

In 1477, with the death of Charles the Bold, Duke of Burgundy, the ruling line failed of male issue, and the great duchy of Burgundy in the south reverted to the Crown of France. The daughter of Charles kept title to her father's other lands, consisting mainly of the Low Countries.

The heiress of Burgundy married the son of the Hapsburg Emperor of Germany. Their son in turn married the daughter of the great Spanish monarchs Ferdinand and Isabella, thus uniting under the Spanish Crown the greatest assemblage of real property the world had yet seen. Included in this domain were the Low Countries, the hereditary German lands of the Hapsburgs, Italy and Sicily, Spain, and the Spanish Indies, which people did not then know consisted of two entire continents.

Thus, in 1555, when Charles V was still Emperor, the Dutch people found themselves under the rule of a foreign prince whose interests spanned the world and whose traditional policy committed him to support of the Catholic Church, newly resurgent against the Protestant Reformation.

The Dutch have ever been a tolerant people, their prevailing religious attitude better expressed by Erasmus of Rotterdam than Luther, Calvin, or Ignatius Loyola. In this greenhouse atmosphere, a diversity of sects flowered throughout the sixteenth century, some swiftly withering, some taking lasting root. The Emperor Charles, born and reared in Ghent, Flanders, was wise enough not to interfere openly with this climate, but in 1555 Charles relinquished the Netherlands, yielding power to his son, Philip II of Spain.

Philip spoke only Spanish. A few months after his father's death, in 1558, he sailed from the Low Countries to Spain, where he remained for the rest of his more than forty years of rule. He was an unimaginative, dedicated, scrupulous man, overmeticulous and rigid, and a fanatic Catholic. His policy of consolidating power in the administration of his property brought him face to face with the great Dutch nobility, who feared for the loss of their hereditary rights and privileges. From the moment of his accession, the tension between him and the Low Countries grew steadily into violence and revolt.

This book's story is fiction. The van Cleef family is a product of my imagination; and while the events in which the van Cleefs act are all drawn from actual incidents, I have tampered with some details in the interests of the narrative. The business in Antwerp, where the Spanish garrison fled from three sails on the river thinking they were the Beggars, happened several years later than it does here. Not Alva's son, but a lesser commander, led the royal army against The Brill. And Willem Lumey de la Marck did not die as I have it; he was bounced from his position as admiral and went back to his native Germany, where the great priest-killer returned to the Catholic Church.

The revolt of the Dutch has inspired two great classics of history: John Lathrop Motley's *The Rise of the Dutch Republic,* and Pieter Geyl's *The Revolt of the Netherlands.* One hundred years separates these works; the differences in attitude and style between them splendidly illuminate the intellectual adventure of those hundred years.

The song on p. 243 is from *Tudor Songs and Ballads from M.S. Cotton Vespasian A-25,* edited by Peter J. Seng, Harvard University Press, Cambridge, Mass., 1978.

Finally, I want to thank the John Simon Guggenheim Foundation, with whose generous support the novel was finished.

THE SEA BEGGARS

Prologue

BEGGARS!" exclaimed Count Horn. "They called us *beggars* for requiring what is ours by right of law and custom!"

The Prince of Orange said nothing.

"The King will set all in order," Count Egmont said, on the Prince's left. "It's these Spanish fools advising the King's sister who think they can remake the Low Countries to their new fashions. They had to accept the petition, after all—that's what matters. Once it reaches the King, he will restore our place here, and chastise these schemers and plotters."

Still the Prince of Orange said nothing. The fresh breezes of early spring in his face, he rode with his friends beneath the elms and linden trees of Brussels, his mind heavy with doubts. He had heard about the petition, although he had kept himself out of it—out of the writing of it, out of the delivery—knowing the Governess mistrusted him already. Margaret would have damned the whole enterprise, had he been attached to it—that gaudy, innocent parade of noblemen and youth who had ridden to the Palais-Royal with their request that the King honor their ancient habits and refrain from installing the Inquisition in the Low Countries.

"If only the Emperor were still alive!" Egmont said, with a gusty sigh.

As well pray that all good men might live forever. The Emperor Charles V had been dead for ten years. Egmont and Horn and probably thousands of others in the Low Countries looked back on his reign as a golden age of harmony and prosperity. The Prince of Orange knew they were yielding to delusions when they did.

Did the past always seem better to men than the present? That was the core of the petition, the request that the King of Spain restore the past of the Netherlands—a past when her rulers had lived here, when the counts of Holland and Flanders, the dukes of Brabant and Burgundy had centered their policy on the good of these provinces, when they had not tried to fit them into some corner of a huge mosaic of states reaching very nearly around the world and having no commonality save the man who governed them all, the King of Spain. So they had ridden to the Palais, the Dutch nobles, with their bit of paper, asking: Please make things as they were before.

The Governess, the King's sister, had resorted to tears, her customary refuge in times of stress. Which led one of her advisers to say, "Madame, are you afraid of these *beggars?*"

"When the King has our petition," Egmont said, "we shall see who the beggars are."

There was danger in such optimism. The Governess had promised to hold off the persecution of heretics in the Low Countries until the King gave her fresh instructions. To take for granted that the King would do as the nobles asked . . .

Horn's gloved hand fell roughly on Orange's sleeve. "Come, William. Why so quiet? You look as if you're riding in a funeral train. Seem happier —there are people watching."

The Prince of Orange pulled on his smiling public face. "Forgive me, friend." Turning his hand over, he caught the older man's brocaded wrist in a brief intimate grasp. "You know I have much on my mind of late."

"Well, get her off your mind," Egmont said, and laughed.

They were riding abreast down the broad, tree-shaded street; on either side stood the homes of wealthy men, the glass windows shining like gold in the late light of the sun. From an upper story a woman leaned and waved her handkerchief.

"Vive le Prince! Messieurs les comtes!"

Egmont and Horn swept off their caps and waved them, and Orange lifted up his hand, smiling. At the shout, half a dozen other doors popped open, and a small crowd poured forth into the street to watch the lords ride by.

"Vive le Prince!"

Orange saluted them; his spirits rose at this boisterous greeting. He turned his mind from his gray inward thoughts to the outer world. It was spring, and Brussels, with its palaces and gardens, its courtly people, was dressed in new bloom; fresh young flowers everywhere danced in the sunlight; the leaves of the trees were uncurling like pale green flags. He waved and smiled to the people who called his name, and resolved to be less gloomy.

After all, the Governess had agreed to cease attacking the Protestants. The King was notoriously slow in his deliberations: it would be months before his answer reached Brussels, perhaps years. And now the street before them was filled with noisy people, in celebration costume, cheering.

"Vive les gueux! Long live the beggars!"

To the left of the Prince of Orange, Count Horn murmured, "That word again."

"What are they doing?" Orange asked. He twisted in his saddle to look around him at the jubilant crowds; clearly they were celebrating the Governess's decision to make no more decisions. Many of them had drunk too much, explaining the high degree of their excitement. Their cheers resounded with the French word for *beggar.* That put him off—to seize on an insult for a rallying cry divided them emphatically from the government. With his friends and their troops of retainers he rode on through the thick and noisy crowd toward the palace where they had been invited to dine.

The gate was clogged with people, and circles of dancers wheeled and dipped in the courtyard between the two wings of the house. Music boomed forth from the balconies, where musicians sat struggling to keep tune in the wash of echoes from the high walls around them. When Horn and Egmont and Orange rode in, the cheering doubled, and Orange had difficulty dismounting his horse and walking into the great hall of the house.

There a great banquet was laid out on long tables, and seated all around them the men who had delivered the petition drank and sang and cheered themselves and their friends.

"Vive les gueux!"

At the sight of the three newcomers the cry went up like a peal of thunder. "Vive les gueux!" In a single leap, the revelers rose to their feet, hoisting their cups in greeting.

They were wooden cups—beggars' cups. Orange frowned, his sense of proper value overturned by such impudence. Around their necks these men wore beggars' chains. They had taken the insult as an accolade—as a common bond.

"Long live the beggars!"

Orange stopped, unready to join this—unwilling to have this salutation pressed on him. It was too late. Forth they rushed, his hosts and friends, his fellows in opposition to the Crown, and carried to him chains and a wooden cup. "Vive les gueux!" The roar shook the rafters. Like a bobbing bit of cork on an ocean wave, he felt himself lifted up and carried away with the rest, his will made nothing. Laughing, they surrounded him, these beggars, and hung the chains around his neck, and pushed the wooden cup into his hand. He knew it was the cup of fate. "Long live the beggars!" they cried, and swelled by their ardor his courage like a rushing wave ran on beyond his reason.

"Vive les gueux!"

He raised the cup and drank it to the lees.

I

IN THE heat of the summer, the great Calvinist preachers went into the countryside, into fallow fields and meadows, and there delivered their sermons under the open sky. From all over the Provinces, pious folk came to listen, whole families, with their children by the hand and their dinners in baskets.

In a barley field near the great city of Antwerp, in Brabant, the preacher Albert van Luys stood up to declare the Word of God. Hundreds of people came to listen; the women sat on the grass in a circle around him, with their little children on their laps, and the men stood behind them in another circle.

Albert van Luys had the true fire of his calling, but the day was hot and long and some of the men had brought beer with them, and gin, and wine in flasks. Some too had muskets, which they fired off now and again, shouting, "Vive les gueux!"

Mies van Cleef had no musket, and drank no more beer than necessary to cool his throat and maintain his strength through the heat of the day. Standing in the ring of men facing the preacher, he dwelt with his whole mind on the sermon: *The day of the Lord cometh like a thief in the night.* Mies had a wonderful power of concentration. Intent on Albert's words, he noticed neither the occasional bursts of musket fire nor the shouts of the drunkards; and he realized only gradually that his son, Jan, had slipped away into the crowd.

That annoyed him. He was a merchant, with a large trade and many employees, whom he expected to obey him without flaw. That his son could disobey him pricked his temper like a needle in his flesh. For a while longer, when he was sure Jan was gone, he struggled to keep his interest on the sermon, but the needle pierced ever deeper into his pride and his rectitude, and finally he stepped backward through the ring of men to the empty meadow.

There he paused and collected himself, a lean man in middle age, balding, his clothes as somber as a monk's and expensive as a prince's. He cast a look around him. The grass was trampled to a pulp; a fine gray dust lay over everything, even the shoulders and backs of the men watching the preacher, whose ranks he had just left. He shook a layer of dust off his sleeves.

At that moment a crackle of gunfire went up on the far side of the crowd. That told him where to find his son. He strode off around the outside of the circle in the direction of the shots.

The field lay along the Antwerp–Mechlin Canal; boats crowded both banks. On the far side, a gigantic mill creaked and wheeled its arms in the gusty breeze. White clouds streamed across the sky. Mies lengthened his stride, pressed on by these hints of a storm coming up over the horizon: his wife and daughter would not enjoy getting rained on.

"Long live the beggars!"

Another musket went off into the air; a man in a flapping black hat waved his weapon over his head. Near him was Mies' son, Jan, squatting on his heels beside another man with a gun, asking questions. Mies' jaw tightened. When he took Jan into a factory with him, or out to the shops, Jan never asked questions. Mies stalked across the beaten grass to his son and taking a handful of his collar pulled him to his feet.

"This is how you value the chance to hear God's Truth expounded!"

Jan shook him violently off, blushing to the ears; his sun-bleached hair bristled with bad temper. Although he was only seventeen, he was much taller than Mies, which perversely angered his father as much as Jan's sinful interest in guns and fighting. He struck Jan on the face with his open hand.

"Go back to the sermon!"

"Don't hit me," Jan said, between his teeth. Past him, Mies saw the men with their muskets, grinning at them.

"Go back to the sermon," Mies said, and wheeling marched away again, toward his place in the circle of men.

Jan followed him. Some last shred of filial piety remained in him. It was not enough for Mies; bitterly he wondered why God had sent him this lout for a son, and wasted a keen mind and a heart for truth on his daughter, who would never be anything but someone's wife.

The sermon was ending. Albert had them in prayers, many in the crowd, even men, weeping for their sins. Mies stopped to look among the gathering for his wife.

Jan stood sullenly beside him. With the briefest of looks into his son's face, the father said, "Be sure your mother does not learn of your truancy."

"Yes, sir," the boy mumbled. His fine white skin still showed the stain of his furious blush.

Now rain was falling. Quickly Mies collected together his family; the sermon had overcome his wife, in whose large-boned frame he saw the pattern by which his son was cut, and she leaned heavily on his daughter's shoulder. Hanneke too had their mother's tawny hair and generous size of bone. She smiled at her father as he lifted her mother's weight from her arm.

"Beautiful," her mother said, and sobbed. Tears streamed down her cheeks. "When Albert speaks of Heaven, he makes me long so for it . . ." In a flood of weeping she lost the power of speech.

"What thought you of the sermon, Hanneke?" Mies asked. Supporting his wife on his arm, he led his family toward the canal where their boat waited.

"His style is very fine," the girl said, "but I think he is not so strong in his reasoning as he might be. There were moments I thought he tried with a great wind of words to blow me over the gaps in his logic."

Mies laughed, delighted with her composed and critical expression. He reached past his wife, to squeeze his daughter's hand. "Trust you to yield not to his fulsome blasts, my little dear one."

Jan burst forward, moving on ahead of them, awkward, as if the size and weight of his limbs outstretched his mastery of them. "I'll help with the horses."

It was in Mies' thoughts to stop him, to remind him of his place, but there was no use in it. He shrugged. "Very well," he said, to his son's back.

They got into the flat-bottomed boat, and Mies arranged his wife on cushions in the stern and sat there with her, his hand on the tiller. Their boatman brought the horses and hitched up the long towline to the harness; with Jan to help him, he had the van Cleefs' boat ready long before the others in the crowd, whose horses neighed and jogged up and down the high bank of the canal while the boatmen cursed and struggled with tangled lines. Stuck in the midst of the fleet, Mies could not see a way clear, and they had to wait for the others to hitch up and move along, to make space for them. Reluctantly Jan climbed down the dusty bank of the canal and stepped into the barge, which dipped under his weight and swung into the boat next to it. He sat beside his sister in the bow, glowering, his eyes downcast, his large square hands gripped between his knees.

Lout, Mies thought, with a hot spurt of anger. The rain was falling harder now. The boats ahead of them were moving at last, and he called to his boatman to drag the barge along the canal, back to their home in Antwerp.

For RUNNING OFF from the sermon, Jan's father sent him down the next morning to the wharf on the canal behind the silk factory, to work at loading and unloading the boats. Although the work was hard Jan enjoyed it; he liked showing off his strength, and while the rough, voiceless men of the regular crew shuffled up and down the steps, four hands to every bolt and spool, Jan leapt back and forth from the wharf to the factory with the great heavy goods balanced on his shoulders and scorned any help at all.

After he had done this for most of the morning, the foreman of the regular crew took him aside and told him to stop.

"If the overseer catches you doing that, he will think we ought to be doing it too," the foreman said. He was a burly man whose bulging forearms jutted out of the frayed sleeves of his shirt.

"It's not that hard," Jan said.

They were standing on the wharf, beside the tufted bollard where the canal boats tied up. Behind the foreman, the short steep ladder scaled the canal bank, and along the top of the bank on either side of it the rest of the crew stood watching what went on between their leader and Jan. The foreman crossed his arms over his chest.

"You're only a boy," he said, "and you have no family. Likely you will take your wage and spend it on beer and whores. We all have to put bread into our babies' mouths. If you work so hard, the factory men will think they don't need all of us, and some of us will be turned off."

Down the canal, someone yelled; a heavy-laden barge was steering around the bend. Jan said, "You should do a good day's work for your wage."

The foreman cocked his fist. "You slow down, or we'll see you don't come back tomorrow."

Jan opened his mouth to inform this brute that he was the son of the factory's owner, but something warned him against that. He looked up at the row of men on the canal bank above him, their faces in shadow, the sun at their backs. The barge passed behind him, parting the canal water with a low murmur; as it passed, its horn gave a breathy honk.

"Very well," he said. "I won't be here that long anyway."

The foreman smiled and lowered his fist. "That's a good boy." His wrist was spotted with old healing sores, flea bites, or scrofula. When he turned to go back up the ladder, Jan saw spots of blood on his shirt. Jan stooped to hoist a bale of carded wool to his back, remembered, and straightened up to wait for help.

That evening he and his father walked home together and his father said, "How did you on the wharf?"

"Fair enough," Jan said.

"Did you talk to any of the other men?"

"A little," Jan said, warily. They were walking down the tree-shaded lane toward their street; the sun had just gone down and the birds shrilled and flapped in the branches overhead, revived in the cool after the day's humid heat.

"Did you notice any one of them who seemed to be"—Mies made a thoughtful face—"a troublemaker?"

"What?"

"One who incited the others to laziness, perhaps, or wild talk."

"No," Jan said.

His father shook his head a little, his lips still pursed, as if over some indigestible idea. He said, "Well, keep your eyes and ears open."

"Am I a spy, then?" Jan asked, furious.

Mies gave him a sharp look. "You are my son. What benefits me does you also, does it not? People who talk sedition are bad for business."

"No one talked any sedition."

Mies said, "There are how many on the wharf? Six? Do we need so many?"

That came at Jan too fast to answer; he opened his mouth and shut it again, wondering what to say. Although he had spoken to the other men only briefly, and the foreman had threatened him, he felt the first formings of a loyalty to them.

"Well?" his father asked.

"What will you do if I say no?" Jan said.

His father walked along, square and solid as one of the big linden trees they passed beneath. "They are overpaid as 'tis. To send some off would help me balance my books a little more favorably."

"They have families. Children to feed."

"So do I."

"You're rich."

"I am not in business to provide a means of life for half the rabble in Antwerp. What a tender heart you have. Then there are too many men on the wharf."

"But I am not there always," Jan said. "When I am not there, surely the work must be harder on the others."

"True," said Mies.

They were coming to the end of the street. Soon their house would be in view, the smells of dinner floating from it; Jan's stomach let out a loud and painful growl. His hunger sharpened something in his understanding of the foreman and his babies.

He said, "What would they do, if you turned them off? Who would care for them? Are they Catholic?" The Catholics gave bread to their poor.

His father laughed. "No, they are good reformed folk, like us, most of them. If we had not settled the issue of the Inquisition, things would be worse than they are in Antwerp."

" 'If *we* had not settled' it," Jan said, an edge in his voice. "You had nothing to do with that."

"Men who think like me," Mies said. "Keep a filial tongue, my boy, or you will see worse than the loading docks." He frowned at Jan; the older man's face was hard as a bandit's. "Keep your ears open down there—I want to know who says what, who makes trouble. Now that you know what to look for."

Jan shut his lips tightly together. They were at the end of the street; ahead of them, other men were hurrying to their homes, and through the last overhanging linden branches the painted eaves of his house were visible, the carved window frames, the door. In an upper story window a pale oval appeared, his sister's face. The place seemed more solid to him now, warmer, a refuge. He lengthened his stride toward it.

M IES VAN CLEEF lived with his family in the house his grandfather had built on Canal Street in Antwerp, three streets away from his cloth-weaving factory. The house was three stories high, with big windows facing the street, carvings around the door, and a wall to hold in the yard, opening in a five-foot wrought iron gate. Mies spent a lot of money on his house, to show how God had favored him, and the house was a formidable presence on Canal Street.

Hanneke van Cleef knew this because as people went by the house they always paused and looked up at it with awe and sometimes envy on their faces. She herself saw the outside of the house very seldom. She spent most of her days helping her mother order the servants and keep the place. In the afternoons usually she sat in the front room on the second floor and read, or looked out the window at the street, waiting for her father to come home.

That was when her life began, when Mies appeared, walking up the street of the big linden trees toward his house.

Today she sat in the window, her elbow on the sill and her chin in her hand, her gaze steady on the corner where Mies would appear, although it was still nearly an hour before the church bells would ring out the end of the day. She was tired of reading, and done with her needlework; the day seemed very empty. She missed Jan, too. Usually she had his company in the afternoons but lately his father had been keeping him at work in the factory.

She wished she were a boy, able to work side by side with Mies. Thinking that, she brought a sigh up that sounded through the room.

"What was that?" her mother said, looking in the door.

"Oh, nothing," Hanneke said.

Her mother came up behind her and set her hands on her shoulders. "A girl should keep busy. Have you nothing to do?" Stooping, the older woman peered out the window over Hanneke's shoulder. "Oh, look—van der Heghe's stork."

Now it was her mother who sighed, watching the angular white bird circle above the chimney of the house opposite and drop to its great nest of sticks. "I'll set Jan to steal that nest this winter, if I must give him money to do it."

"Oh, Mother."

"Well, why should van der Heghe have a stork and not Mies van Cleef?" Her mother straightened, swished at the windowsill with her dust-rag, and sniffed. "They haven't got a penny to part their hair with, I'll tell you that. All pretense and show it is with them." She sniffed again. "They don't deserve a stork." She marched out of the room, batting at the furniture with the dustrag, although not a visible fleck of dust ever lay long on the van Cleefs' household.

Hanneke turned back to the window, suddenly near tears. Storks and dust, that was all her mother cared about—all she could care about; and that way lay Hanneke's life too, a house like this one, except probably not as nice, and envy for the neighbors and gossip and never going out. That presumed she married; if she did not, things would be even worse. She pressed her face to the sour-smelling glass, feeling sorry for herself.

In the street below a boy ran, shouting and waving a sheet of paper over his head.

The window kept his voice out. Hanneke watched him hurry past, his paper like a banner overhead. Little boys could run the streets at will, like dogs, and she thought it very unfair that she could not leave the house without her mother, who never wanted to go out at all. Across the way, van der Heghe's door opened, and the cook came out onto the walk between the rose beds, looking after the boy with his broadside.

Hanneke's gaze sharpened. The boy was coming back; the cook had a coin out and was buying his broadside. Turning her thumb ring around, Hanneke rapped on the glass, trying to get the cook's attention.

"Marta—"

The cook read the broadside and yelled. With a flutter of her white apron, she dropped the paper into the street and ran back up the brick walk to her front door.

"Marta!" Hanneke shouted, and rapped on the glass. "What is it?"

Van der Heghe's door slammed. The boy ran away; the broadside lay in the street, blowing over in the breeze from the canal. Hanneke leapt up out of her chair and bolted from the room.

Her mother was in the back room, putting flowers in a vase. As Hanneke raced by her door, she called, "Johanna! Walk, like a proper Christian woman!"

Hanneke ran down the stairs and to the heavy front door. Her mother's shrill voice followed her, demanding to know what she did. The door was heavy, a barrier, a bulwark against the world. Hanneke pulled it open and went down the walk to the wrought iron gate.

The broadside still lay in the street, halfway between her gate and van der Heghe's. From the other end of the street came the shouts and screams of children playing. Hanneke gripped the wrought iron spikes of the gate, wondering if she could coax one of the children to bring her the broadside; but they were far away. She pulled the heavy spring latch backward, pushed the gate wide, and ran out into the street.

"Hanneke!" her mother cried, behind her.

She snatched the broadside up out of the dust and whirled and ran back to her own yard. Until she had the gate shut again, she did not stop to read it.

The title shouted at her: WORD FROM THE KING! She leaned against the gate and scanned the lines of print below that. A low cry burst from her. She read it again, to make sure she understood.

"Hanneke!" Her mother stood in the doorway. "Get in here this moment!"

"Mother," Hanneke said, and went toward her, both hands out, the broadside gripped in one fist. "Mother, we're lost—the King has refused the petition."

"What?"

"The King has refused the petition! They will bring the Inquisition here—"

Hanneke went by her mother into the downstairs hallway, turned, and faced her. "Mother, they are going to try to destroy us."

Her mother's face seemed to fall still. She clasped her hands in front of her. "Wait until your father comes home."

"Mother—"

"Don't talk to me. Wait until your father comes home."

Hanneke was struggling against a rising surge of panic. She lifted the broadside again and stared at it. But her mother was right: there was nothing to do except wait. Slowly she turned and climbed the stairs again, to go back to her station, to take up her place, and wait.

WORD OF the King's decision came swiftest along the canals, shouted from barge to barge and barge to shore, shouted back again by voices hoarse with disbelief. Jan heard it standing on the third step of the stair up from the wharf.

He said, "Oh, my God."

The loading crew, some on the wharf, some on the steps above him, said nothing. They let fall whatever they were carrying and turned and ran up onto the canal bank; the foreman, coming from the end of the wharf, brushed past Jan on the steps so roughly Jan lost his balance and nearly fell into the water.

"Wait," he called, but no one waited.

On the canal, the long low scow whose boatman had called out the news was sliding away toward the next wharf; from that platform, already the men were crying out in despair and anger. Jan looked down at the litter of dropped bundles on the wharf and scrambled up the ladder to find his father.

Halfway across the high-piled yard to the back door of the factory, he stopped. Why was he looking for his papa, like a little boy afraid of the dark? His hands were damp with sweat. What Mies had said to him only a few days before returned to him like bells ringing in his mind: *If we had not settled the issue of the Inquisition, things would be a lot worse* . . . In the factory before him a loud voice rose, the words inaudible, but the tone one of outrage. Jan went to the gate and let himself out into the street.

If his father challenged him over leaving his work, he would say he went to spy, as Mies had hinted he should do.

The trouble was that he had no idea where to go to do that. He walked aimlessly down the street, in the opposite direction from his home, into the middle of Antwerp. A tinker passed him, burdened down with pots and pans. At the corner, where this street met the broad thoroughfare that led past the Bourse and down to the river, several women in scarves and shawls were talking intensely together. Jan turned into the great street. A boy ran past him, yelling, "The King's a bastard!" in French. The usual press of horse-drawn carts and bustling people on foot crowded the street, but here and there the traffic had slowed and knots of people stood around talking.

Beyond the rooftops that fenced the lefthand side of the street rose the single off-center spire of Antwerp's cathedral. When he saw it Jan's hackles stood on end. Yes. Swiftly he bent his steps there, to the center of the Catholic faith, to the visible enemy.

He came into the square before the cathedral, into the back of a great restless crowd. Everyone seemed to be staring at the ornately carved stone-work of the huge old church. He passed a woman with her little boy by the hand who as Jan went by snatched the child up and hurried away with him.

Along the front of the cathedral the throng reversed itself: in the square they all stood facing the church, but before it were ranks and ranks of men with their backs to it, facing the square. They carried clubs and rocks; they were Catholics. Defending their church. Jan clenched his teeth. He pushed his way through the mob, unwilling to stand still, his heart thumping. He had to elbow a man out of his way and the man wheeled and glowered at him and swore in a keen voice. Others ignored him. Everyone was staring across the little strip of open ground at the Catholics, who stared back at them.

Jan hated them; he did not know how he came to the passion, which seemed to flow through the crowd. He felt himself part of this great wounded beast of a crowd, its expectations poisoned by the King's treachery. Overhead the cathedral's offset spire towered up against the rushing clouds; the men ranged before it to defend it seemed tiny by comparison, tiny and insignificant. Jan started forward. All those around him started forward too, at the same time, with a growl like dogs unleashed, and in time with these others, these other parts of himself, he lost his head and flung himself on the Catholics.

All he wanted was to hurt them; he struck out with his fists at their faces and felt flesh give under his knuckles, and he kicked at them and his shoes found meat and bone. Around him bodies pressed so tight he could scarcely move. One arm was pinned. He lashed out at the people around him. Throwing his head back he howled like a wolf in rage. Something hard thrust into his stomach.

The wind burst from him. He doubled over, falling to his knees on the cobblestones, and at once feet pounded on his back, knocked him flat, ground him into the pavement. He gasped. Once the air was gone out of his lungs he could not swell his body enough to take in another breath. His face scraped on the cobblestones. Desperately he realized he was being trampled. He surged forward, trying to get to hands and knees, and was knocked down again under the weight of the mob.

His eyes blurred. A sharp pain radiated through his side, and his hands hurt. He lunged upward, strong with a panicky mad strength, and got his feet under him and stood. Blind and stupid from pain, he thrust out his arms ahead of him and tore a way through the surging scrambling mass of bodies. His legs hurt so badly he thought they would give way under him and drop him into the street again, and he knew that would be the end of him and fought with every step to keep upright. Abruptly his outstretched arms milled the air. He had come to the edge of the crowd. Forward he plunged, into an alley between buildings, and fell into the dirt and rolled over until he lay against a wall, protected by the wall, and covered his face with his arms and lost consciousness.

AT FIRST it was rage that drove Mies, a red fury; he searched for his son through the streets of Antwerp as if for a deadly enemy. Damn him for running off. Damn him for fighting—because Mies knew that Jan was fighting, somewhere, in the madness that had seized Antwerp this day and that was continuing on into the night. His mind fixed on Jan as if Jan himself had caused the King's decision.

He walked on and on through the city in his search, through the streets clogged with angry people who fought and shouted and threw stones at one another. Before the cathedral, guarded around and around by armed men, he saw bodies on the cobblestones and heard about the mob's charge barehanded against the great building, flesh against stone, life against death.

By then the night was falling. In the growing darkness the friendly, familiar city seemed to disappear; the shrieks that sounded in the night were forest noises, the crash of something breaking, the thunder of running feet, all these alien in Antwerp, where now everyone ought to be at home, at supper, reading the Bible, playing draughts. Now Mies began to be afraid.

He found himself a lantern and went on, calling Jan's name, looking into corners and alleyways, and peering at the faces of every gang that passed him.

Once he opened his heart to fear a thousand fears came at him. Jan was dead, surely, or he would have gone home to eat. Jan had been carried off, or he would not have left the wharf in the first place. Jan was lying somewhere dying, and Mies could not find him to help him—

Someone jumped him, striking him down. Mies rebounded with the energy of dread and despair and laid about him with the lantern. The dark figure of his attacker staggered backward, and Mies leapt at him, roaring. With the lantern Mies clubbed him fiercely down. The lantern's bowl broke and sprayed oil over the stumbling man, which sprang alight, burning, burning, on his coat, his hair, his arms. Screaming, the man ran off down the street, while Mies panted for breath behind him. Mies flung down the lantern's handle and went on.

Whatever happened to him, he welcomed; that was God's will. But not for his son. "Jan," he bellowed, his voice harsh with fatigue and use. "Jan van Cleef!" And got no answer.

IN HER bedroom Hanneke's mother was praying loudly, as if to shout in God's ears would force Him to hear her. Hanneke clenched her fists in her lap and stared out the window into Antwerp.

The street below was dark and empty. The night lay heavy over the city. Whatever was happening out there she saw no sign of. Her father had not come home; her brother had not come home. There was nothing to do but wait.

Now here came the watch, a little glowing ball of light like a shell around the three men with their halberds. Hanneke sprang up from her chair and ran down the stairs to the front door.

"Hanneke!" her mother shrieked. "Be careful!"

Hanneke opened the door and went out onto the walk to the gate, in her mind cursing her mother: how could she be uncareful in her own garden? She leaned against the iron bars of the gate and pressed her face between them, as she had when she was a little girl, and waited.

The watch went by her, the lantern creaking on the end of its pole, and at the next street corner stopped.

"Ten of the clock," the watchman called, "and the city's full of terrors. Stay in your houses, good people of Antwerp, and pray for God's deliverance."

Hanneke gasped; she bit her lip. They were walking on, walking away, taking with them their bit of light and their suggestion of news. She put her hand to her face.

"God, deliver us." From what?

"Hanneke," her mother called.

She put her hand on the latch. To go out there, to go look, to help, perhaps—

"Hanneke!"

All her life they had kept her here, telling her girls did not go out, girls did not seek the world, girls did nothing. Sit at home and learn to sew, read the right books, wait. She sobbed, her eyes hot with sudden tears, furious at them and at herself for accepting it. The rough iron bit into her hand. She would go out there.

"Hanneke, please—I'm frightened."

Over her shoulder she looked back at the house and saw her mother in the doorway, the light behind her, her arms stretched out.

"Hanneke! What are you doing?"

"I'm locking the gate, Mother." Firmly she drew the bolt across the latch and went back up the walk to the house, where she belonged.

THE BANGING on the gate aroused her. She sat up in her chair; she had slumped against the window when she fell asleep. Down at the gate someone stood, rattling the latch and knocking at the bars. She sprang up and ran downstairs to the door.

It was Mies. A glad cry escaped her. She rushed to the gate and threw back the bolt, and her father stumbled in through the open gate.

"Papa!" She flung her arms around him and kissed him.

"Not now," Mies said. His voice was thick with exhaustion; he pulled her arms down and held her away from him. "Help me." Turning, he went back out the gate.

"Oh, God have mercy." It was Jan, lying on the ground beside the wall. Hanneke and her father lifted him up, and the movement brought a yell from the young man like an arrow in the darkness.

"His leg's broken," Mies said; he had Jan by the armpits, while Hanneke tried to cradle his legs. "Be careful."

Jan was crying with pain. Hanneke said, "Oh, I'm sorry, I'm sorry—" He was too heavy to handle with any delicacy and with every step she hurt him more. She and Mies dragged him into the house and took him down to the kitchen, in the rear of the first floor, where it was warm.

"Oh, Jan." She bent over him, his face gray and sunken and marked with horrible bruises.

Mies went around to his feet and pulled his legs out straight, and Jan screamed again. Hanneke took his hand. "I'm sorry."

"Water," Mies said, as if to speak more syllables than necessary was beyond his strength. He bent over his son's body; cloth ripped in his hands. Hanneke went to find water.

When she came back, the cook had come out of her room behind the oven and was kneeling beside Mies to inspect Jan's leg. There was no room for Hanneke. With the cup of water in her hands she stood uncertainly watching them. Behind her a small noise turned her attention that way.

Her mother stood in the hall doorway, in her dressing gown, her nightcap over her hair. Her gaze fell on her husband and her son, and she cried out.

"Mies! Is he—" She rushed forward, flung herself against her husband's back, trying to reach her son. "Is he dead? Is he—"

Mies thrust out his arm to push her away. "Stand back! Give me room, woman—Hanneke, take your mother up to her bed. Where's that—" Twisting around, he saw the cup of water in her hands and grunted. "That's not enough. Take your mother. Cook, fetch some water."

"Mies!" his wife screamed. "Is he hurt? Is he dead?"

"Take her, Hanneke."

Hanneke clasped her mother's arms. "He's alive. He has a broken leg. Come along."

"Oh, God in Heaven." Her mother broke into floods of tears. "Oh, my God—why did I ever have children? Why did I ever have babies?" Sobbing and heaving for breath, she let Hanneke draw her away toward the stairs. On the stairs, going up to her bedroom, she seized Hanneke's arms with her cold hands.

"Don't ever leave me, Hanneke. Don't ever go. Please don't ever leave me."

"I'm not leaving, Mother. Come along."

"Don't ever leave me alone."

Hanneke looked down over the stair rail, into the hall, where now the servant girl had come up from her bed to stand and look curiously into the kitchen; Hanneke wanted to go down there as much as she wanted life— to see, to help, to do. Her mother clutched her tight.

"Don't ever leave me."

"I won't, Mother." One arm around her mother's shoulders, she led her up the stairs to her bedroom.

THE RIOTING in Antwerp did not go on beyond that same dawn, but the city was hot for more trouble, ready for any excuse. To keep peace in Antwerp, the center of the Low Countries, the heart of northern Europe, the Governess sent the one man she knew could do the job, the man she hated and feared most of all: William of Nassau, Prince of Orange.

Magnificent in his brocaded coat, riding a splendid horse, followed by a great retinue of servants and aides, the Prince rode into Antwerp late on an August Sunday. Many said that was a mark of his lack of piety, that he traveled on the Sabbath, but others said it was a mark of his wisdom, because he came into the city on the one day when everyone in Antwerp would be free to come watch his entrance. Certainly the streets were packed with people. But it was not a welcome they gave him. No one cheered; no one waved banners or gave speeches in his honor and presented pageants likening him to ancient heroes. They stood along the streets and watched him ride by, accepted his easy smiles and raised right hand without any answers of their own. Everybody knew there would be trouble, and everybody, Catholic and Protestant alike, expected to see William of Orange on the other side.

"DID YOU go?" Jan asked. He sat in his bed, propped up on pillows, his bad leg stretched out on more pillows before him. Hanneke sat next to the bed on a stool. Between them lay the draughts board. She reached for one of her checkers.

"Father said not to," she said.

"But you did go."

"Mother was sleeping. He came in by the west gate, it was only a little way off."

"Oh, Hanneke," Jan said.

"I had to go! I'm so tired of being kept here like a caged animal—" She set down the checker almost at random. "I was only gone for a little while."

"What if I'd needed you?" he said, and taking one of his men jumped three of hers in a giddy charge across the board.

"Jan!"

"What if I'd needed you and you weren't here?"

She leapt up, her temper swollen, and, having no other outlet, driven to tears. "Why is it always I who must be here?"

"You needn't," Jan said. "Just tell me when you go out, so that I don't call for you and alert the whole house that you're gone. Understand?"

She came back to the stool and sat. "Yes, you're right."

"I'm all behind you," he said, smiling at her. "Go out all you can. Otherwise how am I to know what's going on?"

"Oh, you'll be walking soon."

They had decided that the leg was not broken, only disjointed at the knee. Bandages swathed it like a babe in the cradle.

Hanneke bent over the draughts board. "Anyway," she said, "the day after tomorrow is Assumption Day, you know."

"Oh, really. I had forgotten."

She advanced one of her men. He was ahead of her now by three pieces and she had to be cautious. "The word is that the priests went to Orange and asked him if they should still have the procession, and he said they ought, to make things seem as usual."

Jan chewed his lip. He moved a man, and Hanneke moved again. "Are you going out to see it?" he asked.

"I will if I can. Mother naps every day in the afternoon."

"If anyone looks for you I will say you went out to pick me a pear," said Jan.

He put out his hand, and she took it in a conspirator's grasp. After he made his next move she jumped four of his pieces.

ALBERT VAN LUYS raised his fist into the air. "The King has declared war on us! We must defend ourselves and our faith—all over the Netherlands. God's people are rising in arms against this devilish King and his ministers—"

Among the several dozen men ranged behind him in the council chamber, fifteen or twenty loosed cheers of support for him; but most of them sat silent and unmoved. The Prince of Orange kept his face expressionless.

He saw the task before him as one of building a wall—he had to find the right matter among these people and put those pieces together into something whole and solid to stand against the fate sweeping toward them like a North Sea storm.

He leaned over the table, his forearms pressed against the marble top, and looked into Albert's blazing eyes.

"Yes, you are right," he said. "There have been riots in a hundred places, people have broken into the churches and destroyed the paraphernalia of the Catholic faith, and everyone in the Low Countries is up on his toes, ready to fight."

He widened his gaze to sweep the mass of men behind Albert, seeking out those who had not cheered his call to war.

"But my information is that even here in Antwerp as many of these eager warriors are Catholic as Protestant."

"Traitors!" Albert cried.

"Oh, sit down, you loudmouth," called one of the men behind him.

A grumble of agreement sounded in the wake of that, and here and there men turned to their neighbors and began to argue. The chamber filled up with discordant noise. Albert folded his arms across his chest and set his jaw. He stayed on his feet, but he said no more, staring at Orange. The Prince wondered how much he knew—if he had heard of the Beggar army that was marching on Antwerp even now and whose leaders had sent a message on ahead asking him to open the city gates to them and give them refuge from the Governess's army coming hard on their heels.

He had spoken to an assembly of the great Catholic men of Antwerp that morning. Now he faced a room full of Calvinists and Lutherans and probably Anabaptists too, and he wondered briefly if there were any use in it, or if he ought to have them all arrested and held until the danger was past.

They were still locked in their small private arguments. Albert swung toward them, raising his arms high.

"Prepare yourselves. The conflict is coming. Soon God Himself shall appear in the sky and ride at the head of our army to destroy the Anti-Christ Philip and usher in the Golden Age!"

The Prince watched the faces of the men before him and saw how they closed against that rhetoric, and his heart quickened with new confidence. They did not want to fight, these burghers and merchants and tradesmen; they had too much to lose. His mind leapt to find a way to use that to his ends.

One of them was standing up.

"Your Highness." This man bowed stiffly from the waist. A slender man of middle height, dressed in black, a touch of silver at his throat. A face as hard as a soldier's. "Give me leave to speak."

"Speak," said the Prince, with a smile at the imperious command in that voice.

Like Albert, like all of them, this man spoke in French, the official language of the Low Countries. He said, "In the fighting for the cathedral, a few days ago, my only son was nearly killed. There are boys like him, who want to fight—young and ignorant men, not the paladins of God—only boys who fight anyway, whenever the chance arises. It is not God's way to use such instruments."

The Prince cleared his throat; this was a very fine point, subtle as a shadow, to be made in the face of such broad and sweeping passions. He said, "May I ask your name, sir?"

"I am Mies Willem van Cleef, your Highness; I make and sell cloth. I am a good churchgoing God-fearing man, as everyone here can testify, but I doubt when the final battle for the world comes that it will be fought by green boys, with stones and clubs."

"Traitor," Albert cried. "Spaniard!" With a swirl of his robes he stalked out of the council chamber.

The gathering stirred, as men turned to watch him go, and some even got to their feet to follow. Mies van Cleef stood facing the Prince still, his face grim and his back to where Albert had been. Many men shifted in their places and muttered and moved, but no one followed Albert out the door and the Prince took heart from this.

He said, "Your point is very well taken, Mijnheer van Cleef. I hope your son is well now."

Van Cleef's head bobbed briefly in a kind of courtesy.

"Let us work together, then," the Prince said, "to find some way to protect our young men from one another."

Another man rose in the crowd behind Mies van Cleef. "Did you wish that, your Highness, you ought not to have allowed the Catholics to go ahead with their procession on Assumption Day."

A growl went up from twenty throats, agreeing. The Prince put his hands down on the veined marble top of the table.

"I had in mind the old adage that to keep the peace it serves best to act peacefully."

"We are not at peace," said Mies van Cleef.

"You think the city on the verge of strife?"

Half a dozen men called, "Yes, yes—"

"Then should we not put armed men around the streets, to keep order? Will you help me keep order here?" The Prince ran his gaze from face to face. "They will listen to you—the respected and powerful men of their own faith."

Neatly trapped, none of them said anything. Mies van Cleef sat down again. The man who had spoken against the Assumption procession stayed on his feet, and the Prince nodded to him.

"You, Master Clement, your services are uniquely necessary to this task before us."

"You know me," said Clement de Vere, looking startled.

The Prince smiled at him, and in a mild voice said, "I know you all."

He looked each one in the face again, to let them feel this, that they could not escape from him in anonymity. Mies van Cleef grunted and crossed his legs, one over the other.

"Master Clement is a printer," said the Prince. "The finest Protestant printer in Antwerp, and we shall have great need of his presses to keep the people aware of what is happening and of what is expected of them. We shall also need guards, watchmen for the city's safety. Can I rely on you? Will each of you arm yourself and undertake to give time—much time, I am afraid, knowing you all to be busy men—to keep the peace in Antwerp? To preserve Antwerp from destruction?"

Their faces were blank. They were thinking about it. Still no one had walked out. He leaned forward, ready with his most weighty argument.

"Destruction it will be, if Antwerp should rise as other cities are rising. Heavy blows will call forth heavier yet, from the Spanish monarchy—and they say that even now the King has ordered the tercios of Italy to prepare to march north under the leadership of the Duke of Alva."

"Alva."

That name struck them. They straightened, their faces tight with new apprehension. Mies van Cleef uncrossed his legs. Did he see his only son battling with sticks and stones against the greatest warrior in Christendom?

"Will you help me?" said the Prince of Orange.

"I will," said Mies van Cleef, and rose, the first of all, and came forward to shake the Prince's hand.

DRESSED like a doll in glittering clothes, a jeweled crown on her head, the little black image of the Virgin rode in her car at the head of the Assumption Day procession down the crowded streets of Antwerp. Hanneke watched her from the steps of the Guildhall, where standing higher than the people before her she could see over their heads. She had never seen the famous Antwerp Virgin before. It was smaller than she had supposed. Why was it black? Very old, it was, and silly in its fancy clothes. Priests pulled the car along, and other priests scattered incense before and after it. Troops of boys in white, with candles, sang in the car's wake. After them came scores of common people, praying, scourging themselves, some walking on their hands and knees, doing penance for their sins.

Hanneke bit her lip. Something in this reached even into her Calvinist heart, some ancient longing. The crowd before her stirred; the image was passing directly before them now.

"Mollykin, Mollykin," someone called, in Dutch. "You are taking your last walk."

Laughter in the crowd. The priests ignored it, hauling the car along with ropes over their shoulders. It seemed heavy, although the figure itself was no bigger than a baby and even the jeweled clothes could not weigh so much. Now the singing boys were going by, their candles held upright before them. Too young for discipline, they slid their gazes toward the crowd and some hurried their pace, running into the ones ahead of them. Frightened.

Now here came the penitents, and these suffered much for their faith. The crowd pelted them with rotten fruit and clods of earth and shouted curses and jibes at them. Hanneke slipped down from her vantage point and went away.

She had to be back at once, before she was discovered gone. Yet she longed to stay out here in the city. The excitement in the crowd charged her with vitality. Something great was happening here, an undercurrent of passion, of rising intensity, that she felt along all her nerves, a giddy expectation. As she went through the streets she looked curiously at the faces she passed. Into the shops and doorways. There seemed many more people than usual out in the street. She stopped on a corner, to look around her, and a boy thrust a broadside into her hand.

"I have no money—"

He was already running off. She looked down at the long heavy sheet of paper.

WAR! the top row of print read. WAR! WAR! WAR!

That raised every hair on her head stiff as wire. Her gaze flew down the page.

There was an army coming—two armies. A swarm of Beggars out of the west country was hurrying toward Antwerp; an army of Catholics pursued them, much outnumbering them. Her heart galloped. Folding the broadside into quarters, she stuffed it under her apron sash and went on through the streets to her home.

"LACKEY!" Jan shouted. "Traitor! Spaniard!"

Mies clenched his teeth; he fought the urge to strike at his son's red contorted face. "Sit down. You'll hurt your leg."

"My leg is perfectly well!" To prove it Jan walked in a little circle around the room. "How could you do this, Father? The fate of the whole world hangs in the balance—"

"The fate of the world," Mies said heavily, and sat down in his chair. He leaned on the arm, looking around him at the shelves of books, and wondered again where Hanneke was. Always she was here when he came back, like a piece of the furniture, waiting for him. His son stormed across the room to face him again.

"The time has come to choose, Father—to choose between God and truth and all the evils of the past. You can't just say it's too dangerous. You can't really mean to put the factories and the piles of cloth and the money before God."

Mies shifted in the chair, his fingers tight around the ridged wooden arm, his gaze not meeting Jan's. He said, "I see no sign that God is asking such a choice of me." Mercilessly he refused to hear the inner voice that whispered Jan was right.

"Jan!" His wife appeared in the doorway. "My dear husband. What is this unseemly shouting? I am sure you can be heard even in the street."

"Where is Hanneke?" Mies asked her.

"God is calling us," Jan said, bending forward, his hands curling before him into fists, "to join the army of Christ. If we turn our backs now—"

"Jan," his mother said. "You must not speak to your father in that tone."

"He's a traitor!" Jan roared, and stalked away across the room. Indeed his leg seemed much sounder, although he still limped.

Mies said, "We must preserve Antwerp. Thousands of people depend on us—" Hollow these arguments, meaningless even to him; the only meaningful one the one he could hardly find expression for: his abhorrence of disorder, his vision of the world dissolving into chaos in the acids of hatred and intolerance. Downstairs the door to the street opened and shut.

"You should be in bed," his wife was saying reproachfully to her son. "Your leg is still so sore and swollen—"

"Mama, I'm fine," the boy bellowed, and wheeled on Mies again, his eyes shining, his cheeks streaked with tears. "You will not join us? You will not answer God's call?"

"God's call," Mies said, "is for harmony and peace. Not for—"

"Spaniard!" Jan jerked back his head and flung it forward, and through his pursed lips flew a gout of spit that sailed across the space between them and struck Mies on the cheek.

His mother screamed. Mies gripped the arm of his chair, stiff with rage, his ears roaring, his mind at a white boil. Before him stood his son, weeping.

"Father!" Hanneke rushed into the room and sank down beside his chair. "How dare you?" she shouted at Jan.

"Do you know what he's done?" Jan said to her. "He's joined the Spaniards! He's taking arms against God—fallen in with the Prince of Orange and the Governess, the tools of this world—"

Mies sprang up from his chair, swiped at his cheek, and shouted, "Go! Get out—get away from me, you Godless impious wretched son, you ungrateful devil!"

"You've made your choice, Father." Jan walked toward the door.

His mother threw herself on him, seized his arm, crying, "Wait! Wait!"

"Let go of him," Mies shouted. "You saw what he did—how he treats his own father. Let him go, Griet!"

Jan was struggling to reach the door; his mother clung to him with all her strength, and he had to drag her weight along with him. Hanneke caught Mies' hand and pressed it to her cheek.

"Father, please—where will he go? Father, please."

Mies lowered his suspicious gaze to her. "Where were you?"

"I—"

She lost her breath, but in the red flames that suddenly kindled in her cheeks, in her lowered eyes, he saw what he dreaded to see, that she too disobeyed him, that she too broke from the order of the household and did what must not be done. He thrust her away.

"God is coming," he said. He went to the window, to the light and air, his back to his family. "And He will find impious sons and bold unruly daughters, and all system fallen away." He put his trembling hands on the windowsill and leaned his weight on them. Unaccountably his own eyes burned with tears. He shifted his body, finding himself fearful of resting on the window frame, as if weakened by the weakness of its inhabitants the house itself would not hold up its master's weight. Behind him a door slammed. His wife burst into uncontrollable weeping. His daughter sank into a chair and began to pray.

In ANTWERP all normal life stopped. The Prince of Orange and his recruits patrolled the streets, hoping to keep order by their presence and example, but in the crackling heat of an August night, with phantom armies approaching on every wind of rumor and the wretched poor turned out idle on every corner, a mob of folk shouting that Christ was coming burst into the great cathedral and tore the holy images from the walls, broke the altar, chopped open the shrine of the Virgin with an ax, and hacked the little black doll to pieces. They stole her precious clothes and the outfittings of the altar and tried to set fire to the cathedral itself, although the massive building withstood the feeble torches without a lasting mark. Then the mob ran through the streets of the city, shouting their visions of the coming of Christ and throwing pieces of the broken icons into Catholic gardens, and went to attack a monastery next.

The Prince got there first, with a few of his helpers, and they stood between the screaming Calvinists and the monks huddling and praying in the chapel, and by calm words and the power of command the Prince got the crowd going elsewhere.

Among those who stood beside him that night was Mies van Cleef, the cloth merchant, who searched the crowd with his eyes and yet seemed afraid of seeing something there.

That night passed, and the next, and the next, with no more incidents, although sometimes in the night huge crowds gathered, some Calvinist, some Catholic, and prayed and heard preaching and made loud talk in the streets. Everyone knew an army was marching toward Antwerp, the Beggar army, with a horde of harassing and tormenting Catholics at its back.

On the day when the Beggar army first came in sight of the city walls a mass of Calvinists gathered at the gate, all armed with pitchforks and clubs and pieces of stone torn up from the street pavings, prepared to go out and join them. The Prince went to put himself between them and the gate and ordered them home.

"You must not leave the city," he shouted, trying to lift his voice above their clamorings. "You'll be destroyed. The Governess's army is twice as many as the Beggars and you combined. They are mounted, heavily armed, well led; the Beggars are a rabble. Stay here—do not destroy yourselves."

Then came what he most dreaded, a messenger from the Beggars, asking him to open the gates of Antwerp to them, to give them refuge. From atop the wall beside the gate, the Prince of Orange looked down at the exhausted messenger, riding bareback on a farm horse, and told him no.

"You must let us in," the messenger called, in a voice flat with fatigue and hopelessness. "They are eating us alive. We need shelter—food—we've come so far—"

"I cannot give Antwerp to you," said the Prince. "We must preserve something of our country in the face of this madness."

"You are our only hope."

"Then you have no hope. Go; I cannot help you. None here can help you, but only Christ our Lord. Go, before you are pinned against these walls and slaughtered."

"Go where?" the messenger cried.

"Go home."

"We have no home." The messenger reined his limping plow horse away and rode off down the slope.

At that a wail went up from the Calvinists packed into the street inside the gate, and they lunged forward, broke the gate, and spilled out onto the road and the green slopes along the road, rushing to join the Beggars. The Prince seized the nearest horse and galloped through their midst to their head.

"Stop—go back—you'll be slaughtered!"

Alone, he put himself between them and the Beggar army, now creeping into view along the rounded horizon, and seeing him the mob slowed and stopped.

"Go back." He spread his arms, as if he could herd them all back into the city. "Go back—don't give the Governess's army the excuse to attack Antwerp."

Someone bolted forward from the mob, trying to rush past him, and he swung his horse to block the man's way. "Go back—please—I beg of you."

The man struck clumsily up at the elegant figure on the horse that stopped his progress. The Prince warded off the blows with his arms. "Go back—go back—please—I implore you."

At that a sigh went up from the mob, when they saw him shielding himself from the blows of the Calvinist, not fighting back, not striking down his attacker, and pleading for his attacker's own safety; they even found the power to raise a cheer for him, and turning they made their way back into the city.

A few stole away, hanging back from the fringes of the mob. Most of them returned to Antwerp; the great gates closed, and the bar went across them, and the city shut itself to the Beggars. And after that there was no more trouble.

JAN GRIPPED a pole in both hands, his breath coming harsh and short between his teeth; his eyes were itching with dust. Far down the plain the Beggar army was streaming into view over the horizon. He straightened, prepared to be overcome by the majesty of their appearance—ready to see God's angels in the sky above them. His skin tingled, and his blood thrashed in his veins; at any moment, he knew, something great would happen.

Nothing happened. Far off over the plain the Beggars were running along the road and over the meadows beside it. They kept no order; they wore no armor or insignia. No banners flew over them. No angelic light shone around them. Hesitantly he started forward through the knee-high grass, clutching his weapon, his injured leg throbbing painfully with each step.

A trumpet sounded, far away. He wheeled. This was the beginning, at last, the horns of God blasting on the plain of Armageddon. Now he could see horses galloping up over the rolling land. He called out, raising one arm straight over his head, and ran forward to meet them.

A few strides later he stopped in his tracks.

The horsemen were riding down the Beggar rabble. Not joining them. Not supporting them. Tiny in the distance, they hacked with their swords at the fleeing backs of the army of God. They were the royalists, then, the Catholics, and they were killing with impunity.

Jan let out a low cry. He broke into a run again, headed toward the nearest group of the Beggar army. His leg gave way and toppled him into the grass, and he rose and went on, sobbing for breath, his vision yellowed by the dust that rolled in clouds under the feet of the Beggars and their killers.

Ahead of them a hundred Calvinists were rushing along the road, but the royalist horsemen were rapidly overtaking them. He was too far away to help. Too far away even to die with them. He stumbled over something in the grass and went to his hands and knees, and turning to see what he had fallen over found a body on the ground.

He lunged up onto his feet and raced on, but they were drawing away from him. The enemy horsemen, striking and wheeling, rode on faster than he could run. He passed a man in tatters who writhed and gasped on his back in the slimy grass. Out of breath, his lungs choked with dust, Jan slowed to a walk and then stopped, his gaze on the horsemen, still small in the distance.

They were riding off; their trumpets blared again, a tinny little spangle of noise in the silent afternoon. Gradually he heard the other sounds around him, the whisper of the wind in the grass, the twittering of insects, the croaking of the day birds. A butterfly flapped by him. Slowly he turned and spread his attention around him. He was surrounded by a lot of men, dead or dying, scattered in the grass. No army. No angels, no glory of God, only a litter of bloody meat in the August sunshine. He moaned; a noise he had never heard before and did not mean to make rolled up from his belly and leaked out between his lips. He thought what he saw should burn his eyes out. That would be better. That would mean something. Slowly he dragged his feet back to Antwerp.

"OH, WHO cares?" Jan said. He flung his hand out, loose muscled, flopping his arm down on his knee. "It's all a damned lie anyway, Hanneke." He folded his other arm over his face.

His sister backed away from him, to the door of his room; she wondered what had happened to him outside the walls of the city. Since he had come back he had said nothing. She went out the door to the corridor.

The housemaid was singing in the room opposite. The warm odors of dinner drifted through the house. Slowly Hanneke went down the stairs to the second floor.

Through the open door to her parents' room, she could see her mother, sitting on the tall canopied bed, combing her hair. Her mother smiled at her brightly, like a child, the long brown rope of her hair hanging over her shoulder. Hanneke went on to the sitting room, looking for her father.

Mies was there, in the old chair by the fire. Slumped down into his seat, he did not move when she came in, or look up, or speak to her. She stood a moment waiting for him to notice her. His face was slack and dull as a drunkard's. Aghast, she wondered if he were drunk. He never said a word to her; if he saw her there, he ignored her utterly. She could not think what to say to him. And what if he were drunk? She went down the room to the window.

Night was falling. The sinking sun cast its light against the tall front of van der Heghe's house across the street, gilding the windows. Hanneke looked by habit for the storks in their nest on the chimney.

She gasped. The birds were gone. The nest was knocked halfway off the chimney top. Bits of stick and straw littered the roof line. She turned toward her father, to share this evil, but he was staring into the fire, inaccessible. She looked out again at the house opposite, wondering what had happened —where the birds had gone. It was too early for them to have flown away south. Africa, she had heard, that was where they went for the winter. The name sounded in her mind like a meaningless incantation, a curse in another language. Suddenly she was fighting back tears. She turned blindly to the bookshelf, to find something to read, to forget herself in.

2

WHEN Count Horn rode in through the gate of the Palais de Nassau in Brussels, he could scarcely penetrate the courtyard, which was filled with heavy ox-drawn wagons and servants rushing between them and the palace doors. The servants, he noticed, were loading goods from the palace into the wagons, rather than the other way around, the usual order of things. The place looked as if it were being looted.

He found a groom to take his horse, and leaving his retainers to keep out of the way of all this hubbub he went into the palace in search of his friend the Prince of Orange.

Orange was in his living quarters, on the second story of the south wing, overseeing the removal from the walls of the mirrors and paintings and their packing into crates. When he saw Count Horn, he smiled and held out his hand in greeting, but his face remained grave as ever behind the courtly mask.

"My dear friend." Horn came to his side, his gaze surveying the clutter of packing and goods that took up all the space in the room. The carpets were rolled up and tied fast, and even the ornate fastenings on the windows were coming down. "Are you moving to another palace?"

That seemed impossible. The Palais de Nassau had been the seat of the Princes of Orange for their last several manifestations; no finer house stood in the Low Countries.

Orange still wore his smile, but his dark eyes were hooded and morose. "I am moving my household to Germany, my friend," he said.

"To Germany! Whatever for?"

"This past week I have had news that the Duke of Alva is leading the Spanish armies in Italy north, to take them through the Alps and bring them here. I do not mean to be within his reach when he arrives."

Horn stared at him, his lips parted. With a shake he brought himself out of his astonishment, laughed, and plucking at the snowy masses of lace at his throat adjusted his enormously expensive coat. "You must be joking, my lord. You'd abandon the field to the enemy before he even appears? After your brilliant success at Antwerp?"

Orange had lost his smile. He watched Horn with an impassive face, cocked his hand to a servant standing nearby, and said, "I beg your pardon, my dear Count. I have been unforgivably rude—will you join me for a glass of wine?" A nod to the servant sent him hurrying off.

When they had gone out onto a little balcony, where the sun shone warmly and the evidence of the Prince's activity was gone from view, Horn relaxed. He felt now that this would make a splendid joke—the Prince's loss of nerve at the mere mention of the name of the Duke of Alva. In spite of the disruption of his household, Orange's staff was still perfect in his service; within moments the servant brought a flagon of a very fine pale Moselle wine, and another servant presented Horn with a tray of sweets and fruits for his selection.

"You will be the laughingstock of Brussels, you know," said Horn, lifting a candied lime to his mouth. "And after all the expense and bother of moving everything out, you'll only have to move it all back in again, when the season starts. I hope you don't break that mirror from your salon; you'll never find another as handsome."

"If you want my advice, you'll leave as well," said Orange.

He sat, not on the embroidered cushion of the chair to Horn's left, but on its carved wooden arm; he looked very restless.

Horn laughed. "I am not afraid of Alva."

Orange said nothing.

"We are in control here," said the count. He leaned forward over the silver tray of sweets, his fingers poised, searching out another candied lime. "The Governess had to rely on you to help quell the iconoclasts, did she not? The country is restored to order—"

"There are many who call me traitor now on both sides," said Orange. "The Governess hates and fears me the more because of my work in Antwerp, and the Calvinists hate me for refusing to shelter their army there."

"That will pass." Horn licked sugar from his fingertips. "Alva is a barbarian. The Netherlands is a civilized place."

"Alva is not a barbarian," Orange said sharply. "I know him far better than you do, and he is as subtle and keen witted a man as there is in Europe. Let me tell you something. Years ago, when the Emperor was still alive, he sent me and two others to France, after the conclusion of the treaty between him and Henri the Second, to secure the provisions of the treaty." Orange picked up the wine flask and filled his friend's cup. "One day I found myself in the company of Monsieur le Roi de France in a wood at Chantilly, where he was enjoying a picnic supper, and Monsieur le Roi turned to me and began talking about 'our common plan.' I knew nothing of this plan, but I held my tongue and listened, to know more. Soon it became clear that those who knew me better than Monsieur le Roi had kept the Common Plan from me, because they knew I had no heart for slaughter and persecution, and this plan was for the slaughter and persecution of every heretic in Europe. Beginning with the Low Countries."

Horn licked his lips. The taste of the lime still clung to his mouth. But Henri II was dead, he reminded himself, and so was the Emperor.

"I sat there in the wood in Chantilly," said the Prince, "and listened to him speak of killing his own subjects—some by the sword, some by the rope, and by fire—as if he talked of treading on locusts who devoured his fields, or pulling up weeds in his garden. He thought I knew of every detail. He thought so because one of the other hostages was a chief framer of the Common Plan, and had been sent to France especially to acquire Monsieur le Roi's support for it."

He leaned forward, his dark, hooded eyes sharp. "That hostage was the Duke of Alva."

Horn pressed his lips together. For a moment he entertained a high hot anger at the Prince of Orange for this overdramatic speech, for trying to frighten him.

"He is coming here to destroy heresy in the Low Countries," said the Prince. "The Beggars have given him the excuse, and into the bargain they have quenched all sympathy they could have enjoyed with the Catholics."

"All the more reason to stay," Horn said, in a full courageous voice. "To stay and fight."

"To stay and be wiped out."

"What can he do to us? He can hang a few peasants, but we are the greatest men of the Provinces, my dear Prince—we are Knights of the Golden Fleece, stadtholders, counts, and princes—he cannot touch us."

As he spoke Horn relaxed, reassured. He drew a deep breath, happy with himself.

"I hope you are right, sir," said Orange.

"Of course I am right." Horn finished his wine and set down his cup. "However, if you're leaving—I don't suppose you would sell me that mirror? You'll break it certainly, hauling it off to Germany."

The Prince of Orange laughed. "It's yours," he said. "I'll send it to your palace this afternoon."

"A noble gesture. When you return, you shall have it back."

"Only see that it is not broken in my absence, Count."

"Be sure of it," said Count Horn, pleased.

THE PRINCE OF ORANGE intended to make his departure from the Low Countries covertly, and so he returned to Antwerp for a while, after he had sent all his possessions to Germany from Brussels. But a few days after he reached Antwerp he gathered up his servants and his retainers and rode off to the gate of the city.

The people in the streets knew him at once; everyone in Antwerp knew him, from his work during the iconoclasm and his rule since then, and they loved him. A small crowd followed him as he rode through the city toward the gate. A boy ran up beside his horse, calling, "Where are you going? Oh, where are you going?"

"To Dillenburg," said the Prince, in breezy fashion. "For the hunting. I am only going to Dillenburg, friends—no cause for alarm."

The boy would not be put off; he ran alongside him, still crying out, "Where are you going? Oh, where are you going?" And the crowd grew larger that followed along after him.

He smiled at them; he tried to reassure them, but his smile was tight and forced, and as if he gave off an aura of uneasiness and tension the crowd, swelling in numbers with every step, grew more distressed. They pressed after him to the gate.

"Oh, where are you going?"

"Goodbye," the Prince said, and turned and waved to them. "I shall come back soon—have no fear." He smiled at them; he rode out the gate, still smiling, but many saw the sweat that stood on his brow, and many saw the smile stiff as a grimace, like the rictus of death.

DON FERNANDO ALVAREZ DE TOLEDO, Duke of Alva, gathered under his banner the three tercios of the Spanish soldiery stationed in Italy and marched them north through the Alpine passes. In slow orderly progress, he led these thousands of men, beneath their banners of the Virgin and the saints, from the Catholic south to the reformed north of Europe, and from the rocky heaths of Scotland to the swampy Polish plain, the Protestant Christians tensed like bowstrings. Alva knew the effect of his march, and being a patient man he was content with that for now and kept his troops in good order and made no trouble on the way.

Tall, with hair and beard gone white in the service of his King and his God, he rode usually near the head of his columns. He knew everything that happened in the army and he gave every general order himself. His son was one of his officers, but Alva treated Don Federico de Alvarez no differently from any other Spanish soldier; he expected absolute discipline and unfaltering courage from everyone he commanded, the same discipline and courage he demanded of himself.

In the spring of the year he led his army into the Low Countries.

As he marched toward Brussels, he studied the terrain. His confidence fed on what he saw. He had been here before, and it was easily understood, this countryside—flat and low, the plain swept toward the North Sea without a barrier more formidable than an occasional wood. The roads were excellent, but the canals were a real marvel, connecting every part of the Provinces. On this flat and open game board stood the major pieces of the opposition, the great cities, divided within into hostile classes, jealous one city of another, intensely competitive.

The game was almost too easy. Alva entered Brussels without opposition, without even a stir of alarm among the people who lined the streets to watch. He found that nearly all his immediate enemies were waiting, within easy grasp, for him to make the first move. And Alva moved.

AT BREAKFAST, Mies said the prayer as usual, and they all sat down at the table, and the maidservant brought in the hot dishes. Hanneke spread her napkin on her knees, her hands quick with impatience. She had talked her mother into making a rare excursion out to the market today and she wanted to leave before the older woman changed her mind. She watched her father serve himself the broiled fish, wondering if he deliberately loitered over the choice and the removal of the crusty brown filets to his plate.

He laid the fish knife down along the platter's edge. Sitting back so that the maidservant could take the plate away to Hanneke's mother, he raised his eyes to her brother, across the table.

"You are coming with me today on my shop rounds."

Hanneke lifted her head, startled. Mies' rule of silence at mealtimes was almost never broken. Usually he had settled with Jan what he was to do the night before.

Jan was bent over his plate. When he raised his head his eyes were dark with temper.

He said, "I have other plans."

"Jan, dear," his mother said, in soft reproof. She turned to the fish.

"You are coming with me," said Mies, in a tone that meant to shut down all objection.

Jan said, "I see no reason to obey someone who betrayed his God and his God's faithful—"

There was a thunderous pounding on the front door of the house.

"—and who puts profit and goods ahead of truth and justice!"

Father and son glared at each other across the table. Hanneke gripped her napkin in her lap, her heart pounding. This could not be happening; as well shout God down from the sky as challenge a father over his own table. But it was. The pounding on the door went on, but it seemed to be taking place in another world, unimportant.

Mies said, "I shall accept no more of this insolence. You are coming with me, or I shall resort to such punishments as are suitable for the mis-demeanors of a child."

"When you betrayed our faith and our people, you lost your power over me, Mijnheer van Cleef."

The front door burst open. Now Mies turned his head, blinking; all the family sat up stiff in their chairs to goggle at the strange men who tramped into their dining room.

They wore iron shirts and carried muskets. Soldiers. Hanneke's mouth fell open, and her mother screamed. Mies thrust back his chair. Standing, he strode around the table to the obvious leader of these men, a neatly bearded officer in a black coat.

"What do you mean by this trespass? Who are you?"

"You are Mies van Cleef," the officer said, unruffled. His accent was strange; he spoke in French. He smiled a meaningless pleasant smile at Jan, staring at him from across the table. "You are under arrest."

Mies stood still where he was, but he swayed, as if a strong wind shook him, and his face went white. Hanneke's teeth caught her lower lip. When the soldiers closed around her father, she said, "No."

"You can't take him now," her mother said. "He hasn't finished his breakfast."

Jan passed behind her chair so violently he knocked her forward into the table; he set himself at the men around his father. Mies shouted. In a wild confusion, the soldiers, their prisoner, and Jan all whirled together in a milling of arms and the soldiers' long guns. There was a sharp thud and Jan fell to the floor.

The officer looked amused. His men folded around Mies and walked him out the door, and the officer turned to Hanneke and her mother.

"This house is forfeit to the Crown. You have until noon to get out." He jabbed his thumb at Jan. "We will come for him next." He went out after his men.

Hanneke shot up out of her place and ran around the table to her brother, groaning on the floor. A glance showed her he was well enough. Her mother sat motionless at the table, staring at Mies' empty chair. "Where have they taken him? When will he be home again?" Hanneke went out the door to the front sitting room.

The furniture here was all draped against the dust; the room was used only on feast days. At the window the maidservant and the cook were pressed to the glass looking into the street. Hanneke forced a way in between them.

Out there the soldiers were pushing Mies into a line of other men, each with his hands manacled behind his back and a halter around his neck linking him to the man in front of him. Other soldiers with pikes and helmets stood around them. The men who had taken Mies pulled his hands behind him and fastened him up to the last man in the line. Hanneke bit her lip. He looked dazed, her father, unready and helpless. His breakfast not even eaten. Among the other men in line, she saw faces she recognized. Near the front of the line was Albert van Luys, the preacher.

At a gesture from the officer, a man with a hammer strode up to the door of the van Cleef house, took a roll of paper from beneath his arm, and tacked a notice to the door. The officer barked an order. The column of prisoners marched away, soldiers on either side and coming after. The man with the hammer hurried after them, breaking into a run to catch up. She thought Mies turned his head to look back, but the dust of so many feet made it hard to see; within minutes he was gone from sight.

THE DAY was overcast and cold. Jan shivered without his jacket. At the tower by the river where his father had been taken, he found a crowd of people fidgeting and pacing around, trying to find out what had happened to their own relatives, who had been marched off as peremptorily as Mies. There seemed to be no one who could give them any answers.

The tower gates were locked and barred and the windows were shuttered. People stood before the doors hammering on them with their fists and shouting. Other people talked in little groups. Jan walked through the crowd, his shoulders hunched, the cold driving him on. He wondered if this had befallen him for his impiety—if God had heard his defiance of his father and with the suddenness of a thunderclap had taken Mies away to punish him. The tower was made of grim gray stone, several stories high. He imagined scaling a rope to one of the narrow windows at the top and bearing Mies away on his back.

"They've taken every important man in Antwerp," an old woman was saying, near the gate. "Even some of the Catholics."

"They can't do this; it's against the law." A man in black came up to Jan and spoke earnestly to him, as if they knew one another well. "They can't do this; they must all be released at once."

A clump of men stood opposite the main gate of the tower; their heads together, they were planning something, with many calculating glances at the prison, and Jan went over to join them. They let him without hesitation into their midst.

"We'll need weapons." The big bearded man at the center spoke to all of them, his eyes shifting from face to face. Jan knew him, a brewer from the German quarter. "Rakes, clubs, knives, anything. And something heavy to break down the door with."

The man beside Jan turned to him and said, "They can't do this. We are right to free our people, who are false prisoners."

From behind the tower a trumpet blew. All the men wheeled.

A column of pikemen was trotting up the gentle slope from the river. The sun, just breaking through the dense dark clouds, caught on a helmet here and there and on the long leaf-shaped blades of their pikes. Uncertain, the people around the tower waited and watched them approach. Jan flexed his hands. His mouth was dry. He wished he had a sword, a stick, any sort of weapon. The Spanish pikemen reached the tower, swung their long lances down, and charged into the crowd.

Women screamed; all around the tower, people turned and struggled to get out of the way of the blades. Jan let out a bellow of rage. Whatever these soldiers were, they were cowards, attacking unarmed men and women. Spreading apart his bare hands, he rushed forward at the pikemen, determined to grab one of their weapons and use it on them.

Shrieking, a woman blundered into him, her hands raised to shield herself; he slipped by her and planted his feet. The line of soldiers swept toward him like an ocean wave, close packed, their pikes laid down horizontal in a moving fence of blades. There was no way past them, no way to take one at a time. They spitted a young man to Jan's left and threw him down to the ground and while he screamed trampled over him. Jan thrust his hands out, his breath coming fast, in whines. The wall of blades swung toward him. Blood dripped from the points. He backed up, stumbled, fell, and rolled frantically away.

The memory swept over him of the time he had nearly been trampled; suddenly his body broke free of his mind's discipline. Without thought he sprang to his feet and ran away. There was someone in his path and he knocked her down and ran by her without a glance. The shrieks and curses of other Dutchmen sounded in his ears but he heard nothing except the thunder of his heart. Ahead of him other people were fleeing. They ran too slowly for him; he threw them aside and raced on, on, up the slope toward the city, away from the pikes, away to safety.

W HEN HE reached the house in the Canal Street there were boxes piled on the front step, and his sister was in their parents' bedroom packing jewelry and money and books into the wooden chest from his father's cupboard. Their mother stood over her, wringing her hands and weeping.

"Why are you doing this? There's no need for this. Your father will be home soon—what will he say? Wait for him to tell us what to do." The older woman's face was swollen and twisted with crying. She put her hands out to Jan. "Tell her to stop."

One hand pressed to his aching side, Jan lowered himself to the floor beside Hanneke. She ignored him; she laid books in the chest in a neat brickwork.

"Where are you going?" he asked.

"The Kelmans will rent us a room," Hanneke said. "In the Swan Street, the Joseph and Mary House."

"Tell her to stop," their mother pleaded, crying tears.

"What happened to you?" Hanneke asked him.

"At the tower," he said. "The soldiers came and drove us off. There were lots of people there but they drove us off. Some were killed."

"Are you all right?" Hanneke laid her hand on his arm.

He nodded, his gaze sliding away from hers; he could not face her when he thought how he had fled away from his enemies like a coward.

"Is Father in the tower?" she asked.

He nodded.

"He will be home soon," their mother said. "I'll go watch for him." She fled out of the room.

Hanneke stroked her brother's sleeve; now suddenly there were tears on her cheeks. "What will happen to us? Why is this happening to us?"

He put his arms around her and pulled her against his shoulder, and she wept. "There, now, Hanneke," he said, and rubbed her back.

There was a sudden banging on the door downstairs, and she jumped so violently she spilled books from her lap onto the floor. Jan got up to his feet.

"I'll see who it is."

It was the soldiers, come to take the house. Jan longed to fight them; he wanted to snarl brave words into their faces, but there were ten of them, all with pikes and guns. He hoisted the chest his sister showed him up onto his shoulder, and under the cold foreign eyes of the Spaniards he and Hanneke and their mother with their belongings on their backs trudged out of their house into the street. One of the soldiers said something to his sister as she passed and reached out his hand to pat her breast. She wheeled away, dropping the wooden chest of books into the street. The soldiers all laughed. Jan helped her put the books away again and led her off down the street.

"JUST A few troublemakers," said Alva, smiling. He fixed Count Horn with an unblinking stare and spread his hands. "I must protect my troops from the fanatics who have already proven themselves enemies of the state, capable of any crime."

Count Horn clenched his fist. A glance around the council chamber showed him the other men divided into two unequal groups; those who supported Alva watched with sleek satisfied faces, while the few who opposed him—very few—wore looks etched deep with strain and uncertainty.

Horn coughed into his cupped palm. He had the sensation of losing the ground under his feet, as if the floor had suddenly dropped away.

Stubbornly, he said, "We in these Provinces are governed by laws, my lord duke. Such measures as you have taken violate our privileges."

Alva said, "People who destroy churches and sacred relics do not deserve privileges."

"The Duke of Burgundy is not the Duke of Burgundy without the law!" Horn leaned forward, urgent with his idea; Alva's bland smiling mask infuriated him. "The law makes the ruler. Without the law there is no rule. Don't you see—"

"The King," said Alva slowly, with emphasis, "is master of far more than these few little territories. He cannot be bound by the moss-grown superstitions of one little corner of his realm, or he loses his grandeur as King."

Beside Horn, Count Egmont lifted his head and his deep clear voice. "He rules here because he is Duke of Burgundy—all else is irrelevant here."

"He rules here because he is the son and successor of Charles the Fifth," said Alva. "Because he is King. Because he has the power—the only power —which you will obey, because you have no choice."

Egmont muttered, "Would that Orange were here."

Alva seemed not to hear that. He went on, smiling, smiling, to reassure them. "I am concerned with the safety of my troops—therefore, I have caused the arrest of some few troublemakers throughout the land. Let me promise you no honest man shall be disturbed. And now I ask your leave to dismiss this council until the afternoon, as I am hungry."

Horn leaned over to whisper into Egmont's ear. "Have you heard from Orange?"

"Nothing." Egmont gestured, and the servant behind him moved his chair back away from the table. All around the long polished slab, the others of the council were getting up. If Orange were here, he would have new arguments, subtle disputations of reason and tradition to hurl against Alva, but Egmont was tired and baffled. He could not reach this man, who rejected the very basis of the Burgundian state while pretending to serve its master. "The King has blundered, sending Alva here. He must be made to see that."

Horn did not reply to him. With their aides and their pages around them, the two noblemen went out of the chamber into the large room beyond, where the secretaries sat at their desks and the sentries stood along the walls. As the councillors came out, the secretaries shot up onto their feet and the sentries stiffened to attention, tapping the butts of their pikes on the slick tiled floor. Egmont pulled his gaze away from the soldiers. Their round Spanish helmets oppressed his spirit. He turned to his page for his gloves, his cloak.

A soldier marched up to him. "Count Egmont."

Egmont nodded, holding out one hand, to allow his glove to be drawn on.

"You are under arrest, sir."

From Horn, behind him, a choked gasp; Egmont's head snapped up. "I beg your pardon?"

"Come with me, sir. You are under arrest, by order of the Governor-general."

Egmont gaped at him, his mind frozen by surprise; this could not be happening and in a moment would resolve itself into order and right again, the soldier bowing, leaving him alone. Instead the man reached out a hand to take him by the arm, and Egmont recoiled.

"How dare you touch me! I am a Knight of the Golden Fleece—I am a councillor of the Duke of Burgundy—"

The soldier seized his arm and Egmont threw him off with a violent thrust. "You have no right!" Behind him, they were taking Horn, too. The ground was gone from beneath his feet. He was walking into a void that would devour him. They had him by the arms now. Someone, some Spanish soldier, was actually removing his sword from its scabbard. A hard knot formed in his chest.

"You have no right."

"Only the King has rights." Alva came up beside him, smiling. "The only law is the King's will. Good day, Count Egmont." With a little bow, he favored Horn with a look. "You cannot know, sir, how I agree with you: Would that the Prince of Orange were here." He laughed; he strode away down the antechamber, his back stiff as a pikestaff, arrogant and assured. The soldiers took Horn and Egmont down the stairs.

"I WANT you to come with me," Hanneke said.

"With you? Where? To the prison?" Jan gave an angry mirthless grunt of laughter. "I have been there."

Hanneke was on her knees, packing clothes for her father into a chest; she did not look up at her brother. The room she and he and their mother were sharing, above the Kelmans' kitchen, was so small there was scarcely room for the three of them together. Her mother was still asleep in the cupboard bed; the chest and Hanneke herself took up the center of the floor, and Jan stood in the doorway, watching her.

"It will only be a few hours of your time," she said. "You can spare him that, at least."

"I can. How well you know what time I have."

"You aren't working."

The factory and the shops of Mies van Cleef had been confiscated along with his house.

"It takes time to steal," Jan said.

She said nothing to that. She knew that was how he was getting their food. They had a little money left—not much—but she was clinging to it, reluctant to spend even a penny, with the future so uncertain. She got up from the chest and went to the back of the room, where the books were lined up against the wall, and pored over the titles until she decided on Thomas à Kempis and the *Gospels*.

When she went back to the chest, Jan was gone. The door hung open, the sunlight glittering with suspended dust.

She made a sound in her chest. He could have stayed to help her. Furious, she shut the lid of the chest and heaved it up onto her shoulder. Her mother still slept, to Hanneke's relief; the older woman made such a fuss when Hanneke went out alone. She slipped out the door into the late autumn sunlight.

In spite of the bright weather, it was cold. Her shoulder already aching from the weight of the chest, she started away across the city to the prison.

At the gate a long line of people waited to see the jailers; they carried petitions in their hands, and bundles of clothes and food for their relatives inside the old tower. Down at the other side of the broad damp meadow that lay between the river and the canal was a crew of workmen, clearing the ground for the new fortress to be built there. Hanneke waited in line with the others, gnawing her lip, impatient. Surely by now her mother would have wakened. There would be trouble when she got back.

There was nothing to do, anyway, but argue with her mother. Better that she was here, doing some good. She fixed her eyes on the broad back of the man in front of her in the line and waited.

At noon, at last, she was let in to see the jailer, in the tiny courtyard of the tower: a tall man in a leather apron. He took her chest of clothes and books and tossed it over onto a heap of other baskets and bundles against the wall.

"But—" she said, startled. "Aren't you going to put his name on it? How will you know whom to give it to?"

The man laughed at her, his eyes glinting. "Oh, I have a splendid memory."

"Can I see him?"

"No, no one can see any of the prisoners, little lady."

She stood before him, irresolute; lifting her head, she scanned the blackened stone wall of the tower, the tiny windows crisscrossed with iron bars. Suddenly she realized that Mies would never come out again, that none of the things she had brought for his comfort would ever reach him, that to her he was already dead. She trembled; her soul seemed to shrink inside her.

A touch on her arm made her jump. The jailer was fingering her sleeve. He smirked at her, his eyes unblinking.

"Of course," he said, purring like a big cat, "if I wanted to, I could make some arrangements. If you made me want to." His fingertips stroked her wrist, sliding under the cuff of her sleeve to her bare arm.

She jerked her arm back out of his reach. Her stomach rolled over. With one more glance up at the tower, she turned and rushed away out of the courtyard.

Outside, she stopped; she wondered if she ought to go back—what he would ask of her. She knew what he would ask of her. She could not do that. Not even for Mies—and Mies would not want it of her. Blindly she walked forward through the skeins of people waiting to get inside. They moved out of her way; she bumped into someone and apologized. Her eyes hurt. She was going to cry. The cold sunlight burned her cheeks. Mies would not want that of her. Mies was dead. She wheeled and looked up again at the gaunt stone tower. Tufts of grass sprouted on the black roof.

She should go back. Do whatever she had to do for her father's sake. But her feet were moving, taking her away into Antwerp, back into Antwerp, home to her mother.

When she came into the street that ran by Kelman's house she saw her mother in the middle of it, walking toward her. Hanneke stopped, amazed.

In all her life she could never remember her mother leaving the house by herself.

The older woman saw her and turned toward her, walking slowly, her head down. She looked strange. Her hair was slipping free of the tight linen cap that covered her head and her long dark housecoat was dingy. She was barefoot. Suddenly ashamed of her, Hanneke hurried toward her, to get her away out of sight.

Her mother gave her such a strange look, when she came up to her, that Hanneke paused without touching her and said, "What are you doing here?"

"I am looking for—" Griet said, and stopped.

Hanneke waited a moment for the rest of the answer; her heart was pounding. She cast a quick look in either direction along the street, to see if anyone was watching them.

"For what, Mother?"

The older woman raised her face, gaunt and seamed with age lines. "The way to Hell."

Abruptly tears spilled down from her eyes. Hanneke took her by the arm and led her back to Kelman's house.

In the little room above the kitchen, she helped her mother take off her clothes and get into the cupboard bed. All the while her mother cried like a child. Hanneke sat beside her in the semidarkness, one hand on her shoulder, and thought of her father in prison and her brother fled away into the streets.

"Mama," she said, "this is already Hell."

IN THE darkness deeper inside the dungeon someone was screaming, had been screaming now for hours; Mies had gotten used to that. He kept his back to that. His eyes fixed on the dim slot of light at the top of the door. The only light there was.

His arms hurt from the manacles on his wrists, but his arms had been hurting for so long he had learned to ignore that too. In prison a man learned to ignore so many things, the hunger, the stench, the thirst, the curses and screams. He kept his mind going; he kept his attention on what happened inside his head, what he could manage. He kept thinking about his trial.

When they took him out to be tried, he meant to offer such a defense that they would set him free and everyone else they had arrested. He knew the law. They had made a mistake, taking Mies van Cleef in their net. He would talk his way free and destroy them in the process. They couldn't do this to him.

He lined up his arguments again, for the tenth time, or maybe the hundredth, the arguments so well worn in his mind now, like paths through the tangle of his mind, which led him surely and certainly through the dangers toward the light and safety on the other side. *The other side of what,* he did not question. This could not go on, this screaming and darkness and waiting and hunger and thirst, not forever, and at the end of it surely would be . . .

Something.

His home again, his family, his work. His children. His wife. Out there somewhere, without him to care for them; what was to become of them? Hanneke and her mother: where were they? He imagined them hungry, like him, without his strength of will to resist fear and hunger. Jan would take care of them. In a burst of fury he cursed his son, knowing Jan would not be able to keep the two women safe and fed and housed, the dolt, the stupid fool; why did he have such a fool for a son? And now in the opening made by one passion another swept in, a cold fear, a shaking in all his limbs and a blank terror in his mind. He had to get out of here. Oh, please, let me out of here—

The screaming from behind him struck him like a knife in the heart, and he groaned and wept and banged his head against the wall.

They can't do this to me.

No. They could not. The law said they could not. And now once again he piled up the arguments, brick by brick, into a wall around him, a containment of his fear, a bulwark of his only hope.

J AN LEANED against the wall of the warehouse, his hands behind him, watching the street, waiting. There were a lot of people loitering around the street, poor laborers who gathered here every day in hopes that one of the warehouses all around this quarter would put out a call for daywork. There was very little work to be had in Antwerp since so many factories had been shut down.

It was cold; in the shadow of the wall Jan began to feel the bite of the autumn air. He had left his coat back in the alley where he had spent the night, down by the river; he kept most of his things there, hidden in a broken barrel behind a heap of garbage. There was no room for any of his things in the airless attic where his sister and mother lived, and anyhow he avoided them as much as he could, going there only to take them food; his mother always reproached him for one thing or another, and his sister usually wanted him to help her do something. Something meaningless, like taking books to their father.

He spat into the street. Everything he had heard since the day Mies was taken convinced him that his father would never see daylight again.

The day of the Lord had come like a thief in the night. He laughed, thinking of that, of the unlooked-for truth in that. The day of the Lord had come to steal away even the sunlight from such as Mies van Cleef and the others unlucky enough to be seized in the first pass. Jan had no doubt at all that there would be more arrests—another reason why he spent as little time as possible in his mother's rented room—and he had seen the workmen building scaffolds in the square before the cathedral and did not think they were for pageants and music.

The beer wagon was rounding the corner into the street. He straightened up a little, and his hands slipped around in front of him; he hooked his thumbs in his belt.

It was noontime. The bells would ring within a few minutes all over Antwerp. The streets were crowded with people. Through the dense moving mass of bodies the two roan horses in their belled harness dragged the heavy wagon toward him over the cobblestones. The brasses on their harness glinted. Jan narrowed his eyes. The wagon rumbled past him; he took three steps away from the wall and grabbed the tailgate.

The driver did not see him. He vaulted up lightly into the back of the wagon, yanked the cotter pins out of the tailgate, threw open the back of the wagon, and began heaving the barrels out into the street.

The first one was empty and bounced, and someone in the street yelled. The driver wheeled around in time to see Jan fling the second barrel out after the first. With a screech he leapt up in the seat and uncurled his whip, and Jan ducked and pushed another barrel over, and it rolled off the wagon and hit the street and burst.

The crowd was yelling and laughing now, chasing the wagon, the first few stooping to scoop up the spilled beer with their hands. The driver cracked his whip and Jan jumped away from the lash, seized another barrel, and leapt off the wagon with it.

"Thief! Stop—"

He landed in the middle of the crowd, which surged around him like a friendly sea, enclosing him as they fought to get to the beer in the street. At least one of the first barrels he had tossed out had not broken, and someone was cracking it open and the mob was fighting to get to it to drink. The driver shrieked and waved his whip from the back of his wagon, helpless; his horses, used to their route, plodded on down the street. Jan hoisted up the barrel he had gotten for himself and went off down the alley.

In THE evening Hanneke helped Vrouw Kelman prune her rosebushes; the housewife liked to gossip and wanted an ear to aim at, even if Hanneke knew none of the people she gossiped about. They went around the garden in front of the Kelmans' house and trimmed back the branches of the heavy-thorned shrubs, and Vrouw Kelman talked about people's babies and bad manners and follies.

"Of course," said Vrouw Kelman, in the twilight, as she bent over a bush with the clippers in her hand, "no one's free from folly. Had I known about these soldiers they are sending to us, I should not have rented you the room, dear."

"What soldiers?" Hanneke asked. She gathered up the fallen rose branches and laid them carefully into a basket, to be taken out and burned.

"Oh, this new army. They say all of us will have to take in at least one, and if I had not rented you that room, why, he could move in there. As it is—"

"Who?" Hanneke said, startled.

Vrouw Kelman looked over her shoulder at her. "The soldier I shall be expected to quarter, dear. Do pay heed when I speak to you."

"I'm sorry," Hanneke said.

"Of course I shall not turn you and your dear mother out, not now. And anyway with another mouth to feed, your guilder will come in very nicely."

Hanneke picked up a rose branch and stabbed herself on the thorn. "When will this soldier come?"

"I don't know. It's only rumor, anyway. Don't worry about you and your dear mother. Although I think you ought to see your dear mother stays indoors, or at least inside the garden."

"What?" Hanneke said, stupidly. "Has she been going out often?"

"I wondered if you knew about that. Yes, she's been going off into the street. She's not a happy woman, your mother."

"I'll talk to her."

"The children tease her."

"I'll talk to her."

A whistle from the street brought Hanneke upright, her head turning in that direction. The darkness was almost complete; she could just make out the figure standing by the gate.

"I beg your pardon, Vrouw Kelman, my brother is here."

"Yes, I see that."

Hanneke put down the bundle of clippings and went over to the gate. Jan waited, silent in the darkness, his face masked in the darkness; uncertainly, she said his name.

"Yes," he said. "Here, I brought you some money."

He put out his hand, and she cupped her palm under it and felt the coins drop into her grasp, the metal still warm from his hand.

"Thank you," she said. "Why don't you come inside? We have some beer."

He laughed at that, and she wondered crossly if he were drunk. But he did not seem drunk. He said, "I'll stay out here, just the same, thank you."

"Yes," she said. "I suppose you're right. Have you heard anything about an army coming to Antwerp? That they will quarter a whole army on us?"

"I've heard that, yes," he said. "That's only to be expected. Why, does that bother you?"

"Yes," she said. "You remember what they said, when they took Father, that you would be next. If they're bringing an army here, then they must mean to arrest more people."

"Perhaps," he said. "I have to go, Hanneke. Tell Mother—"

"No." Her hand shot out and clutched at his sleeve. "Listen to me. You have to leave—get away—before they take you too."

He moved, in the dark; his hand closed over hers. "What about you and Mother?"

"I'll find work," she said. "I went by the silk factory this morning—they are opening it up again, now that it belongs to the King. They will give me work there."

"Hanneke, what can you do? You are no weaver."

"I'll sweep," she said. "Scrub floors. Anything." She leaned across the fence to put her arms around him. "Oh, Jan, what if they take you too?" Suddenly she began to weep.

"Hanneke," he said, and pushed the gate open and drew her out to the street. Gratefully she went into his warm embrace.

"Keep the gate closed," called Vrouw Kelman. "You will let out the dog."

Hanneke fumbled behind her to shut the gate. She leaned her head against her brother's shoulder, thinking of the tower, of her father, of the jailer pawing her arm. Of the soldiers who would live in the same house as she did, Spanish soldiers, watching her. Tears flooded into her eyes.

"Don't worry about me," her brother said, and hugged her. "It's you I'm concerned for. You can't work in a silk factory."

"I can," she said, and sniffed, to keep her nose from dripping.

"Who will stay with Mother?"

"I can't stay with her," Hanneke said. "She's driving me crazy."

Now she could not keep from crying, and she turned her face against his shoulder and wept bitterly. He patted her back and murmured to her, and she rubbed her fingers against his sleeve and cried until she was empty.

"Oh, well," he said, and stroked her back. "I'm not leaving, not yet, anyway. Where would I go, after all?"

She had not thought of that. She leaned her face against him and thought.

"There's Uncle Pieter, I guess," Jan said.

"Pieter!" She pulled away and stared up at him. "He's a pirate."

"He's Father's brother. He'd have to take me in."

"But—Father always said he was worthless."

"Father's always said I'm worthless," Jan said mildly. "And there's really no one else, except Mother's family, and they're all Catholics."

That was true. Hanneke wiped her face on her sleeve. "Well," she said, "maybe you ought to stay a while longer."

He laughed; he leaned down and kissed her cheek. "Be good, Hanneke. Say my regards to Mother."

He was going; he was walking away. She opened her mouth to call him back. She felt cold and small without him. Already he was halfway down the street, half lost in the darkness, a shadow moving through the shadows. She turned and went back into the Kelmans' garden.

M IES STARTLED out of a half sleep, banged awake by the sudden invasion of the tower room by a horde of people, clanking in their chains and wailing in their despair, stumbling over his legs and falling against the wall near him. He thrust up his arms, to ward them off, and drew his cramped throbbing legs up close to his body.

"Peace," a man said, in Dutch, and sank down beside him. "Oh, my God."

A dozen feet shuffled through the filthy straw past them, going deeper into the room, and there stirred the other prisoners into calling and cursing and shifting around in the dark. Mies twitched himself from side to side, trying to find a way to sit that did not hurt. He had been here so long—how long, he had no notion—that sores were opening up on the places where he rested against the stone floors and walls. His wrists hurt under the iron manacles; his arms had begun to swell, so that the wristbands that when first put on had hung down over his hands now cut deeply into his taut stinking skin.

He licked his lips, waiting for the hubbub to settle, and when the noise lessened a little he turned to the man beside him.

"My name is Mies."

"Willem."

Through the dark came a hand, which he shook, heartened by this simple amenity.

"Do you know the day?"

"Aye, yes, curse it forever—the day after All Saints."

"All Saints. Are you then a Catholic?"

"Yes."

"Then what are you doing here?"

"Everyone will be here eventually," said Willem.

Mies stared through the dark at him, wondering at that; he wished he could make out the man's face. Did he know him? The voice was unfamiliar. But he knew many people only by face.

"Have you heard anything about the trials?"

Willem said, "No."

The door banged open again, and the warders came in, shouting for quiet. "Keep your teeth together!" A whip cracked. Mies pulled his arms up close to his body and lowered his head to protect himself. It was impossible to see the lash coming in the dark and he had caught the whip more than once across his cheek and arm. The warders tramped around the room frightening the people into silence. There were many more here than before, so many the jailers kept treading on them. The whips cracked again.

Their boots heavy on the rotten straw, the warders marched out the door, and it shut with a boom.

"Well," Mies said, "they can't put many more in without taking some of us out. They'll have to hold trials soon."

"Trials," Willem said, in a voice as harsh as the warder's. "We'll be lucky if we ever leave here again. If they take us out to hang us we'll be better off. Odds are they'll leave us here to starve."

"They've got to try us. That's the law."

Only a rough burst of laughter answered that. Mies reached out and grabbed the man's arm in the dark.

"They have to try us!"

"Leave me alone. I'll call the guard."

Mies let go of Willem's sleeve; the cloth slid away from his fingers and he was left holding the air. His hand dropped again to his lap. He opened his mouth to speak but shut it again without voicing anything more. His body felt as if it were crawling all over with vermin, or cold, or just the understanding he had been holding himself stiff against, all these days and weeks.

There would be no trials. Willem was right. They would leave here to go to their deaths.

He lifted his hands, the heavy chain hanging between them in the dark, and the urge to lay about him with the chain, to pulp the flesh and blood around him, was so strong he nearly got to his feet, although chained to the wall as he was he could have gone nowhere.

He flung himself back against the wall. Banged his head against the wall and moaned. There had to be a way to die. To cheat them of his death. If he had nothing left but to die, let death come now, here, at his own hand. He thrust himself back against the wall again and groaned and sobbed and thrashed his legs. *Curse God and die.* There was nothing left but that. When would it come, oh, God, when?

"Shut up," Willem said, and moved away from him.

Mies swore at him. His arms hurt. He could feel the poisons seeping up along his arms into his body, needles of venom running under the skin. Racing toward his brain, his heart; would they kill him, or the Spanish gallows? Or would he burn, or be drowned, or be buried under rocks? *Curse God and die.*

The doors opened again and the warders came in with chains and hammers, to fasten the newly come prisoners up against the wall. They had a little lantern, to show their work. Mies' eyes followed it, starved for light, fascinated.

They bent to hammer shut the iron ring that bound Willem's chain to the ring in the wall. The light shone on the Catholic's face. Unknown. Mies turned his eyes away, although a moment later the light drew his gaze back like a balm.

The phrase ran back and forth through his mind like a rat in a trap. *Curse God and die. Curse God and die.* He had never admired Job. There seemed nothing stoic in Job at all, no fortitude, no heart. Now bitterly he knew there was nothing much at all in himself, just a bitter despair that could not wait for death.

He groaned, and the warder nearest him struck out with his whip and clubbed him over the face with the butt end. Mies bit his lips together, tasting blood.

Even Christ had despaired on the Cross. Mies leaned his head against the wall. Why did this happen to me—what did I do to deserve this? He picked through all his sins, his boyish defiance of his father, his marriage to Griet above the objections of both families. His greed, his cold charity. He had done nothing that hundreds of other men had not done, and did yet, in freedom still. *Curse God—*

The light went off, deeper into the room. He saw glowing patches of people, squatting in the filth, their clothes like shreds of skin that hung from them. Sores on their arms and bodies and faces. Like his. His back itched where the wall had worn it open. Vermin in it probably. Eating away his flesh. Not worth anything anyway. Just a pile of meat. God deserted me.

Even Christ despaired.

At least, crucified, He had died swiftly. Relatively swiftly. He thought of hanging from nails through his hands and the swollen infected flesh of his arms and hands throbbed painfully against the manacles. I don't deserve this. I'm innocent.

No one is innocent. He thought of the times he had cheated in his business and thought himself clever. Of beating his son out of bad temper when the boy was too slow to do something probably no child would have done well anyway.

God, forgive me, he thought, and suddenly, from nowhere, a light unlike the dirty light of the lantern came on inside his skull. God had forgiven him. That was why Christ died on the Cross.

He shivered; some enormous force swept through him, too strong for his flesh to bear, and nearly made him weep. He lifted his weighted hands to his face. *Oh, God,* he thought. It is true.

Down there at the end of the room, someone moaned, and the whip cracked. The lantern shifted through the filth and darkness, and the hammers rang on iron, chaining up someone else. Mies bent forward, his face against his knees.

All his life he had heard it, that Christ died for him, that Christ had won him life eternal, and never understood, but now he understood. When he needed Christ, all he had to do was turn toward Him and He was there.

He sobbed. The manner of his death to come seemed trivial now. He had found something else. The wild rush of gratitude to God Who had saved him, and Who would take him through that death into Paradise, warmed his body and lit up his mind like the coming of daybreak. The animal sounds of his prison, the stench, the hunger, nothing mattered now. He wept for gratitude; in the first white heat of his understanding he saw that everything was worth this. Falling into prison, losing his life, all this suffering was well worth the understanding that now he had: that God had saved him. He pressed his face against his knees and prayed to God in thanks for having sent him to this place.

HANNEKE was gone. Everybody was gone.

Griet opened the door a little and looked out. The steps that led down to the backyard of this strange house shone yellow in the sunlight. Nobody was there. She could get away now.

She pulled her housedress around her and held it fast with one hand. Carefully, because her feet were bare, she went out step by step down into the yard. It was cold. No matter. In a little while she would find her own home, where it was always warm, and Mies would bring her her slippers and a foot-warmer. Mies was so kind to her, always; if only she could find him again, everything would be all right.

She crept through the yard to the gate and went out to the street. No one had seen her. If Vrouw Kelman saw her she would shout and call for help to get her back into the attic room, but she did not belong there. She belonged somewhere in a tall house with painted shutters and a stork on the chimney. She set off up the street to find it.

Before she had gone very far, two little boys ran out of a yard by the street and shouted at her and threw clods of earth at her. Griet hurried away from them. A dog chased after her, barking.

At the corner, where the little foundry shop was, she picked up a broken iron pot out of the street. She had seen the Spanish soldiers wear pots on their heads, to protect them, and she put the iron pot on her head, in case the children threw stones.

That was a good idea, because now there were more children, and they were throwing stones. She walked off as fast as she could, turned into the next street, and began searching for her house. A volley of pebbles pelted her back and shoulders and she wheeled around, furious, and yelled and made faces and waved her arms.

The children laughed. She did not frighten them enough. When she turned to go on in her search, they rushed after her again, and more stones came, more bits of dirt and even dog turds, horrible smelly things. She broke into a run to get away from them and they ran after her, streaming after her, laughing and yelling. People were looking out their windows at her now. Humiliated, she stopped and turned again to face them, and the children skidded to a stop, a dozen or more of them, ten feet behind her.

"Yeeaaw!" She waved her arms at them. They laughed. A stone whizzed past her shoulder.

Devils. Imps. Her breath whined between her teeth. If Mies saw them he would lash them. Take a stick to them. That was what she needed. She looked around her, saw a stick lying in the gutter, and ran over to it.

"Now," she cried, and lifted the stick high over her head, like a sword. "Now let's have at it, you devils!" She ran straight at them, hooting.

They scattered. The smiles vanished from their faces, and they turned their backs and ran. She darted after one or another, just a few steps, driving them away; her stick swung at their backs. She hit nothing, but the stick made a lovely sound in the air as it passed, and more than one little boy wailed in terror. Griet howled with delight. Long-striding, she dashed after one boy until he disappeared, and wheeled and made for another, until they were all gone from sight. With a yell of triumph, she tossed the stick high up into the air; it fell with a clatter to the ground. Square-shouldered, she marched off to find her house.

THE CROWD was pressed so tight together that Hanneke's basket was crushed. It was hard to breathe. She wondered if the crowd did that or if she were just afraid. Afraid of what? She knew what she had come here to see.

Behind her was the broad high façade of the Fullers' Guildhall; people stood on the roof of it and hung out the windows, waiting. Before her, held open by ropes that kept the crowd back, was the square, and beyond that, the cathedral, its door obscured by the scaffolds that filled the square, and its off-center tower rising up into the sky like some huge scaffold of its own. She thought she was going to be sick. The crowd surged forward and carried her along, nearly off her feet, up to the rope barriers.

"They're coming! They're coming!"

She pulled and shoved at the shoulders and backs around her, trying to see past them. The shout went up from a thousand tongues, and now the crowd pressed up to the ropes and knocked them down and would have flooded across the square, carrying her in their midst, but for a row of soldiers that ran up with their pikes at the ready and forced the people back.

The soldiers calmed them all. Hanneke gripped her basket in both hands, thought of praying, but could not. She looked up at the scaffolds, wagon wheels set up on poles, and no prayer would find its way into her mind. And now they were coming, the condemned, to the throbbing of drums.

Her back tingled, and her hair stood on end. In white shirts, each carrying a cross, they marched up like soldiers into the square. Many were too weak to walk by themselves; others in the row supported them. On their arms and legs she saw the marks of chains. Her heart sank. There were too many of them. She would never see Mies here, in all this mob. She would never see her father again.

The executioners started almost directly before her; they took the first two prisoners and flung ropes up over the spokes on the wheels overhead, adjusted them to balance, and pulled the condemned people up by the necks into the air.

Hanneke screamed. It was awful. They did not die. They hung there and kicked and their faces turned blue and swelled up, and as they jiggled in the air a filthy rain of urine and feces splattered down on the cobblestones under them, so that some in the crowd even laughed. She recoiled. More and more were going up into the air now. She doubled up, hiding her face, and struggled to get away.

Near the building, she stopped, trying to catch her breath—to get her soul in harness again. Over the heads of the crowd she could see the first row of bodies, quiet now, in God's hands, hanging there. Their faces were black. She tore her gaze from them. Not Mies. Not that way.

One hand on the rough stone wall of the Guildhall, she walked along behind the crowd, clutching her basket. She was tired; she had to get home. Get some sleep, before her work started in the morning. What was going on here was over, an end of things, to be forgotten. Forget she ever had a father. Her stomach heaved. Not like that, not Mies. Then in the crowd ahead of her she thought she saw Jan.

She called his name; she struggled to reach him. But the crowd was moving, shifting forward to see those dying in the rows nearer the cathedral, and in their midst her brother was carried farther and farther away from her even while she tried her hardest to close with him. She wailed, desperate: "Jan!" He didn't hear her. Or maybe it wasn't he at all; now she could not even see him, for the press of bodies between them. She sank back, exhausted and defeated, and slowly made her way back home.

IN THE evening after the executions Jan went to the Kelmans' house, to say goodbye to his sister. There were many more soldiers in Antwerp now, and he had decided to take her advice and go away, to their Uncle Pieter in Nieuport.

He went up to the gate, to call her. The night was falling and the breeze blew cold and bright into his face. In the blue twilight he made out some people in the garden, and he was about to call to them to fetch his sister for him when he noticed that one of them was a foreigner.

It was a Spanish soldier. At once he understood; there would be a soldier quartered here on the Kelmans.

His hand slipped from the gate. He turned his head, looking away down the street; for a moment longer he stood there, in case she should see him and call to him, but no one called him back, and he went away down the street, away to Nieuport and his uncle.

IN BRUSSELS there were hangings too, hundreds of dead, ornaments, folk said, for the Duke of Alva's Advent. After the common folk had been dragged out and executed, the executioner stood up on a broad platform in the Grand Place, with all of Brussels looking on, and there on a cloth of black velvet he stood waiting with his ax while his last two victims came out.

The first was Count Horn, who knelt down, and put his head to the block, and was killed. Silence met this act, the execution of so great a man, this downfall from the heights of life to the black pit of disgrace.

They put a cloth over Horn's body, and led out Egmont. "You, too, my friend," said Count Egmont, and went as tamely to the block, to have his head struck off. Then the executioner came forward, displaying their heads in his hands, and called on men to cheer the name of the King.

No one cheered, except a few soldiers; there was a breathless hush, as if all the air had been sucked up out of the square.

In a loud voice the executioner read a proclamation, declaring forfeit and lost all the estates and titles of William of Nassau, Prince of Orange, who had fled from Alva, and announcing that should this Prince of Orange come back to the Low Countries, the same lot would befall him as had befallen these two friends of his, who lay dead on the scaffold.

No one cheered that, either. It did not seem to matter. To most of the people watching, Orange seemed as good as dead. Night was coming. They gathered themselves and took one another by the hand and went away home.

3

THE TIDE was out; on the sloping sandy beach half a dozen little boats lay tilted on their keels. Jan walked along the low bulkhead at the top of the beach, peering out toward the harbor. Nieuport lay at the throat of a little river, behind the banks of dunes that bounded the North Sea, with the harbor tucked into the dredged and widened river mouth. Now the sun was setting, and although the hot light still gilded the peaks of the dunes, the harbor was deep in twilight; all the ships were in, and the nets hung like folded wings from the shears.

Jan kicked a rock off the bulkhead; it fell deep into the soft wet sand of the beach. He had no idea how to find his uncle.

Ahead, the bulkhead curved away to his left, turning upriver, where the town lay. There was a little market in the swell of the curve, which was shutting down for the night. He went through the market, past the gossiping fishwives rolling up their awnings and packing their baskets. The paving stones were slick with fish scales and guts. The smell of the beach came at him, the dry salty smell of dead seaweed and fish, cork and tarred canvas. The air fell calm. Out across the harbor the water was glassy still. Softly the first breath of the freshening breeze cooled his forehead.

He asked three or four people before he found one who could direct him to his uncle's house. With the homeward-going workingmen he trudged up the single street of the town, along the riverbank. The lights of the houses shone on the ruffled water. He went up on a bridge over a canal coming in from the right and turned on the far bank to walk along it.

The third house from the end was built down sheer to the wooden bulkhead of the canal. A dinghy was tied up to the back door. Jan knocked on the front.

There was a light in the house, shining out under the door, and through the oilskin over the window. Someone pulled at the oilskin, looking out.

"Who are you?" a hoarse voice whispered. "I don't know you—who are you?"

"Uncle Pieter?" The boy went a step toward the window, which was on the left side of the door.

"Who are you?" the old man cried.

"Jan van Cleef, sir—your brother's son."

There was a silence; then suddenly the door flew open. "Well, come in," the old man said sourly.

Jan kicked off his shoes and went into a small bare room, smoky from the lantern on the wall. His father's brother blinked up at him, unsmiling. Lifting a leather-covered bottle, old Pieter took a deep pull at it. He faced Jan again, looking slowly up and down him.

"You're Mies' son? Where'd you get such a size on you?"

"My mother's family's tall, sir."

"Stop calling me *sir*." The old man went away across the room and through a door covered with a length of canvas.

Jan looked around him, uncertain. He had seen his uncle just once, years before, when he was only a little boy; Mies had brought him here. He remembered a more respectable house than this, with chairs and carpets and cupboards and maps on the walls. This shabby little house was bare as a mousehole.

"Come on, damn y'!" the old man shouted, and Jan ducked through the canvas curtain and into the main room of the house.

This was rather more inviting. Relieved, he looked around him with a smile. A mat of woven rushes covered the floor, and there was a hearth with a little fire and a pot on a hook over the coals. Two battered chairs and a low table took up the middle of the room. The lamp on it gave off the best light in the room, and to this warm yellow circle Jan went gladly as a child.

"Sit," his uncle said, taking one of the chairs, and picking up a long-stemmed pipe from a dish on the table.

Jan sat down.

"So." The old man's gaze poked at him. "Mies' boy. Well, you look a good stout lad. What brings you out this way from Antwerp? Get caught with your hands in the chambermaid's skirts?"

Jan scratched his nose. He was painfully hungry; the old man's sharp inquiry angered him. He said, "My father's dead, sir."

"Dead." Above the fringe of Pieter's mustache, his waxen-lidded eyes widened a moment, round with new interest. Almost at once he shuttered them up again. Drew on his pipe. The stomach-turning smoke rose in a spiral above the lamp. "Well, a man who spends his time sitting and thinking will wear out faster than one who works."

"He was hanged," Jan said. "For heresy. The Duke of Alva hanged him."

Old Pieter gaped at him. His hand trembled and the pipe spilled a flutter of ash down the front of his shirt. "Hanged—" He threw his head back and erupted into howling laughter.

Jan started up straight, offended. His uncle roared with mirth, pounded his foot on the floor, and thumped his knee. Gradually the fit faded; he wiped his eyes, chuckling, and leaning one heavy elbow on the table faced Jan again.

"It wasn't funny," Jan said. His throat filled with rage and grief. "We're ruined, all of us."

"Well, well." Pieter looked around him at the ashes floating over his sleeves. "Life's a big joke, boy. A big stupid joke." He spat into the fire.

"Where's the joke?" Jan cried. "Ten thousand people the Spaniards hanged—"

"All my life," old Pieter said dreamily, "all my life people have said I was born to be hanged, and only look at my godly brother, Mies, crowned with piety and wealth . . ." His flat palm struck the table. "Now who went to the gallows, and who sits . . ."

He spat again. Jan saw the joke; he saw, too, the deep bitter lines along the corners of the old man's mouth.

"He's better off, probably," old Pieter said.

A little silence spun out between them. Jan's stomach contracted with hunger. His gaze strayed around the room toward the fire; he snuffled hopefully at the air.

"What brings you here, anyway?" Pieter said.

"You said once—remember? Mies brought me here, I was only a little boy, but you said"—Jan licked his lips—"when I grew up, I could sail with you."

Pieter stared at him a moment; another mirthless laugh rumbled up out of his throat. "Oh, I did, did I? And what are we to sail on?"

"You said—I could—on your ship. Remember?"

Again the wet red laugh. Pieter wiped the back of his hand over his mouth. "Impounded. The *Wayward Girl.* Devil give them plagues and never let them die."

"They took your ship?"

"Impounded her." Pieter sucked on his cold pipe, his eyes half-closed. "So, you see. Mies was hanged, and I, I sit and think."

Jan looked around again at the dreary room. Suddenly his mood slipped away into despair; he imagined the Duke of Alva, looking in through a window in the roof, laughing at him. He put his hands up to his face, longing for Hanneke, for his home. His stomach growled.

"Got the bear in you," Pieter said. "Well, well." One hand moved, starting to point to the pot on the hearth, but the gesture died. He nodded to Jan. "There's a mess in the pot. I'll get you a stoup of the juniper, to warm your gut."

"Thank you," Jan said, going toward the fire.

"THERE she is," Pieter said. "Yon by the careening beach." He braced his elbows on the top of the river wall, his eyes directed across the quiet water toward a little single-masted ship.

"What are they doing to her?" Jan shaded his eyes with his hand. The *Wayward Girl* looked rather like a fishing boat. Her hull was round as a bowl at stern and bow, her fore decks flush with the main deck, a little sterncastle standing up over the rear end of her. A third of the way from the top of her mast, the jack yard of a gaffsail jutted out like a cocked thumb. Men worked on her.

"What are they doing to her?"

The old man shrugged. His pipe in his hand, his gaze on his lost ship, he sank into his reveries. Not tall, yet he was stout through the body, with heavy shoulders and a neck thick as a yardarm. When he fell into his daydream, he seemed to shrink inside his clothes.

Jan looked over the river toward the *Wayward Girl.* Her hull appeared freshly painted. The sun flashed on a bright bit of metal by her mast foot.

"She seems pretty good to me."

"Just careened her," the old man said. "They ought to be towing her out to a deep mooring some time soon."

"They're refitting her?"

He looked at her more closely, wondering what the Spaniards had in mind for her. Like most Dutch boys, he had sailed all his life, although in nothing larger than the river-going flyboats that plied the canals and the broad Schelde. The *Wayward Girl* had a clean, trim look not entirely attributable to her new paint and lack of rigging. She looked fast and handy as one of the gray sea gulls that swooped and glided over the harbor around her. The *Wayward Girl.* He loved the name. In a flash, he knew he loved the ship.

Now the Spaniards had her. He sucked on his teeth, wounded in his newborn heart.

"Couple times," the old man said softly, "I've thought over swimming in, at night, and banging a hole in her, so the dirty devil won't get his hands on her, but—"

In one of the tall houses behind them a window rattled open. A shrill female voice shouted, furious. Jan was eyeing the ship, his mind dreamy; not until his uncle pulled on his sleeve, tugging him off down the street, did he realize the woman was yelling at them.

"And don't come back!" she screamed, now that they were moving. "I'll set the watch on you. Riffraff! Dirtying up the street all day long in front of decent folk's houses . . ."

Jan's ears burned and he shoved his hands deep under his belt and hunched his shoulders and did not look around him. He followed his uncle quickly down the quayside toward the harbor, away from the *Wayward Girl.*

PIETER VAN CLEEF had never had a wife or a child: only his ship. As long as he had the *Wayward Girl,* he needed for nothing else, not a way of making a living, nor a good name for himself, nor something to love, but when he lost her he was transformed into a miserable old man, his days empty and overcast with longing.

He wondered what Jan made of him. Beside him the boy walked along humpbacked, his gaze lowered to the ground, his shoes knocking on the pavement. He walked with a loose stride that threw him off-balance a little. He was still growing. When he became confident in his size he would move better.

If he grew. Probably he was hungry. He was always hungry.

Pieter led them away down the street toward the market. He was used to getting along on very little to eat, but a boy like Jan needed good round meals.

He squared his shoulders a little. After weeks of doing nothing he felt better having someone to care for.

It was Friday afternoon and the market was loud with people in from all over the district to buy fish. Pieter walked down the edge of the crowd, looking for any face he knew. By the angle in the street, where the bulkheads spread the river into the open water of the harbor, two men in wide-bottomed trousers were laying out mussels by the bucketful on a streaming bed of kelp.

"Eh. Marten." Pieter nudged the crinkled seaweed with his foot.

The younger of the two straightened up, smiling, and put out his hand. "Hello, Captain. Good afternoon to you."

"Have a good haul?" Pieter said. His cheeks felt stiff from the unnatural act of smiling. He avoided the frowning look of the older man.

"The mussels are Protestant," Marten said, and laughed.

"Hush," said the older man, Marten's father. "Keep your fool's tongue."

Pieter scratched his jaw. "Don't suppose you have any bit of work for an old man who needs something for his gut."

"No," said Marten's father, harsh. "No charity for pirates."

"Father," Marten said, objecting. He stooped over the heap of mussels and began shoveling the shells into a bucket.

"I said no!"

"Well, now," Pieter said, edging away. "I don't want to put strife between a man and his son—"

"The catch is half mine," Marten said, with a glare at his father, and brought Pieter the bucket.

"Thank you," Pieter said. Another thing that came unnaturally. He carried the bucket off down the street; behind him Marten and his father argued in loud voices.

Pieter's nephew had wandered off. Presently he reappeared, and, the tide being in, they went across the street to the wharf. Pieter sat down on the wharf, his legs over the edge, took out his knife, and reached for a mussel.

Jan got his own knife. They sat there with the bucket between them, opening the mussels and eating them off the shell. After a few mussels had slipped down his throat, Jan reached into his shirt and took out a sausage, bit off a chunk, and held it out to Pieter.

The old man goggled at it in surprise. "Where did you get that?"

"Back in the market."

"Someone gave it to you?"

"I stole it."

"Stole it."

Pieter snatched the long brown sausage out of Jan's hand. Springing up onto his feet, he brought the sausage down like a club over Jan's head.

"Hey," Jan cried, recoiling under his raised forearm. "What's the matter?"

"Never steal from your own people!" Pieter smacked him again with the sausage and whirled and flung it end over end out into the harbor. In the cloudless air above him a gull let out a scream of greed and sailed toward the splash.

"I'm hungry," Jan shouted.

Pieter shoved the mussels at him. "Eat." He sat down, shutting up his knife into its whalebone handle.

"I need more than this!"

The old man glared at him. "I didn't ask you to come here."

Jan's face was stiff with bad temper; he looked very young, and much like Mies, who, although delicate and high-minded as a nun, had often shown a choler fit for a fighting man.

"I don't need you," he said. "I can take care of myself."

"You don't steal from your own kind, you big square-headed fool," said Pieter.

"I'll steal from anybody who has anything!"

"Not from your own people."

"My people. They aren't my people—where were they when my father—"

He gulped, his face red and swollen with rage. Pieter poked his finger at the boy's chest. "You have to live here, you fool—if they think you're a thief, you'll get nothing but hard looks and blows!"

"You sound like my sister." Jan got halfway to his feet; he was running away. Then to Pieter's amazement he fell back sitting onto the board of the wharf and burst into tears.

"Oh, there, now," Pieter said, uneasy.

The boy wept voluminously as a woman, all his feeling gushing out in rivers, his hands over his face. Pieter watched him a moment. He preferred the boy's rage, which he could argue with. Finally he put out his hand and touched Jan's shoulder.

"There, now," he said again, feeling foolish.

Jan shook his head; tears splattered his shoulders. "Hanneke," he cried, in a broken voice. "Hanneke. I want Hanneke, and Papa, and my mother. I want Hanneke."

Pieter stroked his back, keeping at arm's length from the unseemly storm of feeling. "Come on, now. A man doesn't cry."

"I'm sick of being a man!"

Mumbling sounds like words, Pieter patted his back a little more; he wondered what sort of water ran in Jan's veins, that he cried for his sister, a big strong boy like this. But now he found himself thinking of his brother, Mies, hanged in Brussels, and of the *Wayward Girl,* and his eyes began to ache painfully with tears of his own.

None of that, now. He got heavily up onto his feet. "Well, let's go find something fit to eat." With either hand he grabbed the pail of mussels and his nephew and towed them off down the street.

"So WE LAID up a while by The Lizard," Pieter said, loud; the beer and juniper in his belly had him stoked to a full roar. "Staying up there to windward of them, and the day broke, and the storm lifted. There was sail all over the sea, there, Spanish crosses, like sheep scattered in a field, just ready to pick off."

He stopped for a deep draught of his liquor. He was sitting on the bench in front of a wharfside tavern; several other men lounged around him, sucking their pipes, and drinking, and looking out across the harbor. Red Aart, whose tavern it was, came along the front sweeping the paving stones, a dirty apron tied around his waist. No one paid much heed to Pieter and his story, which they had all heard twenty times or more, but the old man did not mind their inattention; the story drove up irresistibly within him, like a whale breaching.

"So we went down toward the galleon. She was rolling like a barrel in the troughs of the waves, two masts gone, and the mizzen down over her bow, all the sail and rigging dragging along beside her in the water . . ."

Jan sat on the flagstones with a great tub of water in front of him; he was washing Red Aart's cups and dishes, in return for which, and other small chores, the tavern keeper had promised them the makings of a stew.

"As we was coming up to her you could hear the axes ringing. Trying to cut her away, they was, what hands was left."

Red Aart stood over Jan, watching critically. The brilliant hair that gave him his nickname stood up like a cockscomb on the top of his head. Bending, he scooped up a bowl and waved it under the boy's nose.

"You call that washed?"

Silently Jan took the bowl to wash again. Pieter burned for him: humiliating enough to do woman's work; worse yet to be chided for doing it poorly. He saw the boy's neck flush dark below the ragged line of his fair hair. There was nothing to do, save go on with his story. The old man reached for his tall flared cup.

"So then we came up, quiet as mice, you see—"

"Pieter," said one of the men beside him. "There she comes!"

Everyone sat up straight, even Jan, looking out to the harbor, where the river came in. Pieter let out a choked exclamation. A brace of little galleys was towing up a ship into the harbor, and the ship they towed was the *Wayward Girl*.

Now she was rigged up, with new line and new canvas. Her new paint shone in the late sun, and the water turned over at her forefoot in a little round green wave. The boats towed her toward a mooring in the deep harbor, among the seagoing ships.

No one around Pieter said anything. In utter silence they watched the little ship made fast by stern and bow at her new mooring. The few men on board her slid down her side into the galleys and rowed across the shiny harbor water toward the wharf.

The hands were Dutch, but the black-haired man who stepped smartly from the galley onto the wharf and began giving orders was a Spaniard. He wore a green and white and red-trimmed doublet so new it pinched his neck; he put his finger inside it once or twice to ease it.

Seeing the Dutchmen at the tavern watching, he strolled toward them. With one hand he kept his long fancy sword out from between his legs.

"Well, there they are," he said, in crippled Dutch. "The Sea Beggars. One hand out and their mouths filled with *please.*" He laughed, throwing his chest out, and marched up and down past them, flirting his sword hilt fretted with fine silverwork.

"See her, you old pirate?" His eyes on Pieter, he waved his hand at the *Wayward Girl.* "Old Beggar. That's all you'll ever see of her, dirty old Beggarman. In four days she'll be *La Diamante.*" His white teeth showed in a nasty grin and he jabbed his sword forward, not taking it out of the scabbard, only pushing it at Pieter. *"La Diamante.* My ship, old dirty Beggar-man."

Pieter said nothing. His heart burned like a coal in his chest.

The Spanish officer strutted and bragged a little more, but none of the Dutch would speak to him, and finally he strolled away. Jan had finished with his chore. He sat cross-legged on the broad blue-gray paving stones, his eyes on the *Wayward Girl.* He lifted his head once; his gaze met Pieter's in a short burning look. Standing up, he took the tub of dirty water across the wharf and threw it into the harbor.

"Damned green stripling," one of the other men muttered, looking after the Spaniard. "Never sailed in water over his head, I'll be bound."

"He'll take her out and wreck her," said another man, Joris, who had sailed with Pieter once or twice on the *Wayward Girl.*

"Take her out the first time onto the bars and run her aground," said someone else.

Up the wharf came Marten, the fisherman, staring out at the moorings; when he came even with Pieter, he swung around and said, "Captain, look! They've fitted her with new guns. See? Brass guns, by God!"

Pieter stood up. Sliding his hands over his shirt, he strolled across the street to the wharf, and as one man the others walked with him. They stood on the wharf, eyeing the *Wayward Girl,* which the current was pushing around nearly broadside to them. Pieter spat into the scummy water below the wharf. It was true: amidships, on either side, two long shining guns rested on wooden carriages on the deck, and a fifth gun, smaller, but just as shiny and new, waited in the bow.

Pieter whistled under his breath. "She'll need a new trim, to carry that weight and still show her speed." It ached like sickness that he would not be the man to handle her. An instant later a queer new excitement stirred under his heart. He glanced around him at the other men and saw Jan standing behind him, his mouth half open, his eyes fixed on the ship.

"Aye," Red Aart said. "She's way down by the head, with that big shooter there."

"I'd move that one back to the stern," Pieter said. He threw his chest out, giving room to the wild rising lust inside, and gave his nephew another quick look. "Move the midships guns up a little, ahead of the mainmast."

"She'll be fast as a snake in the water," said Marten.

Jan swung his blazing look from the ship to his uncle. "We can't let her go to the Spanish. She'll tear up our own ships. They'll use her on Dutch ships."

Pieter reached for his pipe and stuck it between his teeth. "Now, boys," he said.

The others were pressing in around him. Red Aart still held his broom; he shifted his grip until he held it like a weapon. "We could sink her. Swim out at night and ram a hole through that fancy paintwork—" He thrust with the broom handle.

Marten groaned. Joris said, "Such a pretty lady—"

Jan said, "Are the Spaniards God's people?"

"Hunh?" The other men turned their incomprehending looks on him. Pieter cleared his throat.

"You mean, steal her from them?"

Jan's head bobbed once in a sharp nod. "Take her to sea. Turn pirate. Attack the Spaniards with their own guns."

Pieter stuck the stem of his pipe between his teeth. "I can't sail her by myself."

"I'll help you."

The other men were staring at them, their jaws slack with surprise. Joris gave a violent shake of his head.

"Christ! You'll never get me into it. The governor's hanging people every day just for thinking. For stealing a ship—"

Red Aart scuffed his wooden shoe over the pavement. "The harbor master has two armed galleys that would blow you to splinters before you made it out of the harbor."

"And if you got that far, the big guns there would make an end of you," Marten said.

Pieter said nothing. He took a little pouch from his shirt, loosened the drawstrings, and dipped his fingers into the aromatic shreds of leaf inside. Carefully he put a pinch of the tobacco into the bowl of his pipe. "We can't sail her alone, anyway. I'd need eight more men at least."

"I've got my tavern," said Red Aart. "And there's my brother. I can't go."

"The Spanish would blow you to bits," Marten shouted.

"Shut up." Joris knocked him in the ribs with his elbow. "Do you want everybody to know what we're doing?"

Pieter got out his firebox. In the midst of the other men, Jan sat with his shoulders hunched scowling at his uncle, his head sunk down like a sullen dog's. Pieter smiled at him, pleased with him.

"The tavern's not much," Red Aart was saying. "But it's mine. And I can't very well leave my brother."

He was talking to nobody; the other men were arguing at one another, each saying some excuse that no one else paid heed to, having excuses of his own to make. Red Aart swung toward Pieter.

"I can't leave my brother."

"Bring him," said Pieter. "I went to sea before I was his age."

"You had all your wits. And what about my tavern?"

Pieter sucked smoke through his pipe. He winked at Jan, sitting silent among the turmoil he had started. The scowl had softened to a puzzled frown. Pieter got up onto his feet.

"Well, well, I'm to my home fire."

"Wait," Marten said. "We've got talking to do yet."

"You do, maybe," Pieter said, and beckoned Jan after him. "My feet are cold; I'm for the fire. Good day."

"*LA DIAMANTE*," Jan said bitterly. "She'll kill Dutch ships, too, I know it."

Pieter said, "When they're done fitting her up, we'll go out and sink her."

At that Jan bit back a curse; he had been learning new oaths from his uncle, words that would have made his mother faint and which it still shocked him a little to hear from his own mouth. They were walking up the street toward Pieter's house. Darkness was fast falling over Nieuport. They passed by the front steps of an old plaster house, the wife standing on the top step on her toes to light the lantern over the door.

The watch was coming. Jan could hear their marching feet. He followed Pieter up over the bridge that spanned the canal.

At the top of the bridge, Pieter stopped so abruptly that Jan walked on his heels.

Not the watch that marched along the street ahead of them. A column of men with iron pots on their heads and double-bladed pikes laid over their shoulders was striding briskly down the way between the canal and the row of houses facing it. As they passed each doorway, a soldier left the column and climbed the step and hammered on the door with his fist.

Pieter swore, one of his dirtier oaths. "Well, well," he said. "Now we'll all be hostelers."

"What?" Jan said. The wild thought entered his mind that everyone in Nieuport was to be arrested; but the houses opened their doors, and the soldiers went in, and no one came out again. "What are they doing?"

Pieter growled at him and led him down across the canal and into the next street. They had to step back nearly to the wall of the corner house to let the soldiers pass. The clank-clank of their iron clothes marked the time of their march. Jan sniffed. They smelled funny—sour, like pickles.

"Germans," said Pieter. "Farts from Hell."

The column past, they went down their own little street. In front of Pieter's door a soldier was waiting. Pieter said nothing to him. He climbed the steps and opened the door, and the soldier barged up past him and into the house. The floor seemed to shake under his feet. Pushing through the front room, he stopped in the larger room beyond, where the hearth was, and the furniture, and looked around, and shrugged his pike and his pack off his shoulders.

"I'll take this room," he said, in ruined Dutch. Pieter and Jan retreated to the chill and bare walls of the front room.

RED AART hated tavern work; he put Jan to doing it, in exchange for feeding him and filling Pieter's cup. He would have filled Pieter's cup anyway. The tavern was his because his father had sailed with Pieter for years, saving up his shares of booty and smuggling in the tavern stores. Sitting on his tall stool at the back of the tavern's drinking room, Red Aart counted the coins in the till, one eye set to oversee Jan's work with the broom, and wondered why there was never any money extra, as he was sure there had been in his father's time.

"Hi, there," he called to Jan. "Don't ply the broom so strongly; you put all the dust up into the air."

His father had shouted the same words to him, and the eminent good sense in it enlarged his feeling of himself, as the few coins clinking in his hand did not.

Jan flung him a surly look, but he softened his strokes of the broom. In the corner, Red Aart's half-witted brother, Mouse, scowled fiercely at Aart. Mouse had taken as good a liking to Jan as a bride to her new husband and spent the day trailing after him.

Lifting his hand, Red Aart let the coins slide into his purse. No meat today. He got down from the stool and went across the street to the fish market, to buy a fish for dinner.

He chose a fine halibut, the eye still shining and clear. Although she knew he was taking it only thirty yards away, the fishmonger made a point of wrapping it in paper. Red Aart haggled the price with her a while. As the money changed hands, Jan came from the tavern and crossed the cobblestones to the wharf, where he stood looking out at the *Wayward Girl.*

"Come take this fish and clean it," Aart called.

Jan wheeled toward him, hot. "I've already worked half the day for you—"

From behind him, Mouse ran up, a runty boy, cockeyed, and took the wrapped fish in his arms like a baby and bore it away to the tavern. Jan and Aart glared at each other a long moment. Finally Red Aart said, "Do you want to eat?"

Jan's mouth twisted in a grimace. He ate enough for two men. Lowering his eyes, he went after Mouse, and Aart followed, relieved. There was something about Jan that made Aart very nervous at the thought of fighting with him, although they were nearly of a height.

He took his stool again, and fell to brooding over the lack of money in the till. Through the back door he could see Jan hacking off the head of the fish. The knife scraped at the scales. A moment later Jan came in, the damp fishy paper in his hand.

"The fishmonger gave you this?"

Aart took it; there was writing on it, printed words. He pursed his lips, trying to look wise. He had spent his childhood years struggling with the mysteries of the alphabet without solving them in the least.

"Can you read?" he asked Jan, and thrust the paper at him. "I don't want to get my hands dirty."

Jan hardly glanced at the paper. "It says the governor is going to tax you one hundredth the value of your tavern, and then one tenth of everything you earn from the trade."

Aart snatched the paper back again and fixed his eyes on the black letters. "He can't do that. I'll be ruined."

"To pay for his troops, it says," Jan told him. He leaned his arms on the counter. His hands were bloody and smelled of fish, and scales, like tiny coins, clung to his sleeves. Mouse had come up behind him.

"He can't do that!" Red Aart said again. A helpless rage burned in his chest. He threw a wild look around his tavern. "It's not worth anything! I cannot pay it—if I have to pay a tenth of my trade, there won't be anything left for me."

Jan leaned toward him. "Then go to sea with us, and keep everything you earn."

The tavern keeper blinked at him, slow to follow this change of lead. "To sea."

"On the *Wayward Girl*. You said—the other day—it's the tavern that keeps you here."

The front door banged open. A score of soldiers tramped in, men of the Spanish army, but mostly German mercenaries. Aart watched them spill out across the room, find places, and bellow for drink.

He slid off the stool, to answer their demands. Facing Jan, he said, with a weak smile, "My custom's growing, you see."

Jan said, "Yes, and you are paying them to come here."

Aart pressed his lips shut. He saw the truth in that; there were three soldiers living in his house, now, and probably these would want credit, if they paid at all. But still—still—

"Herr Obst!" the mercenaries bawled, and beat on the tables.

He went to wait on them, bowing and smiling like a servant. With a grunt of contempt, Jan went out again to finish cleaning the fish.

PIETER had gone to bed very drunk; now he woke slowly, painfully, his mouth burning dry and his stomach sick. He fought against wakening. Pulling his head down he buried it under the blanket.

"What are you doing?" The sibilant rasp of Jan's voice came from the far side of the room. Heavy feet clumped. Pieter groaned; his head was so filled with pain it felt soft and swollen.

"Oh, ho, Dutch boy," said the thick throaty voice of the German mercenary. "You think you stop me? I take whatever I want!"

"Over me," Jan said.

"Shut up," cried Pieter, and the effort pierced his head with pain; his stomach heaved.

Their feet tramped and thumped on the floor; a gasp followed a grunt, and something hard hit something softer. They were fighting. With a great effort of will the old man pulled his mind up from the dull comfort of sleep and rolled over.

The German was wrestling with Jan in the center of the floor. They were of a height; they strained together, their arms locked, in the dim room, until suddenly the German gave way and fell. Jan nearly fell on top of him. Instead he hovered over the German and shouted, "Now get out of here!"

Without a word the German launched himself upward from the floor, in his hand a long knife.

Pieter let out a yell. Tangled in his blanket, he fought to rise, while his nephew met the flashing blade with his bare hands. The German swore in his own language. Jan had him by the wrist and was holding his knife arm out straight; as the two men struggled for mastery their faces darkened and the cords on their necks stood up like rigging on a ship's mast.

The German lunged to the side, his leg snaking out, and kicked Jan behind the knee. The boy grunted; he went down heavily on his knees, his fist still clutching the German's knife hand, but the blade was now poised above him, gleaming in the dark.

Pieter kicked his blankets off. Snorting for breath, he flung himself up onto the German's back and wrapped his arms around the man's upper arms. The German howled. Jan sprang forward and drove his fist deep into the mercenary's belly, and as the German fell slackly to the floor kicked him between the legs.

The knife clattered on the floorboards. Pieter landed on top of the German, who writhed and moaned, helpless under him.

Jan reached down for the knife. When he straightened with it in his hand he started toward the German, and Pieter saw that he meant to kill him.

"No!" Pieter leapt between his nephew and the defenseless German mercenary. "No—don't cut him, for God's love."

"He'll rob us naked," Jan said.

"No. God, if he's killed in this house they'll hang both of us."

The German was lying limp on the floor, unconscious, or feigning. Pieter cast a swift look down at him and getting Jan by the arm pulled him toward the door. "Come along."

"I can't stay there with him," Jan said, on the steps outside.

The dawn was breaking over the rooftops of Nieuport. In the street the housewives were sweeping their steps, calling gossip to one another; the air was cold and fresh. Pieter locked his nephew's arm firmly in his own and led him away toward the canal.

"Come on."

"I've got to get out of here," Jan said. "I can't stay here. I'll kill him or he'll kill me."

"Quiet."

"You should have let me kill him. I owe them some killings—after what they did to my father—"

"Quiet!" Pieter gave him a shake.

"Where are we going?"

"You'll see," Pieter said. "Just be quiet and let me do the talking."

RED AART said, "Well, what about the harbor patrols? If they catch us out there—"

"They won't catch us," Pieter said. "Not if we work fast."

Marten leaned across the table, his eyes bright. "Besides, if they do, we can just jump overboard and swim for it. I say let's do it! Pay the God-damned royalists back a little for what they've caused us."

There was a general growl of assent from around the table. Beside Red Aart his half-wit brother stood, jaw dropped open and crossed eyes dancing.

"All right," Aart said. "When?"

"Tonight," Pieter said. "After the tenth bell."

"And we'll just be going to sink the *Wayward Girl,* right? Nothing fancy. I know you, Pieter van Cleef."

Pieter stuck his pipe between his teeth. "Do you?"

"Not much else we can do, tonight," said Marten. "The wind will be dead foul for the mouth of the harbor, even when the tide's at full ebb."

"It might shift," said Jobst, the baker's son.

"Aye," said Red Aart, "and it might die entirely. The harbor patrols are galleys; they don't need the wind. I don't like the sound of this."

"We'll stove a hole in her and go," Pieter said. He glanced at Jan, sitting silent beside him; the young man said nothing.

"Don't worry about the galleys," said Jobst. "What can slaves do against free Dutchmen?"

"I'll drink to that," Pieter said.

"At ten bells, then," said Red Aart.

"Can I come?" his brother asked.

Pieter grinned at him. "Can you swim?" He reached for the gin bottle in the middle of the table.

4

THE WATER of the harbor was warm as milk, but where the river ran in, it turned cold. At the chill, Jan lost his breath; he let go of Pieter's belt, in front of him. The old man stopped at once to let him catch up.

"Keep close!" The words came in a breathy hiss over the water. "The channel begins here; we have to swim."

Jan nodded. His chest felt tight and he was shivering. The bottom dropped off under his feet. A tug on the back of his belt yanked him sideways. In front of him Pieter was swimming. They were all swimming. Only Jan's height kept his feet on the ground and his head above the water; now he missed his footing altogether and the water lapped his chin and he struck out with his arms after his uncle.

They could not hold belts now, but they kept together, so close Jan's kicking legs brushed the men behind him. He kept his eyes on Pieter's head, cleaving the dark water ten feet ahead of him.

There were eight men altogether, friends of his uncle; he scarcely knew some of them by name. They didn't matter to him anyway. All that mattered was the water, the ship lying in the dark ahead of them, and his uncle leading him to it. That and the desire churning in his belly like another soul, which quickened at the thought of blood.

They were coming to the anchorage. The wind ruffled the surface of the water and ran cold as a dead hand over Jan's hair. A white light bobbed on the shore, a cable length away, but nothing else showed of the town except a clutter of roofs and the church steeple pointing up into the sky. Ahead of the men in the water, the first ships loomed, their masts towering up toward the stars.

The wind was rising. Pieter waved them all into the shelter of the nearest hull.

"Well, boys," he said, when he had them all together and had counted them, "this is the sticking point. Once we go up on deck, we're in it to the teeth. If the Spaniards catch us they'll hang the lot—if they let us live that long. If anybody wants to back out now I don't blame him, or any with him."

Nobody said anything. Jan was treading water close by the hull where they had taken shelter; the smell of the ship's wood, the creak of her anchor cable as she backed off before the wind, laid their impress unforgettably on his fine-tuned nerves. He raised his eyes. High overhead, the vessel's mainmast yardarms cut the sky into open squares. The main braces bellied out on the wind.

"All right," Pieter said. "Let's go. God's with us: we're fighting Spaniards."

He put out his hand to Red Aart. "You keep an eye on that boy, hear?"

"I have him," the tavern keeper said. Behind him Mouse was paddling like a dog in the water.

They all shook hands. In the dark Jan saw only pale shapes where their faces were. They swam away down the side of the hull and below her overhanging stern.

Ahead of them the *Wayward Girl* lay at her mooring, quartered away from them, a lantern on her stern showing the merest bead of light. Pieter swam with his head poked up out of the water, his vigorous arms and legs never breaking the surface, and for an old man he swam fast. Jan strained to keep up. Reaching out with his arms at the top of the stroke, he splashed one hand into the air and his uncle hissed at him in reproof, without slackening his pace. The heads of the other men bobbed like corks after him. They were coming into the lee of the ship. Pieter reached her side. Then on the deck above them something moved.

All around Jan there was a sharp gasp; with that deep breath the others sank down under the water, out of sight. Jan lunged for the shelter of the ship's side, next to his uncle. His hands flat to the fresh smooth paint, he looked straight up and saw a guard, leaning over the rail ten feet above his head, a musket in his hands.

Jan held his breath, thinking of the men out there, under the water. The guard was looking straight at them. If one of them surfaced . . . An instant later, softly, a dripping head rose from the sea beside him, against the ship's side.

The musketeer saw nothing. He walked off. They could hear his footstep through the wooden hull inches from their ears.

Pieter yanked on Jan's sleeve, and the boy slipped away down the side of the ship, toward the bow. The anchor there held the *Wayward Girl*'s bow into the wind; the ruffled water broke in a steady slap-slap of little waves against her hull. Sliding under the anchor cable, Jan reached up over his head as high as he could, gripped the thick new rope, and climbed hand over hand up toward the bow rail.

With one hand he held the rail; inch by inch he raised his head above the level of the deck and looked around.

There in front of him on the foredeck was one of the new guns, drawn back on its carriage and lashed down to cleats on the deck. Her brass shone through the dark like an angel's wing; he could smell the new rope of her tackles. He swept a look across the foredeck and the waist of the ship. The sterncastle was three steps up from the main deck. Directly in front of the steps, by the wheel, was the sentry, leaning on his musket.

Jan's guts tightened. He slipped back down from the rail to the anchor rope and down the anchor rope to the water, where his uncle and the others were waiting.

"I see him," he said. "Give me the knife."

Pieter scrubbed his hand over his face. "Where is he?"

"Give me the knife!"

The old man looked up, startled at his tone. After a moment, his face drawn long, he put the knife into Jan's hand.

Jan hung it carefully on his belt by the thong around its haft and climbed back up the anchor cable; just below the deck the angle of the cable took him within reach of the bottom of the bowsprit, and he scrambled up across it into the space beside the brass gun.

He had never seen a weapon this size. One hand stroked the long barrel. The metal was much smoother than skin.

The sentry was coming forward, his musket in the crook of his arm. Jan crouched beside the long gun and watched him. He was a short, stout man, the sentry, maybe not even Spanish. He stopped in the waist near the mast and turned to look over the side. Jan ran one finger along the blade of the knife at his belt; he unhitched the thong and with the knife low in one hand he moved bent-legged down the deck to the mast.

Only a few feet away the sentry was relieving himself over the side of the ship. Jan tapped on the mast with the haft of his knife.

The soldier wheeled around, the musket flat in his hands. "Who's—" Jan grabbed the barrel of the gun and yanked it out of his grasp. For an instant, still with fear, the sentry looked stupidly into his face. Jan smiled at him. When the sentry's mouth fell open in a shout, Jan plunged the knife up to the hilt in his chest.

Pieter was already hauling himself up over the bow rail; puffing, his eyes narrow with suspicion, he trotted up the deck toward Jan. "What the hell are you doing, boy-o?" Leaning over the rail, he beckoned the others up.

Jan took the knife out of the sentry's chest. Liking the musket, he unbuckled the dead man's belt to get the fittings for it and took the sword as well. Pieter and the others were wandering around the ship, looking over the rigging and the guns and opening up the hatches. Jan threw the sentry's body over the rail and went looking for his uncle.

"Call them together. We have to work fast."

Pieter stuck his fists on his hips. "This is my ship, boy-o."

Jan shifted the musket and the sentry's belt into his left hand. "Yes, sir."

"You remember that." The old man stuck his chin out. In an undertone, he said, "I saw you take that guard. You and I will do very well together, but I intend to give the orders. You understand?"

"Yes, sir," Jan said.

"Now, let's get out of here." Pieter tramped away toward the stern.

Jan stowed the musket and his other trophies against a bulkhead and went to inspect the amidships guns. He felt wonderful; no matter what happened now, he knew he would triumph. He leaned against one of the portside guns, his hand cupped over a brass turning, and waited for the next thing to happen.

"ALL HANDS," Pieter shouted, from the stern deck.

The other men were scattered around the ship. At his yell, they looked around, startled and curious, but nobody moved. Like his nephew they needed some discipline. He filled his lungs with breath and began to bellow orders.

"Marten, Willem—man the mainsail halyards. Flippo, Mark, the jib halyards—"

Instead of doing as he bid they were rushing toward him, in a mass, their mouths full of argument. Only Jan stood silent and watched and waited.

"Pieter!" Marten Lamsbrok ran at him, his finger jabbing the air. "The wind's dead foul! Why spread sail? Let's hull her and go home. We can't—"

"Jan," Pieter called. "Bring that musket."

The others watched with their eyes popping as Jan climbed the poop steps, the long gun over his shoulder like an ax.

"Ah, well," Pieter said, setting his fists on his hips. He glanced at his oversized nephew, who came to stand at his shoulder. "I'll start over again, boys, and this time you'll do it, or, by Cock, the fellow here with the bang stick will see you never do anything else." His voice swelled to a roar. "Marten! Willem! Man the mainsail halyards!"

They jumped. Marten and Willem van Zook had sailed before on the *Wayward Girl* under Pieter and their good turn of foot gave the others an example. Pieter sent a man to the anchor; he looked quickly all around the harbor. There were men sleeping on deck on the galleon, and several lights on the shore, and, more alarming, there was a light at the mouth of the harbor, where the shore battery was mounted. Against his cheek the wind was backing around to the north. He pursed his lips. By now the tide would be sliding back down the river mouth into the sea.

"Up anchor!" He glanced at Jan, beside him, engrossed in the musket. "Can you work that Devil's poker?"

"I can't tell if it's loaded."

Pieter laughed, short. "Well, boy-o, we'll find out soon enough." He laid one hand on the big young man's shoulder. "Soon enough." The anchor was coming up; the tension on the cable had pulled the ship forward a little, her bow aimed deeper into the harbor, past the galleon.

"Up the jib," Pieter shouted.

"Pieter, you old fool," someone shouted, and Pieter gripped his nephew's arm.

"Shoot over their heads."

Without hesitation Jan brought the musket to his shoulder and fired. The blast resounded across the deck and over the water. The muzzle flame licked out into the dark like a fiery tongue. Down in the bow the men wailed; the three-cornered jib sail went shrilling up the mast.

"There, now," Pieter said.

The sail filled and drew, as the men tugged the braces in to keep the canvas face to the wind, and sweetly the *Wayward Girl* answered the urging. Pieter cast a quick look around them. The galleon still lay between them and the channel; it looked dark and inert, but deeper in the anchorage a small boat was rowing through the lesser ships, and lights moved and people shouted on the deck of a galley only a cable length from Pieter.

He shouted, "Shake out the mainsail!"

Jan was bent over the musket, trying to fit a patch into the muzzle, but he wasn't needed now; the men leapt to the halyards, and the huge new mainsail cracked open, falling wide from the jack yard on the mast. Pieter let out his breath, exhilarated.

On the galley there was a shout, and a drumbeat.

"Man the sheets!" Pieter went to the edge of the stern deck, above the wheel. "Jan, take the helm." He looked up the harbor, toward the distant sea. The wind blew full in his face. More than the wind against him, he feared the three big cannon mounted on the shore. He gripped the rail, looking down at his nephew's head as the young man took the wheel.

The ship was moving handily through the water now, headed dead away from the mouth of the harbor; she would pass astern of the dark galleon. The mainsail was luffing a little, which surprised old Pieter, until he remembered that the weight of the new cannon had the ship out of trim. He licked his lips. Ahead the river poured into the harbor.

"Luff off all sail!"

They jumped to the braces and let the sheets fly, spilling the wind out of the canvas. With the wind off her the ship lost her liveliness. She seemed to die slowly, or fall asleep. On the last of her forward momentum, she glided into the onrushing river current, and the forceful water bore her away down toward the sea.

Now they understood, Pieter's crew, and a rough cheer went up.

"Hands to the braces," Pieter roared.

Jan looked up at him, his face solemn. "Here comes that other ship."

The old man was watching the far shore slip by, judging the ship's speed downriver. The tide was ebbing strongly. The ship was swinging slowly around in the broad tug of the current, and he called an order to trim the jib. When the wind turned the ship broadside to the current again, he spared a look over his shoulder at the galley.

The harbor master's ship was putting out her oars. In a ragged line the blades rose dripping into the air, flashing and sparkling in the light of the lanterns at her poop and forecastle. Slowly she moved out of her anchorage. Free of the wind, she could pass the galleon on the bow side, cutting in half the margin between her and the *Wayward Girl.* Pieter bit his lips. He drummed his fists on his thighs. Abruptly, one hand on the rail of the poop deck, he vaulted down to the waist beside Jan.

"Get that musket ready. I'll take the wheel."

Jan reached down at his feet for the gun. "What do you suppose the range is with this thing?"

"You see that culverin in the galley's bow?" Pieter hung his arms over the wheel spokes, keeping the ship steady as he could. He squinted to see forward through the bustle on the deck. "Just don't let them fire on us with that culverin."

"Yes, sir," Jan said.

The *Wayward Girl* was slowly losing speed. The current nudged her off to the side. Pieter's legs tingled, as they often did when he was frightened. What an ass he was, to give up his house and his jug of liquor for this wretched life again. He yelled to his crew to trim the jib.

While he was bringing the ship up into the current again, someone on the foredeck saw the galley.

"They're chasing us!"

All the men but two dropped their work and ran to the rail to see. Pieter roared, "Luff off. Luff off, damn you! Jan—"

The men rushed back to their work. Pieter cast a quick look over his shoulder. Jan had gone up onto the stern deck; he was laying out the powder flask, the sack of musket balls, the patches, and kneeling began to load the musket. Pieter's gaze changed its angle. The galley was coming on, her oars rising and falling like wings. Within minutes she would have the *Wayward Girl* within range of her bow gun.

Pieter gave a yell of rage. His men had finally taken the wind out of the ship's jib, but too late; her way would carry her upriver a little now, closer to the galley, while the rowed ship like an arrow coursed down the tideway at their flank.

"Jan," he shouted. "Keep watch!" Despairing, he flung a look ahead of them, at the narrow mouth of the harbor, where the shore guns hid in the dark.

"She's firing," Jan called.

There was a boom from the galley. A moment later the ball whisked through the air and a fountaining splash shot up from the black water to starboard.

"Don't let them fire on us!" Pieter danced on the deck, spitting with rage as he shouted. "One good shot and we're hulled!"

"She's too far away still." Jan stood calmly looking over the rail at the oncoming galley.

The galley was sweeping down on them. With the *Wayward Girl* nearly broadside to her, she had an enormous target to fire on. Pieter gritted his teeth. He longed for his little fire and his gin. In the light of the galley's forecastle lantern he could see the men working around the big culverin, loading, running her forward, standing up with the slow match—

"Jan," he shrieked.

The culverin thundered smoke and flame. Pieter's whole body tensed, waiting, waiting for the blow. The hiss in the air sounded almost overhead. He whirled; the white eruption of the water where the shot hit burst up on the far side of the ship, a scant two fathoms off. They had fired completely over the ship. They were aiming high, trying to disable the *Wayward Girl* so that they could recapture her.

"Jan!"

The boy raised the musket to his shoulder. The *Wayward Girl* was nearly to the mouth of the harbor, now, still turned broadside to the current and to the pursuing galley. The stink of sulfur crossed the water to Pieter's nose. In the forecastle of the galley the men bent over the cannon, so close he could see the gleam of sweat on their naked shoulders. The bore of the culverin like a preacher's mouth was round with fulminations.

"Jan—"

The boy lifted one hand to him to wait.

Farther away, in another direction, there was another low boom, like summer thunder. Pieter wheeled, his hair standing on end. They had come under the shore battery's fire. He peered toward the dark hilly headland between the harbor and the sea. Where that shot went, he could not tell, and he saw nothing; his back tingled in expectation of the next.

On the galley they ran the gun forward into firing position, and the man with the slow match stepped forward. Jan raised the musket neatly to his shoulder and shot the gunner through the chest.

Pieter emptied his lungs in a yell. His nephew grabbed the ramrod. On the galley's forecastle the gun crew was milling around; someone shouted angry orders in Spanish, and then in Dutch. "Shoot! Shoot!" Jan flung down the ramrod and poured gunpowder into the musket.

From the shore battery came another dull thump. Pieter held his breath. He flung a wild look around him, looking for the ball that could come from anywhere, and saw to his surprise that they were in the mouth of the harbor now, the open sea only yards away.

"Hands to the braces!"

The galley's gun banged, so close that the smoke from the culverin rolled across the water and enveloped the stern of the *Wayward Girl*. Pieter coughed, blinking his fogged eyes; Jan loomed through the smoke, the musket to his shoulder, unmoving, and fired.

There was a shriek from the galley. The Spanish officer fell in a long dive over the rail into the sea.

There was another low boom from the shore battery. Pieter ducked; he heard the whistle of the shot passing close beside his ship. Between him and the galley, the water suddenly burst upward into a volcano of white spray. Jan yelled in triumph and delight, dancing on the poop deck. The white water subsided. Behind it the galley rolled helpless in the thrashing wave, half its bow gone.

"Mainsail," Pieter cried, his voice hoarse with relief. "Trim her down!"

The crew hauled in the mainsail sheets; into the taut belly of the sail the wind poured its strength, and the ship grew light and quick in the water. The shore battery boomed again, but, perhaps distracted by the calamity it had brought upon its own galley, it sent its shot way wide. On the foredeck of the *Wayward Girl* the men were dancing and hugging one another and cheering. Pieter cranked the wheel over.

"Prepare to wear ship!"

Jan sprang down to his side. "Are we out? Are we free?"

Pieter was looking forward, past the wild celebrations on the deck, toward the broad flat horizon of water unbroken by any land. "Yes," he said.

Jan clapped him on the back, and Pieter put out his hand and gripped the boy's arm in rough proud affection. They brought the ship around on a broad reach and sailed away into the masterless sea.

EVERY morning before dawn, Michael opened the ovens and raked over the coals and laid on more charcoal. While the ovens were heating, he went around to the front of the bakery and unrolled the awning and opened the shutters and the door. Now the sun was rising.

The ovens were hot, and his mother would be up, shuffling around in the small dark room at the rear of the bakery, exhaling deep sighs in place of words or prayers. The first loaves were ready for the ovens, little round buns that Antwerpers loved in the midmorning, some plain, some stuffed with fruit or jam. There were forty-two of these; Michael knew already the names and faces of those who would buy thirty-six of them and could have guessed to the moment when these regular customers would appear, who would pay with a penny and who with a real, and what each one would say to him in the course of the transaction.

The other six buns were part of the day's surprises. Michael loved surprises. He slid the tray of buns into the top oven.

He swept the shop and went out to sweep the street in front. Up the way, past the broom hedge, the wine and oil shop was open, and old Philips was out in front sweeping his part of the street. He and Michael waved to each other. Michael did not bother to smile. Philips was nearly blind. He needed only the gesture. Stooping over the broom again, Michael scrubbed away at the cobblestones. Sometimes it seemed that the older he got the less interesting his life became.

But now here came Melisse, a seamstress who lived down the street above the flower shop, a covered dish in her hand. Michael straightened, his curiosity jumping alive.

Melisse wore a dirty apron over her long sober dress. Her hair was pushed carelessly up under a worn coif, and her long thin face was hollow and baggy with fatigue. Coming up to Michael, she tugged on his sleeve and turned back the cloth over the dish.

"My baby's sick, Michael, dear," she said. In the dish was a mess of egg and herbs and milk. "Let me set this in your oven, just for a moment, just to cook the goodness in."

He took the dish; giving a look over his shoulder into the shop, he covered the slop over again. His mother disapproved of charity—and Melisse was gossiped to be a secret Calvinist. Michael smiled at her. "Come back in half an hour."

"Not too long, now," she said. "I don't want the egg to be hard; he won't eat it if it's hard."

"Don't worry."

"But it must be warmed all the way through. Maybe I should stay and do it myself."

"No, no, go on, and come back in half an hour."

Melisse lingered, frowning. Michael took the dish into the shop and set it on the table inside the door. His mother called him. He went back into the kitchen, to help her knead the dough.

Jeanne-Marie hated the sunlight. Her kitchen was like an anteroom of Hell, gloomy and low, the pent air thick with odors of yeast and decaying fruit and old flour and souring milk. The old woman padded on her broad bare feet from the cupboard to the table where she worked, every few minutes fetching up a sigh so tremulous she might have been about to weep. Her clothes were impregnated with flour, and her body shapeless with fat, so that she reminded Michael always of one of her own great floury rolls. When he came into the kitchen she gave him a buffet on the ear.

"What are you doing out there? Who are you talking to? Come work this dough and earn your keep like a decent Christian man."

Side by side they stood at the table punching and pounding the dough, warm and moist at first, sticking to Michael's hands as he pulled and folded it and pumped it with his arms.

Out in front of the place the door opened.

Michael kept his eyes on the dough. He knew what would happen, every step, like an old dance.

His mother shuffled to the kitchen door and peered out. "Michael!" She waved him frantically over to her side.

"Yes, Mama."

"Who is that? Is that Moeller?"

He looked. Of course it was Moeller, who came in every day at this time, with his penny, to buy a fruit bun for his wife and a plain bun for himself.

"Yes, Mama."

"He's a Calvinist. You go and give him what he wants. See he doesn't cheat you." She pushed him forward out the door. "Hurry up before he leaves and we lose the money!"

While he was giving Moeller a cherry bun and the plain bun, two more regular buyers appeared.

"Good morning, Michael."

"Hello, Vrouw Arliss. What may I sell you today?"

"Oh, the usual, Michael."

"Hello, Vrouw Schenck. What may I sell you today?"

"What we always have, Michael."

He wrapped the buns in soft paper, careful not to smear the sweet filling that oozed from the side. A strange girl came into the shop.

"Thank you, Vrouw Schenck. God be with you."

"And how is your dear mother, Michael?" Vrouw Schenck loved to talk.

"Very well, thank you."

The strange girl had gone to one side of the shop and was staring at the loaves of bread left over from the day before. Her long gray skirt was patched, the hem worn, but the stuff was very fine. He craned his neck to see if she wore jewelry.

"Have you heard the latest about Melisse, Michael? I understand her husband has left her again."

He mumbled something to Vrouw Schenck, his curiosity absorbed by the stranger.

"That's what happens to people who don't mind their ways," said Vrouw Schenck, comfortably. "If she'd only—"

The strange girl was leaving. Michael brushed rudely past Vrouw Schenck, saying, "Yes, yes, you're perfectly right," ready to stop the girl at the door. But she had only gone to look at the sweet buns. Embarrassed, he faced his old customer again.

"My, my, Michael," she said, and sniffed. "I can see my friendship's wasted here."

"Vrouw Schenck, I'm sorry—"

The housewife drew herself up like a strutting pigeon and marched out the door. Michael grimaced. It would not do to lose a good customer. He stood looking at the back of the stranger, wondering why he would risk certain profit for the sake of a new face.

"May I help you?" he said.

The girl turned. She was a little younger than he was, and not pretty. Her pale hair hung down in disorderly braids over her shoulders. She said, "Do you sell your stale bread?"

"We give it to the Church," he said.

Her face fretted with disappointment, she glanced behind her once at the sweet buns and started toward the door. Michael got in her way. "Wait." Her dress was rich; he wondered what fate had brought her to search for day-old bread. "Is it for you? Are you hungry?"

From the back of the shop came his mother's sibilant hiss. "Michael!"

He waved at her to be quiet. At his question the girl's face had gone suddenly blank. "I feed it to the birds," she said, with an edge in her voice that suggested he should keep his interest to himself.

"Michael!" his mother called, in a hoarse loud whisper. "Who is she? Is she Catholic?"

"The Church gives bread to the poor," Michael said.

The girl raised her pale eyebrows into polite arches. "How very kind of the Church."

Not a Catholic. He looked her over again, intent, and saw her hands, soft and fine as a noblewoman's. She was making for the door again and he blocked her way.

"Wait. Who are you? I've never seen you before, and I know everybody in this quarter of Antwerp."

"I've got to go," she said. "My mother's waiting for me."

"Michael," his mother shouted. "Get rid of her!"

"Wait." He lunged past the stranger, grabbed the nearest sweet bun off the rack, and brought it to her. "Here."

Her eyes widened, softening her face; slowly she took the bun from him, her gaze unwavering from his, and lifting the bun took a bite. Her hunger overwhelmed her discipline. She stuffed the delicious sweet into her mouth, chewing hard on the sticky mass. Michael smiled at her, triumphant.

"Who are you? Where do you live?"

"Michael!"

She managed to swallow the lump of bread in her mouth. Now that she had eaten of his charity, she could not deny him a little courtesy, and she said, "My name is Johanna van Cleef—I live over in the Swan Street, above the Kelmans' kitchen. Do you know them?"

"Kelman," he said. "Two buns in the morning, a long loaf at night."

She was going. He did not stop her, having now some connection with her after she left the bakery. He smiled at her, and, her mouth stuffed with another greedy bite of the bun, she gave him back a broad cheerful grin. She went out the door.

"Michael!"

"Coming, Mother."

WHEN Hanneke came around the corner into the Swan Street, the Spanish soldier was sitting in front of Kelman's house. Her back stiffened. On straw legs she made herself walk down the gentle slope toward the house; her mother was in that house, her mother.

The Spanish soldier watched her come with his smoldering black eyes. He was very young, her age perhaps, although he had managed to grow a little feathery mustache. He was always dressed in fine clothes, trunk hose and doublet and leather shoes, exotic as a papingo among the plain Dutch people on whom he was quartered. As she came closer, Hanneke's stomach rolled in panic. He had only been here a few days but her fear grew more intense every time she saw him.

Now she was going in the gate, his gaze full of her, his black eyes like the eyes of a jungle animal, hypnotic and evil. She made herself meet his look the whole way from the gate to the door.

Inside, she leaned up against the wall a moment, recovering. He was still there, just the other side of the door. She went back through the house to the kitchen, where the Kelmans' cook hummed over her pea soup, and let herself out the back door, to the little wooden stair up to the attic room.

Her mother was sitting in the window, staring out. The floor and the top of the table and the cupboard bed were spread with bits of clothing, books, and linens. Hanneke closed the door. She had to fight down a surge of hot anger at her mother, who ignored her and began to sing.

Taking off her shawl, Hanneke hung it up on the hook by the door. The room was smaller every time she came back to it. The two women had little enough—a few bundles of clothes, a box of books, a chair, a chest full of embroidered linen for Hanneke's dowry—but with space so dear it all had to be neat, or the room was a chaos. When she did not go out roaming the streets Hanneke's mother spent the day opening drawers and boxes, taking out her possessions and laying them about, and there was never anywhere to step or sit or even to stand.

Hanneke said nothing to her mother. She set about cleaning up the room.

Her mother broke off singing. "Where were you?"

"Out," Hanneke said.

She folded the linen bedsheets intended for her wedding night and laid them back into the cherry wood chest her father had given her when she was twelve. She hated touching these things, seeing them, thinking about the blasted world they tied her to.

"That boy was here again," her mother said.

"What boy?"

She knew which boy: Michael Rijnhardt, the baker's boy, who had been coming into Kelman's backyard every day to look up at the window of Hanneke's room.

"I hope you threw something at him," Hanneke said.

"He looks like a very nice boy."

"He's a Catholic." Hanneke slammed the chest lid shut. Her gaze traveled the room, littered with the fragments of their past life. "Mama, why can you not keep all this shut away?"

"Have you seen Jan?"

"No, Mama."

She lowered her eyes to the chest; whenever she thought of her brother a hard lump formed in her throat. She rubbed her fingers over the deep carved roses on the lid of the chest. She would never marry now. When she was a little girl she had always assumed someday she would find a handsome charming man who would fall entirely in love with her and take her for his wife, but now she knew she would never marry. No one wanted the daughter of a hanged man. When she felt the familiar stinging in her eyes she scrubbed angrily at them with her hand. What right did she have to cry? Roughly she got to her feet, lifting the chest, and heaved it up onto the shelf beside the cupboard bed.

"Help me, Mama." She stooped to gather up the books strewn about the floor.

"Do you know where Jan is?"

"No, Mama."

Her mother climbed down from the window, reached for a book and put it away in the box, reached for another book. Hanneke gathered up the mess around her. Her brother had not come to see them for some time. He was gone, she thought; she had the sense of an emptiness in the city that meant he was gone. She sighed. A soft sound behind her brought her gaze back to her mother. The old woman sat with an armload of her husband's books clutched to her breast and wept. Hanneke tore her attention away. Her mother's grief frightened her. This mirror of her own fear made her fear more real. Furiously she busied herself putting away the rest of the books. After a little while, behind her, her mother began to sing again.

HE HAD been gone too long; his mother would scold him like a child when he got back to the bakery. Michael scuffed his shoe through the inch of new snow that lay over the cobble street, his gaze pinned to the door of the factory. The sun had set over half an hour before and the snow thickened the night as it fell. His mother was right; he should be there to help her, and not standing here in the street like a mooncalf. As he turned to go, the door opened.

Hanneke came out under the little white lantern that hung over the factory door and pulled her shawl up over her head. In the steady silent downsifting of the snow she was only a shape, but Michael recognized her at once; although he had known her only a few weeks he knew her in every nerve end, every sense, as the only thing worth knowing. He went forward to meet her, and she stopped and frowned at him.

"What are you doing here?"

"I'm sorry," he said. "I couldn't help it—it bothers me that you must walk home alone after dark."

"Please, Michael." She walked on past him down the street.

Michael fell into step beside her. Longing to take her by the arm, to guide her and protect her; certain of the rebuff if he tried. It was that distance between them which gave his feeling for her its electric poignancy. He wondered sometimes, if she had accepted him, if he would not have swiftly tired of her.

She was cold. The snow fell on her head and shoulders and she shivered.

"Will you take my coat?" he said humbly.

She shook her head.

"Must you work so late? All the other women have since gone home."

"I must sweep up after them," she said. "That's my duty there."

"What times are these," he said, "when such as you must work."

That drew a swift angry look from her. "I'm glad of my work. At least I can care for myself and my mother."

"I meant—"

"I know what you meant," she said, her chin up in the air. "Your pity is quite misplaced."

There was nothing he could say to that. They walked along down the hill toward the Swan Street, through the light cottony snow; everyone else was indoors and the street was empty. The little round-backed bridge lifted them over the frozen canal. At the height, she stopped and looked away down the canal, frowning; she did this every time they crossed the bridge, and he had concluded that she was looking at the tall stately house down on the next street. Her shawl had slipped back from the crown of her head and the starched wing of her cap was wilting in the snow. She turned and walked on.

"You need not go on any farther," she said. "My home is just over there."

He knew that. She always said that. Just as she always paused, looking at the Kelmans' house, and seemed to gather herself for an assault.

"Perhaps when the snow stops we can go skating together," he said.

"I have no skates."

"I will bring you a pair. My mother's old skates."

Someone was coming toward them, two people, one tall and stooped and the other a child. Hanneke drew back a little, to give them wide room to pass. Michael shifted to one side, shielding her from them, and turned to her again to press his invitation to skating.

"Once the snow stops the canals will be like glass. We'll have wonderful races."

"Mistress van Cleef?"

The tall stooped man came up before them, his shoulders hunched in the cold, his hands stuffed under his coat.

"Who are you?" Hanneke asked sharply.

"I am Clement de Vere," he said. "I'm a printer. I met your father briefly during the—" His gaze shifted to Michael and abruptly he cut off. The little boy beside him looked solemnly up at the three tall people. "I heard you were in need," said Clement the printer. "I came to offer you what help I can."

"I need no help," Hanneke said.

"I admired your father." Again the printer glanced at Michael and cut short what he would have said. Michael thought suddenly: *He is a Calvinist.* He wondered how Clement had escaped the persecutions. "If I can do anything—"

"Nothing," Hanneke said, in a voice thin with strain; and suddenly she burst out, "You've done enough, haven't you? You and all your kind. If not for you he'd still be alive—all this would not have happened—" Her hands balled into fists before her, shaking in the air. "Leave me alone. Please leave me alone." She lunged forward, pushing between Clement and Michael, not running, but walking very fast toward the Kelmans' house.

Clement was left facing Michael in the soft whispering snowfall. He said, "I beg your pardon, sir."

"Thank you," Michael said. "For her sake."

"I pray God she is right, and needs no help," Clement said. "These are wicked times, when women are thrust alone into the world." He took hold of the little boy's hand and led him away through the dark street.

Michael looked after him a moment. He was a good Catholic; he had been to Mass only that morning, and prayed for the King and the purification of the Faith. His mother said he was mad to have to do with Calvinists. Yet they seemed no threat to him, only to themselves. Hanneke was right: but for their own follies, none of the horrors would have befallen them. Perhaps someday she would return to the Faith. He thought not; there was that in her mettle which would not bend. He loved that in her. He loved her. Smiling over that, he made his way homeward through the snow.

SHE DID not go skating with Michael. On the Sabbath she prayed all the morning, and went out in the afternoon to walk and pray. The snow had fallen all the week long but had now stopped, and Antwerp was half-buried in it, drifts against the walls and fences, conical heaps on top of the chimneys that came crashing down as the sun warmed them. From the bridge over the canal she looked down and saw the children sweeping the ice clear; where they had made a clean surface, the ice was already traced with curves and circles from their skates. On the slopes, they ran with their sleds and jumped down on them and flew bumping and screaming over the packed snow.

On the Sabbath they ought not to do so much. She turned away, wishing she could go skating with Michael.

Nonsense even to consider it. She walked home, enjoying the sunlight. That too was probably a sin: enjoyment on the Sabbath. Along the eaves of the houses she passed, the snow was melting into long icicles that dripped and splashed in a kind of music. Someone was playing the virginals in the house next to Kelman's, and not sacred songs either.

The Spanish soldier Carlos was walking in the garden. Hanneke tensed, her mouth dry. Every day, this happened—every day. Grimly she went forward through the gate, and he swung and attacked her with his stare. She stared back. Every step an effort, she walked by him to the door.

He said something, low, in his own tongue. She slammed the door on him.

In the kitchen, the oven was cold; Kelman at least kept the Sabbath that well, forbidding his cook to work. A pot of cold meat stood on the table.

The housemaid sat at the head of it, mending her hose with a needle. When Hanneke came in, on her way to the back door, she said, "That friend of yours was here, Mistress van Cleef."

Hanneke was on the verge of saying, "I have no friend." Instead she said, "Thank you," and went out to the back stairs.

Something hung on the latch of the door to the attic room. She went up swiftly to see it, her heart galloping, and took it from the door: a wreath. In the dead of winter when no flowers grew he had clipped sprigs of holly and wound them together, the berries bright in the glossy green foliage. A thorn pricked her thumb when she lifted it from the latch. She sat down on the top step and sighed.

No one had ever left a courting wreath on her door before. It broke her heart that it had to be now, when she could not take it. What did he think, that she could invite him into the tiny room, the same room where she and her mother slept? In a rage she flung the wreath down into the yard.

It lay there on the snow, bright as a banner, the red berries like blood drops. She sucked the drop of blood from her pricked finger. Leave it there. When he came back to see the fate of his token, he would see that she rejected him. She beat her fist on the stair rail. No one had ever left a wreath on her door before. No one ever would again. It was terrible, terrible: everything evil happened to her, even the good things made evil by circumstance.

She ran down the steps into the yard and picked the wreath out of the snow. It was hers; let people think what they would, it was hers. Someone loved her. She took it back up the steps and inside the room and put it away in the bottom of her dowry chest.

Thereafter Michael met her every night when she left the factory and walked her home, except when his mother found work enough to keep him at the bakery, and Hanneke did not discourage him. She would not let him hold her hand, and they spoke of other things than love.

WHITE THE marble altar, white the linen altar cloths, white the candles that burned above. Carlos prayed to this whiteness as if to God Himself, whose purity and intensity sustained the world, even this imperfect world of the Low Countries. With the others of his column he knelt at the tinkling of the bells and bowed his head and offered prayers for the King, for the Duke of Alva, for the redemption of this foul and evil country from the heretics, and the power of prayer, the memory of other prayer, filled his throat with an uncomfortable lump and brought him near to tender tears.

He crossed himself, standing, and with his fellow soldiers lifted his voice in response to the priests. This was their Mass, the earliest, the first Mass of the day; none of the Dutch were allowed to attend. Probably none of them would have: the Dutch Catholics seemed as alien to him as the

Calvinists he longed to destroy. They cared too much for profit, they were always cheating the Spanish soldiers, or arguing that they took too much of the country's worth, when they were here to protect the country's true worth if the fools would only see.

Here, shoulder to shoulder with his brothers of the sword, Carlos found himself home again, and safe.

He went with the others in a long slow file to receive the Body of Christ, and after prayer and thanksgiving he marched out with the rest to the square before the cathedral to hear the day's orders. There was nothing new; they were all to report to the field by the river for drill, and then to take the rest of the day at liberty. He liked the drill; the liberty he dreaded. Most of the men went to taverns and got drunk but Carlos had promised his mother not to fall into sin. So he spent the day in the garden of the house where he lived, listening to the incomprehensible chatter of the housewife and daydreaming, occupations relieved only by the occasional appearance of his dear one, his heart's desire, his beloved, his Hanneke.

Now, on his way to drill, he walked off from the rest of his column through the side streets to the long low brick building by the canal where she worked. It had appalled him to discover that this was where she came every day, and for some time he had struggled to reconcile this new information with his image of her as pure and delicate and deserving of his love, but slowly he had fit her into a story in which wicked parents denied her, deprived her of her fortune, and cast her out, so that like the princesses in old stories she had to toil with her pretty fingers until the prince should come.

This morning, as usual, she was out in front of the long low building, sweeping the walk. Her back bent, her head wrapped in a white cloth. She would work hard, his Hanneke, without complaint, because she was truly noble, and in the end he would rescue her and she would love him for it. The sound of her withy broom reached him across the empty street, whist-whist-whist, as she stirred the snow along the front of the brickwork.

The sun was climbing above the gabled roof of the building, a pale disk in the cold gray sky. He would be late for drill; the sergeant would call him out in front of the others and berate him, even give him extra marching for punishment. Carlos smiled, thinking of it. He would bear it well, because for Hanneke's sake he would bear anything, any torment, any burden. He lifted his hand to his lips and kissed his fingertips and threw the kiss across the street to the figure bent over its busy broom, and turning he went away through the hostile streets of Antwerp to join his column.

WHEN HANNEKE came home in the evening her mother was gone. The door at the top of the wooden staircase stood open and a line of snowdrift lay deep into the room. She went around the room, as if something there would tell her where her mother was, and shutting the door firmly behind her she started out into the dark city to look for her. She was so upset about her mother that she paid no heed to Carlos, in the front doorway of the house.

The sky was clear and the night was bitter cold. There was no wind. She walked quickly to keep warm, hurrying down one street, then the next, walking every street in turn on the way to her old house, but on the way she saw nothing, and at the house in Canal Street, where now some officers of the Duke of Alva's army lived, there was no sign of her mother.

She called; she went down to the bridge to look along the canal. The cold made her teeth chatter. She was hungry, too, and tired, and longed for her bed. Up and down the streets she went, calling, looking into corners and alleyways. Gradually beneath her anger and resentment and hunger and weariness she began to be afraid.

The watch came by, and she asked them had they seen her mother; they had not. They told her to get home, that they would look—four old men in threadbare doublets, a lantern on a pole above their heads. To placate them she pretended to go back to Kelman's house, but when they had gone she circled around behind them and went on searching for her mother.

In the deep night the city was much different than during the day. Dogs prowled through the lanes and fought over bits of garbage behind the houses; on the rooftops sometimes she saw the low sinuous shape of a cat running by. She saw no people. The houses were closely barred. When she called out her voice sounded off into the darkness with the peculiar hollow resonance that meant there would be no answer. Sometimes she was too afraid to call—afraid to bring attention to herself.

In the dawn light finally she gave up looking and sat down beside a wall to rest, and overwhelmed by the sleepless night she dozed.

A hand shook her awake. "Girl? Oh, girl, are you all right?"

She startled awake, every hair turning, and looked into the face of a little boy, solemn as an alderman. She had seen him before; where, she could not remember.

"I'm all right," she said, and started to get up.

"Come with me," he said. "You can come to my father's shop and lie down."

"I'm all right." For a moment, her mind clogged with fatigue, she had difficulty remembering what she was supposed to be doing. "I'm looking for my mother."

"Your mother."

"She wandered off—she's not—not well. She goes off, sometimes, wandering."

"Do you remember me?" The boy walked along beside her, down the street; they were near the center of the city, and the people going up to their jobs and down to the wharves crowded around them. "My father is Clement de Vere, the printer. My name is Philip."

"Philip," she said, mechanically. The crowd was so thick here she could see only a few feet away.

"My father's shop is just around the corner here. Come and rest a little."

Too tired now to resist, she let him lead her that way. The printer's shop was down the street from the Bourse, where men traded in money. Over the door of the shop hung a sign in the shape of a wooden ruler and a curling sheet of paper. The air inside stank of lead and ink. Clement's boy sat her down on a chair just inside the door and went off into the back of the shop, where the presses stood like trees.

The smell bothered her nose. The shop was dirty, the counters gray with dust, the boxes of type that lined the walls dripping cobwebs. A gray cat slept in a ball on the stool by the fire. The warmth reached her and she started toward it, reaching out her hands to it, sighing. Clement's boy came back with a cup of steaming soup.

Hanneke exhaled an exclamation. Her stomach ached at the smell, and the warmth made her head stuffy. She wrapped both hands around the cup to warm them and Clement's boy dispossessed the cat of the stool so that she could sit down. While she sipped the hot pea soup he sat on the floor and turned the pages of a book.

"What's that you're reading?" she said, when the soup was gone.

He held up the book for her. On the spine was printed DE REVOLU-TIONIBUS ORBIUM COELESTIUM.

"On the turning of the heavenly spheres," she said.

"Do you know Latin?"

"A little. My father let me learn—he had a great respect for learning."

"My father said Mies van Cleef was as brave a man and wise as there was in Antwerp."

"Yes," she said. "Yes, he was."

Now somehow she had let him down, had lost his wife and son, and herself become a drudge in his factory. She stared into the fire, too worn even to care.

"I have to go work on the presses soon," Clement's boy said. "Is there anything else I can get you?"

"No—thank you. I must go home now myself."

"We can go part of the way together."

They went out to the street again and started across the city. The boy still had the book under his arm. Hanneke said, "How old are you?"

"I'm nine."

"And you are reading a book about the heavenly spheres? What does it say?"

"It's a wonderful book. It offers a new system of the world, and many proofs and arguments in its favor—" The boy held out the volume to her, his face eager. "That the sun and not the earth is the center of things, and the earth and all the planets and stars turn in circles around the sun."

Hanneke laughed, taking the book and turning it in her hands; it fell open to a page of neat printed letters. "That's mad. The earth doesn't move."

"His arguments are very mighty," said Philip. "Perhaps it does, and we are so used to it we don't notice it."

Again she laughed; in her fatigue her mind slipped away easily from the powerful architecture of the ideas she had grown up with, and she lifted her eyes toward the sun, blazing in the ice blue sky above Antwerp. It moved; she saw it move, day after day, rolling across Heaven to its rest.

"It only seems to move," the boy said, "because we are moving past it."

Her gaze still lifted to the sky, she let herself imagine that, and the planets wheeling all in concert; if that were so, then now in the sky above her were little worlds, invisible in the sun's veil of light. Under her feet, suddenly, the earth seemed to grind slowly forth into motion.

"It's mad," she said. "It's so mad that if he has proof, then it must be true."

That sounded like madness itself in her ears. She lowered her eyes to Clement's boy.

"Thank you very much," she said. "You found me in extremis and gave me charity, and I am most grateful to you." She put out her hand.

The boy took it, beaming. "I am glad I could help you."

"Goodbye."

"Goodbye, Hanneke."

He went off, turning once to wave, and she watched him go away into the crowded street. A church bell began to ring somewhere. Only nine, she thought, and already reading such grave books. The moment's talk of ideas, of books, took her back to the days before her father's arrest; she felt suddenly much stronger. She remembered talking to him about the things she read. He had never cared much for stars and the motions of the planets, but he had loved to talk of ideas. Still thinking about the stars and her father, she turned into the Swan Street, toward her home.

H E WAS late for Mass, Carlos Demedos knew, and also knew he would not go to Mass at all this day; the sun was fully risen and still the Dutch girl Hanneke had not come home. He had been waiting for her all night, in the Kelmans' garden, and now, gnawed with fear and rage, he left the yard and walked up the street toward the center of the city, watching for her.

Gone all night. He knew what that meant—he guessed even whom she had been with, the broad-faced, blue-eyed baker's boy Michael she had been seeing so much of lately. He clenched his teeth. For Carlos she could not spare a gentle word. To the baker's boy she gave—

She was coming. He saw her at the end of the street, walking swiftly, her basket over her arm. Quickly, without forethought, he moved back into the shelter of the sprawling linden tree beside the wall.

She came toward him, tall and slender as a young tree, her cheeks flushed with the chilly sunlight, her pale hair encased in a tight cap, and his heart contracted. She was so beautiful, to have betrayed him, so young, to be corrupt. When she passed him he leapt out and caught her arm.

"Where have you been? Slut!"

She recoiled from him, her entire body flexing in surprise, and he gripped her skirt in his other hand. A swift glance showed him the street was empty, but in full daylight anyone might come along, at any time, and he pulled her over toward the tree's covering protection. She struggled. Her breath whistling between her teeth, she pulled at her skirt and wrenched her arm in his grasp, and suddenly broke into a babble of her hard-edged throaty talk, pleading with him.

"Slut," he said. "You slut." He understood nothing of what she said. She understood nothing of him; as he snarled at her the helplessness of it all brought tears to his eyes. He loved her, and she had betrayed his love, and he could not tell her so. He flung his arms around her and kissed her.

Her struggling doubled. She flung herself from side to side in his grasp, whining, twisting her face away. The broad touch of her body against his, even through the thick layers of their clothing, brought all his nerve ends tingling alive. He wanted her so much, to hold her, to love her, to have her love him. He crooned endearments to her, and she struck at him with her hands; he tried to kiss her again and she bit at him.

"Whore," he cried, despairing. "Slut."

He bore her down to the ground under the linden tree. She cried out, her arms thrashing, and he pinned her down with his weight. With one hand he yanked at her skirts. She had no right to deny him what she gave to someone else—to the baker's boy. When his hand touched her bare leg she gave out a low wail. A wild rush of exhilaration flooded him. She was in his power now.

Her fist thudded off his forehead. He grappled her arms down again, his breath hot in his lungs. Pressing her down under him, he wrenched at his points and codpiece.

"My girl," he said, his voice harsh with exertion. "My girl. You're mine." His hard manhood freed at last, he aimed it up between her thighs and shoved.

She screamed. The sound spurred him. He rode over her like a god, enormous, full of power, the power welling in him, overwhelming. He poured out his power into her, a gift of love, himself overflowing into her body, bursting beyond himself into the world.

When he drew out, there was blood on his organ. So he had been first, not the baker's boy.

"My dear one." He put out his hand to her face.

She spat at him. Tears slicked her cheeks. Released of his weight, her body rolled limply to one side, and she buried her head in her arms. Carlos got to his feet, looking around them. The street was empty still. No one seemed to have witnessed it, but she had made a lot of noise, and probably behind the walls around them people listened and knew. Pulling up his hose, he fastened the points and hooked his codpiece into place and yanked down his doublet.

The girl was sitting up. Bits of dead leaf clung to her fine wheaten hair. He bent to help her up and she shrank from his touch. Firmly he possessed himself of her hand and pulled her onto her feet. They faced each other, her arm flexed in his grip, and looking deep into her eyes, he thought of taking her and smiled at her.

She swung her free hand at him. He thrust her away, propelling her down the street toward Kelman's house. "Hurry." Her dress was filthy and stained with blood. If anyone saw them, there would be trouble, perhaps for Carlos and certainly for Hanneke. She ran off down the street, and he followed her, one step behind her, to protect her; he had that right now, a matter of pride.

They reached the wall in front of the house, and she dashed in the gate and slammed it shut in his face. When he got into the garden she was gone.

He shrugged. His body was still warm from the fulfillment of his lust. She was here, somewhere; he would see her tomorrow, the next day, the day after, and when he could, he would take her again. In the end, full of him, she would have to love him. He went in through the front door.

WHEN she reached the little attic room her mother was there, asleep in the bed, snoring. Hanneke sobbed. She had forgotten why she had been out all night searching. She looked down at her ruined clothes. It hurt still; when would it stop hurting? She bunched her skirt up in her fist and pushed the wad of cloth up against her groin, to staunch the blood.

She had only four dresses. This one was ruined now, so she had only three left. Going into the corner, where the washbasin and the pitcher stood in a cabinet, she stripped herself to the skin. She was sore all over, her back from the rough contact with the ground, her thighs from trying to hold him out, her breasts from his weight on her. There was blood all over her thighs. She clenched her teeth against the sobs in her throat.

"Hanneke?"

Her mother. Whatever it required of her, she must never let her mother know what had happened. Stooping, her back to the old woman, she gathered up her filthy clothes into a knot.

"Hanneke! Where have you been? Why are you naked?"

"I'm bathing, Mother."

"Where were you all night?"

"I could ask *you* that, Mother. Where were you?"

That silenced the old woman. Hanneke stood still a moment, waiting to hear some answer, but the bed creaked, and the sheets rustled, and when she glanced over her shoulder she saw that her mother had rolled over to put her face to the wall.

Hanneke was supposed to be at the factory, sweeping and scrubbing. She was too tired for that now, too tired and too unhappy. She bundled the bloody cloth away into a back corner of the cupboard and got into the bed with her mother to sleep.

A T THE Kelmans' front gate, Michael found the foundryman from the shop at the corner of the street, collecting all Vrouw Kelman's old pots, and the housewife herself leaning over the wall sharing a morning's gossip with him.

"Well," said the foundryman, "the word is that the Prince is bringing a great army of Germans, and Lord Alva is removing every soldier he can find to go fight them."

The housewife folded her arms on the top of the wall. "That explains why my Spanish boy went off so quickly last night. God keep them."

"Orange is coming," Michael said, surprised into forwardness.

"So they say," said the foundryman. He dumped a broken pot lid on top of the rest of the things in his sack, which clanked. "Lord Alva will master him."

He hoisted the jangling sack up onto his shoulder. Suddenly Vrouw Kelman flung out her arm.

"Wait—wait—I remember one more thing." She ran away into the house, spry as a girl, for all her bulk.

The foundryman turned to Michael; his grin showed the gaps in his big yellow teeth. "So life goes on, eh, young fellow? I'll wager you're glad not to have to go to fight the King of Spain's wars."

"I would he did not fight them here," said Michael.

"Oh, now, better he fight Orange and a pack of paid Germans than send his men around to yank honest folk out of their beds in the night."

"I suppose," Michael said.

He straightened. Hanneke was coming out the front door of the house. His throat was full of words he would hail her with, yet he kept silent, surprised at her manner. She came out so quietly, like a little mouse; she peeped out the door and looked all around the garden, her face pale. Michael put up his hand to her.

"Hanneke!"

She startled. The foundryman said, "Well, well, life goes on." Vrouw Kelman was hurrying up the path from the kitchen door, a clutch of pewter ladles in her apron.

"Hanneke." Michael leaned across the gate toward her. "Why were you not at your work? I saw the leadman—he said you had not come all day."

She crossed the garden to him, still peering fearfully all around her, her face very pale. She said, "I was out the night long looking for my mother —she disappeared again; I thought she was lost forever." Her voice croaked. With the cuff of her sleeve she scrubbed at her eyes. "Where is Carlos?" she asked Vrouw Kelman.

"Did you find her?" Michael asked.

"He's gone," said the housewife. "Poor boy. Marched off to fight, the poor thing. If his mother knew, she'd fear for him terribly."

Hanneke's face slipped from its taut mask of fear into a smile; the change was so marked that the foundryman let out an exclamation, and Michael reached for her hand. "What's wrong?"

"Nothing." She drew her hand out of his reach. "Yes, she came back. I don't know where she was." She pushed the gate open and went to stand beside Michael, looking up at him. "Was he angry—the leadman? Did he say I could go tomorrow to work?"

"He was worried more than angry."

"I had to find my mother, and then I was so tired—" He was reaching for her hand again, and she jerked her arm angrily out of his grasp. "Please, Michael!"

He bit his lips, embarrassed; the foundryman and Vrouw Kelman laughed at him. Hanneke was going off down the street. Michael chased her a few steps, caught up with her, and said, "Now where are you going? Why are you so cruel to me?"

"Please don't touch me."

"Where are you going?"

"To the factory—to tell them I am sorry and will work the rest of the day."

"Don't do that. Aren't you hungry? Come to the bakery—we've made some biscuits. At least come there first, so you won't be hungry."

He knew how she longed for sweets, and now her face was nervous with indecision and she wavered in her step. Without touching her, he herded her toward a side street that arched over the canal on the way to the bakery, and she went along with him.

"I SAW THAT girl Hanneke this morning," said Clement's boy, standing on the far side of the press; he reached across the press to take the top of the fresh sheet of paper that his father held out to him, and between the two of them they fastened it to the tympan, which would hold it while the print was being impressed upon it. "She was looking for her mother, all night long."

"Her mother. Did she find her?"

The boy shook his head. He was small for his age, and grave from so much reading; his face had an old man's solemnity. "I helped her awhile."

"Good for you," Clement said.

"I brought her here and gave her some soup."

"Good." Clement smoothed the paper on the tympan and reaching to the side lifted the heavy iron frame hinged to the long edge of it and folded it over the fresh paper; this was the frisket, which covered all parts of the paper save that to be printed on. He thought of Mies van Cleef's daughter with a heart that leapt. Of all those men who had helped the Prince of Orange during the troubles, Clement alone remained alive and free. He wondered why the Duke of Alva had not taken him and knew it would not last long. Carefully he folded the tympan and frisket together down over the typeform.

"Why was her mother missing, do you know?"

The boy shook his head. "She did not say. We talked about Copernicus. I like her—she is very clever."

"Her father was a clever man."

He ran the inked form under the platen of the press and reached for the long lever that worked it. His son stepped back out of the way.

This letter they were printing came from Orange; Clement meant to have copies of it all around Antwerp by nightfall. The Prince of Orange was marching to the Low Countries with an army. He needed help—the rising of the cities in his favor, the general outburst of the people against the tyrant Alva—and he would not get it. Clement had never known Antwerp so quiet. People stayed indoors now and peeped through their shutters, and at the sound of trouble hid away under the dining room table. Clement raised the press and pulled the typeform out from under it, and unfolded the frisket and the tympan and lifted the printed page up off the pins that held it fast through the whole process. Black and bold, the letters marched like soldiers across the white paper.

This would bring Alva on him, eventually. He shook to think of that —of what would happen to his little boy, alone and cast out, as Hanneke van Cleef was cast out. Yet he could not forgo it; he owed this to the people who had died already, Mies and the others, the hundreds of others. Even if no one read, if no one heeded, yet he had to go on shouting at them: Fight!

He gave the sheet to his son, to hang up to dry, and picked up a clean piece of paper. The smell of the fresh ink as always gave him courage. At least he was doing something. He laid the field of white across the tympan and pushed it down firmly onto the pins.

6

"**H**AW! HAW!"

The oxen lowed, under the whip; with a squeal of bare axles, the wagon lurched up over the rutted road and jounced down again. The carter stood up on his seat and plied his whip furiously. The oxen were tired, and the road ruined by the unseasonable rains, and the oxen lowed again, protesting.

The Prince of Orange swore under his breath. He looked up into the sky; there was perhaps an hour of sunlight left, and his army still was strung out along the approaches to the ford in spite of his orders. The columns would not march in tight rows. Their disarray had them dangerously spread out over the rough hillside on the German bank of the river. He spurred his horse into a gallop across the road ahead of the oxen and up the hillock beyond, to get a broad overlook of the whole business.

What he saw made him swear again. He had hired mercenaries by the lot, veterans of the French civil wars, and probably he had been too eager for numbers and not keen enough for quality. Half of these men sauntered along in no order at all, swinging their pikes, stopping where they would to talk or rest or drink from their belt flasks. The supply train clogged the main road. The soldiers milled around behind it, and at one wagon they had even gotten into the supplies of food and were sitting up there eating the bread intended for their dinners once they reached the Low Countries.

"William!"

Straight and handsome on his dapple gray horse, Orange's brother Louis cantered up and saluted him. "What do you think? Over there's the best campground." He pointed across the river, at the smooth green hollow of the meadow beyond the ford.

"If we can get to it," said the Prince. "Here. You go down there and get those men off the wagon. Lead them up to the river's edge and wait. I'm going down to see the ford. We have to cross the wagons first and we may need to use the men to do it."

Louis wheeled his horse and galloped down across the slope; he rode boldly, if not elegantly, and all the men loved him; as he passed, they cheered him. He raised one arm in answer. William smiled, pleased with his brother, and trotted away down to the river.

Swollen by the recent rains, it ran full to the high bank, the water muddy and swift, and on the far side it overflowed the bank and stood among the reeds and grass of the low ground. The Prince sharpened his eyes for a long look across at the campground. Its green allure might be deceptive. Perhaps it was marshy too. He pressed his horse around toward the wagon train.

Now the vanguard of his disorganized army was meeting the river's edge. For nearly a quarter of a mile on either side, the few horsemen let their mounts drink, and the soldiers were sitting down on the bank and dipping their hands and faces into the rushing water. The heavy ox-drawn wagons were still lumbering along the road, and would be over half an hour getting here. The Prince looked fretfully at the sky again, where the sunlight was already waning, and returned his glance to the river. He did not want to cross that rushing water in the dark.

With a wave to the wagons to stay where they were, he turned his horse and rode into the river. The water was deeper than he expected. His horse stiffened and tried to back off but he spurred it forward and after a few steps the horse put its head down and splashed across.

The water surged up to its belly. The Prince lifted his feet, mindful of his freshly polished boots, and the horse snorted and plunged through the deep. The current struck it. Its hoofs slipped, and it spun around to keep from falling. The Prince caught his saddle with his free hand. If he fell off his horse in front of his whole army he would hear about it all his life. The horse recovered, its ears pinned back, and bolted for the far shore.

Shaking and snorting, it trotted up through the marshy flooded bank. The Prince tapped it with his spurs, and it set off at a rocking canter across the green meadowland. The edge of the meadow was damp, but as the ground climbed away from the river, it dried out: a good place to camp. Near the center of the meadow, he turned to go back.

"No! Damn it!"

All along the river, without orders, without discipline, his army was crossing after him. The first of the wagons was plunging into the swollen current where he had just nearly lost his seat. He galloped back toward them, shouting to them to stop.

They ignored him. The foot soldiers were wading out into the brown water, using their pikes for props. One or two of the horsemen had reached the center of the stream, and even as he watched one rider lost control of his horse and fell with a splash into the river.

"Go back—" On the far bank, Louis was galloping up, to stop the wagons, but two of them had already rolled out into the ford. The oxen bellowed. Perched on the high seat of the first wagon, the driver rolled his whip out across the sky and shouted curses. The wagon lurched. The lead ox went down to its knees, dragging the other with it, and the wagon floated up off its wheels and swung around downstream on the surging river.

A wail went up from the army. Louis was charging to and fro, through the low brush and trees along the bank, turning back the men at the edge of the river, but too many had already gone into the water. The wagon was floating off downstream, dragging the panicked oxen after it. The driver looked around once, threw his whip to the left, and dove off to the right. The submerged wheels of the wagon hit the bottom, the current pushed the upstream side high into the air, and the whole wagon tipped over, spilling barrels and bundles of camp supplies into the water.

The Prince rushed his horse into the river, headed downstream of the wreck, where half a hundred men were struggling in the stream. "Seize hands," he shouted. "Make a line across the current—we can save some of it—"

Some of the men heard him; in the center of the stream a barrier of linked arms and bodies formed, chest-deep in the forceful rushing current. Others ignored him. They scrambled for the shore, wailing and cursing as they went. He forced his mount over the slippery river bottom toward the line of men who were obeying him. His horse lost its footing and fell, and he clung to the saddle with hands and legs, his breeches soaked, the river banging his back. The sky wheeled madly over him. Abruptly the horse lurched back onto its feet again. He swung it around, forcing it back toward the men in the center of the river.

The goods spilled from the tipped wagon were floating downriver, kegs and folded tents, and even a cooking pot bobbing on the current. He reached the line of men just as the first of the goods reached them. Leaning out from his saddle, he caught an outstretched hand, and a barrel struck the man he was holding and tore him out of the grip of the Prince and drove him under the water.

The others screamed. Breaking their cordon, they fought and struggled with the river, trying to reach the safety of the land. The Prince shouted at them but they heard nothing. Another barrel smashed into a man wading waist-deep in the water and carried him off into the center of the river.

The Prince's horse neighed. Thrashing the water, it bolted for the bank, and the Prince made no effort to stop it; there was nothing more to be done anyhow. Ahead of him the last of the soldiers were dragging themselves up the bank, and the goods lost from the wagon were floating swiftly away out of sight down the river. He rode up after his men to the dry land.

Louis came up to him. "Are you all right?"

The Prince took the napkin he held out and wiped his face. "God's bones. What a disaster." He looked upstream, at the disorder of his army, scattered all over the low brushy hillsides; some had already begun to make their own camps here. On this bank near him two or three men lay exhausted and soaked on the ground, gasping for breath. The second wagon to enter the river was stuck halfway into the ford. The Prince shook his head, low spirited. If this was a harbinger of the whole campaign, God was about to try them all very sorely. He gave the dirty linen back to his brother and rode up to help haul the stranded wagon back to land.

NEAT AS a housewife's sewing box, the Spanish camp covered the lower slope of the hill, its fires in rows, its tents in circles around the fires, its men fed and at their work, some standing sentry duty, some cleaning their weapons, some already asleep. The Duke of Alva rode down between two rows of the fires, looking over the camp. Beside him his son, Don Federico, waited for his father's comments. The night had not quite fallen, and he had not eaten; he was hungry. He knew he would get nothing until his father had assured himself of the camp's perfect security.

"Where is Orange?" Alva asked.

"Across the river, two leagues away," said Don Federico.

His gaze fell on his father's hand on the reins. Alva's hands were bony and the veins stood up like ropes, an old man's hands. He was an old man. Why then would he not stay in an old man's palace and let his son do his work? Don Federico looked in the other direction, across the slope, where in the deepening twilight the fires gleamed in rows like golden stitches in a velvet cloth.

"He hasn't tried to cross the river yet?" asked his father.

"He tried," Don Federico said. "The river is still high from the storm and he lost a wagon and some men. It was very disorderly."

He sniffed, disapproving of such incompetence even in his enemies. All soldiers had to know how to do certain basic things, or they were not soldiers.

"Well, you've done a good job," Alva said. "As usual. Thank you very much."

"I don't understand why you had to come out here at all," Don Federico said. "I am thoroughly capable of handling the entire campaign. You could have stayed in Brussels and done the larger business of governance."

Side by side on their fine-bred Spanish Barbs they rode down the lines of fires toward the center of the camp, where the commander's tent was set. Behind them came their aides. Don Federico beckoned, and one of his young men dashed up and saluted.

"Go see that the table is set and the dinner ready when his Grace my father dismounts from his horse."

"Yes, Excellency."

"No need for anything special for me," said Alva. "I'll just have some plain soldier's fare. A hard biscuit and a cup of soup."

Don Federico would have a roast hen, fresh bread, butter, wine, and pears with cheese. He slapped his thigh.

"Why are you here? What if there's a rising in one of the cities, in support of Orange—what will you do then?"

"There will be no rising," Alva said comfortably. "They are too afraid. What do you intend to do about Orange?"

"I'm going to wait until he crosses the river, back him up against it, and hack him into little pieces," said Don Federico curtly. "In the meantime, however, my men have not been paid. Something I hope you mean to rectify."

"I think," Alva said, "you would be shrewd not to allow him to cross the river."

"I can't fight him with a river between us."

"He outnumbers you by almost two to one."

"His men are rabble. Mine are Spanish troops. But if they are not paid, they will not fight. When will you have the money here?"

Alva was looking around the camp again. The age betrayed by his hands showed little in his face. His beard was gray and his hair gray, but the hard ledges of his cheekbones and chin and the intensity of his eyes belonged to a man younger than his sixty years. Don Federico tore his envious gaze away and fastened it on the fine order of his campfires. He would be old himself before his father died and left the world to him—old, and out of time.

"Keep him from crossing the river," Alva said, "and his rabble will become more rabble every day. In the end they will dissolve, like sugar in the rain, without a drop of Spanish blood shed."

They had come to the central campfire. There a table had been put up, and the cook was standing ready beside it, with a page at his heels carrying a large covered dish. Alva made no effort to dismount. He brushed his mustache back, his attention on the tent, the neat stack of firewood, the careful laying out of camp chairs and tools.

"I've never known you to shrink from the shedding of blood," said Don Federico, suspicious now. "When will I have the money to pay my troops? Then each one will fight like six of Orange's fools."

Alva twisted his gray mustache. "I have no money."

His son hissed between his teeth. That was the meat of the problem.

"When Orange is turned back, and these people in Brussels see there is no hope at all, they will vote me my taxes. In the meantime, the King will send a shipment of silver by sea."

"Which you expect when?"

Alva's shoulders moved. He let his reins slide; a groom ran up to hold his horse. "When it comes. There is some difficulty with the plate fleet from the Indies." He dismounted, stepping down away from his son into the darkness, and turned to the table.

Don Federico sat still a moment, staring at the back of his father's head. Things were so simple in battle; one struck and won, or struck and died. The complications that grew up around this simple process infuriated him. Money, and the lack of it; orders, and the reasons for them; policy, and the playing off of cause against cause—none of it meant anything on the battlefield. But now he was to have no battlefield.

"Come and eat," his father said.

With a growl he dismounted and went to sit at the right hand of the Duke of Alva.

IN THE drizzle of the next dawn, the Prince of Orange's brother Louis of Nassau led a charge of cavalry across the ford, and before the Spanish army could respond, seized the wood and the little hill to the north of the Spanish camp. The Spanish feinted, as if to attack, but then withdrew, and the Prince could take the rest of his unwieldy army across into the Low Countries.

They marched up the road that led into the heart of the Provinces. The Spanish army moved with them, but ever out of sight, and Orange knew that at the first sign of disorganization in his army the Duke of Alva would attack him. Therefore he sent on his brother and a troop of cavalry to the nearest town of size, to ask for shelter there.

His brother galloped away in the midafternoon; in the evening, as the army was marching down into a narrow valley quilted with fields and vine-yards, Louis came back, very red in the face.

"They will not let us in," he said.

Orange stiffened in his saddle. He was tired and the rapid coming of the night alarmed him, with his men so far from a defensible camp. "What do you mean?"

"They have shut the gates—they say they will not let you in, as you would not let in the Beggars before Antwerp, and anyway most of them are Catholic."

The soldiers nearest them overheard this exchange, and the word ran off through the army. Orange's fingers tightened around his saddlebow; grimly he felt the lash of retribution in this event.

He faced his brother. "They have the right, I suppose. We must find a campground."

"Up ahead, near the middle of the valley, there is a village."

"Will they let us in?" Orange said, with a fine edge of sarcasm in his voice. He gathered his reins and signaled the advance.

His brother fell in beside him. "I say seize the town. We could do it, especially under cover of night."

"No," Orange said briefly.

"We need the protection of a wall! You know this rabble will not be able to defend an open camp."

"No."

"William, what a scrupulous man you are at the wrong times!"

Orange gave his brother a quick sideways look and kept silent. The darkness was deepening around them; on either side, he knew, the Spanish army lurked.

"Are you going to let a pack of magistrates decide the fate of the Low Countries?" Louis asked, in a hot voice.

"I don't think there's much—"

A yell from the front of the line interrupted him; another yell came, and a horn blasted. Suddenly the troops marching around Orange began to run forward down the road. Up ahead the shouting spread, and there was a scattering of gunfire.

"We're attacked," Louis cried, and wheeled his horse around to bring up the columns marching behind them. Orange swung his horse out of the line and galloped up toward the front of the army.

There was no sign of the Spaniards. In the dark the road seemed clogged with soldiers and wagons; ahead the army had lost all its order and was streaming forward, every man at his own pace, toward the little village in the middle of the valley. There was another barrage of small arms fire. Someone screamed.

Orange let out a yell; now he realized what was going on, and he spurred his horse recklessly along the side of the road, careless of the people in his way. His men were looting the village.

Some few of the officers in charge of the vanguard had brought their troops to a halt outside the village; it was they who fired off their pistols into the air to keep their men under control. The hot blasts of their guns flashed in the darkness, feeble against the mounting oceanic turbulence of the army that pressed around them, surging forward, all eyes on the helpless village. Orange galloped through their midst. Most of them leapt out of his path; one man reeled off to one side, knocked away by a glancing blow of the charging horse's forehoof, and one went down under Orange's mount and was trampled. As he rode he drew his pistol from its holster on his saddle.

He galloped into the village, a loose straggle of huts laid out along a twisting little street. As he rode in at one end, a hut at the far end exploded into flame. Red gold light flooded the whole village, and he saw at once what was happening.

His men were breaking into the houses and throwing the poor peasants' belongings into the street. The peasants themselves were scattered all through the place, some crouched down beside their dwellings, trying pitifully to hide, and some engaged in trying to protect their homes; these were being struck down as soon as they took a stand in their own doorways. A soldier ran by Orange down the middle of the street, chasing a girl who ran screaming ahead of him, and little children wandered through the flickering hellish light, their howls lost in the deafening roar of the flames and the rampaging soldiers. Orange drew his other pistol.

He rode up to the nearest house, where a brawny peasant with a hoe was fighting off several German mercenaries, and lifting the heavy pistol Orange shot the frontmost of the Germans in the head.

That swung the others toward him. He held out his second pistol at arm's length and fired it into the face of another of his men, and dropping the weapon he drew out his sword. The mercenaries charged toward him.

When he lifted the sword they wheeled around and raced off down the street.

A trumpet blasted. A column of mounted men was pushing into the village. Orange wheeled his horse, ready to block the cavalry's way, and saw his brother leading them. With a broad gesture of his arm he urged the horsemen after him and galloped on through the village, attacking the looters.

The mercenaries were no more willing to fight now than they had ever been. At the first sign of Louis' cavalry they scattered and fled into the safety of the darkness outside the village. Orange rode up and down the street, grimly watching the peasants collect their families and gather together what of their belongings they could find intact. The women wept, standing together in groups to console one another; a young man walked along the center of the street, his face lifted toward Heaven, and his arms full of a trampled child. Louis and his men put out the fire, but the hut was entirely consumed, and several of the other buildings had lost their roofs. Orange stopped at the hut where he had shot the mercenaries and dismounted to retrieve his pistol.

When he straightened, the heavy gun in his hand, a tall old man with a beard rushed up to him.

"Get out!" he cried. "Get out! Go!" He waved his arms at Orange as if he were shooing off chickens. "Go away!"

Orange turned to his horse and mounted; he touched his hat to the old man. "As you wish." Swiftly he scanned the darkness outside the village, wondering where the Spanish were, and went to find his brother and his brother's trumpeter.

ALVA STOOD in his stirrups. "They are marching toward France."

Don Federico trotted his horse up beside him; they had come out ahead of their army to this tall hill to see what Orange was doing, when the scouts said he had abandoned his road along the river and was heading south. Alva settled down into his saddle again, smiling. Orange's army was veering off into the tree-masked hills, taking the road south.

"Well, very good," he said. "I think they are giving up."

His son said nothing. He knew his son had wanted a battle, but Don Federico had no understanding of the wider nature of the struggle and could be expected to do only the obvious. Alva reached out and clapped the younger man on the shoulder.

"Follow him. Make sure they don't turn back and try to sneak into my Provinces again. I'm going back to Brussels; I have work to do there."

"Why is he leaving?" Don Federico burst out. "He hasn't been beaten yet."

"Because he has a heart of feathers," said Alva. "He will give up when the way gets hard. That's the sort of man he is. I know him. Now follow him and be sure he goes on into France. I don't care what he does there: I hope he makes a lot of trouble for the Dowager, that's all."

"And you are going back to Brussels," said Don Federico. "When will you send me the money to pay my troops?"

"When it comes," Alva said. He smoothed his beard, smiling. "Be patient. The King will send it soon enough, and I will raise my taxes, and we shall have everything firmly in hand."

7

"FIRE!'' Pieter roared.

Jan said nothing; with the burning match in his hand he hovered over the waist gun, his gaze pinned to the Spanish merchantman wallowing in the sluggish surf a cable length away.

"Fire, damn you!" Pieter brought the flat of his stick down on Jan's back.

"Shut up, Uncle," Jan cried, and as he spoke the next onshore wave rolled under the *Wayward Girl* and lifted her until the dark hulk of the Spanish ship fit square in the notch of the culverin's sights. He put the match to the touchhole. With a hiss and a hellish whiff of sulfur the flame shot away into the brass backside of the cannon and an instant later the great gun bellowed its deafening smoky thunder.

The smoke swirled in around the gun. Jan and the two men working with him jumped forward to drag the monster back inboard to be loaded. From the masthead of the *Wayward Girl* came a cheer.

"Got the other mast! Round as a barrel, she is!"

All around the ship the other men roared and cursed and cheered. Pieter whacked Jan on the rump, this time congratulatory.

"Doomshot! That's my nephew."

Jan with his own hands swabbed the culverin's barrel with a sponge on a staff. He let other people fire the fore and aft guns but he had fallen in love with this waist gun and could hardly bear to let anyone else handle her. Mouse was waiting with the charge. Half-witted though he was, the puny boy was useful for some things. Jan nodded to him and watched while the boy stroked the heavy flannel packet with the gunpowder deep down the gun's long throat.

That done, Jan lifted his eyes to the target.

The *Wayward Girl* rolled and thrashed in the trough of the waves, just outside the surf. Halfway between her and the rocky English beach where the water ended, the Spanish merchantman struggled with the pounding waves.

She had lost one mast in a storm the night before, or the *Wayward Girl* would never have dared take on so huge a ship, three times her weight, carrying over a hundred men. Some of those men were creeping around on the deck, which pitched and bucked with every surging crosswave of the surf; while Jan watched, a few more of the Spanish seamen leapt overboard into the water, to try to swim to shore. Most of the crew clung to the rails and screamed with every wild corkscrew motion of their vessel. Without a mast or a shred of sail to hold her upright, the Spanish ship could roll completely over at any moment.

"She'll run aground any time now," Pieter said. He stuck his thumb into his belt and squinted toward their target. "Once she does, the sea will break her up. We have to get her out where we can loot her. Let's pound her again. Maybe the rest of the crew will jump for it."

Jan muttered, "Would you?" He jabbed his hand toward the shingle beach beyond the surf.

All along the English shore, dark figures stood on the sand, watching, and waiting, and as Jan pointed to them, more slipped over the horizon of cliff behind the beach and came down toward the sea. A few of the Spanish sailors were just wading up through the surf and the people on the beach nearest them rushed up and seized them and fell to beating them.

"There must be fifty of them!" Red Aart shouted. "Who are they?" He leaned across the railing of the *Wayward Girl* to look.

Jan bent over his gun again. If the Spanish ship went aground, those lurking beach bandits could well end up with most of the booty. Pieter tapped him on the shoulder.

"Load up the guns with man killer. Rock shot. Chains." The mean glint in old Pieter's eyes surprised his nephew, in spite of all he knew about him. "Let them say their Hail Marys."

Jan straightened. "Moek! Willy! Aart!"

The men stepped forward, eager, and he sent some to the shot locker and others around the ship, to each of the other guns. "All the guns?" he said to Pieter mildly, and drew a filthy oath from his father's brother.

Mouse tugged on his sleeve. "Me, Jan. Tell me too."

"Get out of my way," Jan said, and pushed him over to the rail. He went up to the bow, to load the old cannon there.

"Sail!" Marten shrieked, from the masthead. "Sail ho—"

Jan sprang toward the rail, every hackle standing. "Where away?" In the waist Pieter howled with rage and kicked violently at the hatchcover.

"Larboard beam," Marten was screaming. "Sail hull down to larboard—"

Jan shaded his eyes, staring across the rushing seas into the distance, but the ship hull down to the masthead was still well out of sight from the deck. It hardly mattered. Whoever she was, she would make no friend of the *Wayward Girl.*

Pieter said, "Well, well. That cuts down a little on our time."

"She's still probably a half a glass away," Jan said, hoping. He went on to the bow gun. Mouse followed him, walking with a peculiar slouching stride that was meant to imitate Jan's.

"Hands to the braces," Pieter shouted.

The men ran around the ship. There were too few seamen to work the ship and fire the guns too, and Jan swore, wondering what his uncle was doing. But when he started back toward the stern, where Pieter was climbing the steps to the poop deck to con the steering of the ship, his uncle shouted curses at him.

"Mind the guns! Just mind the guns and shoot when I tell you, you dumb suck!"

Jan turned back to the bow gun. Mouse was on his heels; Jan pushed him.

"Fetch me the match."

The slow match sulked in its iron box by the brass waist gun. Mouse ran down the ship and brought it up to the bow.

Pieter got the *Wayward Girl* under sail, slipping like a knife through the water, headed away from the Spanish hulk. Standing out to sea until he got room to maneuver, he brought the ship about. Jan leaned against the railing at the bow. His uncle handled the ship as neatly as a wooden shoe in a bathtub. Pieter had made him practice changing course and he had never managed to turn the sails, to lay the ship over and take the new heading without losing the wind and going dead in the water. The great gaff-rigged mainsail luffed a little, drawn too tight to the wind, and Pieter shouted to the man on the brace to let it out a little.

Now the *Wayward Girl* was racing down through the heavy seas toward the Spanish hulk again. On the thrashing merchantman a howl of terror went up, as the crew saw her tormentor approaching, and the men rushed back from the rail. Jan bent over the bow gun. He saw what his uncle meant to do, and that he would have very little time to fire the guns as the *Wayward Girl* passed her target; swiftly he made ready.

In the notch of the cannon's sight the Spanish ship loomed larger and darker. The waves lifted her and dropped the *Wayward Girl,* until the Spanish vessel seemed to hang above them like a great cloud. Then the wave passed on and the two ships slid together, one rising, one falling, and Jan put the match to the cannon and the gun roared.

The shot, dozens of pieces of metal and rock, whistled as it flew. It raked across the deck of the merchantman, killing in a broad swath. The Spanish sailors shrieked and darted in all directions, and more of them dove overboard into the surf.

Jan was already running down the ship to the waist gun. The *Wayward Girl* was flying through the water; Pieter shouted to the men to back the mainsail to slow her down a little, and Jan fired the next gun.

The two ships were so close now that he saw the faces of the Spanish sailors, saw them disintegrate into red mash when the shot struck. The ship rolled toward him just after the shot whipped across the deck, and on the tilted deck he saw the bodies scattered and broken and the blood running in streams. Without hesitating he raced down the *Wayward Girl* to the stern, jumped up the three steps to the stern deck, and bent over the two stern guns.

Standing at the railing of the poop, Pieter shouted, "Aart, go below and bring up two coils of the new cable. Helm, steady as she goes."

The *Wayward Girl* swept past the Spanish ship. Looking down the barrel of the first stern gun, Jan saw the length of her deck; on the boards were a tangle of corpses and screaming wounded and the wreckage of the masts. He put the match to the two bores and the guns thundered almost simultaneously. A veil of smoke hung over the stern for a moment. Coughing, he squinted with watery eyes through the clearing black fog.

The big merchantman rolled helpless. On her deck nothing stirred except a rag of sail that fluttered in the wind.

"Lower the dinghy," Pieter called. He wheeled, grabbing Jan by the sleeve. "You take the boarding party. Rig the tow cable to her bow, if you can—we can haul her off down the coast a little way. I know where there's a cove—"

"Sail," Marten was screaming, from the masthead. "The sail's coming straight down on us! She's Spanish—a Spanish greatship!"

"Oh, God," Jan said.

"Never mind her!" Pieter shook him. "There's no time to spend worrying about her. Get that hulk in tow."

Jan spared one instant's glance out to sea, where the unseen Spaniard was cleaving the water toward them, and ran down to the waist. Aart and Willy were carrying the ship's little dinghy to the rail. On the deck lay two huge rolls of three-inch cable, so new the long blond threads that escaped the twist had not been worn off. Jan helped the other men heave the dinghy overboard.

"Come with me," he said to the two men, and swung his leg over the rail.

"Me too?" Mouse danced on the deck beside him. "Can I come too, Jan?"

Jan's temper surged; he brought his arm back to swat the boy away, but Aart glared at him, and he thought better of it. Maybe if they took him, Mouse would catch a stray shot, eliminating a small but persistent annoyance from Jan's life. "Yes, come," he said, and grabbing Mouse by the arm hoisted him up over the rail and dropped him into the dinghy.

Mouse yelled, from delight or fear; an instant later the other men fell into the dinghy beside him, with the cable. They rowed off toward the Spanish hulk.

Heads and bodies dappled the white-striped surf around the Spanish ship. Most of her crew had gone overboard. Jan hoped none was waiting to meet him when he went up the side. They rowed under her lee by the stern. The ship was catching the bottom now with each push of the waves. Jan could hear her keel scraping on the hard shingle. She rolled down over his dinghy, shutting out the sky, and he gaped up a moment at the huge hulk above him, unnerved, waiting for her to crash down on him. Then she rolled back the other way, and from beneath the waves her dripping weedy bottom rose streaming into his face.

"Wait 'til she comes back over again!"

Some of the Spanish crew swam in the sea near them. Aart leaned out from the dinghy, an oar in both hands, and whacked a floating head until it went under. The others had struck out for the beach, where the English were gathering them in. A row of naked bodies already lay on the cold sand above the tide line.

Jan stood up in the dinghy, with the little boat's anchor in his hand. As the side of the Spanish ship swung down above him, he threw the anchor up over her rail. Midway up her side, a hole three feet wide showed through her timbers, where the *Wayward Girl* had hit her at close range with a heavy shot. The ship righted itself in its wild roll, and the anchor caught on the rail. Jan clung to the rope; he was lifted up, up out of the dinghy.

Like a pendulum he swung hard against the Spanish ship's side. Kicking out his feet, he got a toehold on her slick streaming timbers and walked up over the rail.

The deck was tipping and pitching like a feather in the wind. Everything on it rolled from side to side with every toss of the waves. A body was lodged against the rail where he climbed over; he had to step on its dead hand to get across. The blood gurgled in the scuppers.

"Dios," someone called, feebly, from the direction of the stern. "Dios y Madre de Dios—" Someone else screamed.

Jan leaned over the railing, to look down into the dinghy. "Row along to her bow. I'll meet you there."

Aart waved. Jan went forward; he had to plow through the wreckage of the forward mast and sails and rigging. The rolling of the ship made it hard to keep his footing. There were dead everywhere—underfoot, caught in the snarl of wood and rope, huddled against the bulkhead of the high forecastle. The smell of blood was sickening. A tangle of canvas around a broken spar lay over the steps up to the forecastle deck, and he heaved and lugged at it uselessly until he saw a coil of line hooked around the top step. With his knife he cut it free. The next heave of the ship took the spar off down the deck. He climbed up to the forecastle.

Something boomed in the distance. He wheeled. Off to sea, a little blossom of smoke was shredding away in the wind. Behind it stood a Spanish warship.

Jan caught his breath. He had never seen a greatship under full sail before and even though she was Spanish she was beautiful, her sails piled up like clouds above her, her pennants streaming in the wind. A moment later the shot she had fired struck the sea midway between him and the *Wayward Girl* with a splash that sent droplets flying into his face.

"Come on!" He dashed across the forecastle to the bow of the hulk. The dinghy was just below him, the men looking up with anxious faces. He waved to them to send the cable up, and Aart bent over the rolls and found an end and began uncoiling length on length of the heavy line.

Another rattle of thunder from the Spanish ship. All the men jerked as if struck.

"I'll take it," Mouse cried, and grasping the end of the cable he climbed up onto his brother's shoulders and reached over his head for the chains that hung from the Spanish ship's bowsprit.

"Aart," Jan roared. "Do it yourself."

Too late: Mouse was already scurrying, nimble as his name, into the chains, dragging the cable after him. Jan swore under his breath. He leaned down over the rail to haul the boy on board.

"She's going," Willy cried, dismayed. "Pieter's leaving us!"

The *Wayward Girl* was making sail again, headed for the open sea. Jan shouted, "No, no, he's just putting her on her best tack. Come on—row back—"

A flight of cannonballs stopped his words in his mouth; they hit the sea around the *Wayward Girl* and threw up a curtain of water as high as her jack yard. The ship was moving, slipping away from the Spanish hulk; Jan blinked after her, wondering what Pieter was doing. Maybe he was leaving them. Certainly he was heading dead away from them.

No. Trust the old man. Jan bawled, "He'll come about and sail in past us to pick up the cable. You go out to meet her—"

The two men in the dinghy bellowed, against that entirely. Jan gritted his teeth. Beside him Mouse stood solemnly watching them. Jan twisted to look out to sea, where the greatship was sailing toward them again.

As long as she was sailing up toward them she could not shoot. Jan struck the rail with his hand. He watched the *Wayward Girl*, now rapidly shrinking as she fled away from them.

Her mainsail shivered. Pieter was wearing ship, to bring her back to Jan.

"Go on! Row out to meet him—slip the cable as you go—"

"I'm not going out there," Willy howled.

"Ah, you hen, Willy! Then go there!" Jan pointed to the stretch of rough water in between the rolling hulk and the beach. The *Wayward Girl* drew far less than any Spanish ship; maybe she could squeeze in between this hulk, now scraping bottom, and the sloping beach where the English happily mauled the shipwrecked sailors. "Go!"

That they were willing to do. Clinging to the rail through another gut-twisting roll of the Spanish hulk, he watched them row the dinghy off to the quieter water, where, protected by the hulk from the greatship, they paid out the cable over the dinghy's stern.

The *Wayward Girl* was coming about. Her jack yard swung from one side to the other; her hull wallowed a moment, sluggish, and then lay over on the other flank. The wind caught her great mainsail and swelled it full as a matron's apron.

Mouse cheered. Jan grunted, relieved, and turned back to watch the greatship.

She did not sail fast, but she was so big, her sail so towering above her stepped decks, that she seemed to split the sea and throw the sky behind her. Jan leaned against the rail beside him through another pitch of the hulk.

This time she went hard aground. A shudder passed through her as if she were a living thing that died.

"Come on," Jan said, alarmed. If she went aground they would not easily tow her off. He ran down to the main deck again, where the broken masts and yards lay over everything, and searched for an ax to chop it all free and lighten the ship.

The Spanish greatship was coming about, to follow the *Wayward Girl.* Clearly she meant to close with the smaller ship and grapple with her. Her great bulk lay between the *Wayward Girl* and the open sea, pinning the little ship against the coast, and on her decks men crowded thick along the rails, ready to board her and overwhelm her.

Mouse yelled, "There's another ship!"

He was pointing away down the sea. Jan glanced there and saw nothing and fixed his attention on the *Wayward Girl* again.

Pieter was trying to get his ship back up north of the hulk again, so that he could run down before the wind and take her in tow; but the Spanish greatship, lumbering powerfully along on a near parallel course, farther out to sea, was rapidly running her out of sea room. Jan bit his lips. He drummed with his hands on the rail of the hulk. Pieter was losing the wind. He had to come about soon, or run aground, and when he came about he would fly into the teeth of the greatship and her heavy guns and her boarding party.

"Come on!" He could stand still no longer. Kicking through the rubble on the deck, he found a well-dressed corpse with a saber in its hand, took the sword, and began hacking away the swaddling debris that clogged the hulk's deck.

"Here comes the other ship!" Mouse cried.

He put his shoulder to a broken spar and heaved it overboard, and with it went a mass of rigging and sail. The hulk seemed to rock up, lighter in the water. Mouse shouted again. Jan raised his eyes.

An oath escaped him. There was another ship, running down in the wind's eye from the north. A two-masted cog, whose round bow and stern proclaimed her Dutch built. On her high-stepped fore- and afterdecks were ranks of men with muskets. A gaudy banner of gold and green fluttered from the peak of her mainmast, and other, uglier trophies dangled from her yard ends—bodies, swathed in rusty black cloth. With the wind behind her this strange vessel swept down on the Spaniard, and the Spanish ship swung clumsily around to meet her.

Jan yelled. With the greatship thus distracted, the *Wayward Girl* had a clear path out to the open water, and Pieter seized the moment and brought his handy little ship about and made for the safety and sea room that stretched out beyond the greatship's stern.

The greatship lost the wind. In coming about to meet the strange craft she had missed her course. Her sails slatted and drooped flat against her masts, and she wallowed in the sea like a washtub. The strange ship bore down straight at her. Jan wondered if she meant to ram her. The newcomer was half the size of the greatship. Yet she charged down on the Spaniard with every sail spread.

"Jan!" On the dinghy, bobbing in the lee of the mastless hulk, Aart was standing up to yell at him. "What is going on?"

"There's another ship out here fighting the Spaniard!" Jan swept the sea with his gaze, looking for the *Wayward Girl*, and saw her far out on the water. Her square mainsail shortened to a vertical line. She was turning. "Here comes Pieter. Get ready."

From the greatship came a roar of voices. The newcomer was sweeping down on her. At the last moment the strange ship swerved off a little, to pass astern of her, and the Spanish ship fired her guns.

The crack of splintering wood resounded across the water. A cannon-ball skipped over the waves and buried itself in the sea with a splash that went up like a tree of spray. The strange ship glided past the Spaniard's stern and muskets cracked and snapped on her decks. Along her stern overhang ran the words *Christ the Redeemer.* Still the greatship lay stubbornly dead in the water while her crew scrambled through her rigging and over her yards, trying to fill her sails with wind to give her life again. Between her and the strange ship the stretch of water widened as her course carried the newcomer away down the wind.

From the Spaniard's far side suddenly the *Wayward Girl* appeared, racing down so close to the greatship that Jan howled with fear and anger at his uncle. Distracted, the Spanish had not seen her; one or two of the huge Spanish guns went off, but the *Wayward Girl,* sailing almost under the greatship's rails, fired the bow gun, the waist culverin, and the two stern guns pointblank into the Spaniard's hull, and leaning with the wind she was racing off light as a deer before the greatship could recover.

Jan whooped. "God, the old man can sail!"

"There's more ships," Mouse cried, and pointed.

A whole fleet of strange vessels was strung out along the horizon. The greatship had seen them too. With both her immediate enemies sailing off away from her, she finally gained the wind again. Her pouched canvas billowed and filled taut, and she gathered herself up out of the lap of the sea. The *Christ the Redeemer* was coming about, but she was hardly more nimble than the greatship herself with the wind over her stern, and the Spaniard put her bows straight for the sea and took the wind and ran.

Mouse was dancing on the rail of the hulk, his arms in the air. Jan grinned at him, gay with relief and victory. "Let's go below," he said, "and see what it is we've been fighting for." He ruffled the boy's hair. Mouse smiled up at him worshipfully, and Jan led him over to the nearest hatch and hauled the cover back.

"WOOL." Pieter kicked the nearest of the mountain of bales on the deck. The tide was ebbing, leaving the mastless ship solidly aground; Jan and his men had cleared the deck of bodies and rubble and brought up what of the cargo they could salvage. Bursting in through holes in her hull, the sea had gotten into most of the wool and a lot of the cloth. Pieter went on to the row of casks. "What's this?"

Jan pulled up a slat in the top of the cask he had opened and took out one of the sacks that filled it. Pieter kneaded it expertly with his fingers, feeling the contents through the cloth.

"Pepper. Good enough. Are they all the same?"

"I don't know."

Pieter was looking off across the deck, over the rail, toward the sea. Night was falling. In the darkening air the half dozen ships lying to in the deep water seaward of the *Wayward Girl* were only vague shapes. Jan rubbed his hand on his thigh.

"What are they going to do?"

"I don't know," Pieter said.

The strange fleet had come up on the heels of the Spanish greatship's retreat. They were all Dutch built, cogs and flyboats, showing the gold and green pennant, and when the Spanish ship fled they had calmly assumed a station just outside of the hulk.

"Who are they?" Jan said.

Pieter grunted. He stuck his pipe between his teeth and tramped on down the deck, past the heaps of cargo. "Anything else?"

Jan led him over to a wooden chest by the stump of the mainmast. Aart was standing there, his arms crossed, his back against the butt of the mast. Jan tipped up the lid of the chest with his foot.

"Hunh." Pieter started to squat down, to get closer to the heaps of silver coins in the chest, and thought better of it. "Who else knows about it?"

"You and me. And Aart," Jan said. He shut the lid again.

"Get it onto the *Wayward Girl.* Swim it over if you have to." Pieter threw another narrow look toward the strange fleet.

"Who are they?" Jan asked him.

The old man puffed on his pipe. "Beggars," he said. "Sea Beggars.

Willem Lumey de la Marck and his pack. Pirates disguised as men of religion. You saw the meat hanging from his yardarms?"

Jan remembered the corpses dangling in their black shrouds and nodded.

"Priests. Lumey hates priests."

Jan turned to Aart. "We have to get that chest over to the *Wayward Girl* if we mean to keep it."

Pieter went over to a heap of little kegs and bent over them. "They're just waiting until we do the work here," he said, forcing up the bung of the top keg with the tip of his knife. "Then they'll take it all. God-damned pirates." The bung popped out with a squeak. Lifting the keg, he poured red wine into his mouth.

"I'll take the dinghy," Aart said, and stooped to pick up the chest.

"You will not," Jan said. "They'll know we're doing something." He picked up the chest in both hands; it weighed as much as a good-sized child. "You can't swim with it; you'll go straight to the bottom."

"Here they come," Pieter said, and clicked his teeth together. He thumped the bung back into the hole in the little wine keg.

From the dark fleet that hemmed them in against the shore came a little boat, bobbing across the water toward the hulk. A torch blazed in her bow. Jan frowned, trying to make out how many men sat behind the hot glow of light, but could see only shadows. He wheeled around.

"Here." He grabbed the chest from Aart and put it down again at the foot of the mast. Three long strides took him to a bundle of unfinished cloth that lay against the smashed railing. He yanked it open and tore off an arm's length of it and draped it over the chest. "Now." Picking up his uncle, he set him down on top of the cloth like a little king. "Sit there and don't move."

"Get your hands off me!" Pieter thrashed at him. Jan backed away, looking around, saw nothing else to do, and nodded to Aart.

"Call the rest of the men over here. We'll have a fire and drink the rest of this wine and see what can be done with these people who rescued us."

"They never rescued us!" Pieter shouted.

"They did," Jan said. "And we may as well admit it. Now, sit up, look smart, and don't move off that chest."

The other men gathered around them, and hacking up other parts of the hulk, they made a fire in the middle of the deck, and warmed the wine in a pan over the flames. By that time the fleet's boat had come alongside, and the Sea Beggars were climbing up on the deck.

They strode across the blood-stained deck of the hulk into the firelight, eight men, all carrying as many weapons as they could hold, knives and swords in their belts, and pistols in their boot tops, and two with muskets on their shoulders. Their leader strutted forward on widespread feet. His clothes glittered in the firelight, heavy with gold embroidery and chips of jewels; down the center of his heavy surcoat ran the sacred letter 𝕵, wreathed in emblems. It was a priest's vestment, used at the solemn high Mass.

"Well, well," Pieter said, around his pipe. "Lumey de la Marck, I see."

The man in the priest's coat stopped on the far side of the fire, his fists planted on his hips. "I am Lumey de la Marck," he said. "But I didn't expect to see you here, Pieter van Cleef."

"Did you think I was ashore forever? Here's my nephew, Jan van Cleef, as good a hand with a big gun as any you'll find on the narrow seas."

Jan gave his uncle a surprised glance, startled by the heady praise, and Lumey thrust his hand out to him.

"Well met, Jan van Cleef."

From behind Lumey came a tall man in sober dark clothes of fine cloth and high boots; the hilts of the daggers and the sword in his belt were of chased silver.

"Van Treslong," he said, "of the *Peter and Paul.*" And they all shook hands.

After him came a small round man with a wen on his cheek. "Dirk Sonoy, the *Katerina.*"

They greeted him, and one by one the other captains after him. Jan kept his gaze on Willem Lumey de la Marck. He had heard before of the leader of the Sea Beggars, tales of wild courage and butchery which the bold charge of Lumey's ship against the Spanish greatship gave him some measure of. A nobleman, like many of the Sea Beggars. Jan shuffled his feet together, his hands sliding behind him, uneasy.

Pieter leaned forward on his makeshift throne. "Let's have wine all around," he said. "The night's chill. Aart—Willy—"

There were no cups; they passed the wine in the pan it had heated in, with the dipper from the hulk's water barrel to drink it by. Lumey drank a sip and stood back, running his gaze over the heaps of cargo on the deck around him.

"A fine, big ship," he said, in his booming voice. "A true mare of Andalusia, and what does she carry, Pieter van Cleef?"

"Wool, as you see, mostly ruined. Cloth to be finished, and some spices."

"All we've taken," Jan said, "we'll gladly share with you, for saving us."

"Oh, ho!" Lumey shouted with laughter. He tramped around in the little circle of firelight, his hands on his hips and his gold-embroidered coat sparkling and flashing. "What gratitude this is, from a good crew of Dutchmen!"

"Well said, I think," said van Treslong, quietly, and smiled.

Dirk Sonoy was staring away into the dark. He wheeled around abruptly toward Jan.

"Your ship is the *Wayward Girl?*"

"Yes," Jan said.

"She seems different. I didn't recognize her—I thought she was caravel-rigged."

"No," Pieter growled. He stuffed his pipe full of tobacco and reached into the fire for a splinter. "Fore-and-aft rigged, she always was, but the Spanish took her and rerigged her with the gaffsail. And she sails very prettily for it, too."

Lumey was tramping off down the ship, poking at the heaps of wool and cloth, and nosing into the pepper. Van Treslong moved up closer to the fire and put out his long elegant hands over it to warm them.

"And the Spanish gave her back to you? Kindly folk that they are?"

"We stole her," Pieter said.

From the darkness beyond the fire, where Lumey was, came a whoop of derisive amusement. "What van Cleef does best, by God's hat!"

Sonoy crouched down, the firelight shining on his round red face. "Then you are playing pirate? Join us. The more sticks, the hotter the fire, as the saying goes."

Pieter took his pipe from between his teeth. "Two fools under the same cloak, as the saying goes."

Lumey's heavy footsteps made the deck tremble. "This is all you found on this ship?" He waved his arm broadly at the cargo.

Jan said, "There's still some below, but the ship was pretty well worked over when we finally got her, and the sea's washed into most of it."

Lumey grunted. Beneath his bristling eyebrows his eyes were small and close set like snake's eyes. He said, "You're just a stripling; these other fools are harbor rats. You can't sail alone against Spain. You'd better fall in with us."

"We do well enough," Jan said.

Van Treslong tipped his head back; the firelight shone up under his hat's floppy broad brim. "We need a good fast ship like yours. We've got a scheme to—" Lumey kicked him in the ribs.

"By God," van Treslong said, and snatching a brand from the fire he leapt up and swiped at Lumey with the blazing stick. Lumey howled. Springing backward, his arms flying up over his head, he missed his footing on the blood-slippery deck and crashed down on his backside. The other captains roared with laughter.

"Keep your boots in the barn, Lumey!" Van Treslong threw the brand in a fiery arc out over the rail into the dark sea.

"Hush, hush," Sonoy said, pulling on his sleeve. "He's got his own ways—and you shouldn't hand out your sheets until the wedding's consummated."

"As the saying goes," Pieter said, and sent up puffs of smoke from the chimney of his pipe.

Jan said, "What's your plan?"

"Join us," Sonoy said. "Then we'll talk about it. We share everything equally. Lumey is our commander, because there has to be someone to give orders and the Prince of Orange named him our admiral, but as you can tell, we all say what we think. We're all good honest Christians—"

"Damn the Pope," Lumey said, coming back to the fire. He rubbed his backside with one hand, ignoring van Treslong. His cheeks were red as raw bacon.

"Bah," Pieter said. "I don't care what you dress it in, you're still pirates, and nothing better than pirates. I'll take my chances by myself."

"Oh, no," said Lumey tenderly. "We're not pirates. We have letters of marque from the Prince of Orange himself, God bless him."

"Letters of marque," Jan said. "What's that?"

Lumey's hand plunged inside his coat and came out again with a packet of paper wrapped in cord. "Letters from the sovereign Prince of Orange that we are sailors in his navy, and therefore whatever we do is lawfully done and we can't hang as pirates."

He laughed, exultant, and waved the papers in the air.

"Do your necks still stretch?" Pieter stamped his foot. "Do the Dons still make rope? Then you'll hang if they catch you, you fools!"

Lumey stuffed his letters away under his gaudy clothes. He said, "I don't mean to be caught."

"What's this plan you have?" Jan asked van Treslong.

The tall man straightened up, taking off his hat. "I see no reason to keep it hidden. We have in mind to throw a net of ships across the mouth of the Channel, and when the Spanish fleet comes between The Lizard and the Brittany coast, we'll take them. The King of Spain sends a fleet to Antwerp every half year, with supplies and the pay for his troops."

"How many ships do you have?" Jan folded his arms over his chest. "Those six little ships out there won't do much against a fleet of galleons."

"We'll have forty sail," Lumey said. "And every God-fearing, priest-hating man between The Lizard and the Maas to sail them. Join us, or by Heaven we'll sink you right here."

Jan started toward him, angry, but van Treslong got him by the arm. "Pay no heed to him; he's impatient with reason. But you must see the advantage to joining us, even if all you mean is simple piracy."

"That's all there is to do," Pieter shot at him. "And you who parade about, pretending you are fighting a war against Spain—"

Sonoy distracted him, his mouth full of proverbs, into another line of argument. Van Treslong plucked Jan's sleeve.

"Mark you, there is this: every blow we strike here against Spain hurts both Spain and Alva. Do you hate the Bloody Duke? Do you want to free our cities and our Provinces from his rule? Then you would do well to join us."

Jan said, "Alva hanged my father. I want my revenge."

Lumey pushed in between him and van Treslong. "Either join us, sailor boy, or go to the bottom of the sea! Take your choice."

"God's blood!" Pieter bounced up onto his feet. "For that, I'll never join you, Lumey—for your bullying ways and your big mouth." He tramped up before the bigger man, shouting into his face. "Baron, are you? On the sea you're only as fine as you sail, pirate, and you sail as the wind blows! Don't make more of yourself than there is, pirate—"

Jan tensed, ready to get between his uncle and Lumey, but suddenly van Treslong was looking down past Pieter at the deck, suspicion drawing his face long. Jan lowered his gaze. With a half-smothered yelp he grabbed Pieter by the arm.

"I told you not to stand up!"

Pieter thrust him off, another volley of insults leaving his lips for Lumey. Jan pulled him backward, back over the length of unfinished wool cloth he had dragged after him from the chest, back toward the chest left exposed and obvious before the other pirates.

"You old fool!"

"Why, now," van Treslong said mildly, "I think our hosts here have been withholding something of their bounty from us." He went to the chest and bent over it.

"That's ours," Pieter cried.

"Oh, yes," said van Treslong. "And you brought it out on the *Wayward Girl* to bring on board all your prizes, to give them that certain aura of expense." He tipped up the lid. Lumey bellowed.

"Cheats!"

"Well," said Sonoy, puffing out his round cheeks, "the pisspot's hanging on the door now."

Jan looked around at the intent faces of the pirate captains; he saw there was no argument now that would keep the silver from them, and he shrugged. He smacked old Pieter on the shoulder.

"God, you make me angry sometimes."

Pieter growled. "It's ours!"

Van Treslong was already counting the silver coins out onto the deck. "There's six of us here," he said loudly. "Six ships of the Sea Beggars. I'll divide it up into sixes." Lifting his head, he smiled at Jan and Pieter. "Or is that seven ships of the Sea Beggars?"

A low rumble of angry noise was the only answer Pieter gave. Jan folded his arms over his chest. They had already half convinced him to join them; but he was sorry to be losing so much of the silver. He shrugged again.

"I'm with you." Jan twisted, his face turned over his shoulder, and called, "And my crew, too."

From the dimness outside the firelight the other men of the *Wayward Girl* muttered their agreement. Van Treslong nodded, the silver clinking in his hand.

"Divided by sevens, then."

Sonoy gave Jan a comradely slap on the arm. "Two people can shit through the same hole, you know."

Jan laughed. Pieter stuck his pipe between his teeth again. "As the saying goes."

8

AT NOON, Pieter went down the deck to the wheel, where in a little covered stand the ship's compass was housed, and turned the hourglass over and rang the bell. He marked the watch book and put it away under the compass. Going aft, he leaned on the stern rail and looked out to sea. His hands moved, collecting his pipe and his tobacco pouch and firebox, but he stopped himself, remembering he had no more tobacco. Laying his arms down on the rail, he looked steadily out toward the gray rolling sea.

The *Wayward Girl* lay off the English coast, waiting for the pilot to arrive who would guide her into Plymouth harbor. This was Lumey's idea, coming here, although Pieter had grudgingly to agree to its good sense, since they had to sell the plunder from the Spanish ship. The rest of the Beggar fleet was scattered over the water around Pieter's ship, which was why he kept his gaze pinned straight out toward the sea, where he had to look at none of them.

He hated them. He hated Lumey most, the brawler, the braggart, but he hated the others as well, although he knew them little. And now they had their grips on his nephew. His hands curled over the ship's railing and he clenched his teeth in frustrated rage.

Pirates: what were they but pirates? Nothing wrong with that. Pieter knew himself for a pirate, having been one for as long as he could remember, long before he ever put to sea. It was there in his heart's working, in the structure of his bones, to steal. To live free. So he stole and lived according to his own liking, prepared to take the consequences. But he never dressed it all up in fancy, lofty talk of saving the world.

They would seduce Jan into it, Jan whom he loved with his whole heart. He was tough, that boy, and a natural seaman, a born pirate, like Pieter. He was young, too, and the likes of Lumey and van Treslong and Sonoy would pour the honeyed poison of their excuses into his ears, and it would happen to him what happened to them all.

Pieter had seen it happen to his brother, Mies. A good practical boy Mies had been once, not a pirate, but still a free, wild heart. Then slowly he had gotten notions of religion. Bit by bit he lost sight of the real things of life, the daily hungers, the instants of satisfaction and distress; gradually his mind filled up with a grand, false vision of angels and battles in the sky. In the end it got him hanged. Long before that, he had stopped talking to Pieter, and Pieter had stopped liking Mies.

Behind Pieter now someone shouted across the water. The pilots were coming.

Resolutely he kept his back to them. He hated turning his ship over to a stranger—hated it the more now, when he had lost her once, and thought her lost forever, and only recovered her by force. He had her now, though, and he had won the Spanish hulk with her. Damn Lumey! If he and his Beggars had not interfered, Pieter would have had most of the plunder overboard and kept the silver—enough to make them all rich.

Lumey had the silver now, but Pieter would not give up so easily. In Plymouth there would be opportunities to have it back again. The old man smiled, wanting his tobacco, which he would also find in Plymouth, and wanting his silver. He would have it back, and a satisfaction in regaining it, too. Let them think they were warriors of God. Waving their letters of marque. He'd show them how a true pirate did.

"LOOK, JAN! Look!" Mouse leapt up and down, delighted.

"Shut up," Jan said.

Mouse could not keep still. He had been at sea for two weeks and before then never out of Nieuport. The sail up Plymouth Sound was like a passage into another world. At first the low dark hills on either side had seemed to close in around the ships, and he had kept near Jan, who was not afraid; Jan was never afraid. Then abruptly the hills opened up like hands when they gave you something, and there ahead of them, on the smooth water, a great forest of masts appeared.

"Jan, see? There's a town."

"Shut up, will you?" Jan cuffed him along the side of the head.

Jan was writing in a book; he had been scribbling away ever since the pilot brought them into the mouth of Plymouth Sound. Mouse wanted to ask him what he was doing but he knew Jan would shout at him again, and anyway he probably would not understand.

He stood on his toes to see the harbor. It was bigger than Nieuport, with many more ships. Small boats scurried over the water among the moored vessels. The beach ahead curved around to the left, where the sound went on through the hills. Above the beach the roofs of buildings climbed the slopes like a jumble of steps. He saw a church spire in the middle of the town. Up there on the top of the slope was a big tower, like a castle.

"Jan," he cried, forgetting, and clapped his hand over his own mouth. Jan ignored him, writing.

What was he writing about? Mouse craned his neck to see the page, bowed up from the binding. Marks half covered it. The marks wavered and jumped over the page and doubled and tripled themselves, and he covered his right eye with his hand, which made the marks much tamer. Still they looked only like bird tracks in the damp sand. He would have understood better if they were pictures.

Jan's face, bent over them, was intent and beautiful with concentration. Mouse smiled to himself. If Jan did them, the marks had to be important.

The pilot called orders to old Pieter, who sent them on to Red Aart at the wheel. They were coming about, in the middle of the forest of ships; soon the mast of the *Wayward Girl* would rock and sway with the others. Mouse looked up at the little topsail. They had taken down the mainsail and brought her in under her jib and topsail, which opened at the top of the bare mast like a net for the clouds.

"Ready with the anchors!"

The men dashed around the ship. Mouse kept his eyes on the topsail. The edge shivered, losing the wind; abruptly now it collapsed.

"Down anchors!"

The anchors plunked down into the water. A moment later the little topsail fluttered away down the mast to the deck, leaving the bare finger of the mast behind to point into the sky.

Mouse crowed and clapped his hands together. He felt now they had truly come to rest.

"Jan! Shall we go ashore?"

Still bent over his book, Jan swiped backward at him with his left arm. Mouse dodged the blow. He wished Jan liked him better. He loved Jan; he wished he were Jan, so much that at night when he lay beside his brother on the deck, watching the wheeling stars and waiting for sleep to come, he made up little stories in which a Mouse as big and strong and clever as Jan did wonderful deeds and was everyone's hero.

It wasn't true. Standing on the deck behind his idol, he knew how untrue the stories were and a great misery filled up his head and blurred his eyes. But before he could begin to cry a hand ruffled up his hair.

"Little Mouse, shall we go put our feet on solid ground again?"

It was old Pieter. Amazed, he blinked up at the ship's master, who had never spoken to him before. "Oh, yes." He caught Pieter's hand. "Oh, yes." A warm gratitude replaced his grief, and clinging to Pieter's hand he went across the ship to the rail, where his brother was helping to lower the dinghy.

THE WHARVES of Plymouth smelled, like Nieuport, of rotting seaweed and tar and fish. They were busier than Nieuport's, barges tied up to every pier and from every barge a line of men stretching back to the street, passing bales and bundles and barrels of goods from hand to hand to the waiting wagons. Through this orderly crowd Jan wandered like an invisible man, having no place.

The language tantalized his ears. He stopped to listen to a master in a blue hat curse a half-naked laborer, and the words leapt at him, all but understandable. The rhythm was the same as Dutch, the sounds inside the words the same but the words themselves fell like riddles on his ears.

While he stood there, struggling with the familiar, unknown speech, someone bumped into him from behind. In his own country he would have roared at this insult and fought an hour to avenge it, but here he only lowered his head and walked on.

Across the broad street that curved around behind the harbor, the buildings of Plymouth town began. These were not like Dutch houses. He found their strange looks oddly comforting. He followed a narrow twisting street back into a warren of houses made of wooden beams and thatched in straw. The ditch was full of garbage, rank to the nose. A flock of white chickens clucked and pecked along ahead of him, as if he drove them. He smelled burned garlic. Two men passed him, arguing; they ignored him.

Lost now in the winding streets, he stopped at a place where three streets came together and looked around. A vendor was calling, somewhere, in the singsong of all vendors, but he could not see him. From the second story window of the house on his left a woman leaned to string wet baby napkins on a rope stretched between hers and the next house. A shutter banged.

He went on a few steps and paused; now he could see through the open gate into a yard before a tall old house. In the yard a woman was singing in a fine, pure voice, singing in English that tore his heart. He leaned closer to see. She was washing clothes in a pot, stirring them with a wooden paddle. Behind her a baby sat on the flagstones playing with a little spaniel dog. On the windowsill of the house behind them, a pie had been set to cool.

He took another step toward this place, drawn by old memories. In that house, might he not find a fire, someone to talk to, sweets to eat? Then she turned, the woman, and stopped singing, and gave him so fierce and hostile a look he turned and went off with his ears burning.

The wandering lanes took him around back to the harbor and dumped him in the street like so much garbage. He walked along the wharves again, his head turned out toward the many ships that rested on the quiet water of Plymouth Sound. A woman spoke to him.

He wheeled, hungry for this contact, and opened his mouth to answer, but no words come out: all his words were Dutch, and she was English.

She smiled at him. Over her real face she wore a false one of paint. She asked him a question, and while he fumbled for some way to answer what he did not understand, she reached out and grabbed his crotch.

That he understood. His cheeks and ears went hot as a forge. He tore his gaze from her face and stammered something in his own tongue. She laughed at him. With a flirting twist of her wrist and a toss of her head she walked away down the wharf street.

Jan broke into a run in the other direction. His mind churned with bits of thoughts. He could go back—go with her. But he had no money with him. The urge grew in him to run and run until he ran into Antwerp and up the Canal Street and into the front door of his own mother's house.

Ahead, the street ended; the wharf ended, and he was still in England. He slowed to a trot and after a few steps to a walk. On his left was a tavern. Through the open doors spilled the sounds of men drinking and gambling, laughter and curses, and voices speaking Dutch. In the window was a face he knew, and someone called his name; he belonged here. He swerved to go in.

LUMEY growled over his cards. With one hand he wiped his mouth and reached for his tankard. Before him stood a heap of silver, much diminished from a few hours ago, but still considerable.

Most of what he had lost now lay before Pieter van Cleef, across the table from him. Pieter kept his eyes half-closed and his face noncommittal. He wanted no sign of his delight to show, lest the malice underlying it show too and the others begin to suspect him.

On this round anyway the other players had already dropped out. They lounged on their stools, drinking, paying little heed to the game. Around them the tavern boomed with the noise of the other Beggars, some dicing and playing at cards, and some talking and pawing the barmaids. Fine Calvinists, Pieter thought, and his righteous indignation added a polish of divine authority to his pleasures.

He fingered his cards. "Will you bet?" he said sharply to Lumey.

The Beggar grunted. He was very drunk. The sweat streamed down his veined forehead. His fingers tapped nervously on the paste and paper tickets in his hand. Finally he reached for more silver.

"Five, and I'll take another card."

Pieter nodded, satisfied. While Lumey drew another card from the deck between them, the old man leaned back against the wall behind him and stared at his own cards. He had kings and queens in three suits and four of the Grand Trumps; all he needed was another trump to have a sweep hand, unbeatable unless Lumey held all four Aces; and Pieter knew he could not have the Ace of Wands. He pursed his lips. He could match Lumey's five and draw, and hope to improve his hand that way; but Pieter's design was too elegant to rely on such common chancy ways of winning. He lifted his gaze and scanned the room for Mouse.

The half-wit was sitting by the nearest window, his mouth ajar, his hands idle in his lap. His eyes were always aimed in two different directions so it was hard to tell what he was looking at. Pieter gave a tug to his beard. For a moment Mouse did not move and he thought the boy had fallen into a daze, but then Mouse slid off the window ledge and came over to him.

"Here, what do you want?" Pieter said crossly. He waved at Mouse, as if to send him away. To the other players, he said, "He's an idiot. We should have left him on the shore."

Mouse leaned over him. "What are you doing? Can I play?"

With his elbow he knocked over Pieter's jug. Pieter yelled; he grabbed the jug and righted it again before all the liquor could spill out. Mouse babbled at him—for a fool, he was good at this, although Pieter had spent a patient hour drilling him at it—and stooped to catch the liquor dripping off the tabletop in his cupped hands.

When he tried to pour it back into Pieter's jug the men around the table rocked with laughter. Pieter huffed and fumed, yelled for the barmaid to bring a rag, rescued the deck of cards from the spreading pool of gin. Beneath the table, while he pretended to clean up, Mouse laid three cards on the old man's knee.

"Get away," Pieter shouted, and pretended to kick him. Palming up the cards, he waited until the barmaid was bent over the table and the other men were looking down her bodice before he slipped the new cards into his hand. Mouse had brought him the World and the High Priestess and the Ace of Wands.

"Well, well," Pieter said, when the barmaid had gone. "I don't think there's much I can do with this hand. I'll bank on it, Lumey—ten pieces." He counted silver into the pile in the middle of the table.

Lumey made a variety of low animal sounds. He fingered his cards and rubbed his nose and shifted on his stool, as if he were making up his mind. He would not throw it in, not now. Pieter knew Lumey well enough to be sure of that. Finally he counted out the ten pieces, and old Pieter laid down his cards.

All the other men groaned. Sonoy shook his head. "As the saying goes, Pieter, cakes grow on your roof." They drank to Pieter's luck and, smiling, Pieter hauled in his winnings.

MOUSE was proud of himself; he had done exactly what Pieter had told him, and done it well, because now Pieter was rich. The old man had promised to buy him a knife of his own if he did it properly. Tonight he would have his own knife—no more waiting like a baby while his brother cut his meat for him. He went to the window, where the sun made it warm, and sat up on the ledge.

He still had three of the cards, and he took them from his shirt and held them in front of him. The pictures were very strange, the colors as bright and pretty as the glass windows in the Oude Kirk in Nieuport. Funny things happened in the pictures, hands without arms reaching down from clouds, and people flying. He turned the picture over to look at it better and covered his right eye with his hand.

"What's that he has?" someone said behind him.

He looked around. At the table, the cardplayers were all staring at him.

"By God's blood," Pieter said loudly. "He must have taken them off the table, after the hand was played. Here, boy, give me those. We'll have to deal again.''

Mouse shrank back, clutching the oblong pictures in his hand. Pieter had not told him about this part of it. The five men at the table sprang up and marched toward him. Frightened, he cowered back into the angle of the ledge, and the big man in the gold coat tore the cards out of his fingers.

"Trumps, by Heaven!"

A hand seized Mouse by the nape of the neck. "Where did you get those?"

Pieter was talking so fast the words tripped on one another. "Off the table. Must have taken them off the table when the deck was down—"

"In a priest's punchbowl," the big man shouted. "It was a jig! You cheated me!"

Mouse whined, pushing at the hands that held him, at the big bodies that fenced him into the window space. He threw a beseeching look at Pieter, who understood all this, and could rescue him.

Pieter was backing away. "He's an idiot," he said, and shrugged. "He doesn't know what he's doing."

"We'll find out what he's doing!" The man who held him raised a fist, stuffed with rings like barnacles. "Talk!" he bellowed at Mouse.

Mouse sucked in his breath. He knew he was going to be hurt, and he began to cry. Twisting away from the threatening fist, he pressed his face to the glass.

Beyond the window, out in the street, Jan was walking toward him. "Jan!"

The hand on his neck yanked him around again. "Talk! Where did you get those cards?"

"He's a fool," Pieter shouted. He was sidling away across the room. "He's too stupid to tell the truth!"

Mouse was sobbing. He cried again, "Jan!" and struggled to bury his face in his hands. The men around him pressed closer. He saw the ring-studded fist coming.

An instant later the wall of bodies broke. Whirling aside, the men staggered back, away from Mouse. Jan stood there, breathing hard.

"What's going on?"

The big man, who still had Mouse by the neck, thrust the crumpled cards under Jan's nose. "Your uncle was cheating us, and this idiot helped him."

Jan put his hands on his hips. "He's too dumb to cheat anybody."

"He cheated me!" The big man shook Mouse back and forth.

Jan's face changed, sliding into an uneven grin with no merriment and much anger in it. "Well, if you admit it—it makes a fine story—the great Lumey de la Marck cheated by a half-witted boy?"

Behind them, someone laughed. The grip on Mouse's neck relaxed, and Lumey backed off a step.

"Your uncle cheated me!"

Jan looked broadly around the room. "I don't even see my uncle here."

They whirled. A howl of rage went up from Lumey, who pumped his arms and bit his beard in fury. "The little bastard!"

"He's gone," Sonoy cried. "He took all the silver, too."

Jan got Mouse by the arm. "Come on," he said. Swiftly they went out of the tavern.

"I THOUGHT you said not to steal from your own people," Jan said.

Pieter muttered something under his breath. He puffed on his pipe. The pungent smoke of the tobacco made the air around them hard to breathe. He thrust out his legs before him on the deck. "They aren't my people."

"They're Dutch." Jan held out his hand, palm up. "Like us. And we'll sail with them. That scheme for taking the supply fleet, that's a good notion."

He was eating smoked fish, and he stopped to pick a bone from between his teeth. They and Mouse were the only people on board the *Wayward Girl,* and Mouse was sleeping. He and Pieter sat in the forecastle, looking down the length of the ship. There behind the mast, by the helm, the lantern gleamed over the compass; otherwise no light showed, and yet Jan could have found his way effortlessly throughout the whole ship, could have done the most intricate task necessary to sail her, with his eyes closed. So small a world, he thought, and felt her around him like a case.

"We have no country anymore," old Pieter was saying, beside him. "Get used to that. No country, no family or friends—only the ship and the sea and the winds. That's the truth. If you don't like it, you can make up stories, the way the Beggars do, and try to say it's otherwise, but you're only fooling yourself."

Jan said nothing. He longed for his sister and his mother, for his home in Antwerp; that very longing made him think that Pieter was right. Everything past was gone, and the longing was proof of it. He had nothing anymore save this hardened, wicked old man, and the half-wit boy asleep on the deck beside him. Nothing. He put his head back against the timbers of the ship and shut his eyes.

9

UT YOU can't," Hanneke said, and clenched her fists. "I must work—I have no other way of living. My mother—"

The leadman was shaking his head. "You've been missing days of work anyway."

"But I explained that to you—and I do extra work to make up for it—"

His head swiveled from side to side, his expression implacable. "I can't keep you on."

"Please!"

He reached for the door, to swing it shut between them, and as he shut it in her face he said, "If I were you, girl, I would not remind people my name's van Cleef." The door closed. She was left staring at the stained boards.

He had paid her, at least scrupulous about that, to the last penny she was owed. She held the money in her hand, just barely enough to pay the Kelmans the rent. And then what? They had to eat something. She could not survive forever on the sweet buns Michael gave her. She turned away from the back door of the factory and walked off along the street.

What he had said to her came back; she stood under a tree by the side of the canal and looked into the dark swirling water and knew bitterly that he had let her off because she was her father's daughter. Mies, what a heritage you have given me. She struggled against her rage at her father, who had left her this misery.

The canal's slippery water rushed by, deep and dark from the spring rains. She thought of jumping in, of drowning, and getting out of her troubles that way, and enjoyed the idea for a moment: how sweet to sleep. But of course she could not; there was her mother to care for, and God forbade suicide anyway. She would not sleep; she would writhe in Hell. She walked off along the street to the bridge and crossed over.

In the Italian quarter, where most of the banks were, close by the Bourse, she went from shop to shop asking for work, but no one had any jobs she could do. Some of them even laughed at her, not meanly, but in amazement she would ask. Now and then she came on a shop that was closed up, which did not strike her odd, for a while, until she came to the end of the Lombard Street and saw people carrying furniture and goods out of a building and loading them onto wagons to be taken away.

At that she did stop and put this all together in her mind; she realized there was something ominous in this, that the foreigners were leaving Antwerp. For generations, people from all over Europe had been crowding into Antwerp, the hub of the world, and now, for some reason, they were going.

Only a few streets away, toward the river, was the shop of the printer Clement. He would know what was going on, and she went there.

The shop was loud with the clanging of the presses. Clement and several other men rushed about at their work, methodical as soldiers; the paper rattled in their hands and flashed white in the dim room, and as each lever swayed down the great screw presses groaned like monsters. The smell of ink and lead was painful to the nose. She went to the corner by the fire and sat down on the stool. The cat was curled up in the deep padded chair beside the window.

After a while the door opened and Clement's boy, Philip, came in. Seeing her, he smiled all over his face. Her heart lightened. She hardly knew him; yet he was glad to see her, and he came over to her and sat down on the floor beside her.

"How are you? I haven't seen you in a long while."

They talked a little about the weather and the coming of the spring.

"I've lost my job," she said, when the conversation got around to that. "And I can't find another. Why are the shops closing in the Italian quarter? What's going on? Something's wrong."

Clement's boy folded his knees up to his chest and wrapped his arms around them. "Yes, a lot of people are going away."

"Why? Is there some reason?"

"The Spaniards, naturally," he said, and shrugged. "What else is there?"

"But they've gone," she said, thinking of Carlos, and realized at once how narrowly she had understood the Spanish power in Antwerp.

Clement's boy was watching her with wide grave eyes. His hair needed cutting; it fell over his forehead in a wing, and she put out her hand and brushed it back behind his ear. "What have you been reading lately?"

"A book about trajectories," he said. He looked as if he were still thinking about what they had just spoken of.

"Trajectories. What's that?"

"How things fall."

"Really. How odd, an entire book about how things fall. I cannot conceive of that filling even a page." Her words sounded hollow to her, frantic, planking over a yawning gap in her understanding.

"Well," the boy said, "that's the interesting thing about the new science, that the more closely you look at what seems like a simple thing the more there is to see. Why did they throw you out of your work? Because you are Calvinist?"

At that her chest contracted; she faced the dread she had been avoiding. "Yes," she said.

He put his hand on her shoulder. "My father will help you."

Hanneke smiled at him. Her face was stiff. If she had lost the one job for her faith, then the chances of her finding another were very slight. She thought of her mother, who complained even now of their poor food and close quarters. *I should have taken the canal,* she thought, and turned her gaze into the fire.

A few minutes later Clement was sitting down in the chair, the cat on his lap. "Well, Mistress van Cleef, what brings me the honor of a visit from you?"

"She's lost her job," his son said. "Because she is a Calvinist."

Hanneke said, "I can tell him myself, you know."

Clement's big black-smudged hand flattened the cat's back. "Not just that, I am sure—it is the tax."

"What tax?"

"The Spaniards are requiring several new taxes of us—to pay for the troops they are keeping here. The taxes on goods and land have no bearing on you, but there is a great tax that does, whereby the tenth penny of every sale in the Low Countries must go to the King."

"Every sale of what?" she asked, not understanding at all.

"Every sale of anything. If a loaf of bread is sold, one tenth of the price must go to the King, or if a keg of beer is sold, or a sheep, or an onion, or a piece of cloth, and so the shopkeepers must raise their prices or cut their expenses in some way, and the easiest way is to let go some of their help."

She gaped at him, amazed to have her particular disaster so neatly made part of something huge. "Is that why the shopkeepers are leaving Antwerp?"

"Very probably so," said Clement.

"But then the King must not do it."

Clement smiled at her; his hand stroked down the cat's gray fur. "So we must convince him. I can give you work here, if you want it. Not much, and for little money."

She looked around the print shop; the other printers were away in the back eating their dinners. The floor was thick with dust and bits of metal and scraps of paper.

She said, "I can sweep."

"No, no," Clement said. "This is much more dangerous than that. My—" His head jerked toward the rear of the shop. "My assistants are Catholic, or untrustworthy in other ways. I need help in printing for the cause of God."

"Oh," she said.

"I can teach you all you must know in a few days. But it is dangerous work, and I cannot pay you very much, because it comes out of my purse, and not from commissions."

Hanneke turned her eyes toward the fire again. For doing little more than this, her father had gone to prison. Why was Clement not in prison, not dead too? Her mind leapt at that, as if to solid ground. She swiveled her head to look at him, suspicious. Perhaps he was a seducer, who lured people into crimes and gave them to the Spanish. Why would he be so forward in offering help to her, whom he had never known before this?

She said, "I have my mother to consider. If anything happened to me . . ."

Clement was already shrugging, leaning back, his big square hands giving the cat a shove that knocked it off his lap. "Your decision. Whatever you wish. Will you have some dinner with us?"

"I must be going," she said. Perhaps Michael would give her work. She got up to her feet, gathering her shawl around her.

"Can I go part of the way with you?" Clement's boy asked.

"No," she said, short. "I have things to do."

"Please, Hanneke."

She went between them, going to the door, sure now she was right, and they were a den of traitors. "No." The door squealed when she opened it; she went out onto the street, into the sunlight.

"HANNEKE," her mother said, waited for an answer, and got none.

Gone again. What a wicked girl. All things had gone to wickedness, since Mies went away.

She went to the doorway and looked out. The sun was going down. The air was moist and blustery, banging at the shutters on the house and pulling the door back and forth in her hand. Rain soon. The wind tugged on the door and she let it go; it swung outward with a crack against the outside of the house. She laughed.

Without looking back at all she flung herself out and down the stairs, down into the yard, and away to the corner in the very back, behind the privy, where she had hidden her helmet and her sword. The helmet hurt her head and so she had padded it with dry grass. She put it on and took the long wooden spike of her sword in her hand and went out to find the doorway.

Where it was, what it looked like, she had forgotten; all she knew or needed to know was that somewhere there was a door, and if she found it and went in she would leave this world and go back into the old world where the bread was soft and there was butter to have on it, and herring for breakfast, and a bed with white linen that she shared with Mies, and from day to day nothing ill happened. So she went off to find that door.

The first raindrops fell sharp on her helmet, rat-a-tat-tat, rat-a-tat-tat. She strode down the street, swinging the stick in her hand, her sword.

Rat-a-tat-tat—

Not rain. She spun around, and behind her the mob of small children broke and ran in all directions, screaming.

"The witch! The witch!"

She howled at them. Waving the sword, she charged after them; she took a few steps after one, turned, and went off a little way after another. They ran from her, squealing and crying. Out of breath, she stopped in the middle of the street and brandished her sword at them. Fiercely she snorted through her nostrils at them. They were all gone, hiding behind fences, giggling in the alleyways. She turned and started along the street again.

At once they were after her; a volley of small stones pocked the dusty street ahead of her, and a sharp pain drove into the back of her knee. She wheeled around and did battle with them once more, driving them off.

A dog chased her. She was afraid of dogs and she ran, the children streaming after her, the dog yipping at her heels. Swiftly she lost her breath and wanted to stop but the dog would not stop; it seized her dress in its teeth and tore off part of her skirt. If it caught her flesh in its teeth—

The dark was falling. Her lungs fiery, her eyes blind with tears, she ran around a corner and hid behind a tree.

They seemed to have gone. Somehow they had missed her. She leaned against the tree, struggling for breath. The hammering in her ears drowned all other sound. She longed to sit down.

Slowly the banging in her ears subsided, and below it, she heard the snuffling of the dog, searching for her in the dark.

She howled. Mindless with terror, she leapt away from the tree and ran, and they were all back again, the demons, yelling and snapping at her heels. She lost her sword. Screaming, she hurried down the street, while the hell pack scorched her with their flaming breath and fastened their iron teeth in her flesh. Something struck her hard in the back of the head. She fell. Under the weight of their bodies. Smothering in their fur. She pushed herself up onto her feet and ran on.

"The witch! The witch!"

Desperately she yearned to be home, to be with Hanneke, to have the door to shut after her. She turned into a twisting dark street and ran along it, searching for the house, but all these houses were strange. She was lost. The street climbed under her feet. Wheeling, she looked back, down the long winding way.

Empty. No one followed her. She was alone in the dark.

But when she turned and walked on, suddenly they were back again, leaping from the shadows at her, and she broke into a shambling run. She could feel their breath on her back. Their fangs tearing at her. Ahead the canal bridge. Backed like a camel. Up and up into the night, into the soft rain. She labored up the steep rise in the bridge. Something sprang at her from the dark. Huge. She flung out her arms and embraced it. Hot fur; the stinking blast of its breath in her face. She fell backward and it bore her down, pressing its fur over her face, down forever in an eternal fall.

"THE DAMNED Calvinists," said Michael's mother, lunging and thrusting with her arms at the grainy dough. "They brought it on us."

Michael caught the gleam of her eye, watching him obliquely, and knew where this was going. He rolled a handful of dough into a ball, flattened it with his hand on the baking tray, and picking up the jam pot dropped a spoonful of sugary cherries into the center of the circle. He had six more trays to make, and then he could go find Hanneke, no matter what his mother said.

"It's God's curse on us for letting them live here," his mother said loudly. "For not keeping His way and making the damned Calvinists do the same."

"The Estates haven't voted for it yet," Michael said. "Maybe they won't. Maybe it will never happen." Not even the Duke of Alva could collect a tax that had been rejected by the Estates.

"Pah." Lifting the mass of dough into the air, the baker slammed it down again on the floury board with an emphasis that lifted white clouds into the air around her. "If God wants it, it will happen, never mind what the Estates say. And if it happens, boy, you'll find out what hard work means —hard work and lean profits, because we cannot afford to pay the duke a tenth of our makings."

She had been saying this now for days, since the rumors and the printed broadsides began circulating that foretold the tenth penny. The other taxes, on land and real property, she did not seem to mind: of course they had little enough of that. But the constant bleeding of one out of every ten pennies the shop took in had her fierce, a lioness, more adamant than Michael had ever seen her.

She heaved up one of her interminable sighs, now, and began dividing the dough to rise. "I pray every night your father will forgive me for bringing his business to this."

Lately she had been talking much of his father. Michael, who kept the bakery's books, knew perfectly well that under his mother's direction the shop had done steadily better than under his father's, in spite of the equally steady increase in the prices of flour and sugar and fruit, but if he suggested that she ought not to fear his father's reproaches, she flew at him in a fury.

"Get to work," she said, as if he were not working. "By God, boy, you'll know hard work soon enough, soon enough."

Another great tremulous sigh. Michael bent over the dough, ladling jam into the center of another white fluffy square.

The front door opened. His mother threw her head back. "Who's that?"

"I'll see." He went into the front of the shop.

It was Hanneke. Amazed, he circled the counter, pulling off his apron, and at the look of distress on her dear face he stretched out his arms to her, his hands and forearms gloved in flour. "What's wrong?"

"I can't find my mother." She put her hands to her face a moment. When she lowered them again he saw the dark smudges of fatigue beneath her eyes and guessed she had been out all night again, searching. She slumped against the counter. "Michael, have you a bun I could beg? I haven't eaten anything, and I have no money."

He went swiftly to the tray of buns put out to cool on the end of the counter. "You're missing work again."

"I've lost that," she said. She took the bun and began to eat it; he saw how she forced herself to eat daintily, in spite of her hunger, and his heart took an odd beat.

"Michael," his mother called.

"What do you mean, you've lost it?"

She licked the sugar from her fingers. "I have no work anymore—they let me go."

"You'll find something else."

"I've looked."

"Michael!"

"The only task I've been offered is to help the printer Clement turn out seditious broadsides."

"Do you want another bun?"

"No—no, thank you, Michael. You're very kind to me—I don't know where I would have gone, save to you."

"I'll ask my mother if we can hire you here."

She turned her face full on him and laughed. Her eyes were old with strain and exhaustion.

"Michael!" His mother poked her head out the door. "Oh," she said in another tone, and marched out behind the counter, her hands on her hips. "So it's you again."

"I'm going," said Hanneke, and started toward the door.

"It's all your fault!" The baker waved her fist at Hanneke's back. "I'll lose my bakery, and it's all your fault!"

"Mother—" Michael got between the girl and the door. "Don't go," he said to Hanneke, and faced his mother again. "Mother, she's desperate. At least we can give her some bread—"

"Let me go," Hanneke said, and put her hand on his arm: the first time he could remember her actually touching him. "I have to find my mother."

"As well she might be," the baker said. "The hour's short for you Calvinists, young woman, very short indeed. What's wrong with her mother?"

"Don't go," Michael said, and clasped Hanneke's arm above the wrist. "Let me get you some bread to take with you. Don't go." With a little shake, as if pinning her to the floor, he went off swiftly through the shop.

"What's the matter with your mother?" the baker asked.

Hanneke's fingers twisted in the fabric of her skirts. "She's gone. I can't find her. I have to find her." Her voice rang dull as pewter.

"Run off again, has she? She's mad as a March hare, that's the rumor," said Michael's mother.

Hanneke licked her lips; abruptly she turned her face away, and her hands twisted and pulled at her skirt.

"Well, now," the baker said. "You've been searching all night, by the looks of you. You should rest. And pray to God to show you the right way, and then you wouldn't fall onto these things, by God!"

Michael came back, hurrying, his arms laden with loaves of bread. "Here," he said, and thrust them into Hanneke's hands.

"What are you giving her?" his mother cried. "The entire store?"

"She's lost her job also," said Michael. "She has nowhere else to go, Mother; what do you want of me?"

His mother sighed. Flour lay in the creases of her face, in the wiry tendrils of hair that crept from under her tight white cap. Hanneke said, "Thank you," in a voice that shook. The bread in one crooked arm, she stretched out her hand to Michael's mother. "Thank you, Mistress." Some yards separated them; her fingers reached out to midair. The baker lifted her hand, as if she might take Hanneke's, and her head bobbed and some mumbled words dropped from her lips. Her hand fell to her side again, without making contact with Hanneke's, and the girl went out past Michael, out to the street.

Michael shut the door, his eyes on his mother; she surprised him sometimes, which moved him very much—that after so many years his mother was still mysterious to him. She was staring at the door, as if she still saw Hanneke before her; her face had settled into an unreadable mask, not even human, as if cut from stone or made of stones one on the other.

Catching Michael's eyes on her, she turned toward him. "They are doomed," she said. "Their time is very short." Erect as a soldier, she marched back into the kitchen of the bakery, leaving Michael there alone.

"THE LATEST letter from the Prince of Orange!" Clement's boy raised his broadside over his head and waved it. "Read the latest letter from the Prince of Orange!"

He was walking down the edge of the meadow by the river, opposite the new castle that Alva had caused to be built here, and before him was a sea of people. It was like the fair; everyone was dressed in their finest clothes and carried baskets of their dinner, and jugs of beer, and some were playing music on flutes and lutes, and some were dancing. As if Alva had never come here; as if hundreds of Antwerpers had not danced Alva's jig in the sky. The boy's chest swelled with pride and delight at the resurgence of his city.

"Read the latest letter from the Prince of Orange!"

A tall man in a wide-brimmed hat stopped to buy one of the broadsides from him, but others laughed: "That fool!" Orange had disgraced himself. The word was all over Brabant that Orange had sneaked away from his army in France in the dead of the night because he could not pay the soldiers.

Still, it was a good letter, saying things about the people's privileges and the King's responsibility to the law. Clement's boy waved it overhead and called it out, and here and there someone gave him a bit of money and took away the glossy sheet of paper.

The sun was climbing higher into the sky, and already the air buzzed with heat. An early summer, everyone said. The boy walked through the growing crowd, past the families that spread their tablecloths on the grass and laid their babies down on folded blankets and sat to eat and sing, and he wondered why it was that some summers were hot and others were cold, just as he wondered why the wind blew from the north in the winter and from the west in the summer, and why the days were shorter in winter than in summer. The whole world seemed to him an overwhelming question; he could not draw breath for thinking of a new one.

"Read the latest letter from the Prince of Orange!"

There was Hanneke van Cleef. Gripping his bundle of broadsides, he hurried toward her, calling her name. She turned, hearing him, a tall figure, her face marked with strain.

"Hello, Philip." She put out her hand to him.

"Here." He gave her a broadside. Worried, he peered into her face; she seemed shockingly older. "What's wrong? Is it your mother again?"

"She's gone," Hanneke said, in a queer flat voice.

She sat down suddenly on the ground, looking around her, her arms draped over her knees. With one hand she poked the loose threads of her hair back under her headcloth. Her dress was of fine material, worn so threadbare that holes were opening up in the skirt. Clement's boy held his breath a moment out of sympathy. He wished he were older, to comfort her like a man.

She said, "I've never found her. Not since that night. It's been days and days—I don't think I will ever find her."

"She'll come back."

"No." Hanneke shook her head. "She's gone and I'll never know what happened to her." Her voice was colorless as water.

"I'll help you look for her. I'll—"

"There's Michael," she said, more happily.

He looked where she was looking. A tall young man with a basket slung around his neck was walking down across the muddy grass toward them. In the basket were sweet buns: a baker, a peddler. Hanneke was getting up. She was going to him. With a pang like a tooth in his heart, Clement's boy realized that this was her lover.

"Come on," she said, looking down at him. "Come have a cake—they're very good."

He shook his head, too jealous to speak, his eyes burning.

"Come along." Stooping, she reached for his hand, and he jerked it away and hid it under his knee. She stared at him, her brow puckering; an instant later, the peddler called her, and she went toward him, without a backward look. Clement's boy clenched his fists together. He had never felt like this before. Slowly as an old man, he got to his feet, collected his broadsides, and went off through the crowd.

"The latest letter from the Prince of Orange!" His eyes hurt. He wanted to kill her and the peddler both. "Read the latest letter from the Prince of Orange!"

"WHEN WILL the Estates meet?" Hanneke asked, and licked the sugary taste from her lips.

Michael was handing out buns and taking in money as fast as his hands would move. The crowd around him jostled and laughed and fought for space in the line. "At noon," he said. "By that time, there ought to be thousands of people here."

"All of Antwerp!" A jovial man with a fringe of red-yellow beard nodded to them, taking buns and pouring coins into Michael's palm. "We'll show them they cannot tamper with our trade."

"Look." She pointed across the crowd, toward a wagon where a man was standing, his arms raised over his head. "A preacher. There's going to be a sermon."

"The crowd's made them brave," Michael said.

He had sold the last bun. Shrugging off the straps of the basket, he slung it on one arm, and they walked down the field toward the river.

"A sermon," Hanneke said. "It's like the old days." She could not help but smile; it seemed everything was changing and soon would be as it had been.

Although when she thought of that she shrank from thinking how it really had been.

"Come and let's go dancing," Michael said.

"I'm not supposed to dance."

He snorted at her. "I think you'd be much happier if you were a Catholic."

"That's no reason to be one thing or another. To be happier."

"Why can't you dance?"

A troop of boys ran by them, a dog gamboling along beside, yipping and patting at the children with its forepaws. Hanneke watched them run off. "It's frivolous." She looked for Clement's boy, wondering if he were still bound to his task of distributing weighty messages. The odd look he had given her when she last saw him remained in her mind.

"At least we can listen to music." Michael took her hand.

"This is very serious business." She did not take her hand away. It was pleasant to touch him, to have him with her, to have him love her. She smiled at him, and their eyes met; something warm passed between them. She felt her feelings gather and focus, and looked away before he could see. He squeezed her hand. They walked down toward the castle, where the Estates of Brabant would meet to vote on the new taxes.

LUIS DEL RIO, governor of Antwerp, stood on the upper balcony of the castle and looked out over the great crowd before his gates and frowned. He said, "They would not lift a hand when we were carrying off their friends and neighbors. Only threaten their purses and they rise in righteous indignation like pigs deprived of their slops."

His aides murmured behind him. He leaned against the side of the doorway, watching the dancers. In spite of himself he was drawn to these people, to their easy gaiety, to their high spirits. Animals, they were, indiscriminately reveling in the joys of this world. Spiritual matters seemed beyond them. Yet like children they were hard to hate.

It would be easier for him if he could hate them. He turned his back on them and went into the warm room inside the door.

His aides stood around waiting for orders. The two men from the Estates whom he used to present his demands were standing rigidly before the fire, their hands behind them, and their faces very long. When del Rio came in, they fidgeted; they would not meet his eyes. He gestured to a page to shut the door.

"Now," he said. "The real task begins."

"Excellency—" The first deputy took a step forward, his hands appearing in front of him, to make pale gestures against his dark clothes. "Perhaps you ought to postpone the issue of the taxes. Especially the tenth penny. The people are much incensed . . ."

Del Rio went to his desk, near the middle of the room. "The matter is not in my hands. The Duke of Alva requires that we raise these taxes to pay the army."

The second deputy cleared his throat. "Excellency, there is—we cannot . . ." He glanced at his fellow. "I don't really see how we can expect any success in this matter now."

On the desk was the charter for the taxes, written in red and black ink, handsomely decorated with ribbons and seals, a very elegant document. Del Rio picked it up but did not read it; he knew what it said.

He asked, "What time would be better? Orange's army has been chased out of the Provinces into France. Alva has saved you again from destruction. How better to show the gratitude of Antwerp, of all Brabant, than by voting him this present of money?"

Two or three of his aides said, quietly, "Long live the Duke of Alva."
The two deputies did not echo it.

"Excellency," said the first deputy, his hands performing delicate ara-
besques before him, "with such a mob before the gates, it were hard enough
to entice the Estates to vote for something they wanted, but to vote for
something that repels them—"

"Repels them? Are they so ungrateful that they will not give even
this modest acknowledgment of the Duke of Alva's great work?" Del Rio
tapped the document. "If not for Alva, Orange would have invaded the
Provinces! Tell them that. You would have seen again the horrors of
sixty-six—churches sacked and looted, holy relics smashed, priests murdered." He thrust the document at them. "Do you think safety comes
cheap?"

The deputies swallowed simultaneously, their throats working; they
looked at him dumbly, like chickens waiting to be axed. He snorted, angry
at them. If they would not take his arguments, there was small hope the
Estates as a whole would listen. He kicked the desk.

"Then hear this, if you will not hear good sense. Alva is free now. He's
been gone, off at the borders, keeping Orange from burning down your
homes around your heads, but Orange is gone now, and Alva will come
back." He walked up before the two deputies and put his face into their
faces. "Do you understand?"

"Your Excellency—"

"If we do not have these taxes by your good will and free, my men, we
shall have them by force, as what is due us. Do you understand?"

The deputies' eyes shone. Their lips pressed together in thin lines like
old unhealed wounds.

"Are you threatening us, your Excellency?"

Del Rio let out a roar of angry laughter. He struck the man before him
on the chest. "Yes! That's what I am doing." Wheeling, he walked away
across the room. "God, what does it require to move these people—not
sense, not right, not God or king—"

His aides murmured, agreeing with him, as they always agreed with
him. The two deputies bowed and took the document and backed toward
the door.

"As your Excellency requests."

"I do not request," del Rio said. "I require." His hands on his hips, he
strolled across the room again toward the door onto the balcony. Through
the frosty glass he could see down onto the field, where now men on
horseback were riding toward the castle. The deputies to the Estates were
arriving. As they rode on, the people swept up around them, surrounded
them, blocked their path, and shouted and waved papers at them. In their
midst the deputies raised their hands, yielding.

Del Rio put out his hand to the cord of the drapery. They were stubborn

as stone these people, even the Catholics. With a pull on the cord, he drew
the brocaded drapery shut across the glass doors.

"THE DEPUTIES!"

The roar that went up from the people around her seemed to lift
Hanneke a little off her feet. She wheeled with them, toward the castle; like
them all, when she saw the men in the doorway, she shouted. On her left
Michael gripped her arm. They rushed forward, with the others, toward the
castle.

"What's the vote?" The outcry began at the head of the crowd and
spread backward through the whole mass of people, every voice joining the
yell. "What's the vote?"

In the doorway the smiling man with the beard raised his hand for quiet.
Hanneke held her breath. She clutched Michael's hand tight and got an
answering squeeze from him; suddenly before her, she saw Clement's boy
and leaned forward to catch him by the shoulder and pull him back beside
her, her arm around him.

"The vote—" cried the man in the doorway. "The vote is no!"

The roar that greeted this went up like thunder. Hanneke flung her
arms around Michael and hugged him, and whirling she caught Clement's
boy and lifted him up off the ground.

"We've won! We won—we won—"

The boy's arms went around her neck and he hugged her with a
strength that surprised her. An instant later he was scrambling out of her grip
and running off through the crowd.

"We won!" She seized Michael's hands and kicked her feet in a celebra-
tory dance.

"I thought dancing was evil," Michael said. "Who was that? That little
boy."

All across the field, the gathered people of Brabant were cheering,
drinking, dancing; a gun went off somewhere, and she even heard a cheer
of "Vive les gueux!" Hanneke drew her hand from Michael's, wanting some
distance back between them.

"The printer's son. Clement the printer."

"That Calvinist you told me of."

She nodded. "I'm going home, Michael, if you don't mind."

"I'll walk with you."

She started away along the edge of the crowd. The preachers were
getting up on the wagon again, off by the river, and most of the people were
pushing off in that direction to hear the sermons.

"He offered me work, once," she said, thinking of Clement. "Maybe
I ought to go there and help him."

"That will get you in trouble."

"I'm in trouble now, Michael. I have no money and no work and no family."

"I'll give you bread." He seized her hand. "I'll marry you."

"Michael."

"Then you will have a family."

"Michael, your mother will never consent."

"Will you marry me?"

She looked at him, her head tipped back, and studied the fine honest architecture of his face. Mies would never have considered it—a baker's son, a Catholic, no fit husband for the daughter of Mies van Cleef! When she thought of Mies her mood turned heavy. She turned away.

"I can't marry you, Michael. Or anybody. Not now."

"Why not?"

"I can't."

"Why?"

"I just can't, that's all." No way to explain to him how she felt, stripped of everything, home and family, and even her first feeble efforts at caring for herself: as if she herself were nothing, and if she married him what would she become but a shadow of him? And she did not love him. If she had loved him, then she would have been strong enough to marry him, but she did not.

She said, instead, "Clement's son is so clever—you should meet him."

"A little boy?"

"He's very clever, and reads all the time, and has the most interesting ideas."

"He's nine or ten years old. I'm a grown man. Why are you turning me away like this?"

They were walking along the canal now, on the path that led over the edge of the bank. Ahead a house leaned out over the water, reflected in the smooth surface, and a swan fed in the swampy weeds below the wharf. Hanneke kicked a stone into the water.

"Wait," she said. "Wait until I . . ."

When she made no more of it, he said, "Until what?"

"I don't know. But I will, when it's happened."

"I'm a grown man, Hanneke."

In a flash of understanding, she saw that he had to insist on that because he did not entirely believe it—that he wanted her to marry him because grown men married. She looked up at him, feeling something of a new kinship with him, each struggling with the hollows in their lives.

She said, "Thank you, Michael."

"For what?" he said roughly.

She laughed at him, took his hand a moment, and stood up on her toes to let him kiss her cheek. "I'll see you tomorrow, I hope." Before he could answer, she ran off down the bank of the canal, toward the opening to the Kelmans' street.

"THERE'S Antwerp," said the man beside Carlos. "I wish it were Burgos. And me with silver in my purse."

Carlos muttered an indefinite sound in his throat. Ahead the flat foreign plain gave way to a cluster of spires and towers and red-tiled roofs. The sky was overcast and a raw wind blew, but his heart lightened as if the sun burned bright.

"I'll lay down this stick off my shoulders," said the man marching with him, "but I wish I were doing it in Burgos."

"I'll do it gladly in Antwerp," said Carlos.

The sergeant behind them shouted, "Keep the step! March! You—Miguel, Carlos—if you can't talk and march at the same time . . ."

They marched in tight ranks, all feet in unison, with a boom like a giant striding over the flat land. Heavy on their shoulders the pikes rode all at the same angle. They had not been paid in months, but their pride kept them soldiers.

Up ahead, some long-throated fellow began to sing, and they all sang.

> *"Ho! Bring the fairest ladies—*
> *Here comes the tenth!*
> *Ho! Bring—the deepest kegs—*
> *Here comes the tenth!"*

They had not fought at all this campaign, only marched. Carlos was sick of marching. His boots needed mending and the broken sole had rubbed a blister into the ball of his foot. He raised his eyes to the clutter of red roofs ahead of them, the end of the long road, the color bright against the slate-colored clouds, and his heart warmed again with glad recognition.

> *"Ho! Bring—the little virgins—"*

"I'll never see Burgos again," the man beside him said, in a miserable voice.

Carlos spat. "Stop juicing over it. If you took a mind to it you'd make Burgos of any village."

"My girl's in Burgos."

"My girl's in Antwerp."

He had thought of her every night before he went to sleep, her shy diffidence like a deer's; perhaps by now she loved him. Her white thighs like columns against his. He had slept with her in his heart every night since he left Antwerp.

"You've got a woman there? Is she local?"

He nodded, swelling with modest pride at the note of envy in his comrade's tone.

"Is there room enough for two?"

In midstep he wheeled around, twisting from the hips up, and swung the butt end of the pike in a short half circle that ended between his marching partner's legs. Miguel shouted, stumbled, dropped his weapon with a clang, and fell. Carlos gripped the ten-foot pole of his pike with both hands; with the heavy double-edged head off-balance the pike strained like a living thing in his fists. He tamed it, grunting at the effort, brought it up again obedient on his shoulder, like a woman. Behind him the sergeant was beating and kicking and cursing the luckless Miguel to his feet. Carlos, smiling, smoothed his fingers over the satiny ashwood pole and marched along to Antwerp.

ALL THE way across the city, Hanneke thought of her mother, wondering where she was—if she were alive, if lost and hungry and cold somewhere (although it had been two weeks now since she left, and if she were alive, somehow she must have fed herself). If Hanneke would ever know what had happened to her. That tormented her above even the thought of her mother dying, like turning the page of a book halfway through a sentence and finding nothing but blank paper.

She went across Antwerp to Clement's shop and stood at the door, remembering that she had been short with him when he offered her work before and that now the need for her might be over. She lifted her hand to knock but the door opened before she could touch it; there stood the little boy Philip.

He smiled wide as a player's mask. "Hello, Hanneke. Papa—" Turning, he called into the shop, "Papa, it's Hanneke."

Heavy footsteps sounded in the dark depths of the shop. She said, "May I come in?"

"Of course." The boy stepped aside to let her by.

Now her heart was beating faster. She had to find work, or she would starve; she had to have this work of Clement. He stood there, in front of the foremost press, wiping his big hands on a filthy cloth, his face all in shadow. Forbidding, like a minotaur. She had never found him so before, but now he had something she wanted.

She said, "May I talk to you, sir?"

"Hanneke. Please sit down." He came toward her, with his big stained hands gesturing toward the fire and the chairs there, and as the light from the front window swept up over his face he became, again, a friend. "What can I do for you, Hanneke?"

First they sat down, and the boy ran for bread and beer and a piece of cheese and even some old apples, dry but still good-tasting, and a knife to cut them with.

"The baker has cherries," she said, eating. "Can you imagine? Where they come from I cannot know, so early in the year."

"In Antwerp anything can be bought," said Clement.

"These are bright red ones, too," she said. The harmless words made a bridge between them; dreading to ask what she had come here to ask, she needed this contact, this friendliness. He gave her a sliver of the cheese to go with her apple.

"Can I help you, Hanneke?"

"I need—" She raised her eyes to him. "I need work. I must have some way to live."

"Hanneke."

"I know the need is past—now that we've beaten Alva—but I will do anything. Sweep, and scrub—"

"Beaten Alva," he said, in a voice with a peculiar ring. He sat back on the stool, his hand on his hip. "Alva is coming here."

She lifted her head, startled. Into her mind sprang Carlos' image.

"We have not beaten Alva, girl, not by a long haul. There's a long way to go before we've beaten Alva."

"But—I thought . . ." She put the cheese down on the plate, thinking miserably of Carlos.

"We have only declared the war open, as it were," Clement said. "Now he will try to have by force what he could not get by asking, and we must show him that we will not yield to force."

She was staring at him; the low firelight painted his cheek above the beard. His voice was quiet and well modulated, like a schoolmaster's. She remembered once before when words he had spoken had opened her mind up to this, to see the problem huge, her experience of it only one tiny part of something spanning thousands of lives. She sucked in her breath. In her mind she saw a vast landscape, peopled with tiny figures, each in torment, each fighting or running or praying or thinking: the Low Countries. Into that crowd her mother had vanished, and her brother. In it she must find her part.

"Then you do need me," she said to Clement.

His beard parted in a smile. "I need your help, Hanneke."

"Then I will help you."

"But if I were you, girl, I would go. And I would go now, before Alva comes, because when he comes—"

He reached out his arm to the side and took his son in against him, to lean against him.

"Because when he comes there will be such an evil on this city we may none of us escape."

"Are you staying? And Philip?"

"Yes," Clement said. "We'll put our lives in God's hands."

"Then I will stay too, and help you," she said.

"Very well. Come and I'll show you around the shop."

She stood up, to follow him; her gaze fell on the little sliver of cheese on the plate. Quickly she picked it up and ate it, going after him.

SHE WORKED all day sorting type, learning to read the letters backward, and getting her hands dirty, in spite of her surreptitious efforts to wipe off the worst of the black greasy ink that worked its way into the lines of her palms. She did not want Clement to think she was too fastidious for this work. At the end of the day, she swept up the shop for him—a task he usually left undone—and made a great heap of the dust and scraps of paper and rubble in the street outside the door. At last, tired but feeling better than she had in some while, she went back toward the Kelmans' house.

It was too far, she thought, as she walked. She would have to find a place closer to the shop. Cheaper, too. Or perhaps Clement would let her sleep in the shop; there was room, by the fire, and she could pay him a little for her meals. Do extra work for meals.

Thinking up a line of reasoning to convince him of this, she passed the old elm tree at the corner of the Swan Street and walked toward Vrouw Kelman's house, and from behind her Carlos pounced on her.

She screamed. He had her arms, he was dragging her off across the street, into the shelter of the tree, to do what he had done there once before. For some reason her mother leapt into her mind; for her mother's sake she could not let this happen again, and she struck at him with her fists, kicked at him, and tried to bite him. Her mother—

"Hanneke," he said to her, in a voice choked with exertion. "Han-neke—" Crooning. She writhed from side to side in his grasp. His clothes pressed against her face. She was losing; he was bearing her down under him on a pile of dead leaves. She lost her footing and fell. No—she tore one arm free and groped wildly around her on the ground for some weapon, while he pulled her skirts up, his breath in her face, while his hands stroked her legs. He murmured to her in his language. His hand was against her body between her legs, poking his fingers in there. She gathered herself to scream, and her searching hand found the cold hilt of the dagger in his belt.

She drew the knife up over his back and plunged it down, and he stiffened with a jerk, his head snapping up. A groan escaped him. She struck again, pushing him back, and rolled out from under him. Struck again. Again. In the dark he thrashed there on the leaves, gasping, at her feet. He said her name again, loving and hopeless, and shuddered and lay still.

Hanneke backed away from him; she opened her hand and let the dagger fall. Her dress was covered with blood. He was dead, and she had killed him.

She went down on her knees beside him, her hands out to him, but she could not bring herself to touch him. She had killed him. Whatever he had done to her shrank to nothing in the shadow of what she had done to him. She had sent him on to God, Who would deal with him as He had decided, long before Carlos was ever born—his life, his dream of himself swallowed up in the great plan. All gone. Whatever he had been was gone.

Slowly she got up. What she had just done changed everything. She could not go back to Vrouw Kelman's. When the watch found Carlos' body they would go to the Kelmans' first, and Hanneke was covered with blood. Nor could she go to Clement—lead them to Clement; and as she stood up, shaky on her feet, and went out to the street, she realized she could not go to Michael either. She walked a few steps in one direction, turned, and went the other way. It did not matter now where she went. Her legs trembled so that she could barely stand. Slowly she made her way off into the city.

WHEN THE dawn came she was sleeping in the doorway of a shop near the gate. The sound of marching feet jarred her from her dreams, and she raised her head, her eyes sticky with unshed tears and blood splashes and lack of sleep, and watched the first few ranks of soldiers tramp down the broad street past her.

The sun was rising. The horizontal light struck their round helmets and the edges of their pikes in ripples, like sunlight on the water. The pikes feathered the air. They marched in step, their arms swinging in unison, so that they seemed not to be individual men but one great beast that crawled along the street on thousands of legs, piercing the air with thousands of spines.

Now a banner passed her, a square of cloth that fluttered in the wind with a heavy thumping crack, on it the quartered arms of Spain—Leon and Castile and Aragon and Portugal, the lions, the castles of fairy tales.

She got to her feet. More ranks of soldiers swung past her; they sang, and some shouted at her, and a few made lewd gestures with their fingers. She wondered if they saw she was covered with blood. What they would do if they knew it was Spanish blood.

Another rank of flags was approaching, three huge banners held up by men on foot, while behind them a man on a black horse banged away at two drums slung across the withers of his mount. In his wake came a single rider.

She took two steps closer. The tall figure held her fascinated gaze, his hair shining silver under his flat black hat. He sat straighter than the pike-staffs on his horse. No decoration relieved the black sobriety of his coat. He might have been a Calvinist, so plainly did he dress. His spurs chimed with each step of his horse.

Alva, she thought. That is the Duke of Alva.

She sank back into the doorway, her eyes following him as he rode off down the street. Evil has come here, she thought, remembering what Clement said, and knew it was true.

THE TRUMPETS blared again, ahead of him, behind him; their brass voices echoed off the buildings on either side. Alva rode with one hand on his hip, the reins slack in the other, his eyes aimed straight ahead, through the forest of pikes.

No one had come to greet him. No cheering throngs crowded the street of Antwerp, no schoolchildren performed pageants of welcome, no official made speeches of formal gladness at his coming. Only the cold faces of the buildings watched the entry of the Spanish army.

If his heart raged at the insult, his face would not show it. Trained from babyhood in the service of the King of Spain, he knew better than to show what he felt. He would avenge the insults soon enough; the gilt-trimmed buildings with their ornate stepped roofs and elegant glass windows might stand proud against him now, but he would shame them low as hovels soon enough.

A horseman was trotting up the side of the street toward him: one of his officers. Beyond, through the spreading bare branches of the trees, the high towers showed of the new castle where the Estates met. He touched his lips with his tongue. The excitement in his guts tightened and coiled like a spring. The young officer wheeled his horse around to ride beside Alva's and saluted.

"His Excellency Luis del Rio is waiting at the castle to greet you, my lord."

Alva's head bobbed once. "Very good. You may tell him we will meet him at once."

The young man saluted and reined his horse around and galloped away. Alva's horse tossed its head, wanting to follow, but the duke kept to his slow walk. Only now he let himself smile.

His men filled up the broad field before the castle, rank on orderly rank, and opened a lane between them to the main gate. Alva rode down into the castle, through the unfinished wall, into the newly paved courtyard.

Luis del Rio was waiting there, in ceremonial dress, with his aides behind him. When Alva dismounted, he stepped forward, his smile stiff.

"Welcome to Antwerp, your Excellency."

"You may make me welcome," Alva said, pulling off his gloves, "in a more substantial way. Have you done my orders?"

"Yes, your Excellency. Even now—"

Del Rio gestured toward the gate. Alva turned. Through the gate he looked back up the field, up the broad straight lane between his troops.

Down that lane little groups of his men were coming, and in their midst each group led a prisoner, a halter around his neck. Alva smiled.

"I thirst," he said, and instantly a young man leapt forward with a cup of cold wine.

As he drank, the first of his prisoners marched into the courtyard. Seeing del Rio, the man called out, trying to break from his captors' arms. "I am a deputy of the Estates! You can't do this to me . . ."

Seeing Alva, he lost his voice. His eyes blinked rapidly. Rapidly he was hustled off into the castle.

One after another, by twos, by threes, the other deputies were brought to the castle. Alva stood watching them enter. Every man who cried out, every indignant word, fell like balm upon his soul. Patient as a mother, he waited for the last laggard vote to appear, to complete his gathering of the Estates.

They could not bring them all; some had escaped, hearing of his coming, and some lived outside Antwerp. But they brought enough, and in the end, with two pikemen standing beside each deputy, they signed the proclamation Alva had brought with him, announcing the royal tax on the tenth penny of every sale in Antwerp.

"SHE IS not here," Vrouw Kelman said, when Michael knocked on her door. "Carlos is gone, too." She clutched her dressing gown tight over her breast; her face was older than her years with strain. "Something's wrong. Did you hear the soldiers pass this morning? Something is awfully wrong."

Michael said, "She's not here? When did she leave?" But already the housewife was shutting the door. He turned and went down the walk to the gate.

He started away toward Clement's shop. Maybe she had stayed there the night. He remembered how she said he might give her work there.

When he came out onto the broad street before the Bourse, there were soldiers everywhere, banging on the doors of the shops and marching along the street. He swerved to avoid them. They were after the Calvinists again. Two of them were dragging a bearded man out of a doorway. He turned quickly to keep from seeing that.

In Clement's shop he found the printer hunched over his big press, listlessly setting the bits of lead into the frame.

"Have you seen Hanneke?" Michael asked.

Clement shook his head. "They took my boy," he said.

He lifted his face, smudged with black ink. Through the stains, tears like drops of lead coursed in an unceasing stream.

"Who took him? Why?"

"The soldiers. He was out carrying around broadsides of the Prince of Orange's letter—they took him to the castle."

Michael's throat was dry. He swallowed down his doubts and panic and carefully unkinked his knotted fists. He said, "They'll let him go. He's only ten."

Clement covered his face with his long blackened hands. In Michael the urge grew to reach out and comfort this wretched man whose heresies had doomed his only child. But he had to find Hanneke, and he went away.

He wandered from quarter to quarter of the city, never finding her. Once a double file of soldiers marched past him, and he stood in a doorway and watched them go by, hating them with an intensity that frightened him. Men like him, Catholics like him, subjects of the same king. What had he to fear from them? Yet he knew they were his enemies now.

In the German quarter, where the breweries were, he overheard people arguing about the tenth penny, whether foreigners had to pay it, whether Alva had the right to levy it on them. On the door of the greatest brewery was a broadside of Orange's letter against the tax. Michael stared at it, thinking of the little boy who had brought it here. A big tow-headed German went up to the door and ripped the broadside down. Balling it up in his fist, he flung it into the gutter. Michael walked quickly away.

He crossed the Grand Place again, no longer empty. All across the wide cobbled square, men were unloading lumber from wagons, and hammers were beating nails into wood. The ringing of the hammers echoed off the high fronts of the buildings, with their extravagant gilt decoration, their multitudes of windows that glared back the sunlight. Michael walked through the midst of the rising structures in the Place; he refused to think about them, standing like a new city all around him. As he reached the far side of the square, the clamoring rhythms of the hammers approached each other, met for a few strokes of accidental unity, and diverged again on their separate courses. Michael plunged down a side street, looking for Hanneke.

A T NOON Michael still had not come back. His mother swore under her breath, using a favorite oath of her husband's, and pulled shut the shop door. There were three little and two big loaves left on the racks and she piled them on a tray and took them into the back, to have for dinner when Michael finally did come home.

She emptied the till into a sack and put it under the counter. With a damp cloth she scrubbed the racks until they gleamed.

While she was sweeping the floor, her mind still occupied with grumbling at Michael, who spent all day now with that Calvinist girl, there came a knocking on the door.

She looked through the front window. A man in an odd green coat stood under the bakery sign. Only after she opened the door did she see the squad of soldiers in the street behind him.

"What do you want?" she said loudly, to cover the fluttery panic in her belly.

"The tenth penny of your receipts." The man in the green coat pushed his way in past her, into her shop.

"Not from me," she said, backing away from him, the broom between them. "I'll not pay your Spanish tax."

He went to the till. Behind him the six soldiers marched single file in through the door. The baker wound her fingers around the haft of her broom, the inside of her mouth pasty with fear, while the tax collector rummaged through the till and the drawers around it, looking for money. Abruptly she thought of Michael. What if he came back now? What if he got in a fight with these soldiers?

The tax collector wheeled on her. "Where is the money?"

"I have no money," she said. "I sold nothing today."

"I want the tenth of your receipts for the past week." He loomed over her, his arms swinging at his sides. "And every week hereafter I shall expect the same amount, or better."

"One tenth of nothing is nothing," said the baker stoutly. "I've had the shop closed this week. I've sold nothing." He was too near her; suddenly she found it hard to breathe. She started past him into the back of the store. "You'd better go. I have nothing for you."

He caught her by the arm. Painfully tight, the grip brought her up stiffly onto her toes, tears in her eyes. "One more time," he said. "Where is your money?"

"I have no money," she said.

He dragged her toward the door. Her arm was numb to the shoulder, and a stabbing pain crossed her chest. "I'm a good Catholic," she cried, and stumbled on the threshold. The soldiers surrounded her. The tax collector had a rope. She gasped. But surely they were only trying to frighten her. They would not really hurt her. "I'm a good Catholic," she said again, and they put the rope around her neck.

She screamed. *Michael,* she thought. *Michael*—"I'm a good Catholic," she said again, and they hauled her up to hang by the neck from the sign of her bakery shop.

SINCE Alva had first entered Antwerp, his soldiers had been busy rounding up a flock of victims. Two days after his entry into the city, when the gallows were ready, he had these people taken out into the Grand Place and hung. Hanneke watched in the crowd.

They brought Clement's boy to the gallows and pulled him up by the neck, but he was too light to die that easily. He swung at the end of the rope, screaming, until the executioner jumped up and caught the boy's legs and hung his whole weight from them, and so the boy died.

Hanneke went down by the river. She did not weep; there were no tears left in her. There was nothing left in her at all. She had nothing, neither father nor mother, neither home nor hearth. Alva had scoured away everything save her life from her.

When she reached the gate of the city, swarms of people were already flowing out through it. They carried bundles of clothing and food on their backs and their children in their arms. Their faces all seemed the same to her, blank and dull with the pitiable things they had seen. No one spoke. The little children cried and stretched out their arms toward Antwerp, but their parents walked on, their backs to their city and their past. Hanneke walked with them, going east, toward Germany.

10

HE MOON was setting. With it, the light fitful breeze that had murmured all night in the rigging of the *Wayward Girl* died to a flat calm. Jan shifted his weight, slack on the little perch at the top of the mast, and rubbed his hand over his eyes; he blinked and worked his face to ease muscles stiff from long staring into the distance. He braced his foot on the opposite rail of the lookout and turned his gaze south again over the trackless sea.

Stuck up on top of the mast, the lookout exaggerated every rolling action of the ship; the sea seemed to rise and fall in huge parabolas around him. Jan liked being up here. Now they were standing out far enough from the mouth of the English Channel that the *Wayward Girl* rode the broad ocean swells rather than the choppier waves of the narrow seas, and the action of the ship made him sleepy. He fought a jaw-cracking yawn.

"Jan!"

That was Pieter, at the foot of the mast, his shape foreshortened to nothing but a head. Jan leaned out over the edge of the platform.

"Nothing yet," he called.

The old man stalked away without a word. He was always thus before a fight. Being only one of a dozen ships in the Beggar fleet did not help his mood. Jan glanced around behind him, looking northeast, up the Channel. No sign of them. But they were there, waiting just below the horizon; when the sun rose, perhaps he would pick out a masthead, another lookout. Meanwhile . . .

In the east the sky was turning pale. A lick of a breeze cooled his cheek.

He watched the southern horizon. His thoughts rambled away into daydreams, the ships he would command someday, the battles he would fight, the gold he would spend. He imagined the women who would lust after him, a famous sea captain with a heavy purse. Big-breasted women who would lie in his lap. He slid his hand down under his belt into his breeches. The other sailors talked about it all the time, what they did with women.

Hard and aching, the thing throbbed in his hand. In silent desperation, he pulled on it, ashamed, wanting only to ease it.

The breeze stiffened. The *Wayward Girl* leaned over, a rolling wave passing under her keel. The sky overhead was creamy white. Far, far down the sea, at the very edge of the world, something red moved.

He sat bolt upright; he yanked his hand out of his pants. The world tilted away from him, streaming with dawn light, the horizon a blur of pale sea and white sky. There, among the golden clouds, the spot of red moved like a jewel.

"Pieter!"

Down on the deck, feet pounded. Jan leaned over the edge of the lookout for the lantern hanging off the mast, lifted it up by the wire handle, and unshuttered it, to let the gleam of light through. So close to daylight, perhaps the lantern would not show to the ships watching, far to the north. He masked it a moment with his hand, counting in his head to five, lowered his hand, and let the light shine for a count of five.

"What is it?" Pieter bawled, below.

"Sail," Jan called. "Break out the pennant—I think we'll need it." During the day, they were to use the pennant for a signal.

He hung the lantern up again and stood on the lookout platform, his feet widespread, stooped until he had his balance on the reeling masthead. The wind whipped his hair across his cheek. Turning his eyes south again, he searched a long moment among the furrows and billows of the sea, until the sail leapt out again from the background of cloud and wave; now he could clearly see the red cross on the sail. The Spanish fleet was making its run for the English Channel.

That fleet carried the silver to pay Alva's army in the Netherlands. Jan's chest swelled. To fight the Spaniards was good enough. To get rich into the bargain made it excellent. He bellowed, "Sail ho! Sail off the larboard beam!" Reaching out for the ratlines, he swung his body off the lookout and raced hand over hand down toward the deck.

The crew of the *Wayward Girl* were sleeping on the main deck. At his shout they rolled out of their blankets and leapt to their feet. Jan dropped into their midst. Here it seemed darker, low to the sea, the steep black ocean waves rising above the rail before the ship climbed them and the seas passed under her. The crew hurried around him; their faces bleary with sleep, they stowed their blankets and stretched and yawned and tugged their clothes straight. Mouse popped up through the forward hatch with a fisherman's flat basket full of bread. The sailors fell on it. Behind them old Pieter walked down the deck from the stern.

Jan strolled over to the rail, near the brass culverin, his hands tucked into the sleeves of his canvas jacket. The sharp dawn air turned his skin rough with gooseflesh. He was hungry, but his stomach danced with excitement; he had no wish to eat. He stood by the gun, looking out over the empty sea, until his uncle came up beside him.

"Good morning, Uncle."

The old man growled at him, scratched fretfully at his beard, and hugged his arms around him. "This cold's got me. It's a wonder I can walk." He stamped his feet on the deck; one of his knees cracked like a green tree limb. "Where away's the dirty Don?"

"Off the larboard beam three points south," Jan said. "Hull down still from the masthead. And right in the wind's eye, where you said they'd be."

Mouse ran down the deck to them, his arms laden with cold biscuit. Jan took two or three chunks of the hard bread and put them inside his jacket. Old Pieter waved away the food. He put his hand up to sample the wind.

"Well, well. We've got a few hours yet to say our prayers. Did you signal Lumey?"

"Run up the pennant," Jan said. "It's too day-bright for the lantern."

Mouse bounced and jumped around them, his face glowing, his skewed eyes looking off in all directions. "Let me do it! I can do it—"

The two men brushed by him, ignoring him, and went to the locker at the foot of the mast. Pieter opened it with the key on his belt and bent over the folded cloth inside. Mouse pulled on Jan's arm.

"What can I do? Tell me, Jan—I want to do something!"

Jan removed his arm from the boy's grip. "Don't bother me now."

Pieter straightened, the long red pennant they had made in Plymouth unfolding from his hands. He clipped it to a halyard on the mast and ran it up to the top. Mouse danced around him.

"Can I do it? Let me do it!"

" 'Sblood," Pieter snarled. "Get this little devil away from me!"

Jan grasped the boy's shoulder. "Look, Mouse, we need someone to go up onto the lookout and watch for signals from Lumey. Will you do it?"

The boy's face went bright red with eager excitement. He nodded vigorously and leapt into the rigging, climbing like a monkey toward the mast top, where the red pennant fluttered now.

"Good," old Pieter said. He reached for his pipe and tobacco. "We'll keep a northwesterly course as long as the wind holds. With luck she'll blow fair all morning. The main thing is to keep the Dons well off the French coast so that Lumey and Sonoy and the others can slip around behind them and steal the weather." He tipped his head back, his beard jutting out over his collar. "I don't like the looks of the sky, boy-o."

Jan said nothing. They had gone over and over the plan; he thought Pieter was talking to ease his soul. The sky was clear enough, a few low clouds along the horizon, but nothing to be afraid of. Anyway the ship sailed very well in wet weather. The pungent odor of his uncle's pipe tinged the air and Jan moved away a few steps.

"Well," Pieter said, "let's to it."

Jan walked the few paces up the deck to the wheel. "Hands to the braces! Ready to make sail." With a flourish he pulled free the rope that lashed the wheel. Pieter went by him, up the three steps to the stern deck, to con their course.

T HE CREW raced around the deck, their bare feet nearly soundless on the worn boards. The mainsail and the jib went up with a rattle of salt-stiffened canvas. At once the nimble little ship answered the wind. Pieter felt her tremble under his feet like a hunting dog that hears the horn, and the sea chuckled against her side.

Jan, on the main deck below him, took the ship up a few points higher in the wind, let her fall off a little until the sails luffed, and laid her back on course, all as Pieter had shown him, to get a feel of how she was today, how the wind and the sea suited her. Pieter fought against a smile. Jan was a good sailor. The old man sucked the tobacco smoke into his lungs, enjoying the heady taste. The crew obeyed his nephew as well as they did Pieter —better, some of them, since Jan could knock them down, and Pieter could not.

He knew the guns better than Pieter; he had been at practice, while they waited for the Spaniards, and Pieter had seen him blow empty wine tuns out of the water at the distance of a cable length—no small feat, all things considered, although the guns the Spanish had been kind enough to install in the *Wayward Girl* were the best Pieter had ever seen and had made even Lumey envious.

Jan could shoot and he could sail, but one thing Pieter could not give him. The old man raised his eyes again to the gray lowering sky. The sun had risen but no blue showed through the veil of clouds, and near the eastern edge of the world the sky was black as mourning.

Jan took nothing seriously that he could not control himself. Pieter shook his head. Only time would teach him that.

Their work today was easy enough. The Spanish galleons were sailing up into the Channel, the wind over their sterns and their course laid for the Low Countries. The *Wayward Girl,* handier at sailing off the wind, would play with the huge ships like a dog with a phalanx of bulls, teasing and taunting, drawing them on. If the Spanish did nothing else, the *Girl* would keep them occupied while the rest of the Beggars got behind the galleons. With any luck, the Dons would lose their tempers at the baiting and try to close quarters with the *Wayward Girl,* and then Pieter meant to maneuver them out of formation, so that when Lumey came the four galleons would be helpless to act in unity, and easy victims of the swift and well-armed Dutch fleet.

He stood watching the sea to the south. Now he could make out the topsails of the galleons. The wind filled the pleated sails and drove on the hulls like plows through the heavy seas. Huge as they were, they could not turn too suddenly, nor turn too far, without losing the wind and going dead in the water. He was determined to make them turn, to follow him, to join in long-range shooting if necessary. His skin tingled. As usual, when action offered, he wished himself well away from here, somewhere warm and safe, with the solid ground under his feet. And now the rain was beginning to fall. He went forward a few steps, to call to Jan to alter course, and bring the ship down on the four great galleons sweeping north.

THE FOUR Spanish galleons sailed in a kind of wing shape, the biggest
ship in the middle and slightly ahead of the others. Mouse watched them
from the lookout, his heart racing with excitement. The Spanish crosses on
their sails were clearly visible now from the deck. He had seen no signals
from the other Beggars, but no one had called to Mouse to come down, and
he liked it here, swooping and gliding through the air so far above the sea.
Although now it looked as if it might rain.

Far below him Jan stood by the wheel, a mop of yellow hair on a little
block of body. From here there was no telling how much bigger he was than
the other men. Mouse leaned over the platform, looking down at Pieter with
his cold pipe sticking out from his face, and Red Aart by the stern guns, and
Marten at the main brace on the starboard side.

As he was craning his neck to make out his friends from this vantage
point, the order came to bring the ship about; she lay over and the masthead
swayed, and he had to wrap his arms around the lifelines to keep from
falling.

They sailed across the bows of the Spanish fleet, so close Mouse saw the
men in fancy red and green coats, trimmed with gold, who gathered on the
foredeck of the flagship. The Spanish officers watched the *Wayward Girl* pass
by them and did nothing. *Cowards,* Mouse thought, watching the men in
their bright-colored clothes on the high forecastle. The first drops of rain
struck him.

The wind was cutting now. He started down the rigging and remembered he had not been ordered down. If he wanted to be a sailor, he had
to obey orders.

Jan was wearing ship, to bring the *Wayward Girl* around for another
run past the Spaniards. Mouse pulled his arms inside his sleeves to keep
warm.

The wind was rising. It sang in the rigging like pipes, and it was cold,
cold enough now to make the boy shiver. The ship was slicing through the
water to pass by under the sterns of the Spanish galleons. Now the rain was
falling harder, thick enough to veil the bowsprits of the four galleons in a
gray haze. Mouse squinted to see better. He thought the half-visible flagship
was changing course, and he opened his mouth and leaned out from the
lookout to yell to Jan, and then the wind whirled and swept over the
Wayward Girl from the bow and took every sail aback. The ship lurched, and
Mouse fell off the lookout.

He landed in the main shrouds, but his arms were still fast in his sleeves,
and he could not save himself. He screamed. In his black terror he screamed
for Jan. Sliding through the heavy knotted rigging, he hit a block and
bounced overboard into the sea.

His shirt tore; with a madman's strength he wrenched one arm free, then the other, while the icy ocean closed over his head and he plummeted down into the depths. He thrashed with his legs. The sea covered him. His lungs were nearly empty. Suddenly his head broke into the air again and he could breathe. He used the breath to scream. The ocean enveloped him to the ears. High over his head, the rail of the *Wayward Girl* seemed miles away, her side slipping by him faster than he could lift his arms to swim toward her. His trousers clutched his legs; he kicked out, trying to stay afloat. The rain struck his face. The ship was passing by him, they were leaving him behind. He wailed. An instant later a rope flew uncoiling in the air toward him.

The end slapped the surging wave in front of him. He thrashed toward it, his mouth full of salt water, and caught the fat wet round of hemp. It slipped out of his hands. He floundered through the water after it. The ship already seemed miles away, its plain round stern higher than a rooftop.

His fingers grazed the rope again. This time he seized it with both hands and wrapped it around his waist. While he was fumbling to knot it, a boom of thunder crashed through the rain.

A moment later something hit the water to his left, bounced over him, and fell into the sea to his right; the spray struck his face. A cannonball. The Spaniards were shooting at him. A whine of fear left him. He could not manage a knot in the rope. His hands were too cold, and now the rope was sliding through his fingers again. It swung up taut out of the sea. He dug his fingernails into the twisted fibers, lowered his head, and gripped the rope in his teeth.

The sea rushed by him. His legs felt heavy. Another far-off drumroll of sound: another Spanish broadside. He was dragged up through the air, free of the water, banged painfully against the side of the ship, and dropped onto the deck.

Someone threw a coat over him. They were running all about, shouting orders, readying the guns to fire, and no one paid much heed to Mouse. Shivering and numb with cold, he dragged himself over to the foot of the mainmast and pulled the coat around him and said his prayers, over and over, sunk in a bone-rattling terror.

JAN SAW Mouse fall into the sea, and at once he shouted to the men to throw the sails aback, to take the ship out of the wind. Wheeling, he went in a single bound up the steps to the stern deck.

"What are you doing?" Pieter grabbed his arm.

"Mouse is overboard." Jan rushed to the rail; Red Aart and Marten ran up beside him, and Aart stooped for the line kept coiled by the stern cleats.

Pieter struck the rope out of his hands. "The Spanish are all around us—forget the boy—get to the braces—sail the ship!"

Jan flung a broad look around him. In the slanting rain, the four galleons loomed up like sea monsters from the waves, close enough that now he heard a shout from one of their decks. The flagship was closest. Her broad mainsails shivered; the great ship was coming about, lumbering around toward the *Wayward Girl,* and the *Girl*'s sails were flapping, her power gone. She lay dead in the water as a piece of driftwood.

He gulped. A cold fear gripped him. In a moment the Spanish would be on them. But there in the smooth water of the trough of the wave was a round bobbing head, and an arm shot up into the air beside it, and he heard, or thought he heard, his name called.

"Throw that rope." Bending, he gathered up the snarl of line, whipped it rapidly into coils, and flung the end out toward the boy struggling in the lap of the sea.

Pieter swore at him. Turning on his heel, he marched away across the deck. The rain was falling harder now; Jan could barely make out Mouse's head in the dark water, but he felt a tug on the line.

"Pull!"

He and Aart and Marten pulled on the rope, drawing it in hand over hand. Within seconds, by the slackening of tension in the line, Jan knew the boy had lost his hold.

"Oh, God," Aart murmured. He beat his fist on the rail, leaning out over the stern, his face pebbled with the rain. "God, Mama, Mama, help him—"

Jan shot him an amused look; he had never heard anyone pray to his mother before. He himself was calm now. The decision to save Mouse had driven away his fear. Swiftly he stripped off his canvas jacket and climbed onto the rail, ready to leap into the sea after Mouse.

"He's got it!" Aart pulled on the rope. "I can feel it—he's got it—"

A boom of gunfire drowned his words. All the men on the stern ducked, although the cannonballs splashed into the sea well to larboard of them. Jan leapt down to the deck again. The Spanish flagship was rolling down through the misty rain toward them, her bows splitting the seas. He grabbed the rope.

"Heave!"

They dragged the boy in over the stern; his face was blue-gray, and he lay gasping on the deck at Jan's feet like a dying dolphin.

"Trim that mainsail!"

Jan threw his coat on top of Mouse. Still hunched over, he lifted his head to look up, up at the bows of the galleon. Beneath its bowsprit was a huge red leaping lion with gilt teeth. A musketeer leaned over the rail above the figurehead, swinging his gun around to aim straight at Jan.

"Here!" His uncle thrust a smoking piece of slow match at him.

Jan took the match; he lowered his gaze to the stern gun. It was loaded.

Pieter, even in his bad temper, had lost no time. While the others were saving Mouse, he had brought the stern gun up ready to fire. Jan put the match to the touchhole.

The musketeer saw, and winced back, jerking up his gun. The musket fired, venting a tiny puff of smoke that the wind tore away; and the shot went off into the sky. An instant later the cannon roared. Across the narrowing strip of water between them the ball shrieked in its passage like a woman. Jan heard distinctly the whack of the ball striking the galleon's timbers. The rail exploded in a shower of splinters and wood dust. Jan wheeled around, toward the *Wayward Girl*'s mast and mainsail.

Aart and Marten were hauling in the swinging mainsail. The wind caught it with a crack. A gust of rain lashed the deck. Jan gripped his uncle's shoulder an instant and sprang down to the main deck, behind the wheel.

"Three points to starboard!" Pieter shouted.

The wind lifted the *Wayward Girl* up like a bird on the wing. She bent to her course and slipped away from the galleon into the rain and the mist. Jan glanced back over his shoulder. Above the stern, where his uncle stood, his pipe clamped in his teeth and his arms locked behind him, the towering masses of Spanish sail loomed up, still perilously close. But the *Girl* had the wind. The gap between them widened. The red crosses faded into the driving rain.

A roll of thunder pealed across the sea; the galleon had fired its guns. Something wailed over Jan's head, and he felt the deck shiver under his feet. His ship was hit. The topsail halyards snapped and the little sail fluttered out like a flag. A block crashed down through the standing rigging to the deck, hit the deck, and slid over against the rail.

"Two points starboard!" Pieter shouted.

Jan brought the ship up higher yet into the wind. Trust his uncle's orders. An instant later he felt the wind change against his cheek. The old man had read the sky somehow and known the breeze was veering. The *Girl* was flying now, in spite of the damage done her by the Spanish guns. Rapidly she raced away into the gloom of the rain. Jan sighed.

His uncle said, above him, "That was damned silly—to chance the whole ship for a fool of a boy."

Jan gripped the wheel, which yanked and pulled on his hands; the wind was rising, and the seas were towering up into mountains all around them. "I sent him to the lookout," he said. "If not for me he would not have fallen."

"Pagh," Pieter said. "He's an idiot. God's mistake."

Jan licked the salt from his lips. He was half-naked, and the cold stiffened his muscles; he could feel the ship beginning to lose way against the sea. A following wave broke over the stern quarter and the spray drenched him. He gasped at the chilly onslaught of the water.

"What's the damage?" he called back to his uncle.

"Nothing, compared to what will happen if we don't rig for storm running. Get the mainsail down; we'll run under the jib awhile."

Jan called orders. The storm had engulfed them; there was no need now to worry about the Spanish. No time to think about them anyway. He called to Marten to take the wheel and went forward to supervise the setting of the jib.

II

THE STORM blew all night, shoving the *Wayward Girl* ahead of it, and when it finally gusted away into a pale calm dawn, the ship was far up the Channel, missing a few spars and some of her rigging. The Spanish ships were nowhere in sight, and after such a storm the Beggar fleet was unlikely to be where it was supposed to be.

Pieter said, "The wind's pretty fair for Plymouth. We could look in there and see who's taken shelter from the dirty weather."

The rest of the crew agreed with that, and they sailed off to the coast of England, making Plymouth Sound in three tacks.

Plymouth was packed full of ships as a barrel of herring. The four Spanish galleons lay in the deep harbor. Poor sailors off the wind that the galleons were, yet they fared well in storms and they looked fit as they had when Jan last saw them. On the bow of the great flagship men were working to repair the broken railings. Half a dozen English and French merchantmen shared their anchorage.

Between the waters of the Channel and these big ships, sleek and fat like hens in their roosts, lay the Sea Beggars, a crowd of small, light ships, some considerably storm battered. One at least was sinking: the *John Calvin,* one of Dirk Sonoy's ships, lay to her gunports in the water, while small boats swarmed around her trying to keep her afloat.

Jan leaned against the rail. Old Pieter was steering the *Wayward Girl* into port, under the command of the pilot; Jan, left idle, could turn his whole attention to the work around the *John Calvin.* On the other Dutch ships a constant bustle of men and small boats saw to the repairing of storm damage. On board Lumey's ship *Christ the Redeemer* a complex of ropes rove through blocks at masthead and deckline was hoisting a spar up the mizzenmast.

Jan glanced at the Spanish ships again. He thought if they were clever they would run for it now, while the Beggars were laid up.

Bright pennants fluttered up and down the mainmast of the flagship. Signals to the other ships. Maybe they were commenting on the arrival of the *Wayward Girl.* At this flurry of attention from the mighty Spaniards, Jan's chest swelled; his head grew lighter with a sense of his own gravity. He strolled over toward his uncle, handling the wheel.

"Well, I'm for going ashore and sleeping in a bed for once, as long as we're here."

"Oh, you are. While I'm seeing to the ship by myself, I suppose."

"Uncle, we'll be here for days, maybe for—"

"Will we?" Old Pieter spared him half a glance. "What if the Dons run for it? Stand aside and let me take my ship to anchor."

Jan stepped back. Under her jib alone, the *Wayward Girl* glided over the slack water of the harbor, past the first rabble of the Beggars. Old Pieter called orders in a rasping voice; the hands ran to back the jib. Jan looked toward the town. The sun was setting, bleaching the sky, and the clutter of buildings along the wharf was already dark in shadow. In the town behind, a church bell was ringing.

The *Wayward Girl* drifted toward a clear mooring not far from the *John Calvin.* At a bellow from the old man, Marten let the anchor run.

Jan thought an angry oath at his uncle. Plymouth no longer looked so strange to him. If not home, it was a familiar place to him now, with soft beds and good, hot food—hot food, anyway; he longed to go there as if it were a real home. Already the other sailors were gathering by the mast, where old Pieter stood filling his pipe. Most of the men would go ashore at once. Only his own nephew would Pieter hold on board to work. Jan went below, in a rising rage.

Mouse was there by the water barrel, leaning in over the edge to dip up a cupful of the slimy green water. He slid down onto his feet again.

"Where are we? Can I go up and see?"

His face was gray, and even while he talked, a cough struggled up his throat. Jan got him by the arm and pulled him back down the center aisle of the hold, the only space in the dark crowded cave belowdecks where Jan could walk without banging his head. At the end, in the stern, was the tiny room he shared with his uncle, and now with Mouse. He pushed the boy through the little doorway and made him lie down on the straw tick where usually Jan himself slept.

"We're in Plymouth. You sleep, damn you. I didn't risk all our lives to pull you out of the sea just to have you die on me afterward. Now we can start a fire, and I'll get old Pieter to cook you something hot."

"Plymouth." The boy lunged toward the little window in the stern. Jan caught him by the hair and forced him down on the straw tick. The boy coughed again. He had no fever but his face was the color of clamshells. Jan laid the blanket over him.

"If I catch you up out of this bed again I'll beat you top to bottom. Understand?"

Roughly he bundled the blanket over Mouse's body, tucking it in. The contact, the protective tenderness it roused in him, unsettled him. To hide it he cuffed the boy lightly on the side of the head and, going out, he slammed the door.

When he reached the deck again, most of the crew were already gone, riding the overburdened dinghy halfway to the wharf. The shipyard's tender, nearly as big as the *Girl* herself, was lying along the starboard beam, and old Pieter leaned over the rail bargaining for spars and tar and line. Jan loitered by the larboard rail. The crippled *John Calvin* lay between two big flyboats, roped to their railings; only their support kept the drowning ship above the water. The men who had been working on her had gone ashore. She looked deserted now.

A little rowboat from the wharf circled the *Wayward Girl.* The boy at her oars shouted in English. Jan waved to him to come closer.

"I want some bread, good fresh bread, and some cheese, and meat, beef or mutton, or fish." He felt for his wallet for a coin and thumbed up a silver real, which he tossed into the bottom of the rowboat. "Understand?"

"Bread, cheese, beef, and fish," the boy yelled, in bastard Dutch.

"Fetch it back in half an hour, and there'll be two more like that for you!"

"Eh?"

Jan switched to French, holding up his fingers to sign the time and the money. The boy nodded and bent to his oars. Jan went to join his uncle, splicing the broken halyards.

MOUSE said, "I didn't mean to fall."

"Shut up," Jan said. "Don't be a crybaby."

Old Pieter grunted an oath at them; he was rolled up in his blanket on the bed built into the stern bulkhead. The light from the lantern hanging just outside the little round window shone on his face.

Mouse coughed. He seemed stronger, now that he had good food in him.

Jan sat with his back against the doorpost. The three of them filled the tiny cabin so well he had no room to stretch his legs out, which he longed to do, but he was reluctant also to leave Mouse. Caring for the boy gave him something to do, and it was gratifying that Mouse was obviously getting better, although he had never been especially sick.

Somewhere across the harbor a ship's bell clanged. A few moments later the church bells of Plymouth counted out their solemn measures of the hour. From Pieter's bunk came the gentle rumble of a snore. Mouse was asleep also, his mouth open, his hand curled under his cheek. Jan tucked the blanket under him and went through the hold to the main hatch.

There was no wind. When he came up onto the deck the warmth of the air surprised him. Heavy skeins of fog lay on the flat, calm waters of the harbor and veiled the town and sank over the masts of the ships. Jan walked the length of the deck, glad of the room to move. When he turned, by the forecastle, a light caught his eye.

He went to the rail, squinting into the dark and fog. The light bobbed up and down across the water, making for the *John Calvin,* haloed in the mist.

Jan had spent the evening tying knots and sewing canvas. He took this light as an invitation; without a moment's thought, he peeled off his clothes and vaulted naked over the rail of the *Wayward Girl.*

He entered the water as straight as he could, to keep from making much of a splash. When he surfaced, twenty feet from his ship, the light was still there, bobbing and bouncing toward the crippled Dutch ship. He swam after it, his arms working soundlessly below the water's surface.

The light was a little lantern, half-shuttered, on the bow of a rowboat full of men. Reaching the *John Calvin,* the oarsmen shipped their oars. The other men crouched together in the center of the rowboat, working at something.

Jan reached the side of the rowboat and put his head cautiously up over the gunwale. The smell of burning pitch reached his nose. They were lighting a torch, the men in the rowboat; they were going to burn the *John Calvin.*

Jan got his hands on the rowboat's gunwale, ready to heave his weight up onto it and rock the boat over, but before he could move, one of the men looked around and saw him.

It was Lumey de la Marck. Surprised, Jan gaped at him, and Lumey lurched forward and got him by the arm.

"Get in here, sailor boy!"

That ruffled him, that nickname. Jan swung himself over the gunwale, into the midst of the four men, all bent over a torch and a pot of coals.

"What are you doing?" he asked.

"We're going to burn this hulk," said Lumey.

Jan looked from face to face. Out of the water, now, he was cold. "It's Sonoy's ship. Where is he?"

"Why do you care?" Lumey said, in a voice that grated. His huge paw of a hand lay on Jan's shoulder still, and he shook the younger man, like a schoolmaster giving a lesson. "She's finished, this ship. But there's still something she can do against the King of Spain."

"I don't follow you," Jan said.

One of the other men coughed. "We set her ablaze, right? Everybody will think the Spanish did it, and the Englanders will order the Dons out of Plymouth. Then we take them."

Jan said, "Unh." It seemed too obvious to work. He scanned the faces around him, their features faintly picked out of the gloom by the light from the pot of coals; this was Sonoy's ship, and Sonoy was not here, and as slightly as Jan knew the upright little captain he was still sure he had no part in this. Lumey was staring at him, smiling.

"Are you with us?"

They all looked drunk. It was a drunkard's scheme. Jan wiped his hand over his mouth. He glanced across the harbor toward the Spanish ships. He had been idle for hours, and bored, and this work at least promised some excitement. Besides, what could he do to stop it? He nodded.

"Yes. Do it."

Lumey pounded him on the back. The man with the unlit torch dipped the pitchy end into the coals. Jan crouched down in the bow of the rowboat, shivering with cold. He raised his eyes to the *John Calvin,* whose side rose up over him. The ship gurgled, taking on more water.

"We'd better get away fast," he said. "She'll burn like kitchen coal."

Lumey nodded. "We'll make for your ship, say. When the fire gets going, we can stroke back here and pretend to put it out. Cut the tenders here free." He nodded toward the boat that supported the *John Calvin.* The fire was spreading over the head of the torch and the red light licked his face, the round cheeks bristling with beard, the shrewd little eyes almost hidden under his shaggy brows. He smiled again, showing his gappy teeth. "We'll all be heroes."

Jan said nothing; he had his doubts about that. The man with the torch stood up in the rowboat, swung the flaming club once around his head, and threw it up over the rail of the *John Calvin.* They all heard it thump on the deck.

"Now we're off," said Lumey. Sitting down in the rowboat, he reached under the thwart for a little flagon of wine.

Jan slipped over the side into the water and swam toward the *Wayward Girl.* Behind him the rowboat plied its way on creaking oars away from the crippled ship. In the night stillness the sound of the oars groaning in the locks seemed loud as a voice calling. Jan swam to the stern of his ship, where the ladder was let down, and grabbed one of the wooden rungs. The rowboat came after him.

"Wait here," he said to Lumey. "My uncle's asleep."

He glanced up at the little round window in the stern, hoping that was true.

Lumey smiled at him; the leather wine flagon hung limp and empty in his hand. "Have you got anything aboard to drink?"

"No," Jan said, lying, and went up the ladder to the deck of his ship.

His clothes lay in a heap by the rail. He pulled them hastily on, defending himself, he knew, less against the cold than against suspicion. The *John Calvin* looked dark and inert across the narrow gap of water that separated them. Maybe the torch had gone out. But while he was pressing the water out of his hair with his hands, a flame shot up from the waist of the cripple and climbed furiously into the tarry rigging with a crackle he could hear all this way away.

He ran back to the stern, watching the fire seize the ship; within minutes she was blazing from her bowsprit to her rudders. The greedy power of the fire impressed him. Now he wished he had not agreed to this, but there was no way to stop it: the *John Calvin* was doomed. Below him, in the rowboat, Lumey said, "Well, let's go be heroes," and laughed, a wine-soaked giggle.

None of the others laughed. They stroked back toward the *John Calvin* more slowly than they had left her.

Jan leaned against the *Wayward Girl*'s railing, struggling with his regrets, his gaze trapped by the fire, which now was lapping the tenders on either side. On the shore there was an outcry of voices, and little dark figures ran about. He could see them on the wharf because the hellish red-gold flickering light of the fire stretched across the water and danced over the wharves and poked deep into the town behind.

Clouds of dark smoke rolled upward from the blazing ship, hiding the flames a moment. The breeze scattered the smoke, and the rushing fire shone so bright he had to blink, one hand raised to shield his eyes.

All three ships were burning now, the *John Calvin* and the two tenders. Lumey and the others sat in the rowboat midway between the *Wayward Girl* and the blaze, held away by the heat. Other boats were hurrying out from the shore.

"What's all this?"

Jan jumped. He had not heard his uncle come up on deck behind him. Guilty, he turned, pulling his face into a mask.

"What you see. The *Calvin*'s burning."

"Oh? And how did that happen?"

Jan took a deep breath. It was easier to tell the truth. "Lumey set fire to her. He'll blame it on the Spaniards."

The old man glowered at him. Furiously he dug his thumb into the bowl of his pipe. "And you helped?"

"I came on them doing it. There wasn't much I could do."

His uncle stuck the stem of his pipe between his teeth. "What a fool's caper." He nudged Jan with his elbow. "We'd better get ashore. There'll be a night's yelling over this piece of work, and they'll need help to see it go our way."

Jan raised his hand to Lumey, flagging him over. Suddenly he thought of Mouse. If Mouse knew of his part in this, Mouse would think less of him. Ridiculous, even to consider it, the opinion of a half-wit boy. Jan thrust the thought off.

He followed his uncle down into the dinghy. Mouse had never mattered to him before. He resolved to have him matter nothing once again.

The wharves were crowded with folk watching the fire, townspeople in their nightcaps, their cloaks thrown over sleeping gowns, sailors from the inns and taverns who still carried their tankards of ale in their hands, and even small children, peering through their elders' legs. When Lumey and the other Dutchmen tramped up the stone steps to the quayside, the harbor master met them, wearing a frown as fierce as his ceremonial sword. Behind him was a gathering of Englishmen.

He shouted something at Lumey, gesturing toward the fire. Jan could not understand the English, although a word here and there was close enough to Dutch for him to make it out. Lumey spread his feet wide apart and slid his hands under his belt, already burdened with a weight of pistols. He bawled something loud, to reach the ears of the crowd.

Jan understood the word "Spanish." So did the onlookers, who let out a roar.

The air was raw with smoke and cinders, and bits of burning rope and sail were drifting down around Jan. He moved a little away from Lumey, down the stone quay. Dirk Sonoy came out of the crowd near him, his face turned toward his ship; deep lines furrowed his high forehead.

Lumey was shouting, his right arm jerking and milling in the air. The crowd seemed to agree with him. The harbor master folded his arms over his chest.

Down the quay came a band of men with muskets, pushing people out of their way. Two linkboys lit their path. As they passed, the crowd muttered and swore and shook their fists at them. In the midst of the musketeers walked a man in a broad-brimmed hat and a fancy doublet with a high old-fashioned collar. It was the Spanish commodore, who ignoring the angry crowd strode up to Lumey and the English harbor master and shouted into their faces.

The Englishman, confronted by two noisy foreigners, was backing away. Lumey and the Spaniard sneered at one another. Jan turned to Dirk Sonoy.

"What are they saying?"

Sonoy was still watching his ship, burned now to the waterline; great coils of black smoke rolled from her smoldering hull. Slowly he turned his eyes to Lumey.

"He's accusing the Spanish of burning her. The Spaniard's denying it."

"Naturally," Jan said, with force. Sonoy gave him an instant's sideways look, sardonic.

"The Spaniard's saying they're honorable men, not pirates, and anyhow the *Calvin* was already sunk." Sonoy wiped his mouth on the back of his hand. "He's saying we burned her."

The crowd was hooting and jeering at the tall Spanish officer. The harbor master stood with his arms clasped across his chest, his gaze switching from the commodore to Lumey and back again.

Sonoy said quietly, "I had important charts on board. My letters of marque. And other things."

"I'm sorry," Jan said.

Sonoy said nothing. A small, slightly made man, he stood very straight, to use his every inch, and his expression was always sober; now he looked as if he would never smile again. Jan imagined losing the *Wayward Girl*— losing her like this, by the work of his own friends, and put out his hand to Sonoy.

"You have other ships. The Prince will send you new letters."

"She was my first ship," Sonoy said. He shook his head. "Ay, ay, there's something black in it, too, because of her name."

Jan said nothing more, for fear of betraying his own part in it. He wished now he had done something to stop it; even if he had failed, he would feel better about it now. A few feet away from him, Lumey was beating his hands together and shouting, "Revenge! Revenge!" The crowd picked it up, chanting with him. "Revenge!"

The Spaniard stood with his mouth twisted into a grimace. He gestured with one hand and his musketeers closed around him. The harbor master pushed forward. He shoved Lumey to one side and facing the crowd waved his arms and shrieked the mass into a flattering mutter and then into silence.

He made some loud remarks in English, which Sonoy translated into Jan's ear. " 'I am an officer of the Queen! I am not here to do a mob's will, but the Queen's!' "

At the mention of their sovereign the English raised a cheer as mighty as their chanting for revenge. Lumey scowled. Jan thought, *He has lost,* and was startled to find himself pleased.

"Then we'll go to the Queen!" Lumey roared, in Dutch, remembered himself, and bellowed in English.

That silenced everybody. In the hush, with the Spaniards and the English gaping at him, Lumey raised his arms and wheeled around toward his men. "We'll go to the Queen for justice!"

Another cheer went up from the crowd. Sonoy stepped forward.

"You're mad," he cried, and gestured toward the Spanish commodore. "He'll sail as soon as we're gone from Plymouth!"

"We'll have justice from the Queen," Lumey cried. His face was cherry red; he shook his fist in the air.

Sonoy wheeled on the harbor master and spoke a volley of English. The harbor master seemed more inclined to deal with him than with Lumey, and nodded and spoke and finally reached out to shake Sonoy's hand.

"He'll keep them here until the Queen decides," Sonoy said.

The harbor master was looking at Jan, and suddenly he smiled; he said something to Sonoy and struck him jovially on the arm. Sonoy grunted.

"He says we should take you along. He says she likes them dark but she loves them tall."

"What did he mean by that?" Jan asked, startled.

Lumey threw an arm around his shoulders. "Don't you want to be the Queen's lover, boy?" He laughed into Jan's face and beat him over the shoulders and hugged him. "We'll leave at dawn."

LUMEY and Sonoy and Jan hired horses at the hostelry in Plymouth and took the road to London. The farther they got from the sea the more Jan wished he had not come. The road was wild and lonely, traveling through stands of forest and heath, and over hills higher than any he knew in his own country, and from Lumey's remarks he guessed he was being brought along on this adventure as a bait to tempt the lusty and rapacious English Queen. He longed for his ship, where he was master.

They spent the night at an inn, where they all lay down together in a bed so full of fleas and bedbugs Jan could not sleep for his and his companions' scratching.

"It's a longer journey than I remembered," Lumey said.

They went on, following the old Roman road, straight as a ruled line across the round bare hills and plains. In the afternoon the sky darkened with ugly gray clouds.

"God spare us," Sonoy said. "I'd rather sleep in a hedgerow than another bed like the last, but if it rains we'll drown in the ditch."

"No fear of that," said Lumey. "Yon's Salisbury—I know a lady there, a widow, who keeps a good house, and takes in all who need her charity, for the fear of God. We'll go weep at her door, and she'll give us a clean bed and a dish of supper, mark me."

The rain began. They rode through a steady downpour to a house called Stonegate. There Lumey knocked on the gate, and a porter let them into a little courtyard, already splashy from the rain.

The charitable lady had taken in too many beggars; there was room in the old house for only two more. Lumey grandly volunteered Jan to sleep in the stable, since he was of common birth.

The stable was snug and dry, and warm from the beasts lined up along either wall. Jan sat on a pile of old hay listening to the rain on the thatch overhead and longing for the sea and his ship; he felt himself a different person here, so far from his work and the people who knew him. An old gray cat came up, purring, and rubbed against his arm, and he took her on his lap and stroked her. She warmed him, and he talked to her a little, mostly about Lumey, who was a fool and worse, and felt comforted.

The light faded. He was hungry, and lying in the dark with the cat rumbling away on his knees he wondered where he should go to eat. But then a woman came into the stable, a lantern in one hand and a dish in the other.

She spoke to him in English, and he shook his head, sitting up, eager, his nose working at the smell of beef and onions emanating from the covered dish. She set the lantern down between them.

"French, then, have you? Good. I am Eleanor Simmons, and Stonegate is my home." She put the dish before him. He moved toward it so quickly the cat leapt out of his lap.

"You are very kind," he said in French. "I am sorry to impose myself on you, with no warning, and so late in the day."

She smiled at him. "Not at all. You give me the opportunity to serve God."

She was a tall, thin lady, some few years older than Jan himself, much younger than he had expected from Lumey's description of her as a widow. Her hair was brown and her face plain, not homely, raised from homeliness by the refinement of good birth and gentle manners. He tried not to eat too fast, although the food was delicious. When he was done he put the dish down for the cat to lick.

"You have a goodly appetite," she said. "Are you a sailor also, like the lord Lumey de la Marck?"

"Yes—we sail together."

"How exciting that must be—to travel over the sea to so many different places."

Jan wiped his fingers on his sleeve. "I cannot say, lady, since in my sailor's life I have seen no place but Nieuport and Plymouth."

"Well, perhaps you shall see others." She ran her hand over the cat's arched back between them.

Was that why she lingered, to hear of foreign places? He lay back on his elbow, his mind leaping from thought to thought for one sufficiently entertaining to keep her here; he had no wish to lose her company.

"I should like to go to the New World," he said. "Someday, maybe—"

"Oh, yes." Her face brightened like the moon rising. "The names are enchanting, are they not? Cartagena, and Mexico, and America—"

"Dangerous waters," he said, pleased at her enthusiasm for this talk. "And the Spanish mean to keep us out. But someday I'll go. There's silver and gold, I've heard, lying in the beds of streams like paving stones in the streets of Antwerp, and the people are docile as cattle."

"A new world," she said. "New chances—new beginnings." Her fingers ruffled the cat's thick fur. "It's hard to believe, isn't it, that only a hundred years ago no one even knew it was there—as if God were saving it for . . . someone."

Speaking in another language, perhaps she said not what she meant; but Jan was struck by the look on her face, by the depth of feeling in her voice. He thought, *She longs for something new.* At the same time he became aware, intensely aware, that they were alone together. That he could stretch his hand out and touch her.

She raised her eyes suddenly to meet his, and he clenched his fist in the hay at his side.

"You think I'm foolish, don't you," she said.

"No," he said. "Of course not. You have taken me in, and given me to eat; I think nothing but gratitude."

The other thing, that was sin, and an insult to her; he hid his fist down deep in the hay.

"What is your name?" she asked.

"Jan van Cleef. My ship is the *Wayward Girl.*" He spoke the name in Dutch and then in French.

"How pretty," she said, and smiled. Now she was going; she got to her feet, took the dish from beneath the cat's rasping tongue, and reached for the lantern. "Shall I leave this here?" She drew her hand back.

"Yes—I'd like the light."

"Be sure you don't burn the place down, will you?"

"I shall, lady. Thank you."

"Good night." She went away. He watched her go; the cat curled up in his lap again, vibrating with contentment. After a moment Jan lay back in the straw.

B EFORE dawn Eleanor Simmons took a basket of bread to a poor family in the village under her hill, and walking back through the grass, soaked by the rain that had ended only a few hours before, she passed by the place that gave her house its name: four huge gray stones set on the bare windy plain, one fallen flat, two upright, one lying on top of the uprights like the lintel of a gate, a stone gate.

She hated this place and these stones. The village people came here for trysts and other wicked purposes, and she was sure that the antique pagans who had built it had used it for something awful, for sacrifices, or lewd rites. The stones seized on her imagination, and raised the devil in her; whenever she passed by she found herself envisioning those lewd rites.

She refused to surrender to it, and tried to avoid them. Whenever her course took her past the stones, she went unswerving by them, and warred with her mind all the way. Today she kept her thoughts pure by thinking of the Dutch seamen who had spent the night under her roof, the grateful receivers of her kindness. Especially she thought of the tall young man, whose name she had, unfortunately, forgotten.

When she went into her courtyard, they were standing there with their horses, ready to go. She went up to them, smiling, to have their thanks and farewells.

Lumey kissed her hand, and Sonoy bowed and spoke of God's good mercy shown through her, which made her heart fat with pleasure. By his horse the tall young man stood silent, and when his friends turned to mount he mounted too, without a word to her.

She stepped back, downcast at that. They rode out the gate. Her mood sank lower; she had thought she had made a good impression on him, bringing him to eat with her own hands and talking to him of his voyages; she felt the reproof like a cut. But as he rode out the gate, he turned and smiled and waved his hand to her, and her spirit soared up again. She went into her house, happy.

12

HILE Lumey and Sonoy were talking to the Queen's secretary, Jan went to look around her palace.

There was to be a pageant here, or an execution; workmen were building wooden stages in the garden, and on strings between the tall trees and over the little artificial watercourse they were hanging lanterns and swags of colored cloth. Across the lawn from the stage, a cluster of men were struggling to make a fountain work. Jan went closer to watch. They had the ornamental top of the fountain pulled off and were fitting pipes together in the base. The pipes ran away up the slope in a trench through the green grass, with the sods piled up beside it, leading to a huge wine tun. They were trying to make the fountain flow with wine.

Not an execution, then, unless these English were more ghoulish even than the Spaniards.

As he walked away, they got the pipes connected. A red spurt of wine gushed up from the fountain's throat, and the workmen cheered.

The palace itself was a patchwork of old and new buildings, strung together over the hillside. He walked back into the gallery where he had left his fellow Beggars, to find Lumey shouting red faced at the secretary and Sonoy pacing up and down nearby, shaking his head.

"We're chasing eels with herring nets," he said when Jan came up to him, which Jan took to mean they had come all this way for nothing.

"Two weeks!" Lumey shouted, storming up between them. *"Maybe* she will see us in two weeks!"

Through the nearest door into the long sunlit gallery came two pretty little boys in lace collars, the first carrying a hat with a long white feather, the second carrying a wooden head, topped by a fluff of black hair. As the boys ran past Sonoy, the black hair flew off and landed at Jan's feet. He jumped back away from it, startled. The boy snatched it up, plopped it back on the wooden bulb of the wig stand, and rushed on down the gallery.

"What's going on here?" Jan wheeled around toward his friends.

"There's a disguisers' ball tonight," Sonoy said. "The Queen hosts a German prince, here to offer marriage to her."

Lumey was shouting at the secretary again. Sonoy pulled on his beard, his mouth curled into a thoughtful purse. "There are times," he said, "when a loud noise makes only an echo. Let's go."

Jan was watching a parade of pretty girls go giggling by him, their arms piled up with flowers. A powerful perfume lingered in their wake. He wondered where they found flowers so early in the year. Sonoy got him by the arm.

"Let's go!"

"Where's . . ." Jan twisted to look behind him for Lumey.

The big pirate was still screaming in the secretary's face; now the Englishman jerked up his arm in a signal, and all around the gallery the men in orange velvet who flanked the doors came forward. Lumey stood his ground against them.

"I'll have you know I am a baron of the German Empire—"

Unfortunately he issued this declaration in Dutch. The English guards strode on toward him, six men, six big men, their hands on their small swords. The first two to reach Lumey hooked their arms through his and heaved him toward the front door. Lumey let out a roar of indignation. He wrenched one arm free and flung his fist at the guard on his other side.

Jan started forward to help him; the other four guards were closing fast with him, drawing their swords. Sonoy rushed past them all. Snatching up a little stool as he passed, he dashed in between the guard who held Lumey and Lumey himself.

"For the *John Calvin!*" he cried, and clubbed Lumey over the head with his stool.

Jan shouted, amazed. Lumey collapsed on the floor at his feet, and Jan took a step forward, straddling him, to defend him from the guards. Sonoy gave the stool to the nearest man in orange velvet, who gaped at him, dumb.

The secretary said something crisply, motioning the guards away. Sonoy turned. "Bring him," he said to Jan, and walked away to the door.

"WHY DID you do that?" Leicester stalked away from the window, his shadow long before him. "Valiant warriors for the faith, true hearts in our own cause, and you turn them off. You are afraid, aren't you?" He wheeled toward her, his face flushed with the intensity that served him in place of thought. "You're afraid of Philip."

"Everyone is afraid of Philip."

"That dog. That meeching monk. He lost us Calais; you know that." Fierce as a cheetah, he stalked toward her where she stood in the window overlooking the gate yard. "The Bloody Queen went to help the Hapsburgs, and so we lost Calais. The Dutch could be our chance to recover our empire! Don't you see that?"

The English Empire: one city. One lost city. She put her shoulder to passionate Robin Leicester and turned her eyes toward the Dutch pirates, down by the gate. The two still upright were laying their unconscious fellow across his saddle. She would have to have the story of that; no guards of hers had escorted them out of the palace, as they would have had they taken force

to the Dutch. She laid her hand on the white windowsill. The tall fair man
held her interest, who had carried the other out on his shoulder. Her father
had carried her around on his shoulder.

"The Dutch deserve our help," said her bonny Robin, still prowling the
room behind her in his excess of male vigor. "They fight our enemies and
they are alone. I do not understand why you refuse even to see them."

She knew something of the Dutch, and something more of Philip of
Spain; to meddle between them would need a steady hand and a keen eye,
and a willingness to settle for very little in the matter of reward. Now the
Prince of Orange's navy was riding out the gate, an opportunity checked.
Or a temptation safely avoided. She turned toward Leicester, who saw no
value in ambiguity.

"You heard their story complete. Tell me the lines of it again."

"I had it only in the echo, but even so it heats my blood, as it will
yours." He crossed the room toward her, walking from the shadow into the
light. "Outnumbered and outgunned, they fought the Spanish to a standstill
on the Channel seas until a storm scattered them, and the galleons took
refuge in Plymouth Sound. Next, the Dutch appear"—his hands made sails
in the air—"and stand between the Dons and their escape. Night falls, and
under the shield of darkness, the Spanish flame the greatest of the Dutch
ships, nearly murdering all on board."

She chuckled at him. "I think you need a theater for your full effect,
my lord. Still, you are right, it's a serious matter. I'll send to Plymouth for
an edition in English. And now, sir—"

She held out her hand to him, and with some little grace he gave her
his arm to rest her fingers on. They left the room.

JAN DREW rein and looked back up the road; beyond the rooftops of the
houses that crowded around its walls, the palace of the English Queen raised
its bannered towers into the sky.

"Come along," said Sonoy. "A slow foot makes a long road."

"Captain—" Jan faced him over Lumey, still hanging like a roll of carpet
over the saddle of his horse. "A disguisers' ball—everyone will wear a
costume. Isn't that right?"

Lumey groaned. Sonoy put one foot on his friend's backside and rocked
him back and forth. "Yes, that's what it means."

"Then why can't we go?"

Sonoy's gaze rose to meet his. Lumey was moving now, his head bobbing over the stirrup. Chimes sounded down the road; a beer wagon was
rolling up the way toward them, the horses' harness merry with brass bells.

"We haven't got any costumes, for one thing," Sonoy said.

"We do," Jan said. "We could go as seamen. What's wrong with that?"

"If we're caught, that's the end of our suit with Elizabeth."

"It seems to me our suit's at an end already."

He looked back up at the palace again; the wall hid the bunting and lanterns in the garden from him, the stage, the fountain gushing wine, the improbable flowers, the pretty girls. When night came, and the lanterns glowed, and the girls laughed and danced on the lawns . . .

"I'm going," he said. "I have a clean shirt in my bag."

Face down on the saddle, Lumey thrashed, and a yell erupted from him. He heaved himself upright, grabbing for the pommel of his saddle, missed his hold, and fell into the street. Sonoy murmured in sleek satisfaction.

"Mortified, by God." He swung down from his horse and hauled Lumey onto his feet. "Rise up, rise up, the wind's fair and the sea won't wait forever. Young van Cleef has a notion to storm the Queen's fancy evening."

"What?" Still groggy, Lumey swung his head from side to side. "What?"

Fool. Jan galloped away down the road toward London.

LADY JANE DUDLEY was dressed as Diana, with a crescent moon in her hair and a sheaf of arrows on her back; Elizabeth was one of her huntresses. In the moonlight the white gowns seemed to shine like silver. Pleased, Elizabeth drew back by the arbor to see everything whole.

In among the new-leafed trees tied with flowers of silk and paper, in the patchy glow of the lanterns, her court strutted and preened like a flock of Byzantine birds, all jeweled and ribboned, made tall by strange headdresses and wide by extravagant padding. There by the fountain was someone—Gilbert—got up as Caesar, in a long white gown like a nightdress, a wreath of laurel on his thinning hair, and two fellows trailing after him with bundles of sticks. He went bowing and posturing through a crowd of wood nymphs and fools in clocked hose, stranger than any of Caesar's triumphs. King Solomon backed out of his way, stiff under an enormous crown of ostrich plumes that swayed perilously whenever he moved; behind him, blackamoors held up the litter on which Sheba reclined, her dress flashing and fiery with jewels.

In another part of the garden was a troop of Brazilian aborigines, nude but for strategic placements of feathers and gold. Greeks and Arabs were everywhere, drinking and boisterous, and even some animals—a lion, walking upright with a mane of golden wire, and a unicorn going about properly on all fours, casting glances here and there from glowing eyes.

The musicians behind Elizabeth began to play; she thought of organizing all these visions into a dance. Her eye caught on a strange appearance at the far side of the garden.

It was a tall man, fair headed and half-naked, without a jewel on him anywhere, a rude stone in this treasure chest. Elizabeth went a little closer, intrigued. He wore shirt and trousers of common cloth, but nothing more;

it was the contrast of such plain stuff with the fantastic dress around him that made him look naked. She guessed he was costumed as a sailor.

A moment later she realized he was a sailor, one of the Sea Beggars who had spent the afternoon trying to gain audience with her. After him came the other two, one as soberly dressed as a precisian, and the other, more ordinary in this company, wearing a long embroidered tunic like a Popish priest's vestment.

The Queen's temper warmed. She was minded to have them chased away, and looked for one of her guards; she would have them beaten, too, for such impudence. The nearest guard lounged against a walnut tree across the lawn, flirting with Maid Marian, who was toying with his belt.

The costumes made everything different, Elizabeth saw; they were all strangers now, even to themselves—freed of themselves for the evening. Wasn't that what she had intended? She smiled, her royal anger cooled. She herself could hide in this artifice, rest from her nature and find some amusement to renew her mind. Let the Dutchmen stay. She went down the sloping lawn into the anonymous crowd.

THE FLOWERS were false. They were made of paper and cloth and drenched in perfume, like whores.

Disappointed, Jan moved away from the trees, toward the fountain sparkling and splashing in the center of the lawn. The people there were dancing, a dozen of them drawn up in the figure for a round, the girls on the inside. Their clothes were magnificent. The more he saw of them, the more out of place he felt here, in his canvas shirt: these people wore their fortunes on their backs. He stood watching the circles of dancers heel and toe and heel and leap to the brittle music of viol and lute.

One girl especially caught his eye, so beautiful he held his breath a moment, to see her, dancing on the far side of the circle. She wore a long green gown, her puffed white sleeves spangled with gems and her hair done in braids over her head; he supposed all these English recognized the character at once. The dance brought her steadily closer to him, and he went forward a little, eager to see her beauty in the lantern light, ready to worship her; and then she came face to face with him and he saw her beauty was paint, and her looks, close on, so hard and false he turned his back at once and blundered away through the crowd.

He found some wine and drank it. Where Sonoy and Lumey had gone, he had no notion; strangers surrounded him, talking in a language he did not understand. He walked through the night gardens, avoiding the other masquers. The wine was strong; he drank too much of it. The strangers jostled him. He stood watching them whirl and sway in another dance. In their jewels and feathers and fanciful clothes, they no longer seemed like people to him, but made things, mechanical beings, and monsters.

He wondered if all expectations suffered like this, if all beauty were false. If all heroic deeds began as cheap shams, like the burning of the *John Calvin.*

He went into the trees, to relieve himself. As he stood pissing into a bush, a girl ran into him from one side.

She giggled. She smelled of the strong wine. Her bodice was open down the front and one round breast emerged, nestled in the folds of cloth. She clutched his arm to keep her balance, laughing; with his free hand he struggled to put away his penis. A man burst out of the bushes after her.

"Oho!" The man strode up to them, shouted some angry words at the girl, seized her arm, and pulled her back away from Jan. She tripped on her skirts and fell backward against the newcomer. Jan pulled his trousers closed. The man pushed him.

"Easy, there," Jan said, and backed off a step, looking for the way out of this.

A volley of hot English came at him. The man let go of the girl, who slid down onto the trampled grass, subsiding into feeble drunken giggles. Her companion drew his long sword.

"Now, wait," Jan said, switching to French. "You have this wrong. I did nothing with her." His eyes followed the silvery gleam of the blade. His stomach tightened; he backed up another step, and came up hard against someone else, behind him, who seized his arms.

The man with the sword bellowed and lunged forward, the sword point aimed at Jan's belt buckle. Full of wine, Jan saw this all very slowly, and moved slowly, as if in a dance, sidestepping to let the sword pass by him, wrenching his arms free of the grip from behind him.

Something struck him on the head. In French, he cried, "I am innocent!" and fell. The ground came up hard into his face. He rolled over, dodging the unseen sword point. A foot thudded into his side. His legs got tangled in the brush, and he kicked out; another roll, and he hit the rough bark of a tree trunk.

"Hold!"

That voice rang like iron. He lay still, breathing hard, while his attackers moved away from him.

The iron voice, not loud, spoke on in English. Surprised, he realized the timbre was feminine. Feet moved swiftly around him, pattering away. He lifted his head; he was alone, and not hurt, not badly. He sat up.

Not alone. She stood in front of him, a woman in a long white gown with a sheaf of silver arrows on her back.

She said, in French, "Well, Master Sailor, something shipwrecked in the wine?"

"Thank you," he said. He knew this was the Queen.

"Are you hurt?"

"No, Madame." He pushed himself up onto his feet, one hand to his head, where he had been struck. Now he stood over her, head and shoulders taller, which he shortened in as fine a bow as he could muster. "Thank you, your Grace."

She stood straight and stiff as a pikestaff before him, frowning at him. "Thank me when you have gone safely from me, Master Beggar! I am considering now whether to have you thrown into the ditch, or into one of my dungeons."

His head was beginning to hurt. He said, "The choice is yours. This is your kingdom, is it not?" Grimly he wished himself back on board the *Wayward Girl*, where the choice was his.

"What arrogance! By what right come you here, invade my pleasures, and trifle with the innocent young girls of my court?"

"I did nothing! She came at me, she—" He stopped his tongue, embarrassed; the girl was gone, all his protestations only proofless words. He faced this iron queen in her silvery dress. "Do as you will, lady. God, I would I were anywhere but here, a Spanish gallows but not here."

She said nothing a moment. Leisurely, her gaze traveled over him from head to foot, her face, with its angular bones and feline breadth between the eyes, empty of expression. At last she moved, walking toward him, walking past him.

"Came at you, I can imagine. We have no such beasts in our English menagerie. Sit down here; you seem unsteady yet from your brawling. Or perhaps the wine."

He went after her through the bushes to a little open glade where a stone bench sat under a tree. This one was not gauded up with fakeries, only its own new softly uncurling leaves, and he sat down on the cold bench and put his hand to his head again.

"You are one of the Prince of Orange's men?" she asked, behind him.

"I? No, not Orange—that . . . court dancer, that toy soldier—"

"Oh?" Surprise sharpened her voice. "I took you for a Sea Beggar."

"That I am, lady."

"Oh. Well, a matter of names, as is all the world. You did come here to tell me about the evil deeds the Spanish did in Plymouth, and to have my help in the business."

He lifted his head; it had all begun with that, with that falsehood, the burning of the *John Calvin*. "Yes," he said.

"Well, I am inclined to favor your suit, if there be a way to do so without drawing down on me the untoward blusterings of Spain. I will not have foreign powers making war in my harbors."

He pressed his lips together, remembering all that had happened in Plymouth. She spoke behind him, her voice mild and colorless.

"Spain believes he does the work of God; it is a common self-deceit of power. Daily his arrogance binds more tightly on my own English seamen, here and in the Indies. But this is worse than arrogance—to burn a ship in Plymouth harbor—"

"We burned her," Jan burst out.

Behind him there was now a silence, crowded and heavy, like the air before a thunderstorm.

"I said," he said, more loudly, "that we burned her. She was already sinking. The idea was Lumey's. Sonoy had no doing of it. We burned her, to force the Spanish out where we could deal with them."

With a whisper of cloth she strode around before him, face to face with him. "Why do you tell me this?"

"I am tired of lying," he said.

"By God's blood!" She walked two steps away and whirled around again, her white gown flying about her and the silver arrows flashing on her shoulder. "What insolence is this—first you contrive to dupe me, and then you have the belly to tell me so. What a fool you take me for!"

He shrugged, careless of her; he had cleansed himself, and all his fear and low thoughts were gone.

"You have my leave, Master Dutchman!"

He got up onto his feet, steady now, and sober. "Thank you for saving my life," he said to her, and bowed again, the bow his tutor had schooled him in during his classroom days in Antwerp. She stood like an idol in her white and silver, her eyes brilliant with rage. He went away through the garden.

H E HAD no idea what had become of Lumey and Sonoy, and he didn't care. Going back down to the inn where they had taken a room, he stuffed his clothes into his seabag, slung it on his back, and walked away down the road toward the far end of England.

Most of the night he walked, then slept through the dawn in a field beside the road. In the morning light, he walked on. He followed the Roman road; sometimes other travelers joined him, merchants and chapmen, vagabonds and highborn people on horseback, but usually he went alone, with nothing to do but think.

He remembered what his uncle had said, about stealing from the people around him, but Pieter had not gone far enough in his explanation. To steal, to cheat corrupted everything; one lie fueled another, making truth impossible.

He thought of Alva, his courage, his cold brilliance. There was a grandeur in his evil that Jan could not find in himself. If he were good, it was in modest ways. More likely, he was neither good nor evil, but only something formless in between.

The clouds raced over the sky like greyhounds on the hunt. The rain fell.

It was raining when he came to Salisbury, several days on, and he found his way to Stonegate House. By the time he reached the gate yard the rain had stopped. He stood by the way in, looking into the brick courtyard, where ducks fluttered and splashed in the puddles. A milkmaid was coming up the lane toward him, a yoke on her shoulders, a bucket of milk in each hand. The rain was over, and now he needed no more shelter than one of the huge-barreled oaks that grew up over the lane, but he lingered still. As the milkmaid passed, she smiled at him, and he followed her into the court-yard.

Ivy covered the little old brick house on the far side. The milkmaid disappeared through a low archway in the back. A man in a woolen cap was unloading wood from a wheelbarrow in a corner of the yard, and he straight-ened and spoke in English, with a question rising at the end of his words.

"Mistress—" As he spoke, her name, forgotten until now, sprang to his tongue. "Mistress Simmons?"

In the ivy-covered brick wall, a shutter opened, and a woman leaned out; she called sharply down into the courtyard. The man at the woodpile turned, shouting back, and waggled his thumb at Jan. The woman gaped at him. She pulled the shutter closed. The man in the woolen cap turned to Jan again and smiled and motioned with his hand for him to wait. Jan let the seabag slide down off his shoulder.

"You LOOK wet," she said, leading him up the stairs. "Were you caught in the storm?"

"In several storms, Mistress Simmons."

"Well, then, I'm pleased I have a room to offer you to yourself this time, and not the stable."

Outside the door, he stood looking down at her. "I have a little money. I should be very happy to pay—"

"No, no," she said, briskly. "My husband, when he died, left me with more than I could ever use myself. We had no children; he had no other heirs; what is there to do with it, save God's charity?" She smiled at him. Older than he remembered, her eyes nested in fine lines that fanned out when she smiled. "Make yourself comfortable. We shall have a supper, when night falls, in the hall."

"Thank you."

She opened the door for him and stood on the threshold talking, while he put his seabag down and looked around the little room.

"Have you been already to London? I hope your business transpired as you wished."

He had no interest in telling her the tangled doings of the past few days. "This is very comfortable," he said. "I should have been happy in the stable." The room was just large enough for the bed and a tall old-fashioned French wardrobe; a little hearth faced the window. On the rope webbing of the bed, a straw-filled tick was folded. She came into the room and spread it out on the bedframe.

"Will your friends be coming along later?"

"I don't know," he said. "I left without seeing them." The wardrobe smelled of fresh lavender. He inhaled deeply of the pleasant scent. "This is very fine, Mistress Simmons."

"If there is anything necessary to your comfort, we shall try to supply it."

He was standing at the window, looking out over the wall of the courtyard. It was so different here from his own country: this swelling plain, not flat like Brabant, the trees squat old oaks instead of poplars and elms, no canals, no mills, and yet some things the same, the black and white cows that grazed on the far meadow, the sky's depthless blue, glittering after the rain. He turned toward Eleanor Simmons again.

"You've given me very much, simply in being here," he said. "I came from London with a very bad taste in my mouth, which your hospitality has rinsed away. Thank you."

"You are very kind," she said, and her cheeks reddened. This time, she did go, and he was alone.

BEFORE supper Eleanor walked to the village, to take some bread to the poor there. As she walked back up the plain toward Stonegate, she saw, ahead of her, the young Dutch seaman coming toward her.

They met where the path ran by the old standing stones; when she came up to him, the Dutchman was looking at the huge old stones, frowning.

"What are these?" he said, and put his hands on one stone and pushed as if he might knock it down.

"Pagan things," she said. "It's for this my house is named Stonegate."

She had forgotten his name. It quivered on her tongue to ask him.

He walked around the stones, touching them, and looking up at them. Usually she went by this place in a hurry, but today she lingered. His great height amazed her; the good proportions of his body disguised its size. He jumped up to touch the lintel stone. Measuring the gate with himself.

"I've forgotten your name," she burst out suddenly.

He smiled at her. "Jan van Cleef, at your service, my lady."

That made her laugh. "I am only Mistress Simmons, my lord. Or Eleanor, if it please you."

"It pleases me." He took her basket from her, to carry it for her, and they walked up the path toward the house.

"Enlighten me, sir. Why are you who rebel against the Spanish King called Beggars?"

He walked along beside her, his eyes on the path, which was slippery from the recent rains. "Because years ago, when we were still asking the King politely to honor our rights and privileges, the court scorned us by that name. Now every true Dutchman reverences the title Beggar."

"And you are a Beggar."

"Yes," he said, adamantly.

"I think it most honorable and true to be so, from what I have heard of affairs in your country."

"They murdered my father," he said.

She pressed her hand to her breast, her gaze straight ahead of them on the path. "God help you. I am very sorry to hear it."

"Tell me how your husband died. Was it recently?"

They were coming up toward the house; in the fallow field on the other side of the path, the dray horses grazed, standing to their hocks in the daisies. She said, "He took a fever, five years ago." He had told her of his father; this exchange of pain was good currency. Yet it opened up the old sore again. She and William Simmons had quarreled before he died, and he had gone off so abruptly, in the space of a day, that she had had no chance to mend it with him. Whenever she thought of it, remorse dragged her down in its net of melancholy.

She said, "Now I spend my life in service to others."

Beside her, he stopped abruptly. "There's still daylight left," he said. "Will you sit with me and talk?"

They sat down on a log beside the lane, under an oak tree. He said, "Since I left Plymouth I've had no one to talk to, save Lumey and Sonoy, and they are . . ."

She waited for him to finish; he did not. She said, "Sometimes even here, where I have been nearly all my life, there seems to be no one to talk to."

"Maybe," he said, "there's nothing to say."

"What a curious remark. I assure you, I always have something to say." Did he think she was stupid? She frowned at him.

He stretched his legs out in front of him, moving his shoulders, working his great muscled arms. He said, "There is a world of words, and the real world, and you must not mistake the one for the other."

That was even more curious. "Whatever do you mean?"

"I am not sure. Except it seems to me that sometimes people—I myself, very much—do something and attach words to it, and think by putting the right words to it to make the deed mean other than it does."

"Yes, that seems a common folly of mankind, and nothing new with you."

"There's a boy on my ship, a little slow in the head, named Mouse. While we were chasing the Spanish, I sent him up to the masthead, to get him out of my way, and he fell into the sea."

"Oh!"

"He's safe now; don't cry for him. We had to stop and pick him out of the ocean and the Spanish nearly got us, all because of me, trying to play hero while doing the villain's business."

"But you regret it," she said, and put her hand over his. "You know the wrong."

He turned to face her; his hand turned over beneath hers, and his fingers closed on hers. He said, "Knowing wrong is miles off from doing right."

"God knows the truth in that." His hand was warm, and so large it swallowed hers. Her gaze fell, lest he read too much in her eyes. She fumbled for some honesty to match his. Low, she said, "I try so hard to do God's work, but it's all ashes to me, my charities. I cannot say why—it brings me no peace. It all seems so small, taking bread to this one, medicines to that —a business of number and transport, not of my person. I want . . . I want . . ."

Now she was coming close to the center of her being, and she could not speak it, how she longed to matter in herself again, as she had mattered to William Simmons, long ago. How she yearned for some important work, some sacrifice, to fight, to die for her causes, to have her people's hearts with their gratitude.

He said, "You will have what you want."

"You don't even know it."

"Still, I can see in your face what a great-hearted woman you are." He leaned toward her and pressed his lips to hers.

The kiss was chaste enough, with closed lips, but their joined hands went wanton, squeezing and stroking.

Somewhere beyond the hill a bell began to ring. Eleanor looked up. Her heart was pounding so hard she thought it must shake the cloth of her dress.

"Let us go in," she said.

"Thank you," he said, and rose and helped her solemnly to her feet. "Thank you for talking to me—you make me feel like an honest man again."

Was this the end of it? Reluctantly she let go his hand. His size attracted her powerfully. What he had said worked on in her mind. To play the hero —to live in the world of deeds. Suddenly she thought him wonderful beyond all other men she had ever known, except William Simmons.

They walked back toward the house, silent, both of them, not even looking at one another.

In the courtyard was a noisy tangle of people and horses. Here they could not talk. They separated. Eleanor went slowly toward the kitchen, where she would have the supper to oversee. The wild yearning in her heart mixed with the suspicion that it were better if she never saw Jan van Cleef again, if one kiss could stir her so. She was hungry. Her hands were salty with sweat; she would have to wash. At the brick archway, she turned and looked across the courtyard.

He stood there by the wall, watching her. When she found her gaze on him, he smiled and raised his hand.

Her cheeks went hot as her feelings. Unable to keep still, she wheeled and ran like a child down the steps to the kitchen.

AT SUPPER, other people crowded the table, and Jan had no chance to talk to Eleanor. He watched her all the while, how she ate delicately as a bird, taking only the smallest morsels of the meat and breaking her bread into little pieces. She did not seem to pay much heed to him; only once she looked up, and then catching his gaze on her turned swiftly away.

After the meal he went out to the courtyard, not knowing where else to go, and stood around on the bricks watching the kitchen girls bring the scraps from supper out for the chickens. He thought of nothing but Eleanor. Her eager interest in him, her touch, the kiss, everything that had happened between them seemed to go on and on in his memory; his body ached all over from the exercise of his senses. But she did not care. She had gone somewhere else tonight.

Then, just as he was falling into despair, she came out from the kitchen.

They walked out along the lane again, talking about virtue and how one could know the right things to do. Everything that had chafed him since Mouse fell into the sea now poured out in a rush of words, how he longed for some great exalting work, how instead everything he did disintegrated into trivia and commonplaces and meanness.

The darkness deepened. He took her by the hand, to help her over the rough footing of the lane.

"I wish I were a man," she said. "I'd go with you; we'd fight the Spanish together. But as it is—"

He lifted up her hand and kissed it. "You have the heart for it."

Rain began to fall, and they turned their steps back to the house. Jan wanted to kiss her; he wanted to do other things with her. But there seemed no place where they could be alone and secure enough. He could think of nothing to say. He had never met a woman before who was so apt to his thoughts, to his longings as Eleanor, but perhaps she felt differently. A widow, too, with another lover's memory to honor.

The courtyard was empty; the rain was falling steadily now. She said, "Shall we go to the hall?"

"Whatever you choose."

They went to the hall; the old man who had sat by Jan at supper was dozing by the fire, and two maidservants tittered and played cat's cradle by the window. Eleanor drew back.

"Not here," she said.

"Come up to my room," Jan said.

She moved away from him; they stood on the landing outside the door to the hall, in the dark. She said, "The others will know and they'll talk."

He let go her hand. "Whatever you choose."

Now she turned her face fully toward him; the rain had dampened her hair. She said, low, "Very well." Swiftly she went by him up the stairs. He followed her.

They climbed up to the room under the eaves where he was to sleep. There was a fire laid on the hearth, and Jan knelt to light it. She lit a candle, put it on the mantel, and went to fasten the shutters over the window. Jan built the fire high, his hands trembling, his mouth dry with excitement.

She sat next to him on the hearth and he turned and kissed her.

"We ought not," she said.

"Because of these other people," he said, and went back to poking at the fire again.

She knelt beside him, tilted forward a little from the waist, her face bathed in the glow of the fire. Her lips were pressed tightly together. Her eyes glittered. He thought she was beautiful, not in the common way of beauty, but in her aliveness.

She said, "I do everything now, it seems, for what other people will think."

He took her hand and kissed it, and she moved toward him and he put his arms around her and pressed his mouth to her cheek, to her forehead and eyes and lips. Her arms went around his neck. She lay in his arms, her breath warm on his cheek. He put his hand on her bodice. The thin cloth there was damp from the rain, warm from the breast underneath.

"We shouldn't do it," she said.

"Do you want to?"

"I don't know. I am afraid. I want to but I'm afraid."

"Don't be afraid. I won't hurt you. I'll never do anything to hurt you . . ."

His hand stroked over her, and she moved again, arching her back, her breast rising into the palm of his hand. He pulled the light cloth down and slipped his hand in against her bare flesh, and she moaned. With his mouth he searched out her kiss again, hungry now, her breast filling his hand as he would fill up her body soon, and she was letting him, eager, her hands pulling at her clothes, shyly seeking through his clothes until suddenly she touched his penis, and the surge of pleasure through him nearly made him shout.

He lifted her up. The bed was right behind him, under the window. He laid her down on it and unlaced her gown and her hands leapt past his, pulling away the encumbering dress, baring her round breasts in the firelight. He put his lips to one small erect nipple. She gasped, her hands on his hair, her legs moving, her hips against him. They pushed away her clothes. His hand stroked down over the soft skin of her belly, down to her thighs, where the thick curly hair grew, and when he touched her there she spread her legs apart. He had never handled a woman before, not there, and he groped, uncertain, surprised at the dampness, at the softness of her flesh, and slipped his fingers down between the tender folded skin, and reached up into her body.

She cried out; her whole body arched, letting him in deeper, her hands on his shoulders. Standing up, he shed his clothes and knelt on the bed between her knees, his penis jutting out in front of him. She reached for it; her hand enclosed it, and he quivered all over, his strength gone; led by her hand, he lay down on her, braced on his elbows, and she drew his power down and into her and engulfed him.

It was over for him almost at once. The warmth and pressure all around his organ brought him instantly to the point of bursting, and on the third stroke he gave up twenty years of waiting. He clutched her tight. She was whimpering under him; he knew she wanted him to go on, and he did, amazed at the power of his body, at the effect of his body on her. He held her face between his hands and watched her open like a blossom between his fingers, her eyes brimming with tears, her mouth slack and yielding, until finally her eyes closed and a rosy glow spread over her face, and she was quiet under him.

He kissed her closed, tear-filled eyes. The scent of their bodies was like a perfume in the air around them.

She said, "We've sinned."

"Well, maybe." He rolled to the side of the bed and looked at her body, subtly printed with his, the breasts flattened, the belly red, the wonderful curled place between her legs still a little ajar where he had been. "Are you cold?"

She sighed. "No. Open the window a little, will you?"

He opened the shutter enough to let in the air and the sound of the rain. Lying down beside her again, he touched her breast. In a few moments he would be ready to do it again.

"I haven't even kissed a man since my husband died," she said.

Jan was playing with her nipple. He put his mouth on it, drawing the hard bud upward. "I know you are no wanton."

"Only for lack of opportunity," she said, and sighed again. "I have lain in my cold widow's bed, some nights, wishing—"

"I had never done it before," he said; he did not want her wishing she had not done it. He kissed her mouth again. "If it is a sin it is a mild one."

"How can you say that?" she cried. "A few hours ago we were talking of great deeds and heroes, and now we have fallen into sin again, dragged one another into sin—"

He put his hand over her mouth. Above his fingers her eyes shone with a desperate will to unhappiness.

"You are mine now," he said. "I'll decide what is sin between us and what is not. I'll hear no more of this from you, not if you love me. Do you understand?"

He took his hand away; she lay still, her gaze on him, her mouth curled into a pensive line. His hand lay on her belly, where soon he meant to lie.

"Do you love me?" she said.

"Yes," Jan said.

She put her arms up, to encircle his neck, and drew his head down to kiss again.

"I THINK it must have been a palace once," Jan said, and jumped down from the great stone that lay in the grass before the stone gateway. "Now this entrance is all that's left."

Eleanor laughed. "Perhaps some moralism could be drawn from that."

"What?" He came over to her and took her hand, and they went on along the way to the village.

"I don't know—that everything wicked crumbles into dust."

"Why do you think it was wicked?"

She shrugged, unwilling to lay open her thoughts about the stone gate. And someone was coming up the way toward them. When Jan tried to take hold of her hand she pulled away from him.

"What's the matter?"

She said nothing, smiling; they walked along the path, while the cow-herd and his boy came toward them, an old man and a young, in identical brown broad-brimmed hats. The boy carried a long stick. Their dog loped along before them.

"Good morning, Jem," she said. "Joe."

They chorused, "Good day, Mis's Simmons." Their dark eyes probed at Jan, beside her, as they passed.

When they had gone on by, Jan said, "Are you ashamed of me?"

"No, I—"

"Just of what we did last night?"

"Hush," she said, firmly.

When she thought of the night before, she knew, unsettled, that she had lost power over herself, that he had taken mastery of her somehow; she was determined not to do that again—not to give herself up to him again. Carefully she did not think of the pleasure of his body. Her body.

"Do you want to marry me?" he asked.

That startled her. She looked up at him, his face still so new to her that every fresh angle showed her a stranger. "Do you want to?"

"I love you," he said.

She faced forward again, her heart pounding. Now she wished he would take her hand; she would not pull away from him now. But they were coming into the village, where other people abounded. The moment was gone.

Crisply she said, "I am to the bookseller's. Will you come with me?"

"I'll meet you there," he said, and went off.

She wondered if he were annoyed with her. They were still just barely friends to one another, and he was not English. Maybe it was foolish even to think of marrying him. At once her spirit lowered; she began to fret herself over the right thing to do. For an instant, her temper overflowed with fury at a God Who made everything so hard.

"Good day, Mistress Simmons."

"Good day," she said, not even knowing whom she answered, and went blindly on into the bookstore.

Maybe, she thought, staring at a shelf of books, she was only a whore inside, doing that with him, and so to marry him would drag an innocent down with her. He had said he was a virgin. She reached out for a little blue volume and took it in her hand. On the spine was written *Dido, Queen of Carthage.* She turned it over and over, feeling the leather smooth under her fingers.

At that moment the door behind her slammed open, and Jan like a great blond thunderbolt stormed into the shop.

"Eleanor." He gripped her elbow and made her turn to face him. "She's seized the ships."

"What?"

"The Queen of England. She's taken the Spanish ships for herself! Our prizes!"

Eleanor blinked at him, uncomprehending; then she remembered why he had been to London, and the irony of it struck her and she laughed.

"God, what fools we were, trusting in a crown—in a woman crowned, at that." He rushed up and down past her, his voice shaking with fury. Eleanor gripped the book in her hands. His passionate energy fascinated her.

"I'm going," he said. "I'm to Plymouth—to my ship. The other Beggars will be having a meeting, to decide what to do. I can't let them decide without me."

Her insides contracted. "But—what about me?"

"I'll come back." He laid his hands on her shoulders and looked solemnly into her face. "I'll come back, as soon as I can. Wait for me." Already he was turning from her. Not even a kiss. Shocked, she could not move a step to follow him. Over his shoulder, he cried, "Wait for me. If you take another lover, I'll kill him!" And was gone out the door.

She lowered her eyes to the blue volume in her hand. Seduced and abandoned. Opening her fingers, she let the book slide to the floor.

OLD PIETER said, "I don't see how you expected otherwise." He leaned back in his chair, his hands on his stomach; his gaze ranged over the tavern, where the other Beggars sat or stood in groups and shook their heads and cursed Elizabeth.

It delighted him to see them thus, their hopes destroyed, their work turned to nothing. Now their phantom unity would fade, and he would fall free of the unwelcome cause. Already some were arguing, accusing one another of the fault.

"I say we up anchor and go," he said to Jan, beside him. "You see what use it's been to join with these fools."

Jan said nothing. He had been strangely silent following his return from London. At his shoulder stood Mouse, who had not left his side since Jan came back.

The other Beggars filled the tavern; the barmaids and the tavern keeper had gone into the back, leaving the place to the boisterous Dutch. Near the door, two men suddenly began to throw their fists at one another, and those around them pressed in closer, cheering on the fight. Old Pieter looked on with contentment. In a few moments the whole fleet would disappear, like the white head of the dandelion in a puff of wind, and he would walk from this tavern a free man. Then through the door came Lumey, striding into the pack; he broke apart the fistfight, split the cheering crowd, and subdued them with a look.

The din quieted. All eyes turned on the Beggars' admiral, walking to the head of the room.

"Well, well," Pieter said loudly, "here's the conquering hero himself, returned from successful combat with the Queen! All hail the great man!"

He beat his palms together in solitary applause. The others kept still.

Lumey said, "Ay, the Queen betrayed us. But what would you have done, Pieter van Cleef?"

"Better than you!"

From another quarter of the room came a rough voice in a Flemish accent. "What went wrong? What did you do in London to dash our hopes?"

Another man cried, "Did you sell the Spanish ships to her, Lumey?"

Pieter clapped his hands together again. "I say, let us all go our own way, and have done with the fairy tale of fighting some great war against the Dons!" He glanced at Jan. His nephew sat picking his teeth with a straw, his face unreadable.

All around the tavern, now, men were calling for Lumey to answer, to confess, or to defend himself. Their quarreling voices rose to a deafening roar. The light was dim in here, with only two lanterns on the walls, and the men seemed no more than shadows that moved in the gloom.

A tall, slender figure in a wide-brimmed hat loomed up before them— van Treslong, a senior captain, and a nobleman as wellborn as Lumey himself. He called, "Lumey, answer. How did you fare in London?"

"In no way," Lumey said calmly. All Pieter could see of him was his tarnished and filthy vestment. "She would not even hear our petition. Ask Jan van Cleef. Ask Dirk Sonoy—"

"Sonoy is not here," said van Treslong. "He is refitting his other ship. Apparently you angered him as well as the Queen."

A yell went up from the left side of the room. "Down with Lumey! Hang him in with the priests on his own yardarm!"

Beside old Pieter suddenly Jan moved, rising to his feet; he said nothing, and the others, facing Lumey like wolves ready to spring, did not mark him. They shouted and shoved one another toward their admiral, calling for his blood, while van Treslong in vain waved his arms to quiet them and Lumey glowered and paced across the back wall of the tavern.

"Down with Lumey!"

"Down with the Beggars," Pieter shouted, and beat his boots on the floor.

Jan strode forward. Taller than any other man there, he moved through them and silenced them by his passage. He came up beside van Treslong and said, "Lumey's not to blame. His scheme would have worked. The Queen was partial to our suit, until I told her—*I*"—he looked to see all heard him—"told her it was we who burned the *John Calvin.*"

The silence that fell on the heels of these words was breathless, like the air before a storm. Lumey grunted as if someone had struck him.

"You told her! Why?"

"I am tired of lying," Jan said.

"Knock him in the head!" someone shouted, but nobody moved; a mutter rippled the crowd, intent on Jan and Lumey and van Treslong in their midst. Many had not known before that the *Calvin* had burned by a Dutch torch; they turned to their neighbors and muttered, "Did you guess? Is it true?"

Van Treslong himself, his face white, said, "We burned the *John Calvin?*"

"You fool!" Lumey beat the air with his fist. "I had her in the palm of my hand!"

"Lumey burned her," Jan said to van Treslong. "To throw the blame on the Spaniards, and drive them from Plymouth. It would have worked, maybe, had the Queen not learned the truth."

From the rear of the crowd came another shout against Jan. "Take him! Hang him up—he sold our prizes." A whimper from his left drew Pieter's eyes: Mouse stood there gnawing his knuckle.

Van Treslong flung his arms out to silence the uproar. Jan cast a wide-ranging look around the room. Old Pieter coughed. He said to Mouse, "The boy's a fool." Yet against his will he warmed with pride at his nephew's calm courage.

Mouse said, "We must always tell the truth," and Pieter knew that Jan could do nothing that the boy would scorn.

Jan was turning, in the middle of the room, his hair glinting in the lantern light. His voice boomed out, the voice he used to carry orders on the *Wayward Girl,* and the murmuring crowd fell still again, expectant.

"I'll go by your word," he cried. "I'll stay a Beggar, if you let me, but if you deem me worthless now, I'll go."

A hush answered him. Mouse leaned forward, his lips moving. Then, like an explosion, an oath burst from Lumey's lips, and he strode forward and flung his arm around Jan's shoulders.

"Stay, by God! One of us!"

The crowd raised a single thunderous voice in agreement. Van Treslong shook Jan's hand and hugged him, and the whole of the Beggars pushed forward around him. Old Pieter grimaced. He saw Jan was their darling now, for all his misdeeds, or because of them, as a man loved a woman he could not master. There would be no removing the *Wayward Girl* from the shadow of the Beggars' banner. He folded his arms over his chest.

"We sail tomorrow," Lumey shouted.

"Tomorrow." Jan wheeled, his face suddenly rough with concern. "Have we no more time than that?"

"Do you want the Queen confiscating our ships too? Let her take the notion, and she will—tomorrow! We leave on the morning tide!" Lumey beat on the tavern wall. "Bring the beer! Bring wine and geneva—the Beggars sail tomorrow; tonight belongs to pleasure!"

Looking very gloomy, Jan came back to Pieter's side, and the old man put his hand on his arm. "Changed your mind, I see."

"There's a woman, up in Salisbury."

"Oh," Pieter said, and sniffed. He drew his hand back, envious. "There's a wench in this, is there? I might have known. Well, choose, boy-o, choose—the wench in Salisbury, or the *Wayward Girl.*"

Jan drew back, his face furrowed with indecision. Mouse hung by him, looking up adoring into his face. "Will you go? I'll stay with you."

Jan laid one arm around the boy's shoulders and hugged him up against his side. Pieter grunted. He had never seen his nephew so open with the half-wit boy before. Van Treslong walked up to them.

"You did us a great favor, Master van Cleef—the Queen would have guessed the truth, sooner or later, anyway. We'll see you at the council, after supper?"

"I—" Jan licked his lips. His gaze fell on Pieter, something in his eyes pleading, or just hurt. The old man reached out his hand and gripped his nephew's arm.

"I cannot rule the ship without you, boy-o."

Jan heaved up a sigh from a depth great as the ocean floor. He nodded, first to Pieter, and next to van Treslong. "I'll be there." With one arm he hugged Mouse against him; with the other he clasped his uncle's hand.

13

THE FOG lay thick over the flat water and bundled itself around the topmast so that Jan could hardly see the bottom of the lookout. He walked down the deck to the wheel, where the glass was swiftly running down to its last grain of sand, and stood waiting for the moment to turn it. The piercing cold had driven most of the crew belowdecks; behind him, in the shelter of the poop deck, Red Aart and Mouse were huddled over an iron caldron of hot coals.

"We've lost her," Aart called. "She's gone. Let's make for the open sea."

"When Pieter says," Jan said.

In the ship's log he was writing: *Four bells. Thick fog, no wind. Slack tide. Sandy bottom at five fathoms. Sound of breakers to starboard, no land visible. Searching for Spanish merchantman.*

It was almost the same entry he had made four hours before. Lifting his hand to the bell rope, he rang out four strokes, turned the glass, and closed the log.

"I hate lying off a coast like this in the fog," Aart said.

"When the tide begins to make we'll have to stand out to sea," Jan said; he squatted down beside him, sinking into the little aura of the coal pot, his hands spread to the feeble warmth. "Another half hour of this and we'll be gone."

Aart muttered something under his breath. Mouse edged a little closer to Jan, who slid his arm around him.

He thought now, as he always did when some business of the ship did not hold his mind, of Eleanor Simmons, back in England. What she must think of him, when he had promised her to come back and now had been gone for six weeks without word. He wondered if he would ever go back. He longed to see her again, but the space between them—in time, in distance—seemed too great. Maybe she would have forgotten him. He stroked his fingers through his hair, thinking he should forget about her.

He would never forget her.

Behind him, the hatch flew open, and old Pieter put out his head. "Any sign?"

"Nothing," Jan said. "No change."

The old man walked up onto the deck. He wore a blanket around him for a coat. Tipping back his head, he sniffed at the air. "Where's the wind?"

"No wind."

Pieter scratched his armpit through a gap in the blanket; his fingers were lumpy from the cold. A low rumble of half-spoken oaths left his lips. Heavy-footed, he walked down the deck toward the bow, to talk to the leadman. Jan went to the starboard rail. Sometimes the fog seemed to muffle the sound of surf, but now he could hear it plainly: big waves breaking, two cable lengths away.

This was a bad coast, this Friesland coast, and he wanted away from it. They had come up here chasing what Lumey had declared to be a rich fat Spanish hen, and promptly lost her in the fog, and now Lumey was off somewhere with his ship, and half a dozen others of the Beggars were scattered along the coast, trapped in the windless fog, waiting.

He tramped down the deck after his uncle, who stood with the lead in his hands, examining the traces of the bottom stuck in the wax plug at the end of the weight. Just as Jan reached him, the sound came through the air of a distant cannon shot.

Pieter flung his head up. "Did you hear that?"

"Northward," Jan said. "Damn." There was still no wind. He took the lead from Pieter, who went swiftly away toward the stern, and gave it back to Marten, who was throwing the line.

"What's the last cast?"

"Five fathom," Marten said. "What's going on? Have they found the bastard? Can I get a relief? The cold is biting me, Jan."

Jan raised his eyes to the top of the mast, where the fog screened the lookout; it seemed as thick and motionless as before. "Stay awhile longer," he said. Pulling off his thick woolen mittens, he thrust them into Marten's hands and went at a trot after his uncle.

Pieter had gone to the aft hatch. Pulling it open, he yelled down be-lowdecks, "All hands! All hands up!" Coming up even with him, Jan heard again the distant bellow of a cannon, to the north.

"What are we going to do?" he asked Pieter. The old man struck irritably at him with the back of his open hand.

The crew rushed up onto the deck, exclaiming at the cold and the fog. Pieter paced up and down past them, striking his palms together.

"You hear that?" he cried, when the cannon boomed again. "Lumey has her, the devil. He'll cut her down and take all her loot, and give us nothing but a laugh for our trouble, unless we can get there and help him. There's no wind, so we're going to lower away the small boat and tow the ship."

At that the crew with one mouth let out a howl of outrage. Pieter's gaze slashed at them. "We'll change rowers every half hour. Three men to a crew. Aart, Henryk, Jan, you go first."

The others bellowed again, furious; Jan went down the deck to Marten in the leads, to retrieve his gloves.

They hitched a cable to the bow of the *Wayward Girl* and stretched it out to the ship's boat, and the first three men began to row. Jan was glad of the work. At least it gave them some control over the position of the ship, now that the tide was beginning to make. He took the center oars, because he was the strongest, and set the pace for the others; the hardest part was the first dozen strokes, as they strained to drag the *Wayward Girl* into forward motion. Once she was creeping through the water the rowing grew easier.

Another cannon shot boomed out, and another.

Jan thought of Eleanor Simmons again; he wondered, should he die here, if she would ever know. If she even thought of him now, back in her tower in Salisbury.

"Wind," Aart said, in the stern, hoarsely.

Jan lifted his head. Against his cheek the air stirred, cold as iron.

"Keep pulling," he said.

From the bow of the *Wayward Girl* came another hail. "The bottom's shoaling! Four fathoms and rising!"

That was Pieter's business. Jan kept his back into his work, listening to the crash of the surf off to his left now, and to the occasional thunder of the cannon behind him. The wind was too feeble to drive the ship, but it was blowing off the fog; strips and streamers of it gusted by on the rippled surface of the sea, and patches of clear air showed around the boat.

"Slight of four fathoms and rising!"

"Sail ho!" someone screamed, from the bow of the *Wayward Girl,* and pointed.

Jan twisted around to see. Up there, through the thinning fog, the topmasts and spars of Lumey's ship were coming visible, although the hull still lay buried in mist. She was dangerously close to the shore. As Jan watched, a red flame spurted from her side, and the rumble of her cannon rolled across the water toward him.

"Pull!" He leaned into the oars.

They rowed some dozen or two dozen strokes more, groaning with effort, and suddenly the wind turned and blasted full into Jan's face so hard it froze his cheeks.

"Up oars."

They raised their oars. On the *Wayward Girl,* the crew were rushing back and forth across the deck, trimming her mainsail. The canvas slatted and cracked full of the wind, and the ship drove forward, biting into the sea; the sound of the water rushing past her forefoot was like music. On the deck they were reeling in the cable. Jan raised his arm over his head, more a cheer than a signal, delighted.

"Sail," Aart cried, in a voice that creaked with alarm. "For God's love, Jan—"

Jan looked about. Nearly even with the surface of the water, they could see only a few cable lengths around them. The fog was thinning to nothing in the freshening wind; the sky was turning blue. Whitecaps broke on the tops of the waves.

Out to sea, in the dissipating fog, patches of white stood above the waves, eight or nine of them, ten or twelve, squares of white with red crosses on them. Spanish ships. His back tingled.

"It's a trap," Jan said.

He wasted no more time looking at the Spanish ships. Bending to the oars, he swung the small boat around and made for the *Wayward Girl*. Without word from him Aart and Henryk doubled to their oars.

They stroked madly across the narrowing water. Jan knew what had happened: Lumey's fat rich Spanish hen was a lure, and had gone to ground here in this filthy shallow water to draw the Beggars after her. Only the fog and the failed wind had kept the rest of the Spanish fleet away from them for so long. Rowing in under the lee of the *Wayward Girl*, he could hear the men shouting on her deck, could hear Pieter bellowing orders. As he climbed up the rope ladder to the deck, he threw a quick look over his shoulder, toward the sound of the breakers, and saw the long boiling rows of surf not three hundred yards away.

"God damn it!"

He reached the deck and went with long strides to his uncle's side, by the wheel. Pieter was staring off to sea, where the Spanish ships were waiting. Jan went a few steps past him to the poop deck and climbed the stair, to see up and down the coast.

There to the north was Lumey's ship, and another, maybe Dirk Sonoy's, and inshore from them the Spanish hen. She had gone aground in the shallows, and the two Beggar ships were nearly into the surf around her; Sonoy's ship was struggling to tack off into deeper water, and Lumey was coming about. They had seen the Spanish trap no quicker than the *Wayward Girl*.

South of them were two or three more Dutch sail, victims of the lure. Greedy, Jan thought, and shook his head: if they had not towed the *Wayward Girl* in after the sound of cannon they would be in a better place now, not pinned up against a treacherous shoaling coastline, with the tide making and the wind driving them north.

Pieter said, "They can wait, the bastards. Look at them."

The Spanish were not coming in after their prey. Drawing sometimes twice as deep as the Dutch ships, they were better off standing out and waiting until the tide and the wind and the wild surf drove the Dutch out to meet them. Jan swallowed the panic in his throat. He cast a quick glance behind him again at the beach; beyond the surging line of the breakers, the barren sand rose into steep gray dunes, frosted with snow. Not a good place to be shipwrecked.

The old man came up beside him.

"We have to run for it, boy."

"What do you mean?"

Pieter nodded his head to the north. "The bottom's coming up fast—almost three fathoms now. A couple more hours and the tide will shove us up onto the beach. We have to get out of here." He turned, looking south now, and pointed. "Back there."

Jan looked where his uncle's hand indicated. Behind them the coast curved gently around to the east, flat and dull, fringed with long white rows of breakers. Patches of fog still clung to the sea there.

"Where are we going?" Jan asked, puzzled. "The wind's dead wrong. The bottom's shallower there than here, by the way the waves break—"

"Into the fog," Pieter said. "Get back in that boat and row."

"You're mad," Jan said. "The wind will blow the fog away, and there we'll be, naked as babies. Look at the Spanish, man—" He flung his arm out toward the Spanish fleet; his gaze followed. There were many ships, rocking with the waves, their red-crossed sails slatting in the wind, which was dying once more.

As the wind died, the fog swelled again, rolling out across the sleek water, burying ship after ship in its thick clammy advance. He swallowed. "Very well. Whatever you say."

"Damned right," his uncle said, staring at him. "Get back in that boat and row."

Jan walked back to the side of the ship, where the boat was drawn up; half a dozen of the crew stood there, shivering in the cold and staring out toward the line of Spanish ships. Red Aart leapt toward him.

"What are we going to do? What's going on? Jan, I say we beach the ship and wait."

Behind him, Marten said hoarsely, "I say run for it! If we charge the Dons maybe we can break through."

"There's no wind," Jan said, brusquely. "Marten, Jobst, come with me." He swung one leg over the rail of the ship and groped with his toe for the ladder.

"Where are we going?" Marten and the other man came after him.

"To tow the ship. Come on."

"To tow the ship—how fast can we do that? They'll slaughter us! Where are we going? Pieter's mad. He's gone off his head. It's that tobacco, and the gin, and his age . . ."

But they were following him down the ladder, into the little boat. He sat on the center thwart and reached for the oars, his chest tight. Trust old Pieter, he told himself.

Aloud, he said, "The old man's gotten us through before. He'll do it again. Pull!"

They bent to the oars and rowed hard; when the cable tightened and took the weight of the *Wayward Girl,* the small boat jerked like a caught fish, losing all its forward momentum. They put their backs to the oars again.

They did not have to go far to reach the fog; it was closing in on them again, so dark and dense Jan could see the droplets hanging in the air, roiling up away from the swing of his oars and falling gently onto the back of the man in front of him. The oars creaked; the cable groaned. Steadily they pulled the *Wayward Girl* on through water as still and glassy as ice.

Now it was Aart in the bow of the ship, casting the lead to read the depth of water under the *Wayward Girl*'s keel. His voice reached Jan clearly with each hail.

"Four fathom and sandy. Four fathom . . ."

Jan's back hurt, and his hands were cramping from the cold and damp and the work, but he never thought of quitting. Better to do something, even something painful and tiring, than to stand up there on the deck and wait. The steady rhythm of rowing made the empty time manageable. The other rowers had stopped complaining, now that they were plying their oars; the silence hung around them like the fog.

"Four fathom and rising!"

Jan bent his back, stroking hard at the oars. Abruptly the gloom around him lightened, a breeze touched his face, and with a wild gust of wind the enclosing fog swirled away. Marten, in the stern of the boat, let out a hoarse cry.

"Look!"

The fog was shrinking rapidly away across the water, baring the whole coast again, the sea and the horizon around them. There, out in the deeper water, the Spanish were lying like foxes in wait.

Even as the fog parted like a curtain to expose them, there was a burst of smoke from the side of the nearest galleon, a brief darting flame, and the thunder of a cannon shot.

"Where'd it go? Where'd it fall?"

Up in the bow of the *Wayward Girl* Pieter appeared, leaning out over the bowsprit above Aart's head. "Row!" he bellowed. "Row, you damned fools—"

Suddenly between him and the boat something whizzed out of the air and fell into the sea with a great towering splash that soaked the rowers. The cannonball. Jan filled his lungs with breath. The small boat rocked violently on the turbulent waves.

"Pull!" He leaned forward, sweeping his oars back for a new stroke.

"They're firing again," Marten cried, and stood up in the stern.

"Pull," Jan shouted at him.

"No—we have to—"

Jan stood up and got him by the arms and jammed him down onto the thwart again, the boat bucking wildly under his feet. "Row, damn you, Marten, or I will throw you overboard!"

Marten gave him one look from a face white as the seafoam, grabbed his oars, and bent his back. Sitting down, Jan picked up the rhythm again. With a whine and a splash another cannonball tunneled into the sea a hundred yards away.

"Pull," Pieter howled, from the *Wayward Girl.* "Three points larboard, Jan. Make a new course. Pull, you lazy God-forsaken sons of whores! Pull!"

"Who's he calling the son of a whore?" Jobst said, behind Jan. "The crazy old bastard."

"Up starboard oar," Jan said. "Stroke larboard oar."

The boat swung her bow toward the west. In the distance more cannon sounded.

"Down oars. Pull."

There was a screech in the air like a passing witch and on the big ship a crash of timbers. A shot had hit the *Wayward Girl.* Jan could hear Pieter swearing, up there in the bow. Far away there was a rattle of cannon shot, too many to come from a single ship: the rest of the fleet was fighting Lumey and the other Beggars.

"Pull!"

Another shot hit the sleek water just beyond the ship and bounced over her; Jan saw it bounce again, on the other side, and plow into the shallows. The wind was like an icy hand across his back. He wondered what was happening to Lumey and the others.

"The fog!"

The wind died. The fog swept in again, curling around him like the arms of a cold mother, enveloping him in the gloom and wet. He sighed.

"Three fathom! Rising! Bottom's rising—"

From the bow of the *Wayward Girl,* only half visible in the fog, came Pieter's voice. "Three points to larboard, Jan—"

They changed course again. Jan's back hurt so that he gasped with each stroke; he knew by that how the others were hurting, and he called to his uncle to change the rowing crew. Swiftly, so that the ship would not lose the precious few yards of momentum that made towing her possible, the small boat returned to the *Wayward Girl,* and Marten and Jobst scurried up the ladder; two new rowers leapt down into the boat.

"Jan! Come up—get warm—"

"No," he said. "You need me here." He could not bear to return to the ship, to the inaction and the waiting; here at least he had some mastery over what happened to him. With the others he bent his back to the oars again.

They towed the *Girl* steadily on through the fog. From the north the boom of cannon sounded again, and the man behind Jan swore and prayed in a low voice. The oars rasped in the oarlocks. Jan's arms were heavy with fatigue. He braced his legs against the bottom of the boat to take off some of the strain. When he straightened his back, the muscles stabbed him with new pain. Suddenly there was the thunder of cannon, very close, and instinctively he ducked.

The others wailed. "They're shooting at us!"

In the bow Pieter shouted, "Jan! Bring her up to larboard some more!"

"No," cried the man behind Jan. "The damned Dons are lying off to larboard—he'll take us into the middle of them!"

Jan bit his lip. "We'll take her to larboard. Up the starboard oars."

"He's mad, Jan—they'll—"

"Up the starboard oars!"

On the heels of his words another cannon shot crashed out, very close, and he heard the rattle and crash of wood breaking, on the *Wayward Girl.* Someone shrieked in pain.

"The tops," said the man in the stern, in front of him. "They must be sticking up out of the fog bank. They're shooting at us by the mastheads."

Jan looked up overhead. At sea level the fog lay so thick around him that he could barely make out the bow of the ship, but overhead it thinned away quickly to nothing; he could even see the sun, a pale feeble eye in the gloom.

"Pull," he said.

They towed the ship on through the grim gray mist. Every few moments the cannon fired, but now the direction appeared to have changed; it seemed to Jan now that the Spanish guns were firing from behind the *Girl,* not off to one side—not between her and the sea. Another shot hit her stern and he heard screams and saw bits of wood flying through the air.

His first thought was to thank God that Pieter was up in the bow. The old man was screaming orders at him again.

"Two points to larboard, boy—tow!"

"Pull," Jan whispered; his whole body ached. He wondered if he did any good, rowing when his strength seemed to be gone. "Pull."

Another cannon fired; the shot missed.

"That was farther off," said the man in the stern. "We're pulling away from them. The wind's against them, damn them."

Jan sighed. His arms throbbed so he could not lift them again; he sagged forward over the oars, his head down.

"Jan! Are you all right?"

He raised his head. "Just resting." His voice croaked in his own ears. He lifted his gaze toward the sky.

The fog was being ripped away. The wind was coming back. He held his breath, watching, waiting for the mist to clear. To see where they stood, surrounded perhaps by Spanish ships, or mere yards from the shoals. The wind freshened against his face, blew back and forth in bouyant gusts like the blows of a two-fisted fighter, and peeled off the fog like a blanket, blowing the sea as clear as Heaven all the way to the horizon.

"We're free!" A yell went up from the deck of the *Wayward Girl.* "We're free!"

Jan let out a feeble high-pitched cheer. Without willing it, he rose to his feet, braced widespread on the unsteady boat's bottom, to look around him.

From the *Girl* to the western skyline the sea was empty. To the east, the coastline fell away in a line of low snowy dunes. Up to the north, the fog was still clinging to the water, and there the Spanish fleet lay, over a mile away.

"God have mercy on us." Jan sat down heavily in the boat.

The Spanish ships were firing; they still had some of the Beggars within range. Too tired now to row, Jan sat there and let his fresher boatmates take them back to the *Wayward Girl.* The distant roar and boom of battle sounded as if they came from another world. Old Pieter had gotten them out free and safe, although as Jan climbed up onto the ship, he saw broken railings, and a mass of splinters and rigging and cloth where her stern had been. They would have to go ashore somewhere and rebuild. He went up to the mast, where the water keg was, and dipped himself a drink.

Up north, more cannon fire crackled. Pieter came up beside him.

"They're buying iron," he said, in a voice greasy with satisfaction.

"We should go help them," said Jan, and dropped the dipper back into the keg.

"The wind's wrong," Pieter said, pleased. He thumped Jan on the back. "You did right well, boy-o."

Jan winced, his back muscles cramping from the blow. "So, unfortunately, did the Spanish, it seems like."

"Never mind them." Pieter thumped him again. "We'll go off to Plymouth."

"To Plymouth." He thought of Eleanor Simmons, and his heart leapt. He looked away to the southeast, toward England. "I'm going to bed. Wake me when my watch is on." He stood a moment looking to the southeast, thinking of her, and went below to sleep.

14

WILLIAM of Nassau had been born in Germany, the son of a poor and minor nobleman; it was only the unexpected death of a cousin that made him Prince of Orange. When he fled from Alva he went back to Dillenburg, where he had been born and grown up, to the home of his parents, where his younger brother now was count.

The castle was centuries old. His mother had kept a school there for young noblewomen; as a boy he had shared his ponies with them. From the window of the hall he looked out over the vineyards and hayfields west of the castle and saw an orderly world, where things were laid out in rows and tended by the seasons, a world full as a shell of its nutmeat, with no room for change.

He leaned on the window's wide stone edge and wondered if the Dutch would change.

All Europe was laughing at him. He had stolen away from his army in the dead of the night, because he could not pay them and they were threatening to take him prisoner and hold him to ransom. His own wife made a cuckold of him with stablemen and shopkeepers. What right had he to think he could save the Dutch?

He turned his back to the window and looked around the hall. The furniture here was older than he was, older than his father and his grandfather, heavy square pieces of oak, time stained nearly black. On the floor were rush mats, except at the end by the hearth, where the family was accustomed to sit; there an ancient carpet was spread carefully on the floor flagging. Here he had learned his lessons at his mother's side, reading from the Bible, writing letters on a slate with a piece of chalk. Here he knew what he was: a humble man.

He went up the stairs to the next floor, to the room where he and his brothers had slept as children. Here they had said their prayers at night— Lutheran prayers, because his parents were devout Lutherans; only when he went to Brussels to become the Prince of Orange, at the age of nine, had they consented to let him be baptized a Catholic, because otherwise he would not have entered into the great inheritance. Standing in the doorway of the long low-raftered room, he wondered now at their reasoning. If they had truly believed in their faith, why would they have been willing to see a darling child give up his salvation for a great name and a heap of treasure?

They were Lutheran still. It was Luther's Bible that rested on the table by the bed at the far end of the room—the bed where William of Orange was now to spend his nights.

He remembered battling his brothers with pillows in this room, before their mother came to tuck them into bed; remembered solemn oaths, taken in the moonlight through the window, to keep faith. To small boys faith was only a word. He had not argued when they told him henceforth he would have to go to Mass.

He turned from the room and climbed the stairs again, steps worn hollow in the middle, too narrow and steep for safety. At first the Mass had delighted him—the pomp, the ritual—as his new clothes delighted him, his fine new horses, his wonderful new palace, his new friends with their long magnificent names. He had learned the new confessional with enthusiasm. But when he had it learned and there was nothing else new in it, he lost his pleasure in it, and at the same time he could not find the way back to the faith his parents had taught him.

Slowly he resumed climbing the stairs into the highest part of the castle. The steps were so treacherous that no one came here anymore, except on one occasion: perhaps it was the very arduousness of the climb that kept alive the tradition that when a countess of Nassau was to be delivered of her children, she should be led up here, into this ancient room beneath the roof of the castle. He went into the room where he had been born and stood in the middle of it. The sunlight flooded in the three windows and filled the room. There was nothing else, save an old bed and a little table all hacked and chopped with knives. He and his brothers had gone at it with their belt knives one day, and his mother had threatened to whip him for it because he was the oldest. His father had said, "No, let them be. I did so myself when I was their age."

Here he had been born, in this little room no finer than the hovel of a peasant in the field.

That was honest. That was true. So he had learned, in the years in Brussels, attending on the Emperor, going to Mass, dancing with elegant ladies, carrying messages, waiting politely behind his master, lest his master need a pen, a book, a napkin. All those manners were the husks of life, the outward appearances; life itself was of another nature entirely.

He had found that in the Dutch people, busy at their work, at their games and dances, their hands stained with their earth, their faces brown from the sun, people like his parents. The people who cheered him in the streets, who made up poems in his honor, who loved him from the moment he appeared among them, a foreign boy, shy and frightened, come to be their prince.

He laid his hand on the table, where he and his brothers had cut the edge into deep notches.

He could give up now, and no one would think him less. They all thought very little of him anyway, after his humiliations in the field. He could stay here in Dillenburg and live out his life in peace.

If he went back, what was there? Death, surely, and dishonor, and humiliation. The King of Spain was his lord. To war against him was the oldest crime, Lucifer's crime. Thus would many see what he did.

There was another ancient crime, particular to the wild tribes who had settled in this region and become the Germans and the Dutch, the only capital crime in ancient times: to flee from the field of battle.

He thought of the Dutch, their mild, kindly ways, their tolerance, their natural optimism. Nothing seemed more at odds with these people than the Spanish and the Inquisition. They would resist, in their ways, because it was their nature; and because it was their nature, the Spanish would destroy them.

Out through the window he looked on the warm green fields of Dillenburg, the neat cottages, the spire of the church, as he had from the hall window; but from this height he could see beyond all this tidy order. He saw beyond to the wildness that surrounded it, the thickets and trees and stretches of meadow that lay to the west. That way was the Netherlands. Even as he looked his heart quickened. He knew he would not desert them. No one else would come to their help, but he would, although he knew it meant his death.

"I will keep faith," he said, low voiced. In that voice he and his brothers had sworn childish oaths, long ago, in this room. Now he swore an oath to the distant wildness, to the horizon, to the tormented lands beyond. "I will keep faith. We shall die together, you and I. I will come back."

15

LATE into the day, Michael lay abed, not sleeping; getting up seemed so hard, and for what? To put his clothes on, to eat, to drink, to fill up the day with nothing, and to sleep again? The curtains over his bed were drawn tight, and the sun never penetrated into the room. It was like twilight always, and he lay there and dozed now and then and let his mind wander into safe, old memories.

One afternoon there came a banging on the door that would not go away. He dragged himself out of the bed and slowly put on his shirt, hoping that whoever it was would get discouraged and go; but the banging continued, and shoving his feet into shoes he went forward through the kitchen and into the front of the bakery, and opened the door.

Out there were Spanish soldiers. He swung the door shut, but the man at the door caught it by the edge and held it.

"Are you the baker?"

Michael folded his arms over his chest, afraid; had they come for him now? He looked beyond this man to the row of soldiers in the street. The only one on horseback wore a helmet with a plume. He rubbed his hands up and down his arms, staring at this exotic figure.

"Are you the baker here?"

"Yes," he said. "I'm the only one left."

"Come out here."

"Why?" Michael scrubbed his palms up and down his upper arms.

"Come out here, on order of the governor of Antwerp."

That was the man in the helmet. Michael stared at the white plume again; slowly he went out the door and into the street.

"You are the baker?" The governor said to him.

Michael nodded, looking around at the soldiers. The sun was bright enough to make him blink. The shadow of the bakery sign lay flat and black in the street before him.

"Then why are you not baking?"

Michael swallowed. His gaze fell to the soldiers in their neat row, and to the shadow of the sign in the dust. They were reminding him of what he wanted more than anything to forget, and for reminding him, as much as for their greater guilt, he heated with a fresh-awakened anger.

He looked up at the governor in his white plume and said, "For the tenth penny I won't lift a finger."

The long Spanish face thinned even more at that, and the man leaned forward and said, "Are you a Catholic?"

"Yes."

"Do you know the Church's teaching concerning obedience to the temporal arm?"

Michael pressed his lips shut. His hands slid down his arms and tucked inside his elbows, and he stared at the governor without speaking. Down the street, some of his neighbors had come out to stand in the sunlight and watch.

"Your King commands you," the governor said. "He has the right to raise such monies as are necessary for the defense of his realm, and you have the duty to work to maintain him."

Michael said, "Withdraw the tax of the tenth penny and I will bake bread again, but not before."

The governor sighed. He seemed more patient and bewildered than angry. He looked around him and back to Michael and said, "You are not a man in prime years yet—have you no parents?"

"My father was killed in the image breaking," Michael said.

"Ah. Then you have no—"

"My mother was hung up here from her own sign by the tax collectors for not paying the tenth penny."

At that the governor's lips shut tight. He sat back in his saddle and lifted his reins. "Let's go." With a gesture to his men, he rode on down the street; Michael saw him ride to the next shop, the cobbler's, and send his man to knock on that door, because the cobbler too was not working. Michael went back into the shop.

CLEMENT DE VERE heard from some people about Michael's angry talk to the Governor del Rio and went there in the evening, to the bakery, and knocked. No one answered. He knocked again and again and still no one answered. Finally he climbed over the wall beside the bakery and walked around the side, past the brick ovens cold behind their drifts of leaves, to the little door in the back of the shop.

This door stood slightly ajar already. He pushed it wider and stood there looking at Michael, who was standing in the front of the little room, staring ahead into the front of the shop, toward the recent knocking. In his hand was a jug of beer.

Clement swung the door open, so that it hit the wall with a crack, and Michael jumped. Spinning around, he dropped the jug of beer and it broke on the floor.

"Good evening," Clement said. "May I come in?"

"Who are you?" Michael said, peering at him through the darkness.

Clement went into the dimly lit room; he saw a rushlight on the only table, and taking out his tinderbox he bent over the clay lamp and worked with flint and steel until he had the wick burning. Then, with the hot glow of the lamp on his face, he put the table between him and Michael and said, "Now do you know me?"

The young man's face changed slightly. "Yes," he said. "What do you want of me?"

"Some talk. Sit down."

Michael sat, slack limbed; he looked drunk, but not stupefied. Clement pulled a chair up to the other side of the table and lowered himself onto it.

"Have you seen Hanneke van Cleef?"

Michael put his hand to his face and pulled on his nose and rubbed his mouth. His eyes slid away, searching for a dark corner to hide in. Finally he lowered his hand. "No. Not since—no."

"She's gone, then. Alas for her: she has no Antwerp to flee to."

"Perhaps she's dead."

"Do you believe that?"

Michael shook his head. "But I don't know why she would run away and not tell me."

"She was frightened."

"We were lovers. We were going to be married."

"Perhaps she was afraid of hurting you."

"She should have told me where she was going."

"Sometimes . . ." Clement picked at the wooden tabletop, peeling up a splinter from the surface. "I fled here from Dieppe, in sixty-two, with my wife and my son. My wife died on the way. I did not stay to bury her. Fear, and running away . . ." He put the splinter into the burning wick of the rushlight and watched the flame catch. "It's impossible," he said, and shook his head, "to run and stay calm."

"Why are you here? Just to look for Hanneke?"

Clement shook his head. "No. No, I came here to find you. I heard you defied the governor. I have a job of work for you, if you are up to it."

"I will not work for the tenth penny."

"No, of course not. No one is asking you to. Many the people in Antwerp who are bolting their shops and refusing to work, many more every day. You've seen it."

Michael shook his head, surprised to hear this; a moment later he wondered why he was surprised, because he understood it very well. He grunted.

"Good for them."

Clement's head bobbed. The rushlight, touching only on the high planes of his face and shoulders, made him seem larger than he was. "Yet these folk must still be fed, and somehow we must feed them."

"Why us?"

"All of us. We must feed ourselves, without the Spanish dipping their fingers in."

The splinter was consumed. He dropped the final flaming bit into the lamp, where it blazed up briefly on the oil and was gone.

"The people need bread. You have the ovens and the skill. There is some danger involved—"

Michael said, "You know I am Catholic. What makes you think I will not betray you?"

Clement shook his head. "Because you are Dutch. Are you with me?" He put his hand out across the table.

Michael gathered his breath; the thought of Hanneke was strong in his mind. He remembered his mother, hanging from the bakery sign. Reaching his arm across the table, he took Clement's hand in a hard eager clasp.

THE ROWLOCKS of all three boats were muffled with strips of cloth, but one had come loose, and in the dark the rhythmic rattle and creak of the oar sounded loud as church bells. Michael swore under his breath. Twisting his head, he cast a quick look on ahead of his boat to the frontmost boat, where Clement was, hoping for an order to fix the unmuffled rowlock. No one spoke; the three men in that boat bent to their rowing as hard as ever, leaning forward in unison, down the narrow gap between the sacks of flour piled high into all three boats, their oars rising in the dark, sweeping backward over the river, and falling again to the stroke. Michael turned forward again to row.

They were working their way down the northern bank of the Schelde, where the river bar was shifting and treacherous and few sailors ventured. The three boats slipped in a close file through the still water, Clement leading them. He must have done this before; he knew exactly where to go, and they had not run aground yet. But Michael's oar now and then grazed the bottom, or dug deep into the silt, and the hair on the back of his neck stood on end.

He prayed as he rowed and sometimes cursed himself for doing this at all, when he could have been back in his shop asleep. He promised himself he would not do it again. It was too dangerous. Down this bank of the river there was nothing but the broad flats of silt and thickets of marsh brush, not a light the whole length of their trip, but on the far side was the city, with its wharves and anchorages, a thousand lanterns bobbing on the water, another ten thousand shining on the land, and the harbor watch. How were they to get through the harbor watch? He cursed Clement, too, for talking him into this.

Now the groaning of the rowlock was driving him mad. With a mutter to the man behind him, he shipped his oars and shifted his weight forward, reaching in between the squat sacks of flour to find the lock and the padding of cloth that hung useless from it. Someone else murmured some encouragement. Unable to see much, going all by touch, he wrapped the cloth around and around the iron fork where the oar rode and knotted it fast.

Now it would not move easily, and the rowing was harder, but the racket was stilled. He bent his back to the oars. He was raising a blister on his left hand, too, and he cursed that and forgot about praying.

The man behind him tapped him on the back. He straightened, lifting his oars up, and looked over his shoulder again.

Now they were opposite the center of the city. The water lapped against the sides of the boats, and beyond them, in the marshes, a night bird lifted its voice in a mournful croak; there across the quiet water the lights of Antwerp blazed. Crooked trails of light stretched across the river like fingers pointing at the smugglers. On a ship lying out near the center of the channel a bell rang twice. Michael's ears hurt from listening. He thought he could make out voices on the ships ahead of them. His stomach rolled over, sick with fear.

Coward, he thought fiercely to himself. *God, help me. God, give me courage.* He thought of Hanneke: would she love him if she knew how he felt now? His mouth was dry. His fingers wrapped tight around the grips of his oars were cramping with fatigue, and his back ached.

"We go straight across," the man behind him whispered. "The canal is straight across from us. If we're hailed, ignore it. If we're challenged, then we'll separate. This boat goes to the Duke's Canal, downstream half a mile, and up to the first bend, where there's a wharf, and there wait for orders. Got it?"

The other man, in the stern of the boat, grunted some acknowledgment, but Michael said nothing.

"Go."

They bent to the oars. The few moments of waiting had stiffened Michael's back muscles and his arms, and the first strokes were an agony. Now they were rushing forward into the lights and bustle of the enemy city. In his panic he went too fast and lost the rhythm of the other oarsmen; they hissed at him and one splashed him expertly with a flat stroke of an oar. He tasted muddy water on his lips.

God, help me, he thought, thoroughly frightened now. *God, be with me.* Miserably he longed to be home.

A ship loomed over them; he could hear the river water sloshing against its hull. He smelled oakum and pitch. The sour odor of the wharves grew stronger. His shoulders hurt. He wanted to stop so badly he groaned, but if he did stop the others would turn on him and, worse, would know he was a coward. He wished he had never seen Clement. *God, help me,* he thought, and fell to prayer again, timing the words to the strokes of the oars.

The night was growing lighter; he could see the ears and neck of the man ahead of him, rowing. The city was engulfing them with its bright bustle. Voices sounded ahead of them, and a church bell began to ring and others joined it, a growing chorus of brass tongues. They passed between two more big ships. Like cliffs the first black jetties lifted up around them;

one of his oars scraped wood. Bits of debris floated by them in the water.

"Hold! Who goes there?"

He nearly screamed. He nearly dropped his oars. Ignore it, he remembered, and kept to his stroke. The boat shot forward through the water, a wharf on one side, on the other a broad stretch of choppy water where the canal opened up.

"Hold—up oars, there in the boats, or I'll shoot!"

"Turn," the man behind Michael shouted, and the boat lurched to one side. Michael had no notion which way to turn, or what he should do to help; he sat there paralyzed on the center thwart while his companions swung the heavy craft around to leeward. He raised his head and saw on the wharf that now stood up behind them a row of men with muskets in their hands.

"Watch out!"

The muskets rattled. Michael ducked, his hands rising instinctively to cover his head. A bullet hummed past him. Something struck the boat beside his foot. Behind him a man screamed. The water leapt with tiny fountains from the bullets. Michael sobbed for breath; he felt he could not get enough breath to live. The man in front of him whirled and struck at him.

"Row! Row, you fool—we're betrayed—they were looking for us—row!"

The grips of his oars swung in jerks back and forth above his hands, the blades dipping down into the water. He caught the grips and bent his back to the oars. They were shooting again, up there on the wharf. He leaned into the stroke and raked his oars through the water, and the boat shot forward; that rain of bullets struck in their wake. Something thudded into a sack of flour to his left, and a little puff of white dust went up.

That steadied him. The flour would shield him, somewhat, if he kept moving. The man in front of him was rowing so hard he gasped with each stroke. Swiftly they shot the boat across the open water, past the mouth of the canal where they had meant to go, and into the maze of wharves and jetties beyond.

"The Duke's Canal," said the man in front of Michael, and gasped again. "Remember—in case I—"

For the first time Michael realized the oarsman was shot. Stunned, the young man lost his stroke staring at the body ahead of him, bending to the oars, pulling feebly at the river.

"Row, damn you!" the wounded man ordered.

He rowed. Turning to look behind him, into the bow of the boat, he saw that thwart was empty. They had lost the bow man. His oars hung in the rowlocks, dragging at the water, and Michael leaned back and pulled the oars into the boat to keep them out of the way.

They worked their way down through the dense wharves and jetties of the harbor, sometimes shipping their oars to pull the boat along by hand underneath the wharves, or from piling to piling. Behind them more muskets went off and there was shouting, but no one sounded the alarm near Michael's boat. At the mouth of the Duke's Canal they stopped, close by the bank, to rest.

It was the last rest for the man in the stern thwart. He slumped down over his oars, coughing, and Michael climbed awkwardly up between the flour sacks to him and tried to help him sit.

"I'm dead," the man said. He was nameless to Michael, faceless, only a body. He leaned his head against the young man's shoulder, his breath gurgling in his throat.

"We're safe now," Michael said. "Aren't we?"

The head against his shoulder swayed from side to side. "Betrayed. Someone betrayed us."

Michael said nothing. He wondered if that were true, or if they had only run into the watch. The next time they would have to be more careful. Not use the main canal, for one thing. Slowly he realized that the man leaning against his shoulder had stopped breathing.

He sat there awhile, tired, wondering what to do. There was nothing he could do for this fallen man, except offer a prayer for him—who could have been Catholic or Calvinist or even Anabaptist, for all Michael knew. His chest felt heavy and clogged. He thought of the man's home, his wife and children, waiting for him. *I'll kill a Spaniard for you,* he vowed, and a moment later was horrified at his own thought.

This nameless man had saved him. Michael remembered the paralyzing fear that had gripped him and how this man had rowed and forced him to row away from the enemy fire. Dying, yet he had struggled on to his last measure of strength and saved Michael.

The body in his arms was heavy, but he was reluctant to lay it down. He owed this man a debt beyond paying, the price of his life. Too late now. The boat rocked gently in a little series of waves. The night crowded around him, ghost ridden: all those who had died were watching him. Waiting to see what he did.

His fear was gone. He knew now what he must do. Only one way to pay back what he owed. He would fight on, as this nameless hero had, until he died, or until the Low Countries were free again.

Finally he laid the man down in the bottom of the boat, between the rows of flour sacks, and took his oars and brought the boat around to the Duke's Canal. There was a lock here, a wooden water gate that stretched across the whole width of the canal, and he took the boat to one side and found the way through it. In the dark he fumbled with the stiff weed-grown ropes and the drop gate, and pulling the boat through the narrow opening he hit something that broke with a crunch of rotten wood. In the slack water beyond, he bent to the oars again.

"Hold! Hold, there in the boat—"

The shout went through him like a lightning bolt. Here was his first test. He lunged into the next stroke of the oars. The canal ran by the backs of factories and warehouses; wooden wharves stretched out into the middle of the stream, and he steered toward the nearest of these shelters. A musket went off, behind him.

"Over here," someone was shouting, on the far side of the canal. "Over here!"

Someone else answered, in Spanish.

Michael whispered an oath. He pulled the boat in under the wharf, in among the black pilings like the wet trunks of trees, and drawing the oars into the boat he climbed over the side and sank down into the cold water. The bottom was only four feet under the surface. His feet sank a little into the muck but it was firm enough to walk on. Groping along the side of the boat, he found the painter in the bow and towed the boat on through the dark under the wharf, close by the bank, where the shadow was deepest.

He could smell the blood of the dead man, in the bottom of the boat, the warm sickly sickening smell of the body. The water made him shiver. When he stopped, to listen and to rest, the cold drove him on again almost at once.

While he stood listening, he saw the watch moving up and down the far bank, looking for him, their lanterns swaying out over the canal, throwing gleaming patches of yellow light onto the flat water. They called back and forth, and sometimes men answered on the bank over his head, so that he knew where they were and could hide from them. His feet were numb from cold. He hated the men up there so much he caught himself snarling silently in the darkness whenever their voices rang out. The rope over his shoulder was wearing a rut into his flesh.

Once, someone saw him, or perhaps it was a lucky guess; a musket went off on the far side of the canal, and the bullet plowed into the bank a foot from Michael's face. His stomach heaved. He could be that dead man in there; he could be yielding up that ripe aroma of blood and cooling flesh.

He was that man, he told himself. That man, and every other victim of the Duke of Alva. For a long while he did not move, although the chill crept into his bones and turned his feet and legs to unfeeling lumps; he knew now what a burden he bore.

At last they were gone. He heard them moving away down the canal, calling to one another, and he dragged the boat on to the next turning, out of sight of the enemy. There under the dangling branches of a tree, he pulled himself up into the boat and took the oars once more. Only when he was half a mile on, rowing toward his bakery, did he remember that he had been supposed to wait at that turn for the others. He shrugged. That did not matter. If there were any others left, they were busy enough with their own safety, and he had the bakery, the ovens, the skill to make use of the flour. He could not worry about those other people now, anyway; worrying about them divided his mind and soul; and now he had to be strong. He rowed on, into the fine dawn light, into the warmth of the morning.

NEARLY a week later, Michael stood in the square before the cathedral with a mass of other people to witness the execution of the King's justice. He looked among the rows of men and women brought forth to die, and when he saw Clement there he was not surprised at all.

Clement could barely walk. His arms hung limp at his sides and his face was gray as old paper. He held his head high as a crowned king. When on his way to the stake he passed by Michael, their eyes met for a moment. Michael struggled to keep his face impassive; not a trace of recognition showed in Clement's expression. The tips of his fingers were mashed and raw, and deep blackened burns showed on his palms and lips; he had been tortured.

Michael knew that Clement had kept his secrets, in spite of the torture, because he, Michael, was still free. That was why Clement held his head so high as he walked to his death: he had defeated the Spaniards once again. Michael felt no pity for him. Even when Clement and the others were tied to the stake and burned, he felt only a grim satisfaction in their defiance. His defiance. Scourged of the softness and kindness of his youth, he knew himself strong as any Spaniard. As the smoke rolled up from the fires and the people writhed and burned, he even smiled.

THE GOVERNOR DEL RIO watched the executions from the porch of the cathedral, with his aides around him. The crowd that had come to watch seemed much smaller than that which had witnessed the previous executions, but that did not surprise him, since so many had left Antwerp and so many had died. What did surprise him was the silence of this crowd. Earlier crowds had cried out, moaned, prayed, cursed, surged back and forth the better to see it all, and wept for pity and horror. Today these people stood like soldiers in neat rows and watched and were still as rocks. Their faces were hard. He wondered uneasily what he could do now to make an impression on them. He realized with a rising panic that somehow he had lost his power over them.

16

MAGNIFICENT! Wonderful!" The Duke of Alva paced across the room, his long strides sweeping the carpet. At the far wall he wheeled and glared at the little semicircle of his officers, waiting by his desk. "The Spanish navy has struck a great blow for Christ. At last they have driven the Beggars from the sea."

He swung out one arm like a scythe and knocked down a lamp standard.

"While the Spanish army dawdles and haggles and lets itself be put off by a crew of merchants and storemen!"

A page ran to pick up the iron standard. The clay lamp had broken; a puddle of oil soaked into the carpet. Alva strode back through the office, scowling at the floor, his hands on his hips, his cocked elbows spread.

Luis del Rio, the King's governor in Antwerp, was among the six men looking on. The news of the great victory over the Sea Beggars off the coast of Friesland filled him with relief, and he was unwilling to ask the hard questions that Alva's flamboyant announcement left so ominously unanswered.

Alva said in a low voice, "The navy will have the King's ear for this, and we shall have nothing. Nothing."

Del Rio was watching Alva's face. The old soldier looked tired, and less than triumphant. Perhaps it was only that the victory had fallen to the navy and not the army. Maybe it was jealousy that kept him from rejoicing fully at this great news.

He had fought wars since his childhood, had Alva, and never lost. Not until now. He put all his faith in the simple Aristotelian logic of force: attack weakness, avoid strength, keep your men fit and well armed. By all the laws of his experience, the Low Countries should have submitted to him as tamely as the Indians to Cortez, by the fact of their several natures. But here the roles were different. He despised the Dutch for merchants and traders, but here their mercantile laws prevailed; and it all came down, in the end, not to strength, fear or faith, or even truth, but to money.

"Your Excellency," said Viglius, the councillor, "when can we expect some money from Spain?"

Alva grunted explosively. He turned his back on the half ring of his advisers.

"Your Excellency, the army has not been paid in months. They will not fight. Fortunate we are that Orange and the others have not chosen this moment to attack. We need money to meet the payroll, or the troops will mutiny."

"Surely," del Rio said, "now that the navy has destroyed the Beggar fleet, a shipment of money will come through."

Alva wheeled around to face them, his jaw clenched tight as a shark's. His eyes gleamed. For a moment he faced them in silence. Del Rio thought, *He is wondering how much to tell us,* and a cold tingle of alarm ran down his spine.

"No," Alva said, abruptly. "They have not destroyed the Beggar fleet. They hurt them—that was all. They caught them, finally, and did them some damage. That was all."

He shook his head; his long face worked through a frown. "What about the tenth penny? How much have we collected?"

Del Rio cleared his throat. This was his business. He said, "In Antwerp, almost nothing. In the northern Provinces, some few revenues, but they are poor up there. The great cities are refusing the tax."

"The Estates voted it! They must pay it."

"Excellency, they are refusing to trade. It is a tax on trade. If they will sell nothing, buy nothing, there is nothing to tax."

"How can they refuse to trade? It is their lives."

Alva swung to face him; del Rio lifted his chin, to look his chief in the eyes. "Because they hate us, Excellency. They would rather die than help us."

"God's blood," said Alva. "Would we could slaughter them all."

"Your Excellency." Del Rio leaned forward, intent on what he said, as if he could force his thoughts into the duke's skull. "Even if you slew every Calvinist, these people would stand against you. It is not merely the Calvinists here, it is everyone—Catholics too. What you have done, Excellency, by your oppressions, is drive them together, to confront us as one people."

Alva stiffened. His mouth thinned to an angry slit. "What are you trying to say, Luis?"

"Excellency, I am saying you have failed here. Your policy has failed. In fact your policy has strengthened the opposition to the Crown, and made the King's name despised here."

The long hard Spanish face of the Duke of Alva tightened into a mask. He jerked his head at Del Rio. "Get out."

"Your Excellency." Del Rio bowed deep and started past the other councillors to the door.

"All of you," Alva snapped. "Get out!"

They shuffled away after del Rio into the antechamber, where at once they let out a round of sighs, a gusty wind of relief. Viglius laughed, shaky.

"We'll turn this placid Brussels into the breezy Bermoothes." He put out his hand to del Rio. "Your courage is your escutcheon, my lord."

"Your loyalty wears a bend sinister," said Don Federico de Alvarez,

Alva's son. Gloomy, he walked away across the room to the window, his back to the others.

"What do you think he will do now?" said the governor of Mechlin, with a twitch of his head in the direction of Alva's room.

Del Rio drifted off, letting Viglius manage these idle speculations. At the window he joined Don Federico. They stood side by side, looking out over the park to the busy streets of the capital.

"I can't understand it," said Alva's son. "We win every battle, but they will not see reason and surrender."

"We have lost control of the sea," Del Rio said. "The navy must do more than win honorary battles and inflated triumphs if we are to regain it. And there is another thing. You know the legend of Antaeus?"

The tall man shrugged. "I don't recognize the name." He was not young anymore, although del Rio thought of him as young; he had grown middle-aged in his father's shadow.

"It's a story from Greek times," del Rio said. "Heracles fought Antaeus, whose mother was the earth; as long as Antaeus touched the earth, her strength sustained him, and he could not be beaten." He waved his hand at the tree-filled park, the crowded city, the distant hazy farmlands beyond. "This is the Dutch earth."

"You think we cannot win."

"We cannot win your father's way."

Don Federico spun toward him, taller than he was, tanned from the sun. "God is only testing us. Let our hearts be strong, and we shall triumph. We must triumph. For God's love." His hand chopped the air. "We are the Spanish army! We have fought the Italians, the Germans, the French, the Moors, the feathered warriors of Montezuma, and destroyed them all. We are the greatest force on earth! How can a leaderless crowd of bakers and brewers, moneymen and pirates stand against us?"

Del Rio said, "I admire your zeal. At my age, passion's only a forewarning of indigestion. Let me ask you this—what think you honestly of your father's policy?"

The dark fierce face turned away, out to the window again, toward the open, the sky, the broad plain. "It's not soldier's work—to hang men up to die. If we cannot beat them in a fair fight, we might as well go home."

Grasping the younger man's arm, del Rio embraced him. "God have mercy on you. While such as you live, I have no fear for Spain."

"I am—" Don Federico grimaced. "Out of my time."

"Perhaps."

"What will you do now?"

"What do you mean?"

"I know you, Luis. When you speak as you did to my father just now, it is no idle volley, but the opening salvo to a long engagement. You mean to change his policies. How?"

"I have no faith in my ability to change the mind of Don Fernando de Alvarez."

"What, then?"

"We will write to the King. Ask for his removal."

Don Federico's lips twitched. His eyes burned dark as coals. "Well," he said. "Good. I am tired of being here." He turned and walked away, out of the room.

17

LEAVING Antwerp, Hanneke followed the highway south, sleeping under trees and digging turnips and onions from the fields on either side when hunger drove her to it. There were other people traveling away out of the Low Countries; she found company often with others going into exile.

They talked of the future, where they were going, what they would do. No one really knew, Hanneke least of all.

At the border, she helped a widowed farmwife spin her season's flax, staying there for fourteen days to do it. For her labor she got some clothes and a sack of cheeses, which she took over the border into Germany and sold in a city market for a little money.

The German Empire, a patchwork of hundreds of great and little states, ordered its churches by the principle of *cujus regio, hujus religio,* meaning that the persuasion of each ruler became the faith of his people. The place where she found herself being Catholic, she made for the Palatinate, whose prince was Calvinist. On the way she fell into company with a German family taking the same road north. The wife was very genial and kept Hanneke by her to talk through a whole day's travel. Hanneke, glad of the companionship, questioned none of it. They stopped at an inn that night, and foolishly Hanneke let herself be convinced to put her little hoard of money into the hands of the wife for safekeeping over the night. When she woke in the morning, the whole family, kind and kith and kindred, was gone.

When she asked for them the innkeeper laughed at her. A heavyset man in middle age, he watched her through small pale eyes that never seemed to blink. "Gone," he said. "Sneaked away in the deepest morning, before the sun woke—took your pennies with them, did they?" He laughed again.

She stood still, her hands hanging limp at her sides, and the tears welling like fire in her eyes. Suddenly she wanted her mother with a longing more intense than any hunger, any thirst: wanted her mother and the safety and familiarity of her own home.

"They went on toward Württemberg," the innkeeper said, and waved his arm vaguely down the road. "If you hurry maybe you can catch up with them."

She gulped. Even if she caught them, what would she do? She could not force them to give back her money. She shut her eyes. If she thought hard enough, perhaps this greasy kitchen with its stench of pickled cabbage and old beer would vanish, and when she looked up again she would be back in her home in the Canal Street in Antwerp, before the thunderous knocking on the door broke down the circle of her world, that day so long ago when her father disappeared.

"You can stay here, if you want," the innkeeper said. "There's work to be done. You can earn your keep."

She put her hands up to her face, to hold off the sight of this place; she struggled not to hear him. If she wanted it enough, surely she would have her home again and her mother's arms around her.

An arm did fall around her. She almost turned into the embrace; she almost gave herself up to that safety. Then his hand gripped her breast, and she recoiled from him, striking out blindly, with a blind accuracy catching him squarely on the nose.

The innkeeper howled; he gripped his nose, and with his free hand knocked her down. She fell on her back, her legs kicking up, and in the back of the kitchen the cook howled with laughter.

Hanneke sat up swiftly, tucking her skirts down around her knees. The innkeeper glowered at her. With his huge hairy paw he still held his nose. His voice came muffled past his sleeve.

"You'll change your answer, I think. Stupid wench. Get to work. Sweep the rooms and scrub the chamberpots, and we'll think about giving you some dinner. Go on!" He swung his foot at her, and she leapt up and hurried away from him.

She stayed on at the inn, sweeping and scrubbing for her bed and meals, dodging the drunken and lecherous customers, and doing battle daily with the equally lecherous innkeeper, for the rest of the winter. The hard work tempered her. At first she wept for loneliness, but as the days passed she grew content with herself. She felt herself growing whole again, as if the events of the past few years had shattered her soul into pieces that now began to fit together once more.

The inn was popular; every day swarms of strangers moved in, ate, slept, and went off on their way. She watched them as if from a great distance, from a height. Their lives seemed trivial, unconnected to the great matters of the universe. They went on whole-mindedly pursuing their small interests and ephemeral pleasures, unaware of the huge forces that could crush them in an instant, destroy their lives in a single moment. The catastrophe that had seized her set her apart from the passing herd. Her language set her apart: she understood German, and the Germans understood her, but it was like seeing through a gauzy veil.

She felt herself in readiness, waiting only for the insight of purpose. Twice a day she prayed to God to reveal Himself to her, to tell her what to do. Then one day in the spring, while she was emptying out the chamberpots, she heard someone in the innyard speaking Dutch.

She rushed to the common room window and leaned out to see. Below her was a little party of horsemen. They were plainly, even rudely dressed, and the innkeeper was ignoring their entrance, having sent his son to see to them. There among them was a red-headed man, a little stooped and sober in his manner, whose face she knew immediately although she had seen him only once before, when he rode into Antwerp a long long time ago. It was William, Prince of Orange.

She drew back from the window, one hand on the sill. Her heart was beating painfully hard. No need to run to him now. There would be time enough to talk to him, in the evening. She knew she would talk to him— that great things would come of it. God had brought Orange here to her. Stooping for the stack of chamberpots, she went off to finish her chores.

"Aaaah."

The boot came off reluctantly, like a layer of living skin; Orange wiggled his toes. They had been riding for three days. One of the men was bringing him a cup of wine, and he reached for it, smiling his thanks, his throat parched.

"What a rat's hole." His brother Louis paced up the room, kicking at the rough furniture and the stacks of their baggage sitting around it. "Of all the inns in Germany, we had to find the worst."

"We'll only be here a few days," said Orange. "Until the others come."

"Why wait for them? Why not go on and let them catch us?" Louis dropped into a chair. His face was sour with bad temper. "God's blood. Rather a bivouac in the field than this."

"We need an army to bivouac," said the Prince. The wine was harsh and made his head pound. He held out the cup to his servant. "Water this somewhat, please. Halfway." Turning to his brother again, he said, "I pray you, keep your chafings to yourself—you will infect all our company with your malaise."

Louis growled at him. Raising one arm, he flung it over his eyes.

Orange sighed; he struggled against his own low feelings. Leaning forward, he scratched and rubbed his aching boot-bound feet. The servant had gone for a jug of water. The others of his company sat slumped around the room, none talking, busy with their own private complaints. The shadows in the corners, the gloom that lay over them palpably as the dust of their travel, were more real than the high-flown cause they pretended to honor.

His heart sank. This was what it came to, then, all the great words, all the resolution: a little troop of exiles in a shabby German inn, the largest thing in their minds their piles and boot sores. The door opened.

At first no one moved; they were all too tired to move. The woman who came in among them was only a servant anyway, from her coarse clothes. She came into their midst, tall, big boned as a boy, her fair hair bundled under a rag around her head, and the Prince of Orange saw the ardent temper in her eyes and thought for an instant, *She's mad.* He sat up straight, warned.

"Running away?" she said, her voice clear and sharp in the quiet of the room.

The others stirred, facing her; one by one, in the gloom, their heads lifted toward her.

"Is this your course? When your people are dying and need you, you run away?"

She was talking to Orange himself. He licked his lips, surprised, wondering what he should answer. Her face held his gaze. Her features were common enough, wide-spaced eyes in the broad square face, a heavy-lipped mouth, a large nose: the looks of a woman of the Dutch countryside. Yet her fury glowed forth nobly, a radiance of truth.

"Did you know," she said to him, her words like a whiplash, "that we are dying, that we are being murdered and tortured, that we are being driven out of our homes and down the streets of our own cities by the Spanish? While you run away?"

"Who are you?" he asked.

"My name is Hanneke," she said. "I am from Antwerp. On the day I left, with my hands red with the blood of a Spanish soldier, they were hanging people by the tens and hundreds."

"Antwerp." Someone sighed, in the dusty, gloomy margin of the room, and moved closer.

"We needed you," she shouted into the face of the Prince of Orange, "and you weren't there. You ran!"

"Stop your tongue!"

The Prince's brother Louis sprang forward, hot, to confront her. He flung out one arm toward Orange.

"He has lost everything in your cause, stupid woman—all his money, all his lands, even his firstborn son, sent into prison in Spain. How dare you speak like this to him?"

"Hold." Orange took Louis by the arm and drew him back, and drawing him away he stepped forward himself to take the girl by the hand. "Sit down, Hanneke of Antwerp, and tell us what you have witnessed. Give us fuel to stoke our dying resolution."

For a moment longer she stood like a column of marble, her face blazing with the intensity of her feelings. Her fingers tightened on his. Her eyes grew luminous with tears. The Prince stretched out his other arm to her, and she came into his embrace and put her face against his chest and wept. The others crowded around her, speaking comforts. The Prince, cradling her against him, saw their weariness drain away, their faces alive again with sympathy, with their purpose and their cause; she had brought them back to themselves. God, as usual, had provided what was necessary even in their despair. He touched her trembling shoulders, pleased and grateful.

"I AM GOING with them," she said to the innkeeper.

The German's jowly face swung toward her. "What?"

She waved her hand toward the Prince of Orange's party, assembling in the innyard; the people they had come here to meet had caught up with them, and they were ready to go on. "I am going with them."

The innkeeper spat onto the floor, a practice he did not allow his customers. "So. This is how I am repaid for taking you in and keeping you and putting up with your foul temper all these months."

"I worked for my keep," she said, startled; she had not expected this from him.

"Some sweeping," he said. "A few chores done. Pagh. Go on, anyway; you are a useless girl, anyway."

She turned toward the door, where her few belongings waited, tied into a bundle inside her heavy cloak. Outside, in the sunlight, her new companions waited in the dust.

"Hold," the innkeeper said, behind her.

She turned, and he dug into his purse and took out a coin, rubbed it between his fingers, saw it was a golden guilder, and put it back in the purse. "Nay, hold." He fumbled among his hoardings a moment longer and dug up a silver mark. "Here, take it."

She hesitated, weighing this unexpected action in her mind, and he pushed it at her. "Take it."

She took the money, and he turned away; they separated without more goodbye than that.

With the Prince of Orange, she walked on down the road toward the neighboring duchy, whose master was Lutheran. Here, the Prince told her, he hoped to find support for a new attack on Alva—money for an army, mercenaries, supplies. She understood none of that, and cared nothing for it: all that mattered was that he meant to go back.

"I'll go with you," she said.

She had no horse; she was walking along beside the Prince's stirrup, looking up at him. Abruptly he threw down his reins and swung out of his saddle to walk beside her.

"You shall go back to Dillenburg," he said. "To my mother's home. You'll be safe there."

Before she could answer his brother Louis pushed his horse up between them. "Here," he said. "Let her ride behind me. You must ride, William."

"I am content to walk," said the Prince. He held up his reins to his brother. "Lead my horse, if you will."

"You cannot walk," said Louis. "You are a prince. You cannot walk like a common peasant."

"Oh, can I not?" the Prince said pleasantly. "Why, my brother, I should think that a prince should be able to do more than a common man, not less."

"Exactly," said Louis.

"Then I shall ride sometimes, and walk others," the Prince said. "Lead my horse." He smiled at Hanneke, as if they shared a secret.

"William," his brother said, "you have no sense of your own greatness." He spurred his horse away, leading the Prince's after.

"I haven't any wish to be safe," Hanneke said.

"Whatever do you mean?" the Prince said.

"When you go back to the Low Countries, I shall go with you."

"To what end?"

That stopped her; she had no answer for that. She knew she could not carry a pike or a musket. She stared away across the fields they were passing, where men and women stooped to hoe and plant. The land dipped away down from the road; there on the far slope, where it rose again, a hitch of oxen drew a plow across the golden ground, the furrows darker than the fallow.

She said, "God will tell me what to do."

"I think you do what God desires of you," the Prince said, "in being what you are. You inspire us all."

"Not I," she said firmly.

She wanted more to do than that, more than simply to be, like a statue in a church, something to stir living hearts.

They walked on a little way; it was warm for the season, and the fine dust of the road rose in clouds under their feet. Taking her arm, the Prince moved to the side of the road, where grass grew up beside the ditch, and they walked there, still arm in arm.

"Hanneke," he said, "what will you have me do in the Low Countries?"

"You must drive the Spanish out," she said.

"The King is Spanish. We cannot drive them out entirely."

"Then make them be honest with us. Or we must have another king."

She frowned at that, wondering if that were possible, and a new thought struck her. She looked around keenly at the man walking beside her. "You could be our king."

He shook his head. At the corners of his mouth creases appeared, like a smile beginning. "Then everyone will say I have done it all for my own ambitions. I will not have that said of me. Or of your people."

"We must have a Calvinist king," Hanneke said, "or we will never be safe."

As soon as she said it, she was sure it was true, and suddenly new truth appeared before her, like a new world rolling up over the horizon of her mind.

"I am not a Calvinist, Hanneke," the Prince was saying.

"A Dutch king, at least."

"Nor am I Dutch."

She shrugged, less interested in what he said than the vision growing clearer before the eyes of her imagination. "Certainly we must have a new kingdom."

"A new kingdom," he said, and looking at her he did smile.

"One where everyone could live in peace. Where everyone could work, no matter what your faith, and where children would not be hanged, and where they had to give you a fair trial when you were arrested, and you couldn't be arrested at all except for a very good reason, and—"

"Can we not have the old kingdom still, only make it more just?"

She lifted her face toward the sun. "A kingdom where the true king is God Himself."

"I think," said the Prince, "we are talking of two different realms now."

Hanneke did not reply. The idea she nurtured delighted her; she felt it grow and swell in her mind, quickening, robust. Ahead, the spires of a town appeared above the round crest of the road, and with a few light words the Prince turned to his horse and mounted. She walked along the side of the road, her arms clasped over her stomach, protecting something within her.

T HE DUKE looked dismayed. "By God, sir, it grieves me to see you fallen so low in the world. I knew you had lost much, in the unpleasantness, but to see you like this . . ."

He shook his head a little. The duke was a Lutheran; like many of that persuasion, he let his faith lie small and quiet in the back of his life, a Sabbath matter. He wore satin clothes and the newest in white starched collars, and on his shoes were buckles coated with diamonds. His court also was very rich and orderly.

The Prince of Orange exchanged a bow with him, and they went to walk in the duke's garden. The duke was fond of flowers and had a variety of the very newest sorts, brought from all over the world. Troops of gardeners kept the place immaculate. The two noblemen walked along a gravel path that threaded a way through the clipped hedges and beds of spring violets.

"Alas, you came too early in the year," the duke said. "In July the bloom is magnificent."

"I came," said the Prince, "because there are people dying by the hundreds in the Low Countries, people to whom every moment is vital."

A twig from a pear tree had fallen into the path and the duke frowned down at it, nudged it with his polished shoe, and called a gardener to pick it up. "A very unfortunate situation," he said, over his shoulder, to the Prince. "All Europe rocked when Horn and Egmont were executed. I cannot think when last such noble heads rolled from the block—not since the bloodbath in England, I fancy."

"They died because they trusted King Philip," the Prince said. "I do not. I know Philip, and I am certain now that he will not concede—"

"Ah, now." The duke led him on to a bed of odd-shaped plants, with pale green leaves like knife blades shooting up from the soil. A few lifted red and yellow cups of flowers toward the sun. "These are at last showing flowers. Aren't they marvelous?"

"Philip will not concede anything unless he is forced to," said the Prince. "Yes, they are lovely. What are they?"

"From Turkey. I don't remember what they are called. I sent an expedition there expressly to bring them back. They grow from bulbs, like onions." He bent over the nodding flowers, one hand behind his back. "Unfortunately they have no scent."

"You have my sympathies. Let me remind you that Philip is a Hapsburg, and your Emperor is his cousin."

The duke straightened swiftly, whisking his arm around before him again, and set off down the path. "The Emperor is a reasonable man."

The Prince gave chase. "There may someday be an emperor who is not."

"We are very secure here in Germany. Our religious quarrels are settled."

"When Rudolf dies, who then? He will have no heir of his body. His brother is a fool. His nephews, on the other hand—"

"The Emperor is still in his prime years."

"But when he dies . . ."

They were walking swiftly along the gravel paths, the Prince two steps behind the duke; a pair of gardeners weeding rose beds saw them coming and dodged to one side.

"We have settled all that," the duke repeated, and coming to the end of the path he had to stop and turn. He faced Orange, his hands raised, palms out, as if he would thrust him back. "We do not need more disruptions here."

"I'm not asking you to disrupt your own duchy, or the Empire, at all. Only to remember your fellow Protestants in the Low Countries. I have a young woman in my retinue who—"

"I have no money," said the duke.

"If you would listen to her, she could tell you—"

"Nor have I any available troops. I must ask you—"

"If you listen, she could tell you tales of such horror—"

"I can do nothing!" the duke shouted.

In the silence after his bellow, the two men stared at one another, eye to eye. A sheen of sweat appeared on the duke's brow. He took a napkin from his sleeve and patted his forehead.

"Now, if you will excuse me, sir."

"Thank you for giving me hearing," said the Prince, in a leaden voice.

"You are welcome, sir; I am sure you are very welcome." The duke went swiftly past him, brushing against him, and once past sighed, as if set free of some trap.

"ARE YOU sure it is here?" Hanneke whispered.

"Sssh." The Prince's brother Louis of Nassau waved his hand at her; they walked slowly down the alleyway, picking a path through the darkness around heaps of garbage. Something small and furry leapt up onto the low-hanging roof ahead of them and scurried away. Hanneke hoped it was a cat. She clutched her cloak tighter around her, fighting the urge to look back.

"Hold," said Louis, and stopped before a doorway. He knocked.

The door opened slightly; in the thin sheet of light that emerged Hanneke could see Louis' profile. A voice said in German, "Who is it?"

"Friends," said Louis. "Children of God."

The door opened. "Come in then, brother."

They went into a little room crowded with people. On benches along the walls sat women in dark clothes; at one end of the room, opposite the end where the door was, stood a wooden lectern. When Hanneke and Louis came in all heads turned toward them.

"Peace," Louis said, and lifted one hand. "God be with all here."

"And with you also, brother." A tall man came down the room toward them, holding his hands out. "And with our sister too." He reached out his hands to Hanneke, who clasped them and bowed.

They took their places among the congregation, and the meeting went on, with a prayer and a song. Hanneke looked covertly around her. These plain strong faces might have been Dutch. It had been long since she went to a Calvinist meeting. Her breast ached with a sudden surge of memories. She bowed her head and prayed, thinking of the new kingdom.

The idea had grown to dominate her waking thoughts. The new kingdom seemed so compelling and real that she knew its appearance on earth was imminent. The people were in travail now, and God, the Divine Midwife, would bring forth of them the Golden Age. It would come. She prayed for its coming in a voice that quavered with intensity.

There was a sermon, quiet and well reasoned, about the need to keep the mind and heart pure. A child began to cry, somewhere in the crowd of dark clothes and sober faces, and was quickly silenced. Beside Hanneke, Louis of Nassau leaned forward, intent, his eyes shining. The richness of his clothes and the heavy gold ring on his hand set him apart from these German townspeople. She saw how the others looked at him and hoped they understood that the ring was not an ornament but a mark of his rank.

When the sermon was over, he rose in his place, and every head turned toward him.

"Brothers and sisters," he said. "I came among you as a stranger, and you took me in. My companion and I are forever grateful to you. We are exiles, wanderers, people with no place, our country overrun by savage enemies. Now we come among you to ask you for your help."

The tall man, who had given the sermon, still stood by the lectern. He said, "Tell us who you are, brother, that we may know your history and your plight more fully."

"I am Louis of Nassau," said the Prince's brother. "As for my companion, her history, and her plight, it will serve all simply to know that she is Dutch."

A gasp went up from many throats. Hanneke felt their eyes on her and dropped her gaze, her throat hot and itching with embarrassment.

"The Dutch people are dying," Louis said. "The time has come when we must all give everything we can, or stand by and watch a whole nation perish in the name of idolatry and blasphemy at the hands of the Spanish. We must give, or be party to the massacre. We must—"

From the end of the room there was a crash that brought everyone up onto his feet.

Hanneke wheeled toward the door, every hair standing up on end. The tall man rushed forward; the congregation stirred and shifted their feet, and Louis flung back his cloak and put his hand to his sword. All eyes turned toward the little door where he and Hanneke had come in.

Another thunderous crash rocked it, and the wooden door shattered from top to bottom. It burst inward, flying off its hinges.

In the crowd women screamed, and the whole mass of people pressed backward, toward the wall. Through the opening where the door had been a man in half-armor strode, a torch in one hand and a cudgel in the other. After him came more men in shining breastplates, with torches, with clubs.

"What is this?" Louis marched forward. "Whose men are you? Give way, damn you!" He pulled out his sword, rasping against the scabbard, and the torch light bounced along the blade and glanced off the walls.

"Louis!" Hanneke leapt after him, to stop him.

Before she could reach him, the soldiers fell on him. He braced himself, his sword raised, a lone man between this little army and the cowering men and women of the Calvinist congregation, and the soldiers struck him down. Hanneke shrieked. She rushed forward, past the soldiers now tramping down the room, and knelt over the Prince's brother, her arms out to shield him.

He lay on his side; blood welled thickly from a cut on his forehead, but he was breathing. She gripped his arm and shook him, trying to rouse him. He was unconscious. A scream behind her pulled her attention around.

The soldiers were herding the Calvinists around the room. One reached the lectern and threw the Bible down from it into the middle of the floor and overturned the lectern itself and smashed it with his foot. The Calvinists rushed along ahead of the clubs and the torches. A woman cried out; she had dropped her child and stooped to pick him up, and the soldier behind her knocked her sprawling to the ground.

"Pigs!" A soldier with a black beard marched the length of the room. "We don't want your kind around here. Get out! Get out or fry, you pigs, like the crackling meat you are. Pigs!" He thrust his torch into the wreckage of the lectern, and the dry wood caught fire.

The people screamed. Madly they charged toward the door, away from the flames. Hanneke pulled Louis' arm over her shoulders and staggered up to her feet. Running people, hurrying past her, bumped into her and nearly knocked her down. With the weight of the Prince's brother on her back, she stumbled toward the door. They were fighting, up there, fighting for a way out. Smoke eddied through the room. Her nose burned. The building was set afire. She could hear the flames snapping. Her heart banged in the base of her throat. Run—run—

Coughing, her back bowed under his weight, she hauled Louis out after the screaming mob into the alleyway. There, the soldiers had lined up, so that every Calvinist who came out of the burning building had to run past a row of clubs and kicks. She staggered after the last of the mob. A hard boot glanced off her shin. Something struck Louis on the back; he took many of the blows intended for her. She dragged him out to the street and laid him down there, and turning she looked back down the alley.

The building at the far end was all afire now. Its light blazed the length of the alley. Every piece of garbage, every pebble on the ground threw long dancing shadows toward her. The soldiers were shrinking from the heat, crowding the alley, their clubs hanging in their hands. She sucked in her breath. There could be more people there, trapped in the flames. She stepped forward. The soldiers saw her coming; they raised their clubs, their faces turned toward her like dogs expecting meat. She ran back the length of their line to the door.

They laughed when they saw her coming. One tripped her and she fell headlong. She got up to her hands and knees and scurried along a few yards like an animal before the strength returned to her to get up onto her feet again. A club struck her so hard on the arm it numbed the limb to the shoulder. She rushed into the shelter of the burning building.

There was no one there. She had come back for nothing. The flames enveloped the whole end of the room, so hot her eyes hurt, and her breath was painful. *God,* she thought, *God, is this how You protect Your people?*

She turned to leave; her eyes caught on the Bible, lying in the middle of the floor. The flames shot up all around it, but the book itself was untouched, save for a little char around the edges of its leaves. She ran forward, gathered the heavy book in her arms, and went out the door.

They were waiting for her, the line of soldiers, moving back a little out of respect for the flames. Waiting with their clubs and feet and their leering looks, their laughter; waiting with the flames glinting on their breastplates. Waiting as Carlos had waited for her. She wrapped up the Bible in a fold of her cloak and started down the alley.

She was out of breath, and her legs hurt; she did not run, but walked, holding up her head, waiting for the blows. They did not come. Something in her face drove them back, their arms sagging, their lips losing their mirth. Between them and the fire, she flung her shadow over them, and their breastplates dimmed. The Bible clutched in her arms, she walked slowly down the alleyway and drove the soldiers on ahead of her into the street.

When she reached the street they were gone. The Calvinists stood in a little knot in the cold moonlight. Most of them had fled; only a few were left. Louis was sitting up at their feet, one hand to the cut on his head.

Hanneke went up to the tall man who had delivered the sermon and laid the Bible in his hands. "Is this yours?"

"By God's grace," the man said, and gripped her hand painfully hard.

Louis lifted his head, the blood dappling the side of his face like paint. "You must go to the duke and tell him of this outrage. Whose men were those?"

The other people laughed, rough unhappy laughter. The tall man stroked the leather cover of his Bible. "The duke's men," he said. "The duke sent them. It is no use." He shook his head. "No use."

No use. Hanneke looked at them all, standing with slumped shoulders under the moon, their faces slack with fatigue and despair. *God,* she thought, *when will You bring forth Your kingdom, so that people like these and me will have some place to stand?*

Louis surged up onto his feet. "Come," he said, and grabbing her by the hand went off down the street.

"Where are we going?"

"To see the duke."

She sucked in her breath, startled. He towed her along beside him, her feet flying to keep up with his long swift strides. Yes. Confront the duke. She skipped a little, to catch up with him.

They went through the dark city, over muddy streets and streets slippery with cobblestones, past the hooked and barbel spires of the church that once had been Catholic and now was Lutheran, to the palace of the duke, where Louis' name and obvious nobility got them entrance in spite of the late hour. When they came to the chamber where the duke was taking his late evening cup, the overdecorated footman at the door told them that the Prince of Orange was there also.

Hanneke said, "Good, then."

Louis paused, one hand to his chin. Younger than his brother, he was much handsomer, as if practice had improved the design. He said, "I am not sure we should not wait."

"Wait," Hanneke said. "Did those soldiers wait? People might have died in that fire."

"We don't want to confound my brother's mission."

"If you are cowardly—" She started for the door. The footman, before it, was looking, startled, from one to the other of them.

"What do you intend of my master?"

Louis, scowling, turned his uncertainty and temper on the servant. "Let us through."

"My master does not enjoy being disturbed at—"

"Let us through!" Louis shoved the man violently to one side and rushed at the door. Hanneke followed in his wake.

They plunged through the doorway into a room elegantly carpeted, the walls hung with portraits. A little fire burned on the hearth, where two or three spaniels were sleeping; before the hearth sat the duke and the Prince of Orange, each in a little bowlegged chair, while a servant bowed between them, offering a tray of delicacies to eat.

The duke was turning to look at Louis and Hanneke. He wore a blue satin coat, the sleeves embroidered in gold and silver thread and slashed with pearl-gray velvet, and his beard and mustache were trimmed to perfect curves.

"My lord Louis of Nassau," he said, looking surprised and disapproving. "I did not remember extending my leave to you." His gaze rested on Hanneke; he sniffed.

"My lord," Louis said, and looked at his brother, who was stooped down over his knee to stroke one of the spaniels. "I went to meeting tonight," he said.

"I warned you against that," said the Prince calmly. In his worn brown coat he looked like a commoner. "What happened to your head?"

"I beg your pardon?" the duke said. "My lord, I desire some explanation of this unseemly intrusion—some reason why I should welcome you and not order you out."

"Tonight I was at meeting," Louis stated firmly, loudly. He advanced two steps to plant himself before the duke, but his hands slipped behind his back, and Hanneke, seeing his fingers twine and intertwine, knew how this authority cowed him.

"What sort of meeting was this?" the duke asked, blandly.

"A Calvinist meeting. An assembly of the children of God, for the purposes of worshiping God—"

"Nonsense," said the duke. He waved at the servant with the tray of sweets, and he withdrew rapidly into the corner of the room. "Such goings-on are outlawed in my duchy."

"Nonetheless," Louis said, still louder—shouting now, his voice ringing from the walls. "I was there, with dozens of other men and women, and we were attacked—set on by soldiers who threw us into the street and burned our meeting place."

The duke leaned back in his ornate little chair. "Excellent. So ought all outlaws to be treated."

"Outlaws." Hanneke strode forward, going up between the two chairs, almost into the hearth. "You deem us outlaws, who want only to obey God? Your men, sir"—she stooped to say this into the very face of the duke—"your men tried to burn a Bible."

"Who is this woman?" The duke's lips twisted in distaste. "Some common peasant out of the fields? Who is she?"

The Prince was standing. "With your leave, my lord—"

The duke's voice overrode him. Higher than before it cried, "Who brought this dirty person in here? Who is she? Get her out! Get the dirty wench out!"

The Prince bowed. "By your leave." He started toward the door, taking his brother in tow, one arm out to herd Hanneke before him. "Come on, now, friends—"

She did not move. She stood staring down at the duke, who was waving a scented napkin at her as if she had brought some miasma with her into his expensive little room. She said, "God have mercy on you, and on all your kind. When we are safe in our own kingdom, you shall fall on such times you will pray to God to relieve you of them in death."

"Hanneke—" The Prince had her by the arm. She leaned against his pull.

"Then think of those you might have helped but instead hindered," she said to the duke.

"Get her out!"

"Think of Christ, Whom you might have emulated but instead have crucified a second time!"

"Get her out of here before I call my men to take her out by violence!"

"Hanneke." The Prince dragged her away to the door.

Now she went with him, seeing this was hopeless. Going out, past the white-faced footman into the antechamber, she realized how hopeless it really was, and her mood sank; her body felt made of lead, impossible to move. She trudged along with the Prince and his brother, fighting against tears. The palace was darkened for the night. They walked alone through corridors and rooms lit by single candles set into the walls. In the main hall a woman was down on hands and knees washing the marble floor.

Had she done wrong? For the first time she wondered if she had made a mistake—if some subtler way might not have won what they needed, the support of this rich, light-minded man. Yet it seemed to her that any cause which depended on such people was doomed.

Perhaps they were doomed, all doomed. Perhaps the Catholics were right.

She stumbled. The Prince caught her arm and helped her keep her feet.

Were they right—the Catholics, who claimed to have known the truth all along, who said the Calvinists were sinners who deserted God? Oh . . . oh . . .

She heard herself moaning and clamped her lips shut. Her legs wobbled. Hurrying after her companions down a darkened corridor, she fought the cold invading trickle of doubt. God's will be done. Was it arrogance, to think to know God better than other people did? Satan's sin, to put her own vision first. God's will be done.

At last they reached the sanctuary of the Prince's rooms. She crept into a chair and put her face in her arms, terrified.

"WELL," the Prince said, "fortunately he had already declined any interest in our cause, and therefore your display will have few serious consequences."

With a taper he went around the little room lighting the candles on the tables and the walls. It was a very small room, only large enough for a bed and a chair; perhaps it had been servants' quarters, before the arrival of the penniless Prince of Orange made it necessary for the duke to find some extra space. The Prince wondered where the servants were being kept—in a stable somewhere, perhaps.

He smiled at that; he smiled at his brother, sitting hunchbacked on the bed, his hands clasped between his knees.

"I'm pleased you're not badly hurt. Surely it wasn't as savage an onslaught as you made out."

"It was," said Louis. "I might have died, William. Some of the others pulled me free, or I would have died."

In the chair by the window, Hanneke lifted her head a moment, her face a full moon against a background of shadows.

"You were foolish to go," the Prince said. "Knowing what you put at risk."

"Foolish?" the girl said, in her rough low voice. "To do God's service?"

"You are wise indeed, girl, if you know God's service so well."

She flinched at that, her eyes shining in the candlelight, her face luminous; he thought again, as he had before, *She's mad.* For a long moment their eyes met, the whole space of the room between them. There was no challenge in her look, only a sort of desperation, searching, and longing. Finally she lowered her eyes.

"If you had seen what I have seen you would not suffer fools like this duke to stand in your way."

The Prince grunted. His temper slipped; before he could catch hold of his tongue, hot words were leaping forth.

"Again, it's I who've failed, is it? You come at me with more reproaches —if only I would do this, if only I would do that. What of you, Hanneke? When will you submit to God, and devote yourself to God, rather than challenging me to do it? I cannot save the Dutch; you must save yourselves."

She flung her head back, her cheeks flaming red with the heat of anger. She sprang up from the chair. They faced each other like adversaries. The Prince regretted his outburst; always he preferred to keep his true thoughts secret. She faced him like a lioness, muscular and poised, her hands fisted at her sides.

Then her face changed. Under his gaze the warm red subsided from her cheeks, and her glowing eyes dimmed. Her mouth softened. She turned a little, curving her body away from him, as if to shelter him from the full fire of her temper. Over her shoulder she lifted her head and nodded to him.

"You are right. God has shown me what to do. God has been speaking to me all these months and I have not understood." She smiled at him. "Thank you for making me understand."

"Hanneke," Louis said.

Amazed, the Prince saw she was leaving. She was going to the door; she was pulling her coat closer around her, as if she meant to face some winter blast of wind. He put out his hand to her.

"Where are you going?"

Her face swung toward him again. "Where God means me to go."

"Where is that?"

"To the Low Countries. To my home. To make the New Kingdom." She opened the door and went out.

"Hanneke." Louis got up and started after her. The Prince caught his arm.

"No. Let her go."

"But—"

"Let her go, Louis. She was never ours anyway." The Prince put out his hand to draw the door shut. What she had said rang in his mind. Mad, mad, surely mad. As Christ Himself had probably been a little mad. Belatedly, he wondered if he should not go after her—give her money, words of hope, directions home. Smiled at himself: the mother in him. *Godspeed, Hanneke,* he thought. And pulled the door closed.

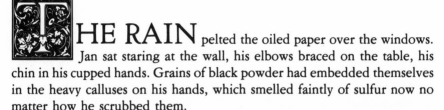

18

THE RAIN pelted the oiled paper over the windows. Jan sat staring at the wall, his elbows braced on the table, his chin in his cupped hands. Grains of black powder had embedded themselves in the heavy calluses on his hands, which smelled faintly of sulfur now no matter how he scrubbed them.

Behind him, old Pieter was playing cards with a few of his crew and with Lumey de la Marck. The slap of the cards on the table and the clink of money changing hands played like music against the hiss and rattle of the rain. There was a burst of laughter, and a tremendous growl from Lumey, who had obviously lost again.

"You are too lucky, you old bastard."

Jan shifted his chair. His backside was numb from sitting. The *Wayward Girl* had been refitted and patched. In a few days the storm would pass, and they would go to sea again, which, though often just as boring as sitting in taverns, at least gave him work to do. And sometimes fighting.

He could go buy a whore—there were three or four in this tavern now, upstairs servicing the other sailors. They said they liked the Dutch sailors because, being so much at sea, they had no chance to pick up diseases.

He thought of Eleanor Simmons, away in Salisbury, and his heart quickened.

If he went there, he was getting himself into something more than a warm bed. He had told her he would come back. If he did not, she could think he had died at sea. But if he did, he would be making some promise with his feet that bound his heart as well.

He could scarcely remember what she looked like. Her hair was red-brown, her eyes were blue, but the shape of her face, the curve of lip and eyebrow, was gone from his memory. He could not love her, if he could not keep her face in his mind.

Yet he had thought of her every day since he had left her, on the *Wayward Girl* at night, standing watch, and since they had limped crippled into Plymouth the thought of her had been growing stronger and more irresistible, like an enchantment.

He remembered of her the soft melody of her voice, the sharing of words with her, the sharing of dreams and longings.

"You old pig!"

Chairs crashed over. He jerked his head around to see Lumey de la

Marck dive across the gaming table, his arms outstretched, lunging at Pieter's throat.

The old man went down under Lumey's weight with a crackle of breaking furniture. Jan sprang across the room. Lumey and his uncle sprawled on the floor; Pieter shrieked, a sound like a knife tearing through canvas. Jan bellowed a wordless answer. His foot swung in a short hard arc that caught Lumey in the side and lifted him up off old Pieter to fall heavily to the floor.

His fists clenched, Jan started after him. A gurgling whine from his uncle stopped him short.

The old man lay on his back in a litter of broken furniture. Blood was pouring out of his mouth. Jan yelled. Dropping to his knees by his uncle, he caught the old man's hand and their eyes met, the blood fountaining up between Pieter's lips. The old man's eyes glazed. He gasped and choked and rolled a little to one side and was dead.

"Rib through the lungs," said Red Aart, behind Jan.

Old Pieter's hand still clutched in his own, Jan knelt there in a trance, waiting for this to end—for the old man to come alive again. The suddenness had jammed up the workings of his mind. He was not ready for it: it could not be.

"Hey!" Lumey bawled. "De la Marck! To me!"

Red Aart and Marten charged him. Lumey fled into the back of the tavern, where others of his men were drinking; they rushed to protect him.

Jan lifted the dead hand to his lips. Bending forward, his face to the floor, he tried to weep off the pressure behind his eyes and could not.

"Now, hold—hold!" Lumey was shouting. "As God witnesses, I did not mean him such harm. He was cheating me—"

Jan gathered up his uncle; the blood had pooled on the floor and got all over his shirt. The old man's limbs flopped and hung down, awkward, like a collection of sticks, the flesh still warm, although the smell of death emanated from him already, the smell of decay. Jan went to the door.

"Aart. Marten. Call the others."

The two big Nieuporters were still standing there, facing Lumey and his men, their faces dark with rage. At Jan's call they turned and followed him out to the rain.

In THE rain, they buried old Pieter in a graveyard below Plymouth height, within view of the harbor. Jan read from a Bible that Marten brought him. He read, not words for the dead, but Psalms his mother had told him, the first few verses of Genesis, passages from Saint Matthew about the birth of Christ: the sweet music of a world that was only memory.

The crew of the *Wayward Girl* stood there crying and cursing, their hats in their hands, while he piled dirt on the old man's body.

Afterward, Marten said, "Well, the ship is yours, Jan."

Jan supposed this was true. He gave the shovel to Marten, who laid it over his shoulder. Mouse stood by the cross at the head of the grave, his face miserable. Jan put one arm around him. The boy pressed his face to Jan's side.

"Will Pieter go to Heaven?"

"I don't know, Mouse."

"He must go to Heaven. I'll pray every night. I will."

"Ssssh."

"Every night and every morning."

Jan patted the boy's back, which was quivering with sobs. The others stood around him, their faces shadowed with their grief.

"What are we going to do now?"

Jan shook his head. "I don't know. I need time to make my mind up." He nodded to them, ranged before him waiting for his answers, and they nodded back, accepting that he had none. He said, "Go to the town; don't get in trouble with Lumey. You know Pieter; he did cheat at cards. I'll be back in a few days."

"Where are you going?" Mouse cried.

"To Salisbury." Jan started away down the hill.

THE PREACHER thundered, "And let us never forget, no sin is more abominable to God than the sin of concupiscence, of lust, of fornication!"

At that, every head in the congregation swiveled around toward Eleanor Simmons.

She went hot from the top of her head to her collar. Fixed her eyes on the wall above the preacher's head, and bit her lips to keep from blubbering. The preacher was right—must be right: for surely she had suffered so much, for that one night of joy, that it must be awful to God, that first He led away her lover, and now He turned the whole world against her.

The preacher was ranting again; he knew the Scriptures less than well, as Eleanor had often reminded him in days when she had some currency in the town, correcting his misquotations and supplying him with chapter and verse. But he made up for the lack of direct communication with God by a full round voice that reached into every corner of the church, and out across the churchyard too. He dwelt at length on the probable punishments for her sin.

She knew that already. She knew it at night when she lay in her bed waiting for sleep and thought of Jan. He had said he would come back, but it had been two months now, with no word. He had said he would come back. Was he dead? He followed the sea, a dangerous path, and he fought in battles against the enemies of God. He could have died.

Or maybe he had never meant to come back. Taken her for a light woman and forgotten her at once. She had been to him like a light woman: what else could he believe?

She would never know, if he were dead. She would never know.

The congregation knelt to pray, and rose to sing, and she did all with them, but her mind was not on God.

After the service she went out into the churchyard with the rest of her neighbors and stood to wrap her shawl around her against the blustery wind. The sky was heaped up with mountainous clouds. Did that mean that a storm pounded the rolling sea, away over the horizon? Somewhere, she imagined, a ship rode the wild wave, its sails drenched with rain.

Something rapped her arm. An old woman stood before her, gray haired, her face a nest of wrinkles around the sharp dark eyes.

"For shame!" The knobby old finger poked into her face. "For shame!"

Eleanor's jaw dropped open. This was Apple Granny, the old drunkard who depended on Stonegate for her daily bread, and here she came to shout shame into her face. The old woman piped up, again, "For shame!" and teetered off toward the alehouse, her head high with righteous indignation.

Someone laughed, behind Eleanor's back. She saw the people around her hiding their smiles. All folk she had done charitably with, at one time or another—all people who owed her kindness. Her heart ached at their dishonesty. Pulling her shawl tight around her head, she started home.

BERNARDINO DE MENDOZA, the ambassador from the King of Spain to the Queen of England, was always conscious of a certain anomaly of rank between him and the lady whose court he chose to ornament with his presence. He was a princeling of one of Spain's most noble houses, his blood enriched by generations of heroes and lords, while poor Elizabeth was only a Tudor, tracing her lineage back a few generations to a Welsh adventurer and a duke's mistress.

That she chanced to be Queen of England—a crown to which, in fact, her claim was not altogether perfect, and which, some thought, Bernardino among them, belonged more truly on the Catholic head of the imprisoned Queen of Scots—was an accident of unsettled times, which jumbled mankind out of all order. That she refused to bend to his superior gifts of statecraft and will was more evidence of her generally heretical nature, which would not conform itself to God's law.

Now he fixed her with a steady stare, to make her feel his disapproval, and sniffed.

"The times require bold strokes, Madame. Kings must use all their power to act, or cease to be kings."

She kicked over her footstool. "Kings owe their first duty to their subjects, sir, as I should not have to remind you. This slaughter of the innocents in the Low Countries—hundreds of men and women; yes, and children, too, say my informants—is the work of one who cannot presume to model his authority after the loving image of Christ!"

"These people are criminals. Heretics, rebels. You yourself are not averse to disposing of such human garbage when it accumulates in England. Yet you pretend horror when another monarch, sorely pressed, does the same." Mendoza curled his lip. "And so betray a small and womanish nature, unfit for manly rule."

"God's wounds," she said, cold voiced. "If it is manly to seize folk in their beds and herd them to the gallows, then I confess to nothing of manliness. I am told the heretics go to their deaths like God's own saints, in pride and dignity, while your soldiers slaver over their booty and riot drunken in the streets. I should be ashamed to call such pigs my own." Her thin, straight shoulders lifted their brocade in a shrug. "But Spanish ways are different, obviously, than most of humankind's. If you have no other business with our Majesty—"

"I do, Madame."

"Well, then, make haste. The heavy burdens of kingship need no further aggravation of idle time."

He sucked in his breath, exasperated. Her father a Welsh upstart, her mother an English whore, what right had she to moral superiority? The Devil spoke through her, the Devil himself.

"As your Majesty well knows, there is the matter of the four ships of His Most Catholic Majesty that were seized in Plymouth—"

"That again." Her hand flitted in the air. "We have talked over the whole issue any number of times, my lord, and we have made our meanings very clear: those ships are forfeit for the conduct of their crews."

"Their conduct! What of the piratical Dutch? Will you go on harboring these criminals, as if they were honest merchants? I tell you, Madame, my king will not long endure these insults."

She said, "Your king has already suspended my credit on the Bourse at Antwerp, which, in view of your king's legendary insolvency, is something of an insult in itself."

Bernardino blew out the breath in his lungs, seeking in his mind some new argument; he stared at her a moment, as if he might push her over by his look alone, and moved away, making a little circle, thinking. The room was cold and empty, of the morning, the carpets rolled up, and the flowers drooping in their vases. Thin cold shafts of sunlight cut through the dusty air to the floor. Tonight all would be gay here again, dancing and drinking and magnificent dress. It was hard to think well in a stripped room.

"These Dutch Beggars are rebels," he said, falling back on an old argument. "They are blasphemers and criminals who defy their lawful king. As a crowned personage, you must see the danger in the precedent of encouraging their rebellion."

She blinked at him. Her face was unreadable; behind that expressionless mask she might have been daydreaming, or praying, or making up a list of court appointments. He clutched his hands together in front of him, longing for a bludgeon and the right to use it.

"They carry letters of marque," she said. "Authorities from the sovereign Prince of Orange."

"Himself a rebel. The enemy of my king, whom you have already affronted by seizing the four ships. If you support his enemies, Madame, the King will have no choice but to take you for an enemy and proceed as his honor dictates."

She stared at him awhile, sleek as a cat. Her copper hair was smoothed and curled under a band of pearls and diamonds. She wasn't even really pretty. Her subjects all said she was, of course, but they were blinded by her devilish, deceitful acts, or by their own ambitions.

She said, "You may convey to our dear brother Spain our compliments and best wishes for his health and well-being, and you have our leave to go."

He glared at her. His sex, his blood, and his brain made him superior to her; how then did he always seem to take her orders? The Devil in her. And God was trying him. He bent his neck stiffly in as slight a bow as he could get away with and turned to go, walking out past a little crowd of servants hurrying in to make the room ready for the evening's revels.

ELIZABETH muttered an oath. The King of Spain was slow to act but once he took up a plan he kept it in his teeth like the bull's nose in the bulldog's jaws. She had her spies in the Low Countries; she knew how desperate was the cause of Spain. She knew how the Sea Beggars were throttling the Spanish lines of supply.

She loved them for it. Spain bestrode the world like the brazen man of myth. To defy Spain at all was madness, but to succeed . . . !

She could not defy Spain. Without allies, without wealth, she had to creep like a little mouse in and out of the chinks in the giant's armor, trusting to his indifference to preserve her. She dared not draw the full onslaught of King Philip's rage down on her little kingdom.

With a silver bell she summoned a page and sent him for Leicester.

There was much to do before she could sit down to her joint of mutton and her ale. Her cousin Mary Stuart was petitioning her again, which had somehow to be dealt with—the Queen of Scotland, who had fled from her enraged subjects into England and now enjoyed Elizabeth's hospitality in a situation Elizabeth preferred not to think of as a prison. Her cousin was a fool. See what came of marrying. Part Tudor, she was: maybe there was the root—her tendency to marry and to kill.

Elizabeth laughed to herself. Her father had always fascinated her, a safe enough interest now that he was dead. Sex and death, the twin powers of the King. Well, there was another, which was money, but that was not nearly so enticing.

Speaking of sex, here came Leicester, stepping high over the roll of carpet down the middle of the floor.

"Ma'am," he said, bowing.

"Robin, I asked you to send to Plymouth for news of the Dutch but I have heard nothing, and I fear you have undone me again. Bernardino was just here in audience, round as a bagpipe with Spanish wind."

"Ma'am, I have a man in Plymouth; I get the news every other day. The Beggars are in port again, refitting and revictualing." He turned the footstool upright and put his booted foot on it. His brow was fretted with ill temper. "It's you who's undone me. You give me these trivial errands—I waste my time doing no more than to put beads on a string . . ."

She made a sound in her chest. "They are here, are they? That's unfortunate." Certainly Mendoza would know of that. Still, every coin had two sides: perhaps there was an advantage to be made here.

"Yes, and rowdy, too," Leicester was saying. "One killed another in a brawl in a tavern, and word is they are quarreling wherever they meet."

"God's death."

She pulled on her rings, annoyed. They really were only pirates, as Mendoza said. The pages came in, bringing armloads of fresh flowers, which they took around the room, in and out of the sunlight.

"By Heaven," she burst out, "why are my choices ever between one thing half evil and half good, and another half good, half evil? Damn these motley Beggars!"

"I say, send an army into the Low Countries," Leicester cried, and jumped up, all fierce enthusiasm. "I'll lead them. We'll make short work of Alva." His face glowed.

"Oh, you will," she said, between her teeth. "Hold, sirrah; you look the strutting roister-doister, sirrah."

His cheeks darkened red with temper, but he bridled himself, standing still before her. She scowled at him. "Where would I find the money? Where the men? You'd send Englishmen to die in foreign lands as lightly as that, would you? God's death! I love my countrymen more than that, I hope."

"I'm tired of running errands," he said, and his gaze slipped away from hers.

"That's the nature of ruling," said Elizabeth. "We are all running the errands of the kingdom, me no less than you. You may serve with a merry heart or a melancholy, but you must serve, or matter not." She wiped her hand over her face, watching him, gentle again toward him, who suffered so much for her sake. "And serve one another as well, that's one comfort."

"You make a fool of me."

"Tchah." Impatient, she waved him off. "Begone. You annoy me."

"As you will, Madame." He swept her a bow full of flourishes and marched out.

Robin, she thought, but did not call him back. She leaned into her throne. The musicians had come in, with their viols and tambours, their lutes and pipes. She would call him later and they would dance. He was good at dancing. He had no mind for statecraft: he could not separate himself from the larger good; he saw only what affected him.

She loved the Dutch and hated Spain, but for England's sake she had to threaten what she loved and yield to what she hated. Well, well, the time would come when things would right themselves. She put out her feet to the stool, where bonny Robin's foot had been. She could wait. She only hoped the Dutch could wait as well.

19

THERE was a child sick in a poor man's hut at the edge of the village, and Eleanor spent the morning there, nursing the baby and holding the exhausted and hysterical mother's hand. At noon, when the child died, Eleanor walked home again, feeling the world heavy on her back as a fiend from Hell.

She stopped at the standing stones to rest. The sun had burned off the morning's mist and the stones were hot to the touch. Moss and lichens grew on them. She rubbed her fingers over the leathery edge of one green-gray patch, her mind on the pitiable baby dying in her cradle. It was wretched to see children suffer. They did not understand; they could not fight back against the demon eating them up. Gone to God, she was, the child. Her lips cracked from fever, her eyes crusted. Eleanor put her hands to her face, despairing.

When she lowered her hands again, a figure moving down the hillside caught her eye.

She straightened, reaching for the basket at her feet; it would do no good to her reputation to be seen loitering here, in this place of sin. Her eyes sharpened. This was no one she knew, walking down the path from Stonegate House, none of the local people, none of her servants. A moment later a glad cry burst from her, her body knowing him before her mind dared recognize him.

"Jan!"

She stood rooted where she was. He strode up the path toward her, smiling. He wore no hat and his pale hair was like tow in the sun. He came up to her as casually as if they had parted only that morning and said, "Well, hello, Mistress Simmons."

She put out her arms to him, and he gathered her up and kissed her firmly on the mouth.

"Oh," she said. "Oh, I thought you were never coming back."

He sat down on the stone where she had been, still holding her hand. "I was at sea."

"Can you stay? Are you here forever, now?"

He pulled her down beside him, his arm around her waist. "Forever! That's a longer time than I can think of." His gaze searched her face; taking her by the chin, he looked deep into her eyes. "You look so pretty, prettier than I remembered." He kissed her again.

She put her hands on his chest and held him away. "Pshaw! Do you take me for a light woman? I want to know what you intend for me. Are you staying with me, to marry me, or will you go off again and leave me here to the humiliations of my neighbors?"

His eyebrows arched up. "Have you been humiliated?"

"Oh, very much," she said, bitterly. "And by people whom I have been the very life and breath to, sometimes."

He squeezed her hand. "I'm sorry."

She waited a moment, expecting more, some answer to her question, but he said nothing; impatient, she blurted out, "Well?"

"I cannot stay very long, dear Eleanor. The ship is mine now; I must take her to sea." He told her of his uncle's death.

"Oh, God," she cried, less in mourning than abhorrence of the sordid flavor of it—to die in a tavern brawl.

"The worst is that he probably was cheating. He hated Lumey."

"Jan, you are a better man than that."

"He was not a good man, my uncle, but I loved him. Anyway the *Wayward Girl* is mine now."

"You keep saying that."

"I'm a ship's master now," he said. He smiled at her, his blue eyes sharp. He seemed much older to her somehow. He said, "I am a man of substance, Eleanor. I can take a wife."

"A wife," she said.

His hands turned over, cupped as if he supported a little world of his own in his hard callused palms. "I want a wife, and a house of my own, to come home to."

"Will you stay with your wife, in your house, and work the land and not go sailing?"

A low laugh broke from him, surprised. "No. I'll plow the sea, not the dirt, mistress. I'm a sailor."

She looked away through the gap in the stones, toward the treeless horizon. Some sheep grazed on the champion ground there. The birds were singing and pecking in the grass around the foot of the stones, busy at their husbandry.

"Will you marry me, Eleanor?"

"And spend my time wondering if you'll ever come back again?" She kept her side to him, her head turned away, her fists jammed into her lap.

"Think on it, please." He reached for her hand again. "Don't say no yet."

She would not give him her hand. Tears rushed into her eyes. She had been so glad to see him; now all the misery in the world filled her. She shook her head.

"Don't touch me," she said.

He left off trying. They sat side by side for a while, without speaking; finally they walked silent back to Stonegate House.

IN HER chamber that night, she made a fire, and sat on the hearth, her heart pounding. Before long there was a knock on the door.

She opened it a little, and Jan said, "Will you let me in?"

"This is why you came," she said bitterly. "Isn't it? This is what you want me for."

"Eleanor, let me in!"

She let the door swing wide and he strode through it, filling up the little room, his boots scraping on the floor. He pushed the door shut behind him.

"What's the matter?" he said. "Why are you angry with me?"

She had no answer; she had been angry with him for leaving, and she was angry with him now for coming back. She could not trust him. Or herself. Merely having him in her room stirred her memories, and her memory charged her lust, loosening her thighs and breeding a warm tingling in her belly.

"Will you let me kiss you?" he said.

"I ought not. It's sin, what we did—" She put her hand over her mouth, to keep from saying too much.

He stood looking down at her, his brows drawn over his nose; there were lines at the corners of his mouth she did not remember from the last time they had been together, when he had seemed to her like a young sun god, strong as nature. Finally he shook his head.

"Maybe I should not have come."

She stooped and put wood on the fire. She thought her heart would break if she spoke to him.

"Have you thought much yet of marrying me?"

"I cannot think," she said, her voice clogged up with feeling. "Not while you're here."

At that he sank down beside her and took her in his arms, and she flung her arms around his neck and they kissed.

He said, "I want to sleep with you."

"I—"

"No, hush." He put his hand over her mouth. "I'll sleep on the other side of the blanket, but I want to hold you." He kissed her again. "Is that sin?"

She locked her arms around his neck. After a while they went to bed. They slept little; they argued all the night.

"I CANNOT leave Stonegate," she said. "Too many here depend on me."

"Depend on you! Who does?" Jan cried.

"Why, the poor folk whom I feed, and my people here—"

"They don't depend on you. You said yourself, when you fell into scorn, they scorned you just as much as anyone else. If you go, someone else will feed them."

He saw at once he had struck something deep in her; her face thinned and sharpened, and her eyes grew harsh as ice. "How dare you say that, when I have devoted my whole life, these past five years—" She struck at him with her open palms.

"I need you," he said, fending off her hands. "I cannot do with anyone else but you. But you cannot stay here. I cannot come up here, three days' walk, every time my ship makes Plymouth."

She rolled over, her face to the wall. "I will not leave Stonegate."

He lay beside her, braced up on his elbow, watching her. There was a candle on the windowsill over the bed, which gave him light to see her by. This struggle with her baffled him. He had expected nothing of it. At their last meeting it had seemed to him he saved her from a dull and thankless life, and now, when he came to rescue her permanently, she fought him violently as a Don.

She said, her back still turned, "You must come here. There is work here, a good life here—"

"You mean, leave the sea? Oh, no."

She rolled over toward him again, tears streaming down her cheeks. "Then you do not love me."

"I do love you," he cried. "Would I have come back all this way, just to be railed at by a harridan, if I did not love you?"

"Oh, so I am a harridan, am I?"

"Eleanor—"

The candlelight glittered on the snail tracks of tears on her cheeks. She said, "I will not marry you unless you come here, to Stonegate, to live here with me. That is my answer." Without waiting for his, she rolled over again and pulled the blanket high up over her shoulder.

Jan watched her a moment and lay down on his back. The bed was too narrow for the two of them, but her warmth reached him even through the blanket and he wanted the closeness with her even if she hated him now. It seemed she did hate him. To force him to come here, miles from the sea . . .

Into his mind flashed the memory of the sea, the green wave rising fetterless and irresistible into the sky. He sighed. He would never live at Stonegate, in a woman's shadow. Staring up at the ceiling beams, woolly with cobwebs, he waited for sleep to take him from his unhappiness.

IN THE morning Jan went out with the other men of Stonegate to the fields, to cut the spring hay. Eleanor sat with the cook in the courtyard, going over the kitchen accounts; nearby, the hall maid was churning butter. The round wooden tub clattered on the uneven paving stones.

The girl sang as she pumped the handle up and down.

"Now listen a while and let us sing
To this disposed company
For marriage is a marvelous thing—"

"Leave off," the cook called to her. "Or sing a pious song."

"Let her sing what she will," Eleanor said.

"Hoho," said the cook. "Is that the way the road tends? I wondered, when I saw the white-haired sailor back again."

Eleanor picked a winged maple seedling from her lap and sent it spiraling off on the wind. "He has asked me to marry him."

"And will you?"

"But sure there is no doubt to know,"

the maid sang,

"Of man and wife the married state—"

"I don't know," Eleanor said.

"He is not English," said the cook.

"If he say yea, and she say no
I hold a groat the wife will ha'it!"

Eleanor laughed at the song, which lifted her spirits; surely it was an omen, and he would agree to her terms. She glanced around her at her home, snug and prosperous, everything desirable.

The cook sniffed. She drank as heartily as any man, and the excess of wine marked her face in red winy veins along her nose. "And you'll leave us here to our fate, I suppose."

Surprised, Eleanor looked up from the accounts. "Not at all. Why do you think it? There is room enough here, surely, for a husband for me."

The cook set her head to one side. "You'll wean a sailor from the sea? It is not done, my girl."

Eleanor opened her mouth to argue, but the rattle of the churn stopped, and the hall maid said, "Hello. Who's that?"

Two strangers were standing there in the gateway. Eleanor rose to her feet. "Good welcome, sirs." One was tall and fair, and the other a boy, with crossed eyes; they both wore sailor's clothes, just like Jan's, and she saw, alarmed, that they were Jan's men.

They came in the gate, the boy slipping into the shelter of the man's shadow; she remembered Jan had said there was a dull-witted boy on his ship, and this was surely he. She fought with her panic. They had come to take him. There was no way she could prevent them from finding him; the reckoning was come, sooner than she had expected, before she was ready.

The man put his fist up to his forehead, in a peasant's salute. He spoke in mumbled Dutch, the only audible words being Jan's name.

"Yes," she said. "He's here." It would do no good to lie. "Come with me," she said, beckoning, and led them out the gate again.

The men were haying in the champion below the hill, near the standing stones. She strode down the path, her skirts in her hands. The sun was bright and warm, and the wind a little gusty: a good day for haying. Down the hillside the men worked in rows, raking up the cut yellow grass.

She kept her eyes on them; the two strangers beside her unnerved her, both their mission and their enforced silence. If he went away now, she would never see him again.

Down there he had seen them coming. Giant among the other men he paused in his work, the rake slanting up through his hand, and straightened, and threw the rake down. He strode up to meet them. His long legs carried him forward almost at a run. Behind him the other men stopped to watch. Even the two big dray horses lifted their heads to watch.

"What is it?" he said to her, coming in among them, and his eyes went to the two strangers. Before she could say anything, he was speaking to them in Dutch; he had passed into their world and left her behind.

She stood there a little separate from them, knowing she had lost him; her hands closed to fists at her sides. What a fool she was: last night, at least, she could have loved him, shown she loved him. He wheeled toward her.

"The Queen of England's ordered us gone. She's closed England to the Sea Beggars, and we have to sail, and we can't come back."

She put out her hands to him. "Where will you go?"

"I don't know." His big hard hands reached for hers. "I have to go at once; you know that."

"Yes. Yes."

"Then come with me. Come with me now, on the *Wayward Girl,* and we'll get married as soon as we can find a preacher."

In her heart, something wild swelled and rose like a bird taking flight. She turned her head, to sweep her gaze over the placid fields, the mounds of hay, the cottage in the distance. The kindly English sky, the English earth. She lifted her face toward her lover's.

"I'll need some clothes, and my books."

They threw their arms around one another and kissed. Eleanor laughed, more to let out the exultant energy that danced hectic in her blood than from any real amusement.

"We have to hurry," Jan said, and they went swiftly off to Stonegate House.

20

J AN GOT to Plymouth three hours before the tide began to ebb, giving them only time enough to fill their water barrels and take on some stores of bread and salted meat, sailcloth and tar and line. The other ships of the Beggar fleet waited for the *Wayward Girl* at the mouth of the sound. The wind was rising out of the east. Jan smelled a storm breeding in the gray clouds that bullied their way into the eastern sky.

Twenty minutes before the tide would turn, he was running along the waterfront from shop to shop, looking for something to make the little master's cabin prettier and more comfortable for Eleanor. At last he bought a bolt of red cloth and a pitcher with flowers painted on it.

They put to sea as the first rain began to fall. The wind drove them west out of the Channel, into the wild Atlantic. The red cloth lay untouched on the cot in the master's cabin; he never saw the painted pitcher again. Against the storm he needed every hand, even Eleanor's, to keep the ship afloat and in the fleet. The pumps worked constantly, and still the water climbed in the bilge. The buffeting winds blew the ship off steadily west; huge seas rose like mountain ranges between her and the other Dutch ships. Now and again the storm faltered, the wind calmed, the seas flattened, and Jan sent his men up the masts to set the sails, and they beat back to the east, tacking for miles to recover a few hundred yards of weathering, until again the savage gale set on them.

Finally the winds blew themselves out. The sun shone through the clouds and patches of blue sky appeared. Save for the men working the pumps, the crew gathered on the deck to thank God for their deliverance. Jan stood with Eleanor beside him, reading out of Marten's Bible. When he was done, he turned to her, ready with reassurances, but her blazing smile met him.

She said, "God is proving Himself to us, Jan, and we to Him."

He grasped her hand and kissed it, pleased with her. The crew cheered them in weary voices, and they sat down to eat, their first food since leaving Plymouth. That was when they found one of the casks of meat bought in Plymouth was rotten, and that bilge water had leaked into most of their bread.

The only Beggar ship in sight of them was the *Christ the Redeemer*, Lumey de la Marck's ship. Together the two vessels sailed eastward, to raise the coast of Europe and judge from their landfall where they were. Just before night three more ships appeared, two of Sonoy's, and one little hoy of Baron van Treslong's, which was badly beaten up and looked about to sink.

The first call from these ships was for water; they had lost all their water stores in the storm.

The ships gathered together for the night. Jan worked nearly all the night long, with three other men, stuffing tarred rope into the strained seams of the *Wayward Girl.* By morning, the bilge pumps were sucking air, and he could order them shut down for a while.

He went down to the master's cabin. Eleanor slept there on the cot, wrapped in his big boat cloak, her head pillowed on the bolt of red cloth. When he came in, meaning only to look at her and make sure that she was warm, she stirred, looked up at him, and sat, putting out her arms to him.

He sank down into her embrace, and they kissed. She pressed her cheek against his face.

"My love," she said. "When will you come to sleep?"

"Soon, I hope," he said. He kissed her again. "When I do, Eleanor, I think we ought to sleep apart, until we find a man of God to marry us."

She hugged him, her arms around his neck. "When will that happen?"

He shook his head. "I don't know. We cannot go to England, nor to France, and my own country belongs to the Devil." He forced himself to laugh. "When you came with me, you gave up everything else, dear Eleanor."

"Nothing of any worth," she said, in a husky voice.

His heart jumped at that; he had thought she would regret it, coming with him, but he saw now that something in the storm had kindled her spirit. They sat awhile, in silence, kissing each other now and then; finally she lay down again to sleep, and he wrapped the boat cloak around her and with a kiss on her forehead left her there.

WHEN SHE came on deck, Eleanor drank in the keen salty air like a draught of wine. For a moment she stood looking across the deck at the sea and the sky, so utterly changed from the days of storm. The deck still rocked under her feet and she walked carefully toward the rail.

Now the sea lay around her in wide calm swells, blue-green under the sun, that lifted the *Wayward Girl* in swoops up to the sky and let her down again into the trough of the wave. The sky was bland as milk. Against her cheek the wind blew a light warm breath. She thought of the storm; the waves had climbed up into walls that towered over the ship, the wind driving hard lances of rain against her face, the sky black with clouds, demonic.

At the rail, she stood watching the other ships. There were fifteen of them altogether now, each rocking and dipping in its own dance with the sea, each one different. None was near enough that she could see people on board. They were like separate worlds.

The ship was, she thought, the world pared to its elements. No overgrowth of extraneous custom blurred the stark outline of the eternal struggle. No embellishment or habit of society could moderate the constant intervention of the hand of God. The sailors gave themselves up to the unequal battle with the sea; whom God chose survived.

The infinite horizon filled her with a sense of gigantic purpose. The very emptiness of the broad sea, which dwarfed the little wooden ships, satisfied her with its obvious order and proportion.

A mumbled voice beside her diverted her gaze.

The slow-witted boy, Mouse, stood there, holding out a chunk of bread and a wooden bowl of some indeterminate stew. She smiled at him, suddenly hungry, ready to share this new companionship.

The bread was so hard she could not bite into it. The boy talked to her in his own language, which was so close to hers and still unintelligible to her. Taking the biscuit from her, he dipped it into the broth in the bowl, lifted it, and pretended to eat, and gave it all back to her.

She soaked the bread until it was soft enough to eat. It all seemed very tasteless, and the meat looked and smelled foul. She smiled again at Mouse, who beamed at her. While he stood watching her, she forced herself to eat of the meat.

Her throat refused it. By a fierce effort she swallowed it anyway, and instantly her stomach sent it back up. Turning to the rail, she hung her head over the side and vomited convulsively.

She heard a soft gasp from the ship's boy, and felt a light sympathetic pat on her back. When she straightened up, breathing hard, she saw only a glimpse of him at the far end of the main deck, darting into the space behind the poop deck stair. Somehow she had frightened him. Her stomach hurt. She leaned against the rail, trembling, her throat raw. Remembered her lofty thoughts of only a few moments before, and in the tortured coils of her guts she found the strength to laugh.

LUMEY said, "For the arrows of the Lord are in me, the rage whereof drinketh up my spirit, and the terrors of the Lord war against me."

On his ship there was nothing left to drink but wine, which he had a jug of and now lifted up for several swallows.

Jan grunted at him. "Better to drink nothing than that, you fool. God knows we'd be better off without you."

"Leave off," said Dirk Sonoy. "Now is the moment to love one another. Better a raven than a swan among crows. Without one another we are surely doomed."

The other captains muttered in agreement. They were sitting in their ships' boats, pulled together rowlock to rowlock and bow to bow in the midst of the fleet. Today the sea was quiet as a baby's cradle, the wind too weak to fill a sail. Sonoy leaned forward over his chart again, spread on the thwart before him. He had broken his arm somehow in the storm and it was wrapped up and bound across his chest under his shirt. Treslong, sitting opposite him in the bow, held the edges of the chart down with his wide-spread feet.

Sonoy tapped the chart, which showed the Narrow Seas and the bordering coasts of England and France. "We can put in here, perhaps, in Cornwall, and fill our water casks; if we hurry, do it at night, we can be in and out before anyone's the wiser."

Jan leaned over to look, his weight tipping his dinghy up onto its round side. "God's love, Captain, I am taking no ship of mine in on that coast. There are such rocks and reefs—"

"I know the coast."

"At night?"

Sonoy jabbed the chart with his thumb. "The villagers here are sympathetic to us. Once I had to go ashore here, and I had a very fine greeting from them."

"That was before their Queen threw us to the Devil."

"They repaid me evil for good," Lumey droned, "and hatred for my love. Set thou the sinner over him, and the Devil—"

"Shut up," Jan said, curt, and turned back to Sonoy and van Treslong, who as usual were masters of the fleet during Lumey's incompetence. "Why can we not sail up to the German coasts, where people would be friendly to us?"

"That's a long way, van Cleef, and no guarantee of a kindly welcome."

Van Treslong said, grim faced behind his huge ginger mustache, "The Germans are under the Hapsburgs."

"What do you say?" Jan asked him.

"I say look for a fat ship to take. Spanish, if possible—anything that comes, if necessary. Fill our stores as best we can by piracy."

This was so inadequate that Jan guessed at once van Treslong had some deeper scheme that he meant to bring forth more in its maturity. He looked hard into the other seaman's face. Van Treslong blinked at him and slowly under his mustache smiled.

"When we reprovision," Jan said, "what then?"

Sonoy was bent over his chart, ignoring him. One of the others said, "Then death to Alva and the King of Spain!" and others vented a round angry cheer.

"What have you in your heart?" van Treslong asked.

"Sail west," Jan said. "To the New World. Make our place there, in a virgin and innocent place."

Several of them laughed at him; the others, even Sonoy, stared at him with wide eyes, caught on the dream.

"The Spanish rule there too," someone said.

"There are few Spanish, and lots of land."

Van Treslong put out his hand. "A bold idea, van Cleef. Maybe someday we will." At that the others looked away; they fell to arguing over the idea. The clatter of voices swelled. Jan took van Treslong's hand.

"We could do it."

"Maybe. In the meantime some of us are near to starvation, and we must feed ourselves."

Lumey flung the empty wine jug high over his head; it spun end over end down into the sea. "The wind," he said, croaking. "The wind is coming up."

Jan raised his head. Down so near the level of the waves, he felt no more than the ruffle of the wind like a hand touching his hair; higher, in the riggings of the nearest ships, the freshening breeze plucked at the lines like harpstrings, and the sails that had hung drooping from the yards gathered their bellies full and grew plump and white as a housewife's apron.

The captains cheered. They scrambled around in their boats, rocking and slapping oars and gunwales together. Lumey bawled, "We'll take a line to weather The Lizard. The *Wayward Girl* to lead."

Jan thrust his oars out through the rowlocks and stuck his feet against the stern thwart. "Lumey! I've an extra cask of water; steer by me and we'll drop her to you."

"A gracious gesture, by God!" Lumey saluted him with a raised fist.

"You're no use to us drunk," Jan shouted. He put his back into the oars.

THEY SAILED into the Channel, looking for a prize. The wind stayed fair for the northern run. They found no ships to seize. One evening they raised the coast of France; bonfires burned on every hill, warning them off.

Eleanor said, "I am a weakling. I'm unfit; I cannot eat this meat." Her hands covered her face.

"Eat my bread." Jan gave her his piece of biscuit and took the chunk of salted pork from her bowl. He drew her into the circle of his arm; they sat in silence on the stern deck, looking out across the sea.

That was the last of the meat anyway. Thereafter they had only bread and water, and very little of that.

Eleanor said no word of complaint. When they sat together every evening, she smiled and told him stories of her past life; her face was pinched thin as an old woman's, and her eyes grew huge above the hollows of her cheeks. When he kissed her, her lips were so dry he wondered if she could feel the touch.

Days went by. Mouse fell sick and Eleanor put him to bed in the master's cabin and sat by him and prayed and talked to him, learning Dutch from him, and made him eat her bread and drink her sip of water. Jan went aloft himself every time the sails were set; he knew some of his crew were losing their strength. He hoped by his example to keep them working. Marten spent hours trying to snare the sea gulls that came less and less often now to wait for garbage in their wake. Some of the other men fished, catching nothing.

On the twentieth day after they left Plymouth, a sail appeared, bearing a red cross, to the north of the *Wayward Girl.* Jan sent up a flag, to signal the ships behind him, and raced toward the Spanish vessel. It was a merchantman, twice the size of the *Girl,* with three times the men on board, but Jan knew no caution: he wanted food and drink for Eleanor and for Mouse.

The merchantman tried to run. Clumsily she struggled around onto the other tack while the *Wayward Girl,* reaching along the wind, shot like an arrow toward her. The awkward Spaniard wallowed out of the wind's eye, her sails slatting, and missed stays. Every sail flopped. Jan shouted in triumph.

"Starboard three points!" he called to Marten, who was steering. "We'll give her a bit of iron, and she'll cry like a baby. Forward gun, ready to fire!"

The three men crewing the bow gun were still struggling to load her. Panting, Jobst yelled, "Wait—one minute more—"

Eleanor came up onto the sterncastle. "What—oh! A ship!"

She went to the rail and leaned out to see. Jan swore and banged his hands together. "Jobst!"

"Almost—"

The Spaniard was crawling with men, up and down the rigging, hanging on the yards, as they worked to get the sails drawing again. They had rigged a spritsail, but the heavy-loaded ship resisted even that pressure to line up with the wind.

"Jobst!" Jan screamed, in a temper; he saw they might sail right past the Spaniard before they could fire, and then have the trouble of coming about and beating back against the wind. Given so much time, the Spaniard might get away, or Lumey, in the *Christ the Redeemer,* who was just behind the *Girl,* might get to her first.

"Hands to the braces!" He would slow his ship down.

"Look," Eleanor cried, and pointed to a white scarf fluttering from the main yard.

"They're giving up." Jan wheeled around, filled with a spurious new strength. "Marten! A point more to starboard. Jobst, keep the gun on her. By the main braces, let her go!"

The hands on the mainsail let go the lines, spilling out the wind, and the ship slowed smoothly, gliding down on the Spaniard. Along the merchantman's rail, a swarming crowd gathered, many waving white handkerchiefs. Jan ran to get his pistol.

With half a cable length separating the ships, he crossed in the dinghy, two of his men with him, their belts stuffed with pistols and knives. The Spanish captain met them at the top of the ladder, his face set like stone, snorting his words down at them as if he were giving the orders. Jan got him by the shoulder and swung him around to face the *Wayward Girl.*

"You see that gun, Señor?" Speaking French to this foreigner, Jan pointed to the brass culverin in the Dutch ship's bow. "Resist me, and that gun will blow a hole through your ship a whale could sound through, and all these pretty ladies . . ."

He swept his arm toward the crowd along the rail; among the seamen were a number of gentlemen in black Spanish dress, and women too, with shawls draped to veil their faces. The Spanish captain sniffed at the culverin, but beyond the *Wayward Girl,* now, loomed the black masts and sails of the *Christ the Redeemer.*

The crowd along the rail saw her too, and cries of fear and despair went up from them. Jan made a face. He saw some priests in the crowd, and mindful of Lumey's games with priests he got the Spanish captain by the arm again.

"Get those blackbirds below." With a glance at the *Christ the Redeemer* he went down himself into the hold, to find the merchantman's stores.

As WELL as the common stores of seamen's fare, the Spanish ship was carrying live chickens, pigs, kegs of wine, real bread, crocks of butter, and honey, food for the elegant passengers. It seemed like a feast, all piled up on the deck of the *Wayward Girl,* but when it was divided up among the ships of the Beggar fleet it shrank away to a day's eating.

"What else was there?" Lumey shouted, tramping up and down Jan's main deck, a slab of bread and butter in one hand and his sword in the other. "What have you hidden from us, sailor boy?"

Jan was eating chicken, barely cooked over the hastiest of fires. "You're on my ship, Lumey."

"I say he's holding something back." Lumey's arm wheeled out, inviting the other men around them into the argument. "I say he found more than this; why else would he refuse to let anyone else on board the prize? Hah! Answer that."

Jan had stripped the Spaniard and let her go, since he could not feed or even guard the swarms of people on board her. The merchantman would make for a port in the Low Countries, only a few days away.

Sonoy sat on his heels by the mast, his head against the rope wrapping, watching some of Jan's crew roast a whole pig on a spit. "Whatever he took, he earned; he seized the ship. The sweet goes to the man with the cake in his mouth."

"Hah!" Jan shouted at Lumey. He stalked away up the deck to the sterncastle ladder, where Eleanor was sitting, eating bread and honey. Mouse crouched at her feet, his cheeks sticky.

"Recovered?" Jan nudged the boy with his foot.

"He was giving all his food away." Eleanor bent and hugged the boy. "He is a saint."

"He's a fool," Jan said, "but God loves him."

She raised her head to give him a glance barbed with bad feeling. Jan sat down beside her. "What's the matter now?"

Before she spoke, she ate the rest of the bread and licked her fingers of the last of the honey. Finally, her hands in her lap, and her eyes turned away from him, she said, "You are nothing but pirates, really, aren't you?"

"What?"

"All that fine talk about helping your people, and fighting the Spanish for the sake of your faith—all you are is a pack of pirates."

Her voice trembled, either from fatigue or the weight of what she was saying; it was in his mind to laugh at her, to tell her she had known always what he was, but that quaver in her voice held him back. He thought of old Pieter, who had said much the same thing as this but with an opposite emphasis. His heart sank. Was that all there was to it—an empty shell of words and wind to pretty up plain robbery? He supposed she was right, as old Pieter had been right.

She got to her feet and went away down the stern deck to the hatch, and disappeared below. Jan slapped his hands on his thighs.

"Women," he said to Mouse.

The other captains were gathering around Sonoy at the mast of the *Wayward Girl.* The delicious aroma of the roasting pig surrounded them; gently the skin crackled, crisping in the fire, and the fat exploded in pops like small arms. Jan licked his lips. He hoisted Mouse onto his feet and pushed him ahead of him down to the others, where Lumey was strutting and throwing his chest out and snorting his suspicions.

"Keep civil," Jan said, between his teeth. "This is my ship."

"Mind your betters, sailor boy."

Sonoy lifted his head. "Hold, you two—van Treslong's got a plan."

Jan turned, uninterested at first, still clutched in the gray mood Eleanor's words had brought upon him, but now he remembered thinking before that van Treslong had something deep in his mind, and he went over to the group of captains. "What's going on?"

Van Treslong fiddled with his red-yellow mustache. "We're standing just over the horizon now from the coast of Holland. There's little harbors all over those islands, and none of them have garrisons of any size. I'll warrant there isn't a Spaniard in the whole of the waterlands right now, just the local Catholics in arms. I say we sail in and take one of the sea towns and reprovision there."

Jan let out his breath, a little disappointed; that was daring, but still piracy. The others leaned forward, intent. A quick look into their faces told Jan they were very warm to this.

"Where?" Sonoy said.

Van Treslong shrugged, twisting his mustache around his finger. "Flushing. The Brill. There's a dozen different places."

Sonoy's face was shining. "To go back home again," he said, under his breath.

At that Jan's spirits brightened. He had not set foot on a Dutch shore in over a year, and even if Holland were not Brabant, yet it was nearly the same. His mind raced forward, toward the practical application of this scheme.

"We'll need pilots. Those waters are treacherous."

Van Treslong smiled at him. "Half my crew grew up in Zeeland. I myself spent much of my boyhood in The Brill; my father was governor there."

"That was a while ago," said someone else. "The Maas changes with every tide. If we go to The Brill, we'll be sailing up the river."

Beside Jan, Lumey erupted in a great yell of laughter. "By God, you'll all sail straight into the Spanish throat! You're mad. We cannot go blind into a Spanish port—"

"Not Spanish," Jan said. "Dutch."

"There will be people who support us, too," Sonoy said. "Many in the waterlands support us."

"You're mad," Lumey said. "But if you insist on doing this, then let it be The Brill; she has the best harbor on the coast—save Flushing, and Flushing's almost in the Duke of Alva's lap—but The Brill is far away."

"The Brill it is," van Treslong said, and put out his hand, and one by one the others laid on their hands, looking deeply into one another's eyes, and nodded.

The Schelde, the Maas, the Rhine—the great rivers flowed up from the south through the center of the Low Countries, and where they poured their several streams into the North Sea, they broke the land into a fleet of little islands. Flat and low, they kept their faces ever to the sea, where a great tide or a wild storm or even a single monstrous moondriven wave could rise up to drown them utterly. With the solid ground for anchors, the people had over the centuries built dikes around the tidal marshes, pumped the sea out, and made new land, but it was a precarious footing, the sea ever seeking to reclaim its own when the people tired of watching.

To Eleanor Simmons, used to the constant, solid English countryside, these half-drowned lands were strange as China.

She stood on the sterncastle of the *Wayward Girl,* listening to the pilot direct the course of the ship and writing down what he said. It was still early morning. The sky was pearly with fresh light. A steady breeze was blowing and the tide was making, so Jan had set only the jib and the mizzensail, to creep in over the water.

There on the larboard beam a low dark mass rode on the river: an island of barren silt. Beyond it on the far bank Eleanor could see the wide arms of a mill against the sky. Quickly she made note of that; Jan had told her to write down every landmark.

The pilot said, "Three points starboard, there, wheel."

Behind Eleanor the rudder lines creaked. It was so quiet she could hear the warble of the sea passing under the ship's stern. Jan came pacing up the deck toward her, his hands on his hips. Three big pistols jutted from his belt. He wore a fancy white shirt of linen, booty from the Spanish ship, and sailor's breeches of dirty canvas and no shoes. He shouted, "What's the bottom?"

Someone amidships relayed the questions, and from the bow, where the man was casting the lead, the answer came back: "Five fathom and rising! Black silty bottom—"

The pilot said, "It'll be three fathom before we wear the tip of The Brill."

Jan muttered something. His forehead was damp with sweat. Eleanor knew better than to speak with him; he had been half wild all morning, and being so enclosed in land, with the tide and the wind pushing him steadily up the narrowing river, he had all the aspect of a beast being dragged into a cage.

On the land to the left—to larboard, she reminded herself—was a low round tower; she made a note of that in her book.

"There's The Brill," said the pilot sharply.

Off the starboard bow the land was jutting out to meet them. A high seawall thrust across the river current to break the tidal flood; beyond it rose thatched roofs and mottled walls and the tops of little trees. Eleanor wrote as fast as her fingers would move. She had never seen a Dutch town before. The shape of the buildings was different—taller, narrower than English buildings. The pilot was taking them out a little from the seawall, where the white surf banged and crashed and threw foam up into the air; as the *Wayward Girl* turned, Eleanor caught a glimpse of the rest of the Beggar fleet, sailing behind her. Crowded together, they seemed more even than they were.

Now the *Wayward Girl* was gliding past the seawall, and the wharves and riverfront of the town of The Brill opened up to view. Jan rushed to the railing.

"No Spanish ships," he said, relief heavy in his voice.

The whole broad riverfront was covered with people. When the *Wayward Girl* sailed into their ken, a great yell went up. They could not know yet who this was; Eleanor wondered at their wonderings. She wrote what she saw, although she wanted only to look, to see everything.

"Sail," someone yelled, from the waist, and there was a general laugh from the crew.

A ferryboat was swinging across their path, a flat barge propelled by sweeps. The half dozen people on board gaped at the ship looming over them. Jan ran to the side and looked out.

"Bring him alongside! Marten, point a gun at him and get him under our lee."

Marten, in the bow, had a musket, which he brandished at the ferry. The master of the little barge was hanging on his sweep, staring up at the ship that towered above him; his jaw hung open like a flytrap. At the sight of the gun he flung his arms up over his head.

Two or three splashes rose from the far side of the barge. The gun's appearance had sent some of his passengers overboard.

Under Marten's gun, the ferryman brought his flatboat around beneath the *Wayward Girl*'s rail. Jan leaned out and yelled, "Have you anything to eat?"

Eleanor laughed. She folded her arms comfortably on the rail and watched the ferryman search a locker and bring forth a round yellow cheese.

"Who are you?" he called, and tossed the cheese up over his head, where Jan could catch it.

"The *Wayward Girl*, Jan van Cleef, master, sailing under letters of marque from the Prince of Orange."

"Orange!" The ferryman wheeled toward the few passengers left to him, who stood close together on the barge behind him. "It's the Sea Beggars!"

The people gave up a wail. The ferryman looked back to Jan again.

"What do you here?"

Jan flung a look across the water at The Brill; he shortened his gaze to meet Eleanor's eyes. His face tensed with decision. Leaning over the rail, he shouted to the ferryman, "Go in there and tell those people we are giving them two hours to surrender the town to us."

"Two hours!" The ferryman backed across his barge to look downriver at the rest of the fleet. "How many men have you?"

"Oh . . ." Jan scratched his chin, his eyes narrow. "About five thousand or so."

"Five thousand men!" The ferryman flung his hat into the air. "God be blessed—God be thanked." He seized his long-bladed stern oar and swung the barge slowly around, away from the *Wayward Girl*, and steered for The Brill.

Jan laughed, and raising one arm called for his boat. He still held the cheese, which he brought to Eleanor.

"Here. Divide this up properly with everyone, and see Mouse eats his.

I have to go talk to Lumey and the rest." He smiled at her, his tension and temper dissipated in the exchange with the ferryman. "What do you think —have we five thousand here?"

"Counting God and His angels." She took the cheese and with her left hand pulled his knife out of his belt. "Go tell your fellows what you've gotten us into now."

He laughed again, high tempered, and bent down and kissed her, a loud smack on the lips. "There will be a minister here, somewhere."

"Good," she said. "It's wasteful to sleep in two beds, when we could be using one."

He went down to his dinghy, and she sat on the deck to cut the cheese into pieces.

THE FERRYMAN, whose name was Koppelstok, went up from the quay through the townspeople that crowded the waterfront; having seen him speak to the strange ship, everyone assailed him with questions, which he ignored. The excitement beating in his breast was too great to lose in words. He went straight up the street to the town hall, where the magistrates had gathered in a nervous cluster on the front steps, some of them still fastening their coat fronts.

"Koppelstok!" cried the chief magistrate. "Those ships! Whose are they? They don't look like merchantmen to me."

"Heavens above," the assistant magistrate said. "They're only fishermen, come in to escape a storm or something." He looked very pale; his fingers pulled constantly at the flat brim of his hat. "Tell him, Koppelstok. My wife's invited her mother's uncle to dinner today, and I should have been home to sit down with him half an hour ago."

Koppelstok planted himself on the steps, enjoying his moment of preeminence, and looked from one to the other of the officers, with whom he had been engaged all year in a nasty argument over his licenses. In rolling tones, he said, "Well, they aren't merchantmen."

The chief magistrate wrung his hands together. "I knew it."

"And they aren't fishermen."

The assistant magistrate dropped his hat on the ground.

"They say they are the Sea Beggars, and we have two hours to deliver up The Brill to them."

Behind him a many-throated yell went up, because a huge crowd had followed him here from the riverfront to hear what he would say; and having heard it, they turned and scattered in all directions through the town, shouting the awful news.

"The Beggars are coming! The Beggars are coming!"

The magistrates flung up their hands. The chief magistrate, a pious Catholic, crossed himself and muttered an oath like a little prayer.

"What shall we do? What shall we do?"

"They say," Koppelstok said, with malice, "that they have five thousand men on board, armed head to foot."

The assistant magistrate was sidling away down the steps; others of them took his example, and fled off the other way, into the town hall. From the church tower two blocks down came the rolling clamor of bells.

"Five thousand men!" The chief magistrate wiped his forehead. "God have mercy on us. God have pity on us." Turning on his heel, he ran up the steps to the town hall and disappeared inside. Behind Koppelstok, a wagon rumbled down the street, piled up with furniture, headed for the land gate. Another appeared in the crossroad. Koppelstok went back down the street to the waterfront, to hide away all his valuables.

B Y THE late afternoon, when Jan and his crew led half the Beggars in a rush onto the waterfront, The Brill was deserted, except for a few dozen Calvinists who cheered them from the river's edge to the land gate. At the land gate, Lumey was just breaking his way in, knocking open the gate with the butt end of a mast. The two groups of Beggars met in the street and milled around a while, uncertain now what to do.

"Where are they all hiding?" Lumey asked. He waved his sword around him, practicing on the enemy air.

"They ran away," said a gray-bearded man whom Jan recognized as the ferryman who had taken his message to the town. Standing on the steps of the church, he peered around at the sailors gathered in the square before the gate. "Where is the rest of your army?"

Jan thrust his pistol under his belt. He had eaten nothing in two days but a sliver of cheese; he began looking around him for something to steal. "This is all."

The ferryman blinked at him. "You said—"

"I lied." Jan started back down the street toward the waterfront, where Eleanor would be waiting for him.

The ferryman trotted after him. "You said you had five thousand men!"

Jan flung him a sharp look. "What difference does it make? The lie worked as well as an army would have. Is there a minister of God in the city?"

"But—aren't you here to fight Alva?"

Jan stopped, exasperated by this persistence. Ahead, the street opened onto the broad stone quays of the harbor; by the water stood a woman, her hair covered by a shawl, a boy beside her, waiting. He raised one hand to her. Facing the old ferryman, he said, "Go find me a minister."

The old man's jaw thrust out, warlike. "I thought you were—"

Jan grabbed the front of the old ferryman's coat and hoisted him up onto his toes. "Go find me a minister! A sexton—a deacon—anyone who can marry me." Opening his hand, he let the old man fall with a thud to his heels and strode away, down the street toward Eleanor.

HE BROKE into one house after another, until he found one with the dinner laid out and ready to be eaten. The soup was cool and the beer warm, but that mattered nothing to him. The ferryman returned with a minister, who stood in front of Jan and Eleanor and said the appropriate words, and then they all sat down to the feast—Jan, his new wife, his crew, and the minister and the ferryman as well.

The ferryman said, chewing, "Well, you made fools of everyone. There isn't a soul left in The Brill but God's people."

Jan said, "They can have it back when we've stocked our ships."

The old man watched him steadily through narrowed eyes. "You're going away again, then? Just leaving, without even a shot at Alva?"

"Alva's a hundred leagues off in Brussels," Jan said. He wished Koppelstok would shut up; his talk made Jan very restless. Once they left The Brill, the Beggars were back where they had begun, homeless, captives of the sea. He put boiled turnips on Mouse's plate, to his left. "Eat," he said, and struck the boy lightly on the shoulder. "Put some muscle on you." Mouse lifted his face in a wide shy smile, his eyes crisscrossed.

"I thought the Beggars were fierce," said the ferryman. "Now I see you're only—"

Jan poked at him with his fork. "I'll sew up your lips if you keep nagging me."

His crew laughed, and Koppelstok fell still, glowering at them. Jan stood up to cut the mutton. He would worry about The Brill later. Maybe some arrangement could be made—they could pay the local Calvinists to keep the port safe for them, once they went to sea again. He chased that thought from his mind. The huge bulk of the people here were Catholic.

While Jan was putting a slice of mutton on his plate, van Treslong came in, alone.

"Congratulate me," Jan said. "I am a married man."

The baron shook his hand, and taking off his hat bowed very courteously to the bride. Mouse moved off to give him the seat on Jan's left hand at the table. Van Treslong took a bit of meat and a cup of drink.

"What do you here?" Jan asked. His stomach was painfully full and he thought he might be about to be sick. Leaning back on the stolen chair, he groped in the space to his right for Eleanor's hand.

Van Treslong wiped his fingers on the tablecloth. "You'll learn, in time."

Eleanor squeezed his hand. Jan reached for his cup and drank the last of his beer. "In a very short time I will not be here."

"Where, then?"

"Upstairs. Enjoying my host's clean Sunday sheets. What brings you to me?"

Heavy footsteps sounded in the front rooms of the house. Van Treslong said, "I think you are about to learn it."

Lumey came in, half a dozen of his men behind him. His face was bright red from drink. His sword was thrust through his belt. Trampling into the room, he looked around the table and let out a yell of understanding.

"By God's eyes! A wedding feast. I'll kiss the bride." He started forward.

Jan drew out one of his pistols and laid it on the table. "You'll kiss my backside first, Lumey."

His crew roared with laughter. Van Treslong pulled his long mouth longer in a smile and Lumey snorted, standing on widespread feet, his great belly out in front of him, his head thrown back like a counterweight.

"Mark you, how he's grown beyond his station!" He waggled one finger at Jan. "But I forgive it, for the weight of his cannon. The which is why I'm here, sailor boy. The night's coming, the tide will turn in three hours. Now we must fill our holds with plunder and take to the sea."

Jan pressed his lips together. His gaze slid sideways to van Treslong, whose face behind the ginger flow of his mustache was sleek with interest. To Lumey, Jan said, "I'd in mind to stay awhile longer."

"Don't be a fool, sailor boy. When they find out we're so few in number, they'll be back. They'll have the Spanish in their front rows, too. We're only safe at sea. Let's go."

Van Treslong said nothing, only his face speaking for him, the cheeks taut, the eyes bright as lamps. Jan held Eleanor's hand in his, wondering how much of this she understood, and thinking how she had called them *nothing but pirates.*

He scratched his chin. The Spanish would come, that much was true. He did not see how they could hold The Brill against them. But . . .

"We were starving on the sea," he said.

"You fool," Lumey cried, wheeling on van Treslong. "What have you said to him?"

"Nothing," said the baron. "All these are my witnesses."

Lumey struck the tabletop with his fist. "How long do you mean to stay, sailor boy? Three days? A week?"

Jan was struggling with his thoughts; there seemed nothing solid to decide on, only death or wandering over the sea. Eleanor held tight to his hand. He looked from face to face of his crew around the table. They would do as he said. He thought of the sea, and its peace, and the storms of the sea, when every ship needed a harbor.

He thought of the taverns of Plymouth, full of foreigners, whores, and lonely sailors. His gaze ranged over this room, the dark polished wood, the solid table and chairs, the little round portraits of the previous occupants, like his own mother's dining room. This was Zeeland, not Brabant, but the people here spoke his native tongue, and they ordered their lives by customs he was used to.

As he thought, something happened in his mind. His whirling ideas took shape, and he found a place to stand on and see forward and backward at once.

"We came here as pirates," he said to Lumey, and to them all. "We took The Brill like pirates, ready to rob and go. Well, maybe the time's come to be greater than pirates. We could go back to the sea, and taking The Brill would be nothing but a snap of the fingers in Alva's face, and another song for Beggars to sing. But we can stay here, and make a stand, for us, and for all our people; and even if we die, then people will see what is important enough to fight and die for."

Van Treslong clapped his hands together. At the far end of the table Koppelstok leapt to his feet. "Well said!"

"Stay," Marten cried, hoarse voiced, and the other men lifted their voices and their clasped hands. "Stay. Stay."

Lumey straightened, his face working. "By God, you have a heart like a church bell, boy." He shook his head. "We'll see how strong it sounds when Alva's at the gates." He turned and marched out of the room.

Jan's right hand was still in Eleanor's, and her grip was tight and hot. He turned to her and she smiled, her face brilliant with pride and courage. He saw she had understood it, all along, everything. He wondered if she understood the odds against them. Putting his arms around her, he drew her tight to him, urgent now to use the time, and to cheers that boomed like thunderclaps they kissed.

21

THE RISING sun found Alva on the march, riding south at the head of a column of infantry toward Louis of Nassau, who was trying to sneak over the border from France with an army of Huguenot rabble. News had reached him from The Brill, but The Brill was far away, and unimportant; Alva would deal with that at his leisure, when his border was secure.

On either hand were green fields, young corn growing, and strips of cabbage and onions. The road led him down between two rows of trees, through which the sunlight slanted. Alva was thinking about Louis of Nassau's impatience and courage, which led him often into attacking when he had not the resources to attack, a weakness Alva meant to use to destroy him.

The thoughts gave him a sense of peace. For months he had been pent up in little rooms, fretting at problems that seemed to grow on the solutions he attempted to apply to them; now at last he had something to do that he understood.

"My lord," said his son, riding just behind him.

Alva lifted his eyes. Ahead, the road wound down between rows of trees, and on every tree trunk a piece of paper hung.

An aide galloped ahead to bring one to Alva, and he spread it on his saddlebow; he did not signal a halt, and the column moved on, steady, inexorable, south toward Spain's enemies. The paper was still stiff, the printing clear. If it had been hanging very long, the morning dew would have pulped it and made the ink bleed. Someone had put up these broadsides only moments before Alva saw them. Irritated, he swung his head from side to side, scanning the empty fields. They were out there somewhere, hiding, the villains who did this. Watching him. He lowered his eyes to the broadside.

"What does it say?" He held the paper out to Luis del Rio, on his right.

> "On Saint Fool's Day, as it passes,
> The Beggars stole the Duke of Alva's glasses

"Brill means spectacles in Dutch," said del Rio, in a badly timed display of superfluous knowledge.

Alva crumpled the broadside. "God's death on these animals." With a curt nod to the aide he sent for his map of the Low Countries, and three more aides hurried up the column with it. All the while everyone marched on, without pause, toward the battle in the future.

The map, held up between the hands of two aides while the third led their horses on, resolved the problem of The Brill into a series of movements over land and water. Alva tapped the waxen cloth with his forefinger, confident of his dominance over it. Still, he did not like what he saw. Those islands and sandspits up and down the coast of the North Sea would be easy to defend, should the Beggars chance to extend their power over them, and The Brill was in the center, well located to extend from. Coldly Alva told himself that from such a holding even the Prince of Orange could withstand the onslaught of an empire.

"Don Federico," he said crisply. "We shall squash these impudent Beggars now, once and for all. Let them find it was a mistake to venture within my grasp. There is an army at Bergen: take it, and wipe out this thieves' nest at The Brill."

"Yes, my lord."

His son's voice rang like a clarion. Federico always enjoyed commands far from his father's overlook.

Alva turned his eyes on del Rio, riding beside him. "You are to return to Antwerp and gather the army quartered there. March them north to The Brill to support Don Federico's troops."

"Yes, my lord."

"God be with you."

"God is our sword and our shield," they said in unison, and saluted him. They left him there. Alva rode along a while, staring at the map, wondering why every moment spent studying the position of The Brill should bring him more alarm. With a twitch of his hand he sent the map away and turned his face south, toward Louis of Nassau, toward what was important, more important than The Brill, if only because he understood it better.

22

AT NOON, Luis del Rio, the King's governor in Antwerp, entered the silent city. With two columns of mounted lancers at his back he rode along the main street toward the heart of the city, where stood the tower he was building. No bells rang, no crowds of citizens rushed out to greet him—not even a beggar appeared to ply the governor's generosity for a coin. He rode through Antwerp as if through a graveyard.

As he rode, he remembered how he had first seen this city, standing among her elms and poplars like a bride in her bower; then the streets had surged with carts and coaches, merchants on foot surrounded by their retainers, packmen bawling out their wares from door to door, messengers racing to and from the Bourse. How it had amazed him then to hear Greek and German spoken here as freely as Dutch or French! The streets for all their traffic were clean as church floors; the houses, trimmed with paint and gilt, were kept like monuments.

Now the wind tossed dead leaves and garbage along the pavement and the houses were decaying into rubble.

The people had left, the many-tongued merchants, the packmen, the rich and the poor; not all had left, but enough to hollow out the city like a shell. Of those who stayed behind, no one bought or sold, not in real ways, not since the tax fell on them. How they lived from day to day the King's governor could not tell and was afraid to think about.

He was coming to the heart of the town, by the brown tide of the Schelde. On his left the street opened up on the great square before the Bourse, whose doors were nailed closed. A winter fire had gutted the building and collapsed the roof; even the pigeons had deserted it now, although a stork's nest rested on the peak of the end wall.

There was a woman walking down the street ahead of him.

The sight was so unusual it held all his interest. The ground dipped down under her feet, falling away toward the river, so that she stood up against the empty sky: a tall woman in a shawl, leaning on a staff. As he came even with her, she stopped to watch him pass. A bundle hung on her shoulder. He had seen so many leaving; it startled him to see someone return.

They passed by one another, not fifteen feet apart. A tall woman, with a broad plain peasant face, who leaned on her staff and calmly watched the

Spaniard ride by. Something in her look held his attention. He twisted in
his saddle to keep his gaze on her as she fell behind him. Some power in
her face, in her tall shape. Yet she was only a woman of the people. He
straightened up, assuming a more military bearing, to ride into his citadel,
where at last someone would cheer.

HANNEKE watched the King's governor go past, thinking not of him but
of the devastated city around her. It was almost like a foreign place to her,
so different was it from the city where she had grown up.

She went down past the empty Bourse into the brewery district, where
the wooden tanks stood empty and collapsing from neglect, their iron bands
sprung, and their hollows noisy with birds; the canals and pipes of the
waterworks were full of lily pads.

In the street behind the Brewmasters' Guildhall there were people, at
last, not Spanish soldiers, but Dutch; a little boy sat on the edge of the
pavement beating disconsolately at the cobblestones with a stick, and a
woman was pulling a two-wheeled cart down the walk from a ruined house.
Beyond, several doors down, a man sat in the doorway of the bakery, staring
at nothing.

Hanneke quickened her step, her eyes on his face. Slowly she recognized him, feature by feature. He was much changed. Coming to a stop
before him, she waited for him to notice her, but he was sunk deep in
thought, his forehead gathered into a frown, and he ignored her.

She said, "God's greeting to you, Michael. Don't you recognize me?"

He looked up. His cheeks were clawed with deep harsh lines. Like a
burst of light the recognition of her hit him, and he got heavily up and came
slowly out into the street to meet her, saying nothing. The intensity of his
look unnerved her, and she began to speak, to parry that fierce stare, but
before the words were half begun, he surrounded her in an embrace and
hugged her to him with a crushing strength.

She pressed her face against his shoulder. For the first time she felt truly
home.

At last his hard grip eased, and they stepped apart, their hands on one
another's arms. She said, "I'm so glad to find you here—everything seems
so changed."

"Oh, yes," he said, thinly. "Very changed. Come inside. There's nothing we can say out here."

He led her into the front of the shop, where he and his mother had sold
their cherry buns and soft sweet bread; now nothing stood there but the
empty shelves, thick with dust. Michael opened the counter and they went
into the rear of the shop.

A fire burned in the hearth. He drew a stool up to it and made her sit.
Hanneke slipped her bundle down from her shoulder with a sigh. She

watched him rummage in the back of the kitchen and return with a small loaf of bread, a jar of jam, and a little wooden pot of beer.

She sniffed. This room, once ripe with odors of yeast and flour, now smelled of nothing but cobwebs. She said, "Are you not a baker anymore, Michael?"

"Not since my mother died," he said. "Since they tied the tenth penny to our necks, I have not sold a crumb of bread."

Sitting on the hearth, he cut the little loaf in two and put one piece solemnly before her. She made no move toward it.

"Then how do you eat?" she asked. "What of your custom—the people who depend on you?"

"We smuggle in the bread we eat," he said. "Everything we need, we bring in by secret ways, at night."

"We."

One of his broad sloping shoulders rose and fell. He took the lid from the pot of beer. "Those of us who are left. Calvinists, some of them. Clement was a great man among us, at the beginning. Now he is dead; someone else has taken his place. As each one dies, there is always someone else to take his place—what is the saying, about the demons in the swine?" An unpleasant smile crooked his mouth. " 'Our name is legion, for we are many.' "

"You are the demons, and the Spanish are the swine," she said. "It is apt, I suppose. What of your mother?"

"The Spaniards murdered her."

Hanneke's mouth fell open. "Your mother? But she was—"

"The day you disappeared, I went everywhere looking for you, and when I came back, she was hanging from the sign."

"Oh, sweet Heaven."

"Where did you go? Why did you go without telling me?" The words burst from him with a long-restrained fury. For a moment he faced her, wounded, soft as the boy he had been when she left. "All this time I have wondered—I have dreaded knowing—why did you leave me?"

She said, "Carlos—the Spanish soldier—he attacked me, and I . . . killed him."

She watched his face for some sign of revulsion. The boy Michael would have been revolted; but this harsh, haunted man was not. His face flattened with satisfaction. "Good blow."

"I was afraid—if I went to you, they would blame you for it, so I went out of Antwerp."

"A good-struck blow." He gripped her hands and kissed her.

"I think not," she said. "I wish I had not done it."

"Bah. He was Spanish. But where have you been?"

"Away," she said. "Looking for a place to rest, at first, and then I saw what must be done, and I came back here."

"And you are here now," he said, and took her hand and kissed it.

When she did not draw back, he leaned toward her and pressed his lips to hers. She trembled, but she let him do it; she knew this stranger would demand of her what Michael had only asked for.

"Tell me where you have been. Did you go far?"

"Far enough," she said. "Far enough to see I had to return here to do God's work."

He leaned back. He was much thinner than she remembered him, which made him seem much older. "And what work is that? Are you still Calvinist?"

"Yes," she said, surprised. "Aren't you?"

"No."

"But—how can you fight the Spanish and not be Calvinist?" She shrugged. "Are you demon, or are you swine? I cannot see—"

"You don't see," he said, roughly. "But you will, when you've been here awhile." He caught her hand and held tight to the fingers. "I'll make you see, Hanneke."

She stared at him, their hands still linked, with the feeling of seeing him across the black void of an abyss. The wind came and rattled the window. A sifting of pale flour floated down from the rafters. Hanneke turned her gaze to scan the gloomy silent room. The old woman was here still, somewhere, watching over her son; the past still had him by the heart. She tugged her hand free of his grip.

"Michael, the time has come to break free of the old ways. God is calling on us to make His kingdom on earth—"

"I need no new kingdom," he said. "Only to make the old one the way it ought to be—the way it was. I need you, Hanneke. I need my woman to give me comfort, while I fight for what belongs to me."

"Michael," she said. "No."

He was reaching for her hand again. "You can't have come back after so long, and not give me what I need. I've been waiting for you for so long . . ." Painfully he clutched her hand and pulled her toward him, his face lean with hunger.

She sprang up to her feet, her hand imprisoned in his grasp. They faced each other like battlers. In an instant, she saw that it was true: they were enemies. He was Catholic, bound to the old ways, and she was free of that. God had set her free.

In an undertone, she said, "Michael, let me go."

"You can't have come back now and not be what I want," he cried.

"Michael—" She jerked her head around, toward some thin sound from the street. "What's that?"

He lifted his head to listen. In the silence of the bakery, all sound seemed damped away to nothing. Hanneke raised her eyes again, toward the ceiling coated with flour, as if she might meet the gaze of the old woman, watching. Then again she heard the distant blast of a trumpet.

Michael pulled her toward the door. "Outside."

They went out through the side door, past the brick ovens in the yard, out to the street. There, three Spanish horsemen were riding down the center of the street toward them, one with a trumpet and two with the long red pennants of the army, curling and uncurling like serpents in the air above them.

Hanneke and Michael stopped at the low wall along the side of the street; now before the half-ruined houses on either hand, other people appeared, sheltering behind gates, beside fences, and under trees, half hiding from the soldiers.

They stopped directly before her; the trumpeter put his shining horn to his lips, and the metal shriek rang out.

"Soldiers of the King! Soldiers of the King!"

The cry was in Spanish, but every Dutchman understood it, having heard it a thousand times before. Hanneke closed her fingers on the fence. The generals were summoning an army, making ready to march. She wheeled toward Michael.

"Where are they going?"

He lifted one indifferent shoulder, his eyes sharp. "Who cares where they go? As long as they go. Tomorrow, we will bring feasts in."

Hanneke watched the soldiers ride away, the pennants rippling from their pikes; the sun caught the brass trumpet in an instant's blinding flash. "They must be going to fight somewhere. Maybe Orange is come again."

Michael made a sneering sound in his throat. With the side of his shoe he kicked at the leaves piled against the base of the fence. For the first time she saw how thin he was; his shirt hung over his chest like a sail over the hollow air, his spine like a mast, his ribs like curved yards.

He said, with contempt, "Orange. He will not come again—not that fool. It's the Beggars, up in The Brill—that's where these will go to fight."

With a gesture he indicated the street. Two Spanish soldiers had wandered out of the houses across the way, yawning and pulling on their red doublets.

"The Brill," Hanneke said. She had some vague notion that was a seaport in the north somewhere. "The Beggars are in The Brill?"

He nodded, still watching the soldiers, who were making their way off down the street.

Hanneke sucked in her breath. She had been traveling for what seemed weeks and had heard nothing of this. The news struck her slowly, with a gathering force. The Beggars were in The Brill: The Brill was Calvinist. Was Dutch again. She took a step toward the street, after the soldiers.

Michael gripped her arm. "Where are you going?"

Over her shoulder, she said, "To The Brill."

"What? To The Brill? You're mad." Roughly he yanked her around to face him. "You just came home, Hanneke. This is where you belong. Here you must stay."

She looked into his face and saw a stranger. The merry good-hearted boy she had known had disappeared behind the dour face of this man shouting orders at her. She wrenched her arm out of his grasp and ran through the gate.

"Hanneke!"

She gathered up her skirts out of her way and ran down the street after the soldiers.

THE MOMENT he stepped out the door, del Rio knew something was wrong; he had been dealing with soldiers too long not to hear the ugly temper in the mutter of noise that arose from these men. He went out to the middle of the courtyard, where the groom held his horse. The soldiers were gathering in the parade ground just beyond the south gate, and as he mounted he put himself in view of them over the low unfinished wall.

They were not standing in ranks. Already some thousands of the men quartered in Antwerp had appeared, and the parade ground, sloping off a little toward the muddy Schelde, was red with their jackets. But rather than forming the orderly rows their training required of them, they were massed in clumps, talking. Del Rio's back tingled with premonition. Most of these men were not Spaniards. Most were German mercenaries, and they had not been paid in months.

He gathered his reins and signaled to his officers, mounted in the courtyard beside him, and slowly they rode out of the half-finished citadel onto the parade ground.

The trumpeters went ahead of the staff, flourishing their long belled horns, so that the red ribbons danced in the sunlight. A blast of brass-throated sound rang out. The troops stilled. Here and there, lines formed among them, as the horns awoke their obedience. Del Rio rode forward toward the high ground, where he could survey them all.

Now he saw that the edges of the gently sloping field swarmed with people—the townsfolk, come to witness. Even the bridge over the river was black with them. Nor were the soldiers gathered here any near the number of men quartered in Antwerp; easily one third of King Philip's army had not answered the call.

"Men of Spain!" He raised one hand over his head, to command their silence. The lieutenant on his left rode forward to translate his words into German, most of these men of Spain speaking no Spanish.

"Men of Spain! The King has called us forth to serve God and the Crown against those who threaten our faith. I know you will reply as you always have . . ."

He had given so many of these speeches that the words fell without thought from his lips. His eyes took in the restless mob that faced him, grumbling, angry, and growing angrier; until abruptly a tall fat man with a yellow beard leapt up out of the mass of men in front of del Rio and shouted, "Where's our money?"

The shout that these words brought from the other soldiers resounded like a thunderclap. Del Rio's Barb stallion reared up, snorting. While del Rio fought him quiet again, the soldiers yelled and clapped and whistled like night creatures; the trumpeters played shrieks on their trumpets, the commanding sound lost in the tumult.

Then suddenly the soldiery broke forward, like the sea rushing in over the beach. They flooded around del Rio and his horse and his officers and seized them and shook them to and fro. Del Rio drew his sword. It was whipped out of his hand before it had cleared the scabbard. His horse reared again, and as del Rio looked out over a mob of red doublets and shouting faces he began to pray.

"Our money!" The yellow-bearded man roared at him like a great German bear. "Our money! Our money!"

An arm's length from him the young lieutenant who had been translating wheeled around, his face shining with terror, and flung out his hand to his chief. "Help me!" An instant later a pike took him through the chest. His body flopped like a speared fish. The howling mob hoisted him up overhead and trooped off with him.

"Our money! Our money!"

"There is no money," del Rio shouted. His hands were slimy with sweat; his back itched, expecting the dagger point between his shoulder blades. "Go to The Brill—destroy the Beggars—they have your money!"

"We won't move a step until we're paid!"

Beyond the soldiers, now, del Rio saw, with a certain small surprise, the townspeople were crowding closer. One, a woman, had even pushed in among the soldiers, to hear what they were saying. He dragged his attention from this. He forced his voice steady, his face calm; he looked down on this mad mutinous army like a father on disobedient sons.

"The Beggars stole your money. Destroy them, and the King will give you all you desire, for love of your valor. If you do not, if you continue to defy his wishes, then—"

The yellow-bearded man caught the bridle of del Rio's horse and dragged the slim head down and sideways in the milling of his arms. "Then we will sack Antwerp!"

Another raw-throated yell went up from the soldiers. The woman elbowed her way even closer. Her face was bright with fury, her eyes direct and clear; she looked up into del Rio's face and shouted, "You cannot let them. The city is in your charge—on your head, if harm comes to these people who are your responsibility."

Del Rio blinked at her; he had seen her before somewhere, but his unsettled mind would not connect her with any other memory. A woman of the people. His horse staggered. The yellow-bearded man was wrenching the poor beast's head around again.

"Our money! Our money, or Antwerp burns!"

Now another outcry rose, this from the townspeople, not the brutal yell of the soldiers, but a wail of terror and rage kept silent too long, bursting forth now irresistibly. They pressed closer around the soldiers, and del Rio saw, in the calm of despair, that they outnumbered the soldiers, and they carried weapons—not pikes, but clubs of wood, and rakes from their gardens, and knives from their kitchens. There were as many women among them as men, which gave their collective voice its higher pitch, its birdlike clarity. He tore his gaze away, back to the yellow beard.

"You are treading the edge of disaster. Now, while you can, form ranks, obey your officers, and make yourselves an army again—"

"The Beggars!"

The clear feminine voice rose above all the racket like a flag above the surge and chaos of the crowd. It was the woman of the people. She had climbed up on something, not far from del Rio; she was pointing out over the crowd toward the river, and her voice pierced the clamor.

"The Beggars! The Beggars are coming!"

A gasp went up from the soldiers and the townspeople alike, as if they drew one breath into one set of lungs. Every head turned. There, on the muddy Schelde, beyond the supply barges tied up at the citadel wharves, a white sail glided, and beyond it another, and beyond that, another still.

"The Beggars. The Beggars are coming!"

The townsfolk roared. They rushed forward in a single mass against the soldiers, and like reeds before the scythe the men of Spain went down.

"Wait," del Rio shouted, but his voice was lost in the screaming and shouting of the men around him. They were running. The yellow-bearded man still had del Rio's horse, and he dragged it around by the bridle and led it in a wild plunge down the parade ground. The other soldiers followed in a ride toward the shelter of the citadel.

"Wait," del Rio shrieked. No one heeded him. He waved his arms and wrenched at his reins; he twisted to look across the surging crowd at the river, where the three sails, drifting closer, revealed themselves to be no more than garbage scows. No one stopped. With the townspeople hewing and clawing at their backs, King Philip's army fled in a wild rout into the new fortress, del Rio hustled along in their midst, and slammed the gates, and hid.

HANNEKE did not think it would last very long. She sat with her knees tucked up to her chest on the pounded earth of the parade ground and watched the people of Antwerp dancing in rings on the lower meadow. They had done a wonderful thing; they had driven off the evil that had hung so long over their heads, but she did not think it would stay away long.

Nearby her was the dead horse she had stood on when she called the name of the Beggars and brought a phantom navy to these people's aid. A dozen women in bloody aprons were butchering it; they would eat meat tonight. The men were breaking into the supply barges along the river, and would find more food there. But it would not last.

What would last was in the north, where the Beggars had taken a city and could stand, their backs to the ever-nourishing sea. Even now, she knew, from the shortened speech of the Spanish governor, the Duke of Alva was planning a counterattack on The Brill; and that would be the measure of the future, not this business here in Antwerp.

It was there that she was called to go. What called her she had no name for: only, as she sat looking over the slope, the rings of dancers, the women cutting up the dead horse, the children, who finding bits of wood, pretended to fight, the young mothers nursing their babies, the old men standing deep in talk, the citadel behind them, the broad brown reach of the river like a hem along the foot of the slope—she saw in this variety an order, like the order of the starry sky at night, too large for a human mind to comprehend, but clear enough to God. In that order she moved like a wisp of dandelion seed that sailed the wind.

Her brother. She had not heard from him in years, but he had gone to sea. She gave no hope, no longing expectation to finding him ever again, but the wind that brushed her cheek and urged her north was the air that filled his sails. She stood up, shaking the dirt from her dress, and started away down the road.

23

H EAVE!"

The men threw themselves against the rope; with a whir and a groan the block rolled the slack line through and took the weight of the big brass cannon. Jan leaned over the edge of the rampart to watch the gun climb slowly up through the air toward him. With one outstretched hand he motioned the men to pull.

They leaned into the rope, hoisting the cannon, nose first, up into the air, while the three sailors around it supported it in their arms like a great brass baby. Behind Jan there was an ominous popping of wood. He screwed his head around toward the mast they had rigged against the city wall to carry the block and tackle. The mast popped again.

"Avast! Let her down." Frantically he milled his arms at the four men on the rope.

They let the rope slide. Singing through the rollers, it flew slack, and the cannon sank down toward the ground; but the mast was splitting, end to end, with a scream like a murdered man. Jan leapt down off the wall. The cannon fell in its net of ropes. The men around it took the weight on their arms and it bore them down to their knees, their mouths flying open at the shock. Someone watching wailed. Jan flung himself at the big gun, wrapped his arms around the barrel, braced his legs, and planted himself. The cold weight dropped into his embrace, crushing his shirt, driving him down. He gasped. Other men rushed in around him. With their help he lowered the great gun down to the street.

"Aaah."

His breath exploded from him in relief. The other men clapped him on the shoulders.

"I thought I was dead," said Marten. Naked to the waist, he held out his arms, where bands of bruises already purpled the flesh where the gun had fallen. "Until I saw you there."

He flung one arm around Jan's neck and hugged him. Jan nudged him away with his elbow.

"Enough of that. We need another sheer. Two masts, this time—lash them together." He looked up at the rampart over his head, where the gun was to sit. It seemed an immense distance. He thrust off his doubts and pointed to various men of his crew.

"You and you, go fetch the masts. Get sound ones. Marten, bring me thirty fathoms of line—anchor cable, if you can find it." He wiped the sweat from his face on his sleeve. A long rip opened the white linen from shoulder to elbow. He fingered the edge. "My wife won't like the looks of that."

"Your wife is glad enough it's just your shirt." Eleanor came up the street toward him, smiling, but pale as the shirt itself. A basket hung on her arm. "I brought you dinner. Have you time to eat?"

He took her up on the rampart to share the meal with her. They sat looking out over the fields outside The Brill. Cows grazed on the meadow grass below the wall. The land stretched flat as a table out to the dike; not a tree grew on it. Jan ate bread and the good yellow cheese of the district.

Two women in white starched coifs were coming along the top of the dike toward the city, baskets on their arms, probably from the onion fields on the far side. A dog gamboled along ahead of them, its head turned toward them. They were townspeople, some of the few who had come back to The Brill after the Beggars seized the town.

He wondered what the rest would do—if they would come back. He hoped not all. The house where he was living suited him very well, and he had no desire to give it up to its rightful owner.

"Who is that?" Eleanor pointed.

Jan shaded his eyes with his hand. Coming along the flat lowland was a troop of horsemen.

"Lumey," he said. "Back from another raid."

Eleanor leaned over the basket, looking for the knife, and cutting herself another slice of bread spread fresh butter over it. She wore a blue dress, the cloth smooth and plump over her breast. "Is he your leader?"

Jan moved his shoulders, having no answer he liked to that question. Now that the double file of horsemen was closer, he could see Lumey himself in the lead, his beard bright with ribbons. The gaudy coat he wore was the embroidered vestment of a Catholic priest. The line of prisoners he dragged in his train was doubtless made up of priests. Jan turned his head and spat over the wall.

"Good cannot come of his bloody deeds," said Eleanor, her eyes lowered.

In his heart Jan agreed with her, but he would not say so; Lumey was their leader, by word of the Prince of Orange, and if they argued with that now, where would they stop arguing? Now they needed unity, of mind, of purpose, of leadership. Lumey gave orders well enough, when the need called for it. Jan stood up, brushing the crumbs from his thighs. As he always did, he turned to look north, where the dike curved around to shut out the sea.

The wind was fierce out of the north today, driving the waves hard against the rocks on the outside of the dike. White fingers of spume flew up over the earthen wall.

"Here come your men," Eleanor said.

He went down to rig the sheer to the wall and raise the cannon up into place to defend The Brill.

"I HAVE heard," Lumey said tenderly, "that priests have no balls. What do you say to that?"

He sat in a chair before the first of his victims, a young man in a cassock, his eyes round and glistening with fear. He was tied by the arms and waist to an upright beam of the house. Jan squirmed to see this. The chair he had taken was too small for him. He cast a longing look at the door.

"Well, he's not talking," Lumey said, genially. "We'll have to see for ourselves."

He held a broad-bladed fish knife in one hand, and reaching it out he slipped it into the front of the priest's sober dark gown and with a twist of his wrist slashed it open from the priest's waist to the hem. The young man whimpered. Against the wall behind him, the other captives mumbled their prayers and strained against their bonds.

Jan said, "You're mad, Lumey."

Around the room, the admiral's other guests agreed with that. Lumey only laughed. With the saw-toothed fish knife, he lifted up half the priest's garment.

"By God! It was a lie all this time. He does have balls."

The knife probed the priest's genitals. Jan's hand slipped down to his crotch. The small hairs crawled on his nape and the insides of his thighs. Sweat pebbled the face of the young priest; he was staring away, over Lumey's head, into the darkness, his eyes glassy.

"Well," Lumey said. "Priests should have no balls. I shall remedy this one's defect right—now—"

The shriek from the young man's lips struck through Jan like a shock of lightning. He leapt up out of his confining chair and made for the door.

"Woman-hearted, are you, sailor boy?" Lumey roared in exaltation, and held up the dead parts on the tip of his fish knife. Jan opened the door. The other priests lined the wall beside it; some overflowed with prayers, and one had fainted, and more than one were cursing like seamen. Jan gave them an instant's sympathetic glance.

"Keep courage," he said, and went out to the street.

Baron van Treslong was already out there, leaning up against the wall that separated the house from the common thoroughfare, twining his fingers together. Jan stood beside him a long moment before either of them spoke.

Van Treslong said, "God help me, I know they are Papists, but I would save them if I could."

"We've got pistols," Jan said. "Let's go back in there and stop this— this—"

"You are still young," van Treslong said, and taking Jan's arm he steered him away down the street, away from Lumey's house, where now as they left another shriek rang out. "Things are still very simple to you, Master van Cleef."

"They are Dutch," Jan said.

The dark houses on either side were deserted. Their footsteps rang hollow in the empty street. Van Treslong's arm was linked with Jan's, a heavy pressure like a chain. Suddenly he longed for the sea and its simple order.

"If we offend Lumey, he will leave," said van Treslong. "Together with his ships and crews, and probably several other captains and their ships and crews. And then how will we hold The Brill? Besides, Orange made him admiral. Only Orange can remove him."

They turned the corner. To the left now was the harbor, where their ships rocked at anchor, their masts gaunt against the starry sky. Jan kicked a stone across the wharf.

"Orange," he said, scornful. "That nothing prince."

"Hold," van Treslong said. "Speak well of the Prince of Orange."

"Why should I? What does he, but sit in safety at some friendly court and write us letters that send other men out to die? We took The Brill. We have seized our fortunes by God's grace, not Orange's."

"Hold," a harsh voice called behind them, and they wheeled around, separating. It was the watch, manned by local Calvinists, who walked up toward them under their lantern and peered into their faces.

"Good evening, Captain. Good evening, sir." Tipped their hats, and went off down the street. Jan watched them go, bouyed up by their respect; he began to feel a little better about Lumey.

Van Treslong came back to his side. "You have never met the Prince."

"No."

"Then let me ask you this, if there were a man in all things so unlike Lumey as an angel to the Devil himself—who is gentle even to captive enemies, who thinks ever of the long view and the people's good, who counts his own advantage last of all his necessaries, and who understands statecraft as a needlewoman does her handiwork—would you not want him to help us make our country free?"

He flung a quick glance at Jan, who shut his lips and would not speak; he saw he was being led along like a child.

"Think on it," said the baron. "We must make our country free of the King who has always ruled us, free of Spanish law and Catholic order—make a whole new kingdom, as it were, the way a set of carpenters and masons builds a house from the ground up."

They turned into the broad main street that ran past the town hall to the land gate. Jan shoved his hands under his belt. Van Treslong's words fascinated him; he had given no thought to any of this before. It had never occurred to him that they would have to shape their country again. It had seemed to him that countries had shapes as people did, from their birth, that could not change.

"Can you do it?" the baron said. "I cannot. I do not know what to do —who should do what the King did, in the old way, or even what it was he did, really. How to order church and state so that both thrive, how to keep the peace without tyranny, how to hear the voices of all the sorts of people, how to make new laws and judge the old ones, how to speak to other countries and have them speak to us—I know nothing of this. Orange knows. He is no soldier. But he'll make a king."

"Hunh." Jan walked on awhile, van Treslong at his elbow and his eyes lowered, thinking of all this—thinking, too, that van Treslong knew a deal more than he admitted. He shook himself.

"Why are we talking like this? There will be no new kingdom. When Alva gets here, we'll all be dead."

Van Treslong said, "That's in God's hands."

"You brought us here. Taking The Brill was your idea. Did you plan it all simply that we should die?"

The baron said, "I planned nothing. I only asked of you, of all of us, that we—you put it best, van Cleef—that we be *greater than pirates.*" He smiled; they were in the main street, beside the canal, and the few houses where people still lived shed the light from the lanterns over their doors in trails across the water. Jan could see the baron's face in the faint glow. "If we die, yet we cannot fail. Everyone now will know what we have chosen to die for. Others will make the same choice. In time, there will be enough. More than enough."

Jan said, "A human sacrifice."

"I hope not."

"Damn it, I don't want to die. I just got married."

"It's your choice."

They walked on toward the gate, where voices were rising; Jan at first paid no heed to that, his head heavy with arguments and counterarguments. Reaching the open square before the gate, he caught the voices in his ear and stopped.

"We cannot let you in!" someone was calling, on the top of the wall. "Wait until morning."

Faintly, another voice answered, unintelligible, from beyond the wall. Van Treslong stepped forward. "What's this?"

On the top of the wall, the sentry wheeled around. "Captain—my lord —some woman's come, she wants to join us. Shall I open the gate and let her in?"

"A woman," Jan said, and grunted. "Another mouth, and a weak arm."

Van Treslong called, "Open the gate for her; we are in no position to deny people, and it's cold out there."

The sentry went to the winch that worked the gate. Jan went back to thinking about the talk with van Treslong. Suddenly he longed for Eleanor's company. She had no such unsteadiness of mind as he; when she had decided she was solid in her choice, and she had decided to stay here in The Brill. He sighed, tired of debates. The gate was creaking open. Through the widening gap came a single tall woman with a staff in one hand and a bundle over her shoulder.

"Welcome to The Brill," said van Treslong.

"Welcome to the end of your life," Jan said, harshly.

She let the bundle slip from her shoulder to the ground. "Thank you, sirs. I have traveled long to come here; it is very good to have arrived at last."

Her voice was familiar. Jan took a step toward her. His heart leapt like a deer startled up from its resting place. "Hanneke?" In the darkness, all he could see was her shape. "Hanneke?"

She turned to him; she came into his arms. His sister. He brought her body against his like a piece missing from himself, and deep in the embrace they laughed.

"WHY DID you come here?" Jan asked. "You walked all across the whole country, to come here and die?"

"There are worse things than dying," she said. "Mother died."

They were walking up the street toward his new house; van Treslong had discreetly left them alone.

"Dead," Jan said. "How?"

"It's on my shoulders. I left her alone too much. You know how helpless she was, how she relied on Papa. She was worse, after we left the old house." Her voice was mild, almost without feeling. Jan wondered at the change in her; she had always been so high of feeling before.

She said, "They have destroyed Antwerp. It's a dead city. No one has anything to eat, and people are starving in the streets. All trade's stopped. The people are so bitter and low of spirit—"

She stopped, staring away down the street, seeing something she alone could see. Her lips trembled.

"Why did you come here?" Jan said. "Of all Europe, why The Brill?"

"God brought me here," she said. Her voice was soft, but as she spoke it quickened, vibrant. "Just as He brought you and all these other people, to do His work, to build His kingdom on earth." Her lips curved in a smile that vanished almost before it appeared. "Where else is there in Europe to be?"

He reached out his arms and she came into his embrace; the warmth of her body shocked him, somehow, as if she burned by the power of her idea. He struggled to see what she saw—something ahead of them, something to gain, to fight for. He saw plainly that it was the past that had driven him here, the past and the losses he had suffered, but the past and the things he had lost could not sustain him. He needed what she had, something to fight for, some idea of the time to come. What van Treslong had: the New Kingdom.

Jan could not believe it. He was afraid to believe in it, afraid of failing. Of being wrong. But his sister was here, warm in his arms, his sister. He pressed his face to her wind-tumbled hair.

HANNEKE lay sleeping in the second-best bed; Jan drew slowly back from her, reluctant to leave her. Eleanor felt the sting of jealousy. Until now, she had never known he had a sister.

She lifted the lamp, to light their way, and without speaking they went across the house to their bedchamber.

Here, she put the lamp on the corner of the table by the big hooded bed and sat on the bed's edge to let her hair down. Jan came up behind her. She turned her back to him and he took the pins from her hair and undid the braids and spread her hair out over her shoulders. She sat with her hands between her knees, her eyes half-closed, luxuriating in the caress of his hands in her hair.

He said, "I am sorry I brought you here. To this."

"Hush," she said sharply. It annoyed her that he apologized for it—as if all were his doing, and she had not chosen. He was undressing her now, his hands moving slowly over her clothes, undoing laces and buttons, and slipping off one garment after another. She shut her eyes. He bared her shoulders and bent to press his lips to her skin. He licked her neck and she trembled, alive with desire.

In a few moments they would lie together in the bed, bringing one another to the fullness, the overflowing completion of their love. For the last time, perhaps. Knowing that, she burned for him, for the immediacy of his touch, for the responses of her body to his touch, alive.

He drew her clothes down around her waist; sitting behind her, he kissed the nape of her neck, and his hands glided under her arms and around to cup her breasts. She trembled. She tipped her head back against his shoulder; her hands slipped down behind her, over his thighs. Let the world end. Tonight they were the world, she and her husband. Standing, she dropped her clothes down to the floor and stepped free of them, facing him, her arms at her sides. He took off his clothes, impatient, his gaze never leaving her. She loved the way he moved, so quick and sure, light as an animal; she loved his body's lean muscular elegance. Let it all end; this was prize enough, this all-demanding, fragile, mortal love. Ready for him, she stretched out her arms and gathered him to her.

IN THE morning the sunlight was yellow as butter; it fell on the tablecloth and gleamed on the crockery and the spoons. Hanneke sank down on the chair beside the window and lifted her eyes to this stranger who was serving her, her brother's all-unlooked-for wife.

"Where is Jan now?" She spoke French, as her brother did, to Eleanor.

"Down by the wall, mounting his cannon there," the Englishwoman said. She would not meet Hanneke's gaze; her eyes followed her hands, cutting bread, putting butter and jam beside it, lifting broiled fish onto the plate. "Did you sleep well?"

"Very well, thank you. I have not slept in a bed in many weeks."

"This is a most comfortable house."

"Yes, it is."

Silence fell. Eleanor lingered a moment longer, her hands moving in small purposeless gestures, while Hanneke ate the first bites of her breakfast. She could not look up from the bread. What did one say to a woman suddenly discovered to be one's sister? She said nothing. Eventually Eleanor went off into the next room, where soon the noise of a great bustle of work began.

He was not the same Jan, either; he seemed so much older. Hanneke picked a herring bone from her tongue with the tips of her fingers. She should have stayed in Antwerp, a place she knew.

But the sunlight was so warm, this table so clean, and the food so good —she did know this. She knew it from earlier, much earlier, from her childhood, this order of meals and houses, of calm womanly work. Except it was another woman's work; not her mother's, but this strange woman's work.

Eleanor came back and lifted away the dishes as Hanneke was done with them.

"No," Hanneke said. "Let me do that; I shall help you."

"Oh, no, no, no." Eleanor whisked the dirty dishes out of her reach and into the kitchen.

Hanneke closed her fist on the linen tablecloth. She felt unwanted here, unneeded. Quickly she got up and went off through the house to the door.

Before she could leave, Eleanor was there, in her shawl, a basket on her arm, looking elsewhere. When she spoke to Hanneke, her gaze swept her, their eyes meeting for the instant necessary for communication.

"Are you going out?"

"I thought," Hanneke said stiffly, "I would go find my brother."

"I am going there. Let me walk with you."

They went out to the street together, their eyes directed forward, and walked along with some feet of space between them, to avoid touching at any cost. This street ran over a canal; they had to stop at the bridge, to let a cart pass over, and while they waited they stood side by side, not touching, not looking at each other, certainly not talking.

Hanneke thought: *What does she think of me? She must hate me. She is jealous of me, because Jan loves me.* And immediately, she thought, *He loves me more than her,* and was pleased.

Before a house on the far side of the bridge was a big wagon drawn by two horses, from which a man and a boy were unloading furniture into the house. A woman appeared in an upstairs window, throwing open the shutters. Eleanor saw this, pressed her lips tight together, and walked on more quickly. Hanneke wanted to ask her what it meant; but now she was reluctant to cross the margin of silence between them and she kept still.

They went on by a church, with a lofty spire; the doors were blocked with a heap of pews and an altar rail.

Now Hanneke was full of curiosity. She burned to ask questions of Eleanor, but her pride refused her. She peered down alleyways and over fences and watched every person she saw as long as she could, wondering what they were about. Were all these people Calvinists? The church that was shut up was obviously Catholic, which seemed to imply that there were no Catholics left here.

Beside her, Eleanor walked with her face closed in behind a prim frown, her basket swaying on her arm. What did Jan love in this ice maiden? Hanneke faced forward again.

When she did, she saw something in the street ahead that made her gasp, and stop in her tracks, and Eleanor stopped beside her.

"In Heaven's name," Hanneke said. "What is this?"

From the eave of a tall house on their left, half a dozen naked bodies hung. A little group of children in the street before them were staring up at the corpses and throwing rocks and chunks of dirt at them.

"What does this mean?" Hanneke cried.

Eleanor turned toward her, her eyes full on her, the first time she had looked Hanneke in the face. "Those are the men that Lumey took and killed. Lumey, the admiral of the Netherlands." Her voice trembled with indignation. "He is a beast, and they must do without him. It is the greatest test of us, of our cause."

Hanneke had not expected to hear her speak of a cause. She turned her eyes from Eleanor to the hanging men. "Who are they?"

"Priests. Catholic priests. Lumey has a special hatred of them. He does ill to every one he finds, and he goes about seeking them whenever he can."

"We shall not make the kingdom with deeds such as this," Hanneke said.

Eleanor gave her a piercing look. "No. That is my concern exactly." She reached out a long thin hand to Hanneke.

Jan's sister took it and was surprised by the hard rough palm, the feel of bones sharp under the skin. She said, "We are women. We see some things more clearly than the men do."

"Tell the men that," Eleanor said, acidly.

The two women went on together, side by side, down to the harbor, where several men sat in the stocks. Eleanor had brought them bread and beer, and water to wash their faces with. Their heads and hands pinioned in the stocks, they could not feed themselves, and the two women fed them. Eleanor told Hanneke what each man had done to earn his punishment. Hanneke wiped the dribbled beer from their chins with her sleeve.

The harbor was quiet. A few ships rocked at anchor; a little crowd of children loitered in the shade of the nets drying by the wharves, waiting for the women to finish with the prisoners and leave them helpless again to the children's tormentings. Hanneke walked along the stone seawall, looking out toward the horizon.

"That is our ship," said Eleanor. "The *Wayward Girl.*"

"What a name," Hanneke said, and laughed. "She's very pretty."

"Old Pieter named her, I am sure," Eleanor said. "Your uncle."

"I never met him."

"Jan loved him. And from what I hear of him, none was more fond of wayward girls than he."

Hanneke laughed again. The two women walked along the edge of the harbor and soon found themselves outside the town, passing below the end of the land wall at the spot where the sea and the river mingled. On the dike that held the sea out and kept the land below the wall of The Brill, they walked along enjoying their newborn companionship. Eleanor clasped her arms over her breast; the sea wind fluttered the loose ends of her headcloth.

"You spoke of a kingdom," she said. "What do you mean?"

Hanneke said, "God means us to make a New Kingdom on the earth, where godly men and women shall live in peace."

"You know this."

"I am certain of it."

"Then you think we shall withstand Alva, when he marches on The Brill?"

"God will decide that," Hanneke said. "If we fail here, He will raise up someone else, somewhere else."

Eleanor said nothing for a while. The dike was just wide enough for the two of them to walk abreast along the top; on the one side was the singing rowdy water of the sea, and on the other the barren low salty earth reclaimed from the sea.

Eleanor said, "I am not afraid. I don't know what will happen, which is, as you say, in God's hands. I am not afraid, whatever might come."

They had reached the sluice gate, a wooden patch in the stone and earthen dike. The ropes were rotten and crumbling to dust. Hanneke put her foot on the top of the sluice gate, to see if it would hold her weight, and the wood cracked a warning. She stepped back, turning toward Eleanor.

"I think we have come all we can."

Eleanor was looking across the dry land. "Here comes Mouse."

"Who is he?" Hanneke watched a small figure running toward them from the town.

"A lad from the ship. They all think he is half-witted, but he seems whole enough to me—only a little off the center, as it were."

Hanneke laughed at the choice of words. "So are we all, somehow."

Again she and Eleanor looked one another in the face; again a sympathetic understanding passed between them. Mouse ran up to them, a shaggy-headed cross-eyed boy the age that Clement's boy had been.

"This is Jan's sister," Eleanor said to him; she laid her arm around his shoulders. Now she spoke Dutch, slow and stumbling.

The boy pressed himself shyly to her side. "Hello," he mumbled.

"Hello, Mouse," said Hanneke.

He looked up at Eleanor; his neck was dirty. He said, "Jan says you are to come to him on the wall with his dinner now."

Eleanor patted him on the shoulder. "Run and tell him we are coming." She smiled over his head at Hanneke. The boy raced away toward the wooden wall of The Brill, and the two women, arm in arm, walked after him.

"Were they all infantry? Did you see any cannon?"

The newcomer chewed the mouthful of bread he had been eating; he claimed to have walked all night and day to reach The Brill, coming from the mainland. He also claimed to have seen several columns of Spanish soldiery marching north, pikes on their shoulders and helmets on their heads.

The bread swallowed, he said, "I saw only what I told you, sir. I know nothing of armies; I saw only the soldiers and their pikes."

Jan clapped him on the shoulder. "Well, you came here in time to learn something more about armies than that, anyway."

"I am ready to fight." He was a young man, in a plain brown coat, with steady eyes—only one of the trickle of people who had been coming into The Brill now for days.

"You'll need a place to stay." Jan turned, scanning up and down the rampart, where his crew were busy mounting the cannon; they had taken guns from every ship in the Beggar fleet to defend the land wall. Marten was fifteen feet away, sawing a hole through the top of the wooden rampart to push the muzzle of a long gun through.

"Marten!"

"Here." The sailor straightened.

"Take this fellow home with you," Jan called, "and see he's cared for."

"I will." Marten raised one arm. The stranger started toward him, pulling off his coat as he went.

"Can I help you?"

Jan faced out over the wall, looking east, toward the mainland. He folded his arms along the top of the wall and leaned his weight on it, frowning. This man was not the first to report to him that a Spanish army was marching north. Somewhere, beyond the low flat horizon of the dike, lines of soldiers were pounding the roads to The Brill, thousands of them, hardened troops who would kill everything they found. Men like Lumey. He thought of Eleanor, in the hands of a man like Lumey. Or his sister, or Mouse, or for that matter himself.

In his head he ran up a list of the people in The Brill who could fight: the Beggars themselves, about four hundred men, counting even Eleanor and Mouse; the local people, like old Koppelstok, the ferryman, who was helping on the rampart, and the other Calvinists, who sometimes seemed more zealous in breaking into their Catholic neighbors' houses and stealing all they could than in preparing for a desperate fight; and the steady incoming flow of Calvinists from other parts of Zeeland and Holland and even the farther Provinces. How many of them there were he could not judge accurately, but he knew he was hopeful in supposing that more than five hundred people stood against the Spanish army.

And his guns. He dropped one hand to the brass culverin by his side. She was his favorite, his first love, and while the other captains had sent the oldest and least trustworthy guns off their ships to the wall, he had brought this long beauty because he was proud of her and would make the Spanish afraid of her. He slapped her cold hard side. Probably they had no guns, the Spanish army. Looking east, into the bleak distance where the dun-colored earth met the overcast sky, he strained his eyes to see the first pricks of their weapons, and he smiled.

"ALL THE make-believe is over," Lumey shouted. He paced across the front of the church, where the altar had been. The church being the only place in The Brill large enough for all the people, they had called the meeting there. "The Spanish are marching our way, thousands of them, armed and practiced at their arms."

He whirled around to face them, his new vestments swaying around him. A devilish priest, Jan thought, and smiled to himself.

"So," the old pirate shouted. "Now's the time when all men must choose, and choose well, for once and all. Do you stand here and let the Dons have you, or do you go to sea and live to fight again?"

Jan turned his head to look across the mass of people packed into the front of the church. A baby was crying, on the far side of the huge hollow space, but otherwise no one spoke. Their faces were solemn. Men and women and children, there were less than five hundred of them, and the Spanish army numbered in the thousands.

Lumey began to pace across the desecrated altar again. "Those of you who decide to stay—brave fools that you will be—you have a few other decisions to make. How to make your stand. Where you want to die. The women . . ." At the far wall he wheeled. The candles on the walls made his stolen garments glitter. "The women have to have some means of killing themselves and their babies before the Spanish reach them."

From deep in the crowd came a low moan. Lumey smirked; he liked that. He went on.

"The seamen must make some provision for destroying their ships. Burn them, hull them; they must not fall into Spanish hands." He shrugged. "There's no saving the guns."

Jan could hear people crying now, in the crowd. He glanced behind him, where his sister and his wife stood side by side. Their faces were smooth and bland as statues. They were ready. He put out one hand to each of them, and each one quietly grasped his fingers.

"So," Lumey called, stamping up the middle of the church. "Now's the time. Those of you who are going to stay here in this coffin of a town, line up with van Cleef, there, the tall one. Those of you with wits and understanding, come here with me."

Jan lifted his voice. "Lumey has his own cast of thought on this; I have another. We Sea Beggars have not set foot in the Netherlands all these years. We know only that the Spanish have taken our homes away from us. Some of these people who have lived here through Alva's terror can tell us more —how Alva's ground them down and tried to break their spirit."

He looked across the church, wondering if they were even listening to him. Many more were crying now. He cleared his throat.

"If we run now, before the very name of Alva, then he knows he's crushed the best part of us. Now, I don't want to die, and my wife is here, and my sister, and I don't want them to die, but if we fight here, live or die, we will show Alva he cannot break us. We'll give heart to every Dutchman locked in the tyrant's grip."

Silence met his speech. He finished, lamely, "That's all I have to say."

The crowd seemed not to move. One or two people came forward to stand behind Jan, joining the defenders of The Brill. A few more followed van Treslong and Dirk Sonoy up the wall toward him.

Van Treslong came up to Jan and put his hand out. "You could have said something about God, van Cleef. Surely God will help us here. People need to know things like that."

Jan shook his hand. "I don't think God will make this anything special, and from what my sister says He's offered very little help to any Dutchman, these past three years."

The shuffling of feet resounded through the church; the congregation was moving in a dark tangled mass, indefinite of direction. Maybe they were just going out. Someone he had never seen before came up to him.

"You're right." She was an old woman with a hooked nose and no teeth. "I'm too old to live much longer anyway." She clasped his arm and went to stand behind him.

Here came Koppelstok, the ferryman, who said, "By God, van Cleef, I thought you were nothing but a bag of wind, like yon priest killer, but you've proved yourself to me." He struck Jan a comradely slap on the arm and passed by him with the others.

After him a slow parade of people wound, men whose fears and doubts still worked in their faces, and women with their children, white and grim. Jan turned to van Treslong. "We'll have some with us, after all."

Van Treslong smiled at him. "Some. Look you, we have them all."

Jan raised his head. The shifting, awkward mass of people had crowded together on one side of the church. They could not fit in the space behind Jan and so they pressed together in the space before him, turned, and faced across the church at Lumey. Between them and Lumey the floor spread wide and empty. The admiral stood wide legged facing them. Behind him were three or four of his own seamen, and no one else.

Now one of those seamen swore and spat and at a long-legged walk, almost a run, cleared the space between him and the crowd and joined Jan's side.

Lumey looked behind him. Saw how few there were behind him. He wheeled. His face was fierce with a new vigor.

"By God," he shouted, and his voice boomed in the pitch of the church, "you will not make a coward out of me!" His men behind him, he marched across the church; he fell in with the others around Jan.

THE WAITING was the worst, especially at night. The town was different at night anyway. The sailors from the Beggar fleet took over the taverns and drank and ranged up and down the street shouting and fighting and looking for women. They had already gotten in trouble with some of the local people, and in turn their captains got in trouble with Jan, who had thrown the sailors into the stocks. In the morning two of the captains were in the stocks.

Mouse said, "He carried them there himself. The Baron van Treslong went with him, holding his pistols, to make sure no one tried to stop him." He giggled.

Hanneke was staring at the men in the stocks, heads, arms, and legs fastened into the wooden frame. Finally she gave a little shake of her head. "Jan is certainly much changed. A few years ago he would have been in there with them."

She went off down the street. Beside her Mouse ran capering like a little goat, his arms flapping. She said, "Who made Jan the master here? I thought Lumey was the master."

"Lumey only gives orders when he must," said Mouse. "That's why we all obey him."

She cast a sharp look at him. Eleanor was right: this boy was keen of wit as any of them. Only his stupid looks gulled the others into believing him dull.

Now he said, "Do you want to see my secret place?"

"Your secret place? But if you show me, it won't be secret anymore." She had no desire to play childish games with this boy.

"You'll keep the secret, won't you?" He grabbed her by the hand. "Come along. It won't take very much time. Please?"

Reluctantly she let him drag her off down the street toward the Catholic church. There was little to do; Eleanor was busy keeping her house, and afterward she and Hanneke were to cook. Jan was working on the wall still. Hanneke let Mouse pull her down the street and into the church.

"This way." Still clutching her hand, he drew her after him down the aisle of the church to a little door on one side of the altar.

Hanneke said, "I don't really care for places like this, Mouse." She looked up at the paintings above the altar, of Christ and His angels rising toward Heaven, their robes boiling around them like sea waves. Mouse pulled her in through the little door.

A narrow winding stair climbed away from them into the top of the church. Now she knew where he was taking her, and she groaned.

"Mouse, will you make me climb all the way up into the steeple? Oh, Mouse."

She followed him up through the narrow channel of the staircase. The air smelled of mildew and dust and there were no windows, the only light coming from far above them, dropping soft and diffuse down through the staircase. Her legs began to throb. The boy scampered on ahead of her like the little animal of his name. She half expected to see a long brown tail whisking along behind him. At last they reached the top of the church steeple, where the bell hung.

Here there was no floor, only a narrow catwalk along the four walls of the steeple and a threadwork of rafters supporting the bell and the roof. Mouse leapt nimbly from one precarious footing to the next. "Look here! Look here!" On all four sides the steeple was open to the wind and the sun. Hanneke leaned on the sill of one of these windows and looked out.

"Oh!"

She had not expected, somehow, to be so high above the ground. The view enchanted her at once. She was looking down on the town, on the streets where she had walked only minutes before, as if from a cloud, or from Heaven itself. Over there was the curving line of the harbor, with the blue sea glittering in its lap, and the ships lying at anchor, and the men in the stocks mere dots on the pale brown stone of the street. To her right the river ran, its surface turbulent with the contrary forces of the wind and the tide;

she could see all the way across it to the black marshes on its far bank and the mill in the distance.

Eager now, she scrambled along the wall to the corner, to the next window, to see in another direction; that brought her to face the landward wall of The Brill, where the men were climbing up and down and working on the cannon, whose barrels gleamed in the sunlight like mirrors. She could see beyond the wall to the dry-land dike; beyond that were the onion fields, where several people worked, so small and far away she could discern nothing of them save the rhythmic rising and stooping of their bodies as they pulled weeds.

From so high, she could easily see the trench between the dry-land dike and the wall of The Brill, where the sea had rolled until the people built the new dike and pumped out the water. There black and white cattle grazed.

She leaned her arms on the sill, smiling. The sober industry and obvious accomplishments of these people cheered her.

"Hanneke," Mouse said, beside her. "What's that?"

She was watching the cattle; for a moment she did not look up, not until the sun, striking some bright metal, flashed a signal into the edge of her vision.

She raised her head. Mouse was tugging on her sleeve and pointing out past the dry-land dike, toward the dark mass of trees that marked the edge of the distant marshes. She squinted. Something was moving there, vast and indistinct, the sun sparkling here and there on it.

She gasped, swelling her lungs with breath. It was an army, a force of marching men, with the sun striking light from their armor and their pikes. It was the Spanish army.

"Hanneke!" Mouse cried. "Hanneke—what is it?"

"Go." She wheeled toward him, catching him by the shoulders. "Run and tell my brother—" Her gaze sped by him to the bell. "Go and tell my brother that they come!" Leaning back into the window, she curled her arms out over the sill to hold herself, braced her back against the wooden frame, and swung her feet out to the bell and pushed.

Mouse leapt by her, reached the door, and vanished down the long tube of the staircase. Hanneke thrust with her feet at the bell. Heavier than she expected, it hardly moved at all at first, and she grunted with the effort of pushing. Slowly it swayed away from her, and she relaxed, let it swing back toward her, soundless still, and pushed it away again. She felt the clapper strike the metal wall beneath her feet, and the deep voice woke.

Bong—bong—bong—

She twisted to look over her shoulder, out past the wall of The Brill, toward the army that crept toward her. Still far away, it lapped up over the land like a foul tide.

Bong—bong—bong—

Below her, in the street, people were running now, shouting, screaming. Running toward the wall, and on the wall she saw more people rushing about, tiny specks of movement. Between them and the advancing flood of the Spanish army lay only the barren ground, the onion fields, the dry-land dike over which now those people who had toiled outside the wall were running home to safety, the women from the onion fields, the boy with his black and white cows.

Bong—bong—bong—

Her gaze stuck on the broad shallow trench of reclaimed ground between The Brill and the dry-land dike. The sea had rolled there once. Ever eager, it lapped and bit even now at the dike that restrained it, longing to roll there again. She lifted her eyes toward the evil tide of Spaniards creeping over the land toward her. Her heart was hammering. Swinging away from the bell, she jumped toward the door and the stairway down.

24

AN HEARD the bell toll; he sprang up onto the truck of the gun he was outfitting and looked east. What he saw raised the hair on his head and put a coiling snake of panic in his belly. Two long columns were making their way up the road toward him, visible to him now only as two rows of pikes beyond the dry-land dike. Even without seeing the pennant above them, he knew who they were.

He leapt down from the gun. The women from the onion fields were racing in toward the gate, their faces white, wailing with fear at what they had seen coming after them. A boy with a stick dashed out to herd the cows on the barren ground together and bring them inside the wall.

"Marten! Man the gate. When everybody's in, bar it fast. Where's Lumey? Jobst, fetch van Treslong here. Where the devil's Lumey?"

He went along the rampart, from gun to gun, making certain of the supplies of powder and shot by each one, with his own hands checking the lashings that bound each cannon to its truck. Around him everyone seemed to be going mad. People screamed and shouted and ran up and down the wall; he had to push men out of his way to get to some of the guns. On the street below the wall a crowd was growing, their faces lifted toward him, pale and frightened. Mouse was fighting his way through the press of bodies, and down the street behind them Hanneke was running toward the gate.

A great yell went up from the wall beside the gate; the men there had seen the Spanish coming.

The rampart trembled under pounding feet. Jan turned, standing by the last of the cannon; there were too many people on the wall, and he shouted to them to clear it and let only the gun crews stay on the quaking wooden rampart, but no one heard him. The gate was opening to let in the women from the onion fields and the boy with his black and white cows.

As they went in, Hanneke ran out. She had an ax in one hand. Jan shouted at her, but she did not hear him; she started purposefully across the barren ground toward the sea dike. He leaned over the wall and bellowed her name.

She wheeled, raising her face toward him, and waved her free hand.

"Hanneke! Where are you going?"

"To open the dike," she shouted.

"Hanneke!" He twisted his head to stare a moment at the dike. It was a good idea to open it, but in the course of their march the Spanish would reach the far end of the dike too soon. They would kill her. Someone else would have to go.

When he turned back toward her to order her inside again, she was already running away toward the dike.

"Hanneke!" he screamed. "Hanneke, come back!"

She wheeled once more and waved to him. He filled his lungs and shrieked her name, gripping the top of the wall with both hands, leaning out toward her. She waved, her white arm raised like a flagstaff. Oh, Hanneke. Turning, she ran lightly toward the dike.

"Hanneke!"

He turned and bore into the crowd pressing up against the wall, clogging the rampart. If he could reach the gate, go after her. He cast a fearful look toward the Spanish. Their pikes jabbed the sky just beyond the land dike; they were gathering there, under their fluttering banners, as leisurely and confidently as hunters after game. He clawed at the people in his way. Swiftly he glanced over his shoulder at the figure of his sister, running toward the sluice gate.

"Captain! Captain!" Someone rushed at him with questions.

"Jan, over here!"

She was too far away now. She was gone, and the Spanish were before him, and people were shouting questions at him. Now here came Lumey, climbing the ladder to the rampart. Jan wheeled.

"Get all these people off here! Only the gun crews can stay on this part of the wall. Get the rest of these people down on the street and arm them."

Some of his crew were nearby and turned at once to do his bidding. He gave one last look toward his sister, now small in the distance, still running, her hair falling free of her headcloth, bright in the morning sun. He faced the Spanish. They were here at last; now finally he would know the answer to the questions that ached in his heart. He gathered himself, made himself think he might die, and to his surprise found himself ready. Let the Spaniards come. He turned toward Lumey, red-faced, stamping down the rampart toward him.

DON FEDERICO drew rein, signaling the columns behind him to stop. Ahead was a low earthwork; over the top of it he could see to the little town beyond, built on its flat promontory between the river and the sea. Its landward wall was an old wooden rampart, built in an earlier, more barbarous time when people fought with clubs and arrows.

The Spanish general folded one arm over his saddlebow and looked from one side of the battleground to the other. There were people running across the fields outside the wall to the gate, and a comical little herd of cows, cantering in the bony awkward way of cows, hurried over the flat ground away from him; so the Spanish army had been noticed. Good. It would inspire fear in the enemy, perhaps even lead them to surrender at once.

His horse stamped, impatient. The slow march here from the far side of the island had scarcely stretched the stallion's legs, cramped after the long ride in the barge. Around him, behind him, the ranks of soldiers shifted their feet with a manifold clinking of corselet and helmet and talked in low voices, excited, pointing to their target.

Don Federico, to his satisfaction, saw an easy victory here. The wall would stop nothing, not even the charge of infantry, who would break through that gate in moments, and there could be no more than a few hundred defenders in the whole town. No matter that Federico had only half an army, del Rio's troops from Antwerp having inexplicably failed to appear.

Alva was wrong, though, for once. He had misjudged the seriousness of this problem. The Brill was more important than an invasion from France of poorly led foreign troops. If this town were allowed to stand, even to go lightly punished for its insolence, all over the Netherlands other towns would rise against the Crown. Don Federico intended to prove himself, here, more valuable than his father wanted to think: here he would throttle a genuine revolt.

He summoned his aides. "I see no difficulty in this. We will mount an assault on the main gate. Don Diego, I command you, take your musketeers over to that high ground"—Don Federico pointed to a long low earthwork extending along the riverbank, north of the town—"and prepare to give us an enfilading fire to cover our advance."

He snorted, amused, seeing movement on the wall. The gate was closing. In their haste, the defenders had left someone outside, who danced and gesticulated at the foot of the wall. They were terrified in The Brill. They were wise in that; Don Federico meant to leave nothing standing higher than one stone upon another.

"They are waiting for us. We shall have some fighting to do. I trust your men are all shriven." Excited by the prospect of battle, he could not keep back a tight smile; he saw in the faces of his aides the same impatient eager readiness, a keen edge. "Go, in God's name." He crossed himself, and they dispersed to their posts.

LUMEY was tramping up and down the rampart by the gate, his gaudy vestment splattered with old blood, ribbons in his beard. When Jan came up to him, he was turning away from the gate, which he had just ordered closed.

The admiral's face was bound up in a twitchy frown. He swung toward Jan and barked, "There's nothing for me to do here. You and van Treslong can do this." He banged on the wall. "The guns don't move—the Spanish are straight in front of you—shoot when they come in range." He started away toward the ladder to the street, now boiling with excited people.

Jan grabbed his sleeve. "Where are you going?"

Lumey flung out one arm like a blade toward the Spanish in the distance. "They must have come here in boats. I'm going to find them and hull them. God be with you." He jerked free of Jan's grip and hurried away down the ladder.

The Baron van Treslong had come up the rampart to Jan's side. Amazed, Jan stood staring after Lumey, who plowed through the mob in the street, turned a corner, and was gone.

"Is he running away?" Jan asked.

Van Treslong grabbed his arm. "No—but he knows nothing of fighting on land. He is a sailor. Let him go. You captain the guns here; you are the master of that. I shall get these men ready to fight off an assault, if they charge the gate." He threw one arm around Jan and hugged him tight. "Good luck. God watches over us; whatever comes is by His plan."

Then he too was gone, down the ladder into the street, where his voice rose sharp with orders.

"Jan—Jan—"

He swung around, toward Eleanor, who was pushing and shoving through the thickness of bodies that lined the rampart. She flung out her arm toward him, and he caught her hand.

"Gather up all the women and the children," he said, hustling her toward the ladder. "Take them down to the harbor. If any here survive, you can escape by sea."

He twisted to look back over the wall at the Spanish army, which now was ranging itself along the landward dike. There were thousands of them. If they broke through, the women here would suffer long and pitifully before they died. He wheeled back to his wife.

"Jan," she said. Her face was wild, her hair flying in wisps around her cheeks, the color high in her fine-grained skin.

"If none of us survives," he said, "you must—you must—"

He flung his arms around her and held her so tight she groaned.

"I can't find Hanneke," she said, standing back.

"She's gone."

"Gone! Where?"

"To her destiny." He held his wife's hands in his; he looked deep into her face. "I love you very much, dear Eleanor."

"I love you, Jan."

"Go. And do as I said, if . . ."

Her face tightened, grim with resolution. "I will." She squeezed his hands in hers, turned to the ladder, and went down to the street. Jan stood there a moment longer, watching her go off into the town. When she disappeared into the swarming masses of people in the street, he turned back toward the wall, back toward the Spanish enemy.

From the pasture outside the wall, Hanneke could see nothing of the furious bustle on the rampart, but she could hear it: the boom of feet on the wooden platform, the shouting, the prayers, the clatter of weapons. She thought she heard her brother's voice. With the ax in her left hand, she set out for the seawall at the far end of the pasture.

From this level, the Spaniards were invisible at first, but as she walked she noticed above the land dike the pricks of their weapons lancing the sky and she heard the tramping of their feet. She broke into a run. The ax was heavy and she slipped and fell once to her knees on the dry salty earth. The knife-edged sea grass stung her legs. She held up her skirts with her right hand and ran awkwardly forward. Her breath came short.

Behind her Jan was screaming at her. She ran faster toward the dike.

Just as she reached the end of the seawall, a little troop of Spanish soldiers appeared at the other end. They carried muskets. She saw at once that they meant to line up along the top of the dike, to fire on the rampart where the Calvinist guns were so that the defenders could not shoot their cannon while the main army attacked. She ran up onto the dike, scrambling along the steep stony slope, her feet knocking loose clods of dirt and rocks to shower down behind her in a little cascade.

When she reached the top of the dike, the musketeers saw her, and a whoop went up from them. One threw his weapon to his shoulder and fired at her. Where the bullet went, she did not see; she ignored it, running along the top of the dike to the sluice gate.

Another musket fired. The bullet plinked off the stony ground by her feet.

Half the length of the dike separated her from them; they would never reach her in time to stop her. She lifted the ax and swung it in a round arc toward the top of the sluice gate. Down the dike, a Spanish voice snapped orders. She heard the rattle of their armor as the men knelt down to fire from rest. Hauling up the heavy ax, she drove it down against the iron-hard wood of the gate. Chips flew off from the notch she had made in the top.

The muskets went off in a light crackle of sound. The bullets swarmed around her like bees, ticking off the ground, and something burned into her thigh. She heaved up the ax, struck hard into the gate, and split it down from top to bottom. Again the muskets banged.

Like a needle through her, a pain lanced her chest. The gate was groaning, the weight of the water behind it pushing against the cracked wood, but still it held, and she swung the ax up, extending her body full length to get all the power she could behind the blade, and the bullets whispered in her ears and tore into her cheek and her arm. She drove the ax down into the gate with all her strength. A chunk of wood jumped up and sailed away to her left, and the gate broke, and the sea poured in.

She gasped. She could not move, balanced on her bleeding legs, teetering, the ax falling from her hand. She turned her eyes now from the broken gate through which the green water rushed to the musketeers at the end of the dike; she could hear the bullets strike her flesh, but she knew they were beaten. She had beaten them, she and the Dutch earth and God's sea. Slowly she fell down onto the dike, laid her head to the ground, and was still.

ON THE wall Jan saw her break open the sluice gate, and all around him the others saw and cheered, cheered the water rushing in onto the pasture, but Jan did not cheer, because he saw his sister die. The first. He faced the Spanish over the stretch of scrubby pasturage and said, "Fire."

Beside him, Mouse reached out the slow match to the big brass culverin and lit the powder. The gun swallowed the scrap of fire and bellowed smoke and shot into the air.

The roar of the gun silenced the cheers. Jan went on to the next gun, Mouse at his side with the slow match. He did not think of Hanneke; he felt her dying like a knife in the heart, a fire in his own guts, a fury.

"Low," Mouse said, and pointed.

The shot from the brass culverin had struck the dike below the line of Spanish soldiers, kicking up a spray of rocks and dirt high into the air; the enemy troops scattered away from it, and a horse reared and bugled in panic. Jan said, "Fire."

This gun was an old iron gun from the *Christ the Redeemer.* Her voice was different—all the guns had different voices—this one a throaty roar and a rumble, and her shot whistled in the air, eerie, like a live thing.

The Spanish recoiled at the sound of the shot, the line swaying back away from the dike, but this gun was set higher and her belly's worth of iron flew over the dike and struck square into the mass of men retreating from it. There was a roar from the men on the wall of The Brill, and Jan's lips drew back from his teeth in an unpleasant smile. Pieces of bodies lay on the top of the dike, thrown there by the shot.

He said, "Good. Keep this one as it is, and fire as it's ready." Stepping past the gun crew, Mouse at his side, he went on to the next cannon.

They had brought this gun, a light demiculverin, in from the smaller of van Treslong's ships; it did not fit its truck, and they had spent most of a day trying to rig it so that it would not jump off its bed when it was fired. The gun crew stood back as Jan came up to them. He glanced out at the Spanish, who were re-forming their lines; they would charge soon. They were only waiting now for the musketeers to line up on the seaward dike and open fire, to drive the defenders back off the wall.

They began to fire now, as he watched, and all along the rampart the gun crews ducked below the cover of the wall. At the far end, a man screamed and pitched back off the rampart into the street. Instantly another man took his place.

Jan said, "Fire."

Mouse put the slow match to the bore of the demiculverin, and the gun went off with a howl.

As it went off the iron barrel rocked sideways, breaking away from its mounting; it swung around and struck the wall, and the wall gave way. The gun crashed through it, the ropes that bound it popping like small arms. Jan lunged after it, to save it, caught the heavy brass lip around the muzzle with both hands, and braced himself, his feet against the wall. The wall gave way. With the gun he pitched out into space.

He yelled. Desperately he twisted in midair and fell against the wall. He slipped a yard along the smooth wooden surface, his hands scrabbling for a hold, and one hand caught on the broken edge of the wall below the rampart. His body swung loose against the outside of the wall.

This was his answer, then. He was to die here. He thought of Eleanor; there flashed into his mind the picture of Hanneke lying on the top of the seawall. His feet kicked at the wood, helpless. The Spanish were firing on him. A bullet struck his left arm and he lost his grip.

He was falling. Then from above him on the rampart a hand grabbed his wrist and held him.

"Jan!"

He looked up, flailing at the wall with his feet and his free hand, and saw Mouse, bending down through the break in the wall to hold him.

"Let go!" If he fell he would drag Mouse with him. He knew the half-wit had not the strength to hold him long. One of his feet caught on a knot in the smooth planking of the wall and pushed him upward for an instant, up toward the gap in the wall; he swung his free hand up and caught on to the wall.

Mouse did not drop him. Standing up for leverage, the cross-eyed boy grasped Jan's wrist with both hands and pulled, and a moment later others of the men on the rampart rushed over and caught Jan's arm and his clothes and hauled him up through the gap, through the pelting Spanish bullets, back safe onto the rampart.

"Are you all right? Are you hurt?"

Heaving himself up onto his knees, he flung his arms around Mouse and hugged him fast. Mouse pressed against him.

"I saved you. I saved you, Jan."

Jan kissed him. Standing up, he gripped the boy's hand. "You did that, certainly. Come along." Stooping to take shelter from the top of the wall, they went on to the next gun, which fired low.

"OH, WHAT will happen to us, what will become of us?"

"Hurry," Eleanor said, and herded the young women with their babies on ahead of her toward the wharf, where the others were waiting. Some of the children had broken away from their mothers to play on the boats, and she shouted to the other women to keep them close. Behind them, in the town, there was the thunder of cannon.

"God help us." The more timid of the women began to cry, and several knelt down on the stone wharf to pray. Eleanor walked up and down past them, twisting her hands together.

She could barely speak to them; none of them spoke French, and her Dutch was still uncertain. She wished Jan had found someone more suitable for this and let her help him on the wall.

The cannon fire now was nearly continuous. Above the roofs of the town, a massive cloud of black smoke was rising, and she thought she heard the light crackle of small-arms fire.

She could not stay here, waiting, doing nothing. She went back to the women and, waving her hands at them, did what she could to tell them to keep together and stay there; then she went off through the town, looking for stray people she could save. There was a huge shout from the wall, half cheer, half panic; she wondered what was happening. She wanted to be with Jan at the end, but he had told her . . .

In the little square before the town hall, she came on the stocks, and the sailors still writhing in them.

A hoarse shout broke from her throat. She ran up to the wooden frames and tugged at them. The men bellowed at her in Dutch. They wiggled their arms and legs comically at her, their faces red. The stocks were locked, of course; she could not open them with her hands, and she ran into the house across the street and rummaged through the kitchen until she found a stout knife.

Running out to the stocks again, she pried open the locks with the blade of the knife. The men climbed stiffly out of the yokes and ran away down the street, toward the sound of fighting. One stopped to grab Eleanor by the shoulders and paste a wet kiss full on her mouth. With a laugh, he ran limping after the others.

Eleanor went back into the house across the street and got out all the knives she could find, good long-bladed knives with sharp edges, and took them back to the wharf. There weren't enough to arm all the women, and many of the older children, too, could fight. She went back to find another kitchen to rob.

LUMEY bent his back to the oars. The current of the river was so strong that he could make no headway against it, and so he had steered his little boat over to this bank. Here the water was shallow and still and the dark trees overgrew it, their branches dripping moss that dragged over the boat and his shoulders and head. The smell of the marsh was nauseating. He stopped to drink from the jug of wine he had brought, grunted to clear his throat, and picked up the oars again.

In the distance, he could hear the boom of cannon and the lighter music of muskets. They were fighting, back there, fighting in a way that profoundly annoyed him. On ships there was always the business of maneuver, judging the wind and the sea, changing sail and plotting a course, but here, damn it, what was there but a bang-bang punching contest?

The Spanish would win. He knew it; everybody knew it. They had the men and the metal and they would win, and the good work the Beggars had done all these years would be lost. At least the Dons would have to swim home. He hoped van Cleef and his other hotheaded friends would have the sense to hull their own ships before the Spanish took them.

It made him cry, actually cry tears, as he stroked the flat-bottomed boat with its load of liquor and little kegs of black powder on through the stinking marsh; he cried to think of his beautiful *Christ the Redeemer* falling into Spanish hands. He cried sensuously, enjoying it. He stopped to drink some more and cried all the while, until his boat ran aground.

Getting out, he stepped into water six inches deep and mud much deeper than that, up to his knees. With the boat's painter over his shoulder, he slogged on through the rotten black swamp, ducking streamers of moss and dangling branches like evil arms that tried to hold him back.

Now he did not cry, because now he saw ahead of him through the latticework of the trees the masts and square sails of the Spanish barges.

He stopped, catching his breath, applauding himself for his craft in knowing where they would be. Actually, anyone who knew the Spanish would have guessed they would come from the mainland at the narrowest point of the intervening water and anchor here, but in case they had shown more sense, he had meant to go on rowing around the whole island until he found them; yet here they were. He went back to the boat for his jug.

More cannon fire rolled from the land behind him. They probably thought he was a coward, running away from the fight. He had run away. He was a coward. He did not understand land fighting and never had; he had always been uneasy on the land. But he saw, with the shrewdness of long years of experience at fighting, that the land was where the great battles would be fought now. Something had changed, in the taking of The Brill; the course of the struggle with the Spanish had changed. The years of piracy and raiding were over, and a new kind of war had begun.

Not Lumey's war. But Lumey meant to make a grand exit from it.

He tucked the jug inside his coat and pulled the boat forward. The water was deeper here, and he could get back into the boat and row. He did not. He tied the boat up to a wet smelly branch and trudged through the mucky swamp toward the barges, to see how they lay.

The swamp dried up a little, here, making a reasonable landing place. Here the river swept on by to the north, and the island's eastern shore fell off to the south, forming a wide, calm anchorage—not deep, but deep enough for several dozen flat-bottomed barges. They were all crowded

together, probably tied together; the army must have unloaded those far-
thest from the shore across the nearer ones. He could see men sitting around
a little fire, off in the middle of the anchored barges, drinking: the boatmen.

He wiped his hands on his thighs. Pleased, he assessed his mind and
found nothing that shrank from this. They had recoiled from his usage of
priests. Now let them see that he used himself as violently as any other. He
sloshed back to his boat.

He did not get into it at once. First he gathered up all the long fuses
that led from the little congregation of kegs in the stern, tied the sulfurous
lengths together, and lit them with his tinderbox. When they were sputter-
ing and smoking healthfully alive, he climbed into the boat and bent to the
oars.

The smell of burning fuse was better than the smell of the swamp. He
began to laugh. With all his might, he pulled on the oars, and the boat shot
forward through the calm water, whisking down on the barges. Lumey
roared with laughter. The fuses spat and glittered as they burned. He did
not pause now even to drink. They saw him coming, the boatmen; he heard
them yell, but they were too late. His boat crashed into the first of the barges.
Leaning out to grab the high gunwale, he pulled his boat with its trails of
raw smoke around to the barge's bow and slipped between that bottom and
the next; and by that means, as the fuses grew shorter and shorter and the
boatmen shouted, he worked his little boat in among all the big unwieldy
barges, until the fuses, crackling and sparkling, disappeared inside the powder kegs.

Then, only then, Lumey reached inside his coat for his jug. But he never
drew it out again.

DON FEDERICO clenched his fist on his reins. He was tired of waiting.
His stomach churned from waiting too long.

He looked down the length of the pasture toward the riverward dike,
where the musketeers knelt in two long rows, firing on the wall of the
town. They were all in place now and shooting well in order, but their fire
was not doing its business. The cannon on the wall still fired with an even
rhythm, blasting the flat pasture in front of Don Federico, the land he had
to cross to reach the wall, from which they had forced him to retreat. He
bit his lip, wondering what had gone wrong. The musket fire should have
driven the defenders back. It must be killing some of them. He swore
under his breath.

When he had seen the girl chop open the sluice gate, he had told himself
it hardly mattered. The water moved slowly, and they would hold The Brill
before the flood covered the pasturage between him and the town. But now
the water was lapping up nearly halfway over the scrubby ground, and the
hole was widening in the dike. Diego was withdrawing those of his men who

had crossed over the sluice gate to the far side of the dike, evidence enough that the dike was giving way there. In a little while, the whole place would be inundated, and The Brill could be on the far side of the ocean, for all its accessibility to Don Federico and his thousands of men.

He had to charge now, in the face of the cannon fire, lose whatever men he had to, take the town in a single rush, before the sea shut him off.

"Trumpeter! Sound—"

Before he could continue there was a low growl of sound behind him, far off. He twisted in his saddle. With a jangle of metal all his men turned too, to look behind them. The rumble swelled up behind the lacy fringe of trees that marked the swamp through which they had passed; it exploded into a great crash, and from beyond the trees there rose such a cloud of black smoke, peppered with bits of debris, and such a thunderous wash of sound, that Don Federico let out a yell.

"The boats!" One of his aides ran toward him, pale as a woman. "They've blown up our boats!"

Don Federico swung around in his saddle, his blood racing. Well, that left him no choice. He leaned forward, cocked like a pistol, toward The Brill. "Trumpeter! The charge—sound the charge—"

His men heard him. Even before the trumpet blasted, the men were shouting. Long held back, they burst forward, their pikes swinging down, and hurled themselves toward the little town that stood before them, at last given over to their rage.

"HERE THEY come," Jan shouted. "Fire as you will."

He ran down the rampart toward his culverin, jumping across the guns and stacks of shot in his way, men darting out of his path. Mouse ran at his heels. They reached the big brass gun and turned.

The Spanish came like a horde of demons, their pikes pricking the air, their voices raised in a weird ululating howl. They came like a wave of water, so many of them there was no discriminating individual men among them; Jan saw them as a single great moving mass. He bent down over the culverin and sighted along her barrel.

This gun, so far from the dike, had suffered no casualties; some of the guns at the far end of the wall had lost their crews to the musket fire. The water flooding the field would cover that end of the wall. He looked up at the men around him and said, "Fire."

Mouse leaned forward with the slow match. The gun bellowed. All down the wall the other guns went off, sending forth their shot in a ragged line of iron and stone across the intervening distance. The round hit the Spanish line, and blew holes through it, but the holes filled up at once with other men, coming on as swiftly as a fire through high dry grass, coming like an avalanche. Jan looked for a weapon. They would be fighting hand to hand soon. His men rushed around him, sponging the cannon, rolling powder packet and shot down into her long hot throat.

"Fire!"

The cannon thundered, and through the onrushing ranks of the Spanish army the shot sliced a red zone of bodies—screaming men and writhing, thrashing arms and legs. Yet they came in, enraged by their losses; they swung their pikes down level, and charged at the gate. Jan shouted. No time now for the cannon. Grabbing the ramrod, he vaulted down off the rampart into the street before the gate.

The others followed him, flooding after him toward the gate, which thundered and bowed inward over its bar under the impact of the army. From the street behind Jan, van Treslong ran, leading his own little army in a ridiculous order of columns. The gate burst open.

Jan shouted. Wielding the ramrod around his head, he rushed forward into the gap, and the first two Spanish pikemen who came through it he struck across the middle with the ramrod and hurled backward into their fellows.

An instant later, there were men all around him, his own people, standing shoulder to shoulder with him. The pikes lunged at their faces. With his ramrod he beat down the shining blades, and reversing the pole, he thrust the butt hard into the teeth of a soldier in front of him, felt the ramrod's butt break bone and flesh, and saw the soldier fall.

"My sister," he shouted. "For my sister!" Stepping forward, he trampled on that body while he struck and parried blows with another man behind it.

The gate jammed the charging Spanish close together, kept their arms pinned close, their pikes bound awkwardly, and Jan meant to hold them there, in the gate. He flailed at them with the ramrod; one fell back, but another lunged at him, the pike sliding over the haft of the ramrod, coming at him like a silver snake. He dodged it. The pike slipped past his elbow and bored into a man behind him. Jan grabbed the haft and yanked, and the pikeman came off-balance after his weapon. Jan got him by the throat and threw him backward onto the blades of his own men.

Now he had the pike for a weapon. He had never used one before; he thrust with it and saw how it sliced away the soldiers in front of him. They lunged at him, three at once, still confined in the narrow space of the gate. All around him his own friends fought them. He braced himself. No time to think, to plan. Seeing a face before him he drove the pike at it, awkwardly overhand, and the blade split the face with a shower of blood and caught somehow and was wrested from his hands.

Weaponless, he flailed out with his fists, ducked the oncoming pike of a Spaniard screaming prayers, and wrestled with him. Lifted the thrashing body in his arms just quick enough to catch another blade with the back of the soldier's armor. The armor did no good. It broke under the impact and the blade came through and he pushed the dying soldier away at arm's length while the blade pierced through back and chest and came out on Jan's side, aimed at him, filthy with blood. He flung the body sideways and that carried the pike away too.

Still he had only his bare hands, and the Dutch around him were falling back, or dead, lying in the street, lying under the feet of the Spaniards pressing inward. He staggered back a step and tried to brace himself and could not. Back another step. He was losing. He thought of his sister, of Eleanor, of his ship. Flung up his arms to block a pike coming at him, and fended it off to one side, and somehow directed it into the body of one of his own men. He wailed, despairing.

"Hold on—hold on!"

The high clear voice penetrated the tumult like sunlight through a shadow. From both sides, screaming, their hands flashing with knives, came the women.

He shouted. He surged forward, the men behind him lunging after him, and the women flung themselves on the Spanish from either side of the gate, and the Spanish faltered. Jan caught up a pike from the ground. He drove forward into their midst, seeing Eleanor in those women, wild to protect her. With the pike before him, he slammed the Spaniards back through the gate. A woman screamed in his ears.

"Eleanor," he shouted. "Eleanor!" Blind with new fury he charged forward and thrust them backward another step, and another. The men around him were howling. The women joined them. At Jan's side, now, a little girl was fighting, her white arms ending in long butcher knives.

The Spaniards staggered back, through the gate, and they splashed into water. The sea was rising behind them, flooding the pasturage. The men in the last ranks wheeled, their voices high and shrill with panic, and the sea lapped at their knees. The Dutch were swinging the gate closed on them. The sea swirled and dragged at them. Their trumpets blasted, urging them on, but the sea had them. Desperate, they raced toward the dry land, back beyond the landward dike, the safety of the onion fields. The sea rose around them and those that fell did not rise, held down in their armor under the waves.

Jan roared; he sprang toward the ladder to the rampart and clambered up beside his gun again. She still lay back in her trucks as her last shot had thrown her, and he had lost the ramrod. He ran to the next gun to take its ramrod and went back and cleaned the gun and loaded her, his hands trembling. Over his shoulder he saw the Spanish struggling in the rising sea. Many had died in the gate, and many more were drowning, but still some of them had reached the dry dike on the far side. He thrust the shot deep into the culverin and went looking for the slow match.

Now for the first time he saw the great plumes of black smoke rising from the trees behind the Spanish army, and he knew Lumey had burned their boats. He roared. A wild exultant laughter surged up through him, and he flung his fists up into the sky and shouted and stamped his feet on the rampart. His men were rushing up around him; far down the wall, a gun fired, and its scythe of shot cut down the Spanish struggling up from the mire to the safety of the land. All along the rampart men cheered and bent to the guns and fired.

Eleanor came toward him, blood staining her gray dress, smiling. He had made himself ready to die. It took him some effort to accept life again. All around him his people were cheering and leaping and hugging one another. He reached out for Eleanor, his life, and she came to him.

25

YOUR sister died."

He nodded, kicking at the sand; they were walking along the beach. There was a storm coming in, and the waves were pounding up well past the line of shell and weed that marked the usual high tide. He said, "She saved us. Had she not cut the dike, they would have taken The Brill."

He slid his arm around his wife's waist. For Hanneke he felt both grief and joy; for himself only grief, that he had lost her again, so soon after they had regained each other.

"Mouse told me he saved your life."

"He did." Jan gave a little shake of his head. His left arm throbbed painfully now; after the fighting was over he had found, to his surprise, that it was wounded through. "God help me, I felt sorry for him all this time, or contempt for him. He saved my life. There's a lesson in that I do not mean to forget."

She hugged him, her cheek against his chest. He did not say to her, You saved us all. She knew that. Everyone knew that.

They walked along the beach, into the teeth of the wind. The storm was sweeping in from the north. Great slate-colored shelves of cloud hung over the sea, and the setting sun stained the western edge dark red. A wave crashed against the beach and washed up toward them, a curling soapy edge of foam, and he steered her out of the way.

"Now what will happen?" she said.

"We have sent for Orange. When he comes . . ." He said no more. He had no idea what would happen next; it was all new, with no footing in the past, no way to judge it by the past. As if he had died in The Brill, his life was starting over. Like the fierce storm wind, a steady excitement enlivened him. Eagerly he looked forward into the future. It was right, he thought, that this new kingdom should be born here, on land the Dutch had made, on the edge of the world.

"Look!" Eleanor raised her arm to point. "An omen."

The sun had sunk down under the edge of the cloud roof; its clear piercing light shot across the sea with a brilliance that blazed on every wave top and turned the sand to gold.

Jan made a sound in his chest. "We'll have a long storm before the sun shines well on us again." He wanted it; he needed the storm, the power of the storm to weigh his own power against. "Come along," he said. "I have to make my ship safe."

They turned and went back toward The Brill.

Many Days later, the Prince of Orange entered Holland. The Sea Beggars met him at the border, to give him their homage and to recognize him as their leader. Jan van Cleef waited with the other captains, ready with some cold words for this aristocrat who arrived to take the glory after the deed was done.

They were standing on the flat northern shore, where the Prince was landing in a small boat. A harsh wind blew out of the north and drove the waves onto the beach with a boom and crash of sand-filled surf. The little boat nosed in through the breakers and struck the ground with its keel, and three men leapt out to drag it onshore.

Another man climbed out, knee-deep in the surf, and walked up to the rank of waiting captains. As he came, he smiled, and reached out his hand, first to van Treslong, and next to Dirk Sonoy.

"My friends," he said. "I come here not to lead—you have proven you need no leaders but God Himself. I come to serve, as best I can, in our common cause."

He put out his hand next to Jan, who was fumbling with the made-up speeches he had been turning over in his mind all morning. In the face of the Prince of Orange he could remember nothing that seemed fitting. The Prince, seeing his hesitation, lowered his hand.

"Do you have some reservations of me, Captain?"

Jan blurted out, "Many have died here, sir. Do you mean to stay here now, and keep faith with them, and not flee when the going's hard?"

The other Beggars muttered, angry at that, but the Prince of Orange's smile only broadened, the lines at the corners of his eyes deepening into fans of wrinkles. Gently, he said, "I am here to make my grave in this land."

Van Treslong strode forward. "Your Highness, van Cleef's lost his sister, at The Brill; he is distraught—"

"He has won his rights here," said the Prince. "I ask of him only the chance to win mine." He reached out his hand again to Jan. "Have I the honor of your company, Captain van Cleef?"

Jan took his hand in a hard grip. "God be with us both, sir."

"And we with God; we shall not fail." The Prince nodded to him. With a gesture to draw them all after him, he walked up the beach, into Holland.

All the candles had gone out but one. The Duke of Alva leaned his forearms on the table and stared into the saffron light, his mind despairing.

He had driven back Louis of Nassau; he had won every battle he had fought. The news of his son's disaster at The Brill had seemed at first like a minor annoyance. Another army would take The Brill. What did it matter? Why did it matter so?

The letter from his King lay open under the candlelight, the words marching neatly from side to side, the words that ordered him back to Spain, that told him he had failed.

He knew that—knew it in his stomach, in his bones, and in his heart—but he could not see how he had failed. He had won every battle. No one dared to stand against him. He slid his hands up to cover his face, blocking out the light.

A Note on the Type

This book was set via computer-driven cathode-ray tube in a type face called Garamond. Jean Janson has been indentified as the designer of this face, which is based on Claude Garamond's original models but is much lighter and more open. The italic is taken from a font of Granjon, which appeared in the repertory of the Imprimerie Royale and was probably cut in the middle of the sixteenth century.

Composed, printed, and bound by
The Haddon Craftsmen, Inc., Scranton, Pennsylvania.

Designed by Virginia Tan.